PLAYING THE DEVIL'S MUSIC

A STELLA COLE THRILLER

ANDY MASLEN

TYTON PRESS

For Jo

Where dance is, there is the Devil.

— Saint John Chrysostom, ca. 349–407

PROLOGUE

JÄGARASEN, VÄSTMANLAND COUNTY

Blood roaring in her ears, Detective Inspector Stella Cole pointed the snub-nosed pistol at the Internal Affairs chief.

Without the duct-tape bindings, Assistant Police Commissioner Nik Olsson would have collapsed at her feet.

But there he stood, pinned in place between two parallel stacks of wooden crates, arms outspread across their tops. Waiting for death like a cow in a slaughterhouse killing pen.

He raised his head. In his bloodshot eyes she read a beseeching gaze. *Don't do it.*

His face was as pale as a corpse's. In just a few seconds, the gun barrel pushed against his cheek would discharge its lethal load and then there would be no face at all.

'Please,' he croaked.

Shutting out Nik's pleas, she tightened her finger on the trigger.

Then she fired.

1

STOCKHOLM, FOUR MONTHS EARLIER

The party was into its second hour. They were celebrating closing a case – a gangland hit – and then the murder squad's door opened.

As heads turned, the murmur of disgusted voices rippled beneath the disco beat issuing from a sound system someone had borrowed from the media briefing centre.

Stella looked up as Nikodemus Olsson entered the press of bodies.

His entrance was as unwelcome as it was unexpected – for who would invite the head of *Avdelningen för särskilda utredningar,* the Special Investigations Division AKA Internal Affairs AKA 'the Rat Squad' to a detectives' party?

The atmosphere dimmed perceptibly, the way a spring day in Stockholm could be rendered winter again as lowering storm clouds obscured the sun.

But Nik, thin of frame, clean of jaw, eyes burning with the

zeal of a mediaeval witchfinder, could withstand much greater forces than those ranged against him now. His thin lips curved into a smile as he made his way to the drinks table, actually two desks cleared of paperwork and pushed against the wall.

He cracked the tab on a can of Diet Coke. Took a cautious sip as if even a sugar-free drink might offer him too much pleasure. Then threaded his way to where Stella was standing.

She had been talking to Jonna, her friend and assistant. But Jonna had been whisked off to dance by a younger detective. Micki Gustafsson was new, a replacement for a once-promising young detective named Tilde.

Micki, bless him, hadn't worked out that Jonna was gay. Stella grinned as she watched him trying his best moves on her assistant, who favoured Stella with a wink over Micki's shoulder.

Standing just a little too close, Nik looked down at Stella. He shifted his gaze to the can of lager in her right hand.

'You're enjoying the party, I see.'

From any other officer in the station, the remark would have been a harmless observation. To be taken at face value. They might be holding a bottle themselves, or a shot glass brimming with aquavit.

But from Nik, the nearest thing the SPA had to a bone fide puritan, the simple six-word sentence was freighted with layer upon layer of meaning. None of it pleasant.

—*You've been drinking alcohol on SPA property. Not an offence but a lapse in judgment.*

—*Maybe you have a problem with drink. Don't worry. A lot of officers do.*

—*I myself prefer to keep a clear head.*

—*Because I'm a moralising prick with a broomstick up his arse.*

Stella grinned. Oops. That last thought most certainly wasn't Nik's. She nodded at the silver can in his smooth, pink-skinned hand with its perfectly manicured nails.

'You want to go easy on those, Nik,' she said, irritated that her voice was slurring, just a little. 'I read somewhere that those artificial sweeteners give you cancer.'

He sniffed. Then leaned closer, until his face was so close to hers she could see the individual pores on his sharp-ridged nose.

'I know what you think, Stella. You're the golden girl. Or, what do they call you? The Queen of Weirdness? Fluent in Swedish. A star detective. We're lucky to have you. All that. You think your clearance rate means you're armour-plated. That your past won't catch up with you. But believe me when I say that I am looking very closely at you.' He sipped from his can of Diet Coke. 'Roisin Griffin didn't come all this way on some hunch. I've been talking to some people in London and I am starting to piece together a very disturbing picture of certain ... events ... that happened before you left.'

At the mention of Roisin's name, it was Stella's turn to recoil. The Northern Irish detective inspector had been a member of her team at the Met. Talented, hard-working, but, ultimately, overambitious. And, finally, corrupt, selling information on cases to a sleazy reporter from the *Sun* to further her career and damage Stella's. It hadn't worked, and, in the end, Roisin's envy had cost her her life.

Nik closed the gap once more, backing Stella against her own desk. His eyes burned.

'I already told you about Rosh,' Stella stammered. 'She was obsessed.'

Nik pushed his face into hers.

'Do you know what Franz Kafka said about obsession, Stella?' he hissed. 'He said "Don't bend. Don't water it down. Don't try to make it logical. Don't edit your own soul according to the fashion. Rather, follow your most intense obsessions mercilessly." I think that's what Roisin was doing. And I intend to discover where her obsession would have taken her.'

'Get to hell, Nik,' she snapped, pushing him away from her.

'Oh! I see. We're back to using violence, are we?' he said, overloud, so that a few nearby cops turned their heads to see who was getting into it. 'Well, maybe you've had too much to drink. We don't want to fall back into our old ways, do we?'

So he'd dug up her old medical records. Bastard. She had to bite down a caustic reply threatening to burst free from her lips.

If Nik had left it there, the evening might have ended more or less peaceably. Just a bunch of very drunk cops spilling out of SPA headquarters onto Kungsholmsgatan, heading for a curry house or a bar. But Nik, even more than Roisin, was not one to rule his obsessions. He let *them* rule *him*. Knelt before them: a willing servant before his master.

'It's not your fault,' he said, more emolliently. 'I mean, losing your husband and baby daughter to a hit and run. Well,' he smiled unpleasantly, 'that would be enough to turn anyone away from righteousness. I suppose we should be grateful that this time it's only alcohol you're abusing, and not pills.'

Stella was not conscious of reaching to her right. Her hands were already flat on the desk behind her. Supporting her as she leaned backwards to avoid having to inhale Nik's signature scent: soap-and-sanctimony. It would feel, later, as she replayed the events in her head, that her hand had moved of its own volition.

Either way, it came up gripping a pistol.

As time slowed down, troubling thoughts chased each other through Stella's head.

Was it wise to point a gun at an assistant police commissioner?

Probably not. No, strike that. Most definitely, *assuredly*, not.

And if said APC was Nik Olsson?

Make that a bank of red lights. Accompanied by blaring sirens and a blue-and-white striped barrier pole clanging down into a steel support.

With a feeling of unreality, heightened by the cans of Oppigårds Grim lager she'd consumed, Stella considered Nik's face, disfigured by a flinch so total every feature seemed to be screaming at its neighbour to get out of the way.

Jonna was there, hands upraised. 'Stella! Put the gun down!'

Her expression, mouth open, blue eyes wide, was enough to shock Stella back into herself again.

She'd been ready to shoot Nik in the face. Or had she? Her finger lay alongside the trigger guard, not curled round the trigger itself. Yeah, because that excuse would fly. She'd broken a cardinal rule of gun safety.

Seized with a fit of shaking, she lowered her arm, and let Jonna uncurl her fingers from the pistol's grip. With the gun safe in her friend's hands, Stella collapsed back against the desk. Her legs were trembling and sparks were flying round the periphery of her vision.

Nobody spoke. Taylor Swift still blared from a speaker until someone snapped off the music.

And then, a triumphant smirk on his face, into which the colour had returned, Nikodemus Olsson, Assistant Police Commissioner and head of the Rat Squad, arrested Stella.

2

Stella slept fitfully, her copshop evening meal of brown bread and smoked herring sitting uneasily in her stomach. And now it was morning. What the fuck had she done?

In some ways it would have been nice if she'd been so drunk, so paralytically, catastrophically drunk, that she had no memory of the party. But sadly, she could remember every damned second.

The evening split cleanly into two halves. The half where she was bantering with Jonna and Oskar, telling him he ought to invest in a new wardrobe. And then, abruptly separated by that moment of madness, the half in which she'd shoved her service weapon into Nik Olsson's face.

This was it. No way could she style this out. Claim it was banter that got out of hand, or a simmering rivalry under which alcohol had turned the heat up.

For a start, Nik wasn't drinking. He *never* drank. And, more seriously, banter that got out of hand was supposed to result, if anything, in some over-ripe language. Drinks being hurled into faces. Maybe even a few wild punches being swung.

Not sticking a gun into a senior officer's mug.

Oh, God. She'd be kicked off the force at the very least.

Probably prosecuted. She knew the Swedish penal code as well as Nik and there were plenty of ways he could use it. And after being convicted, she'd be deported. There'd be no way she'd get her old job back. Not to mention the slight problem of her having been exiled by none other than the British prime minister, Gemma Dowding.

Disaster.

The lock clanked. Filling the doorway was a short, barrel-chested man. One of the custody officers. His name was Erno Jacobsson, but everyone called him Eeyore because of his lugubrious manner and long, sad face. He beckoned her out.

'They want you upstairs, Stella.'

His voice was filled with compassion. Suddenly she wanted to cry. She fought back the tears.

On the way up the stairs, Eeyore turned his head.

'Pity you didn't pull the trigger. You'd have done us all a favour.'

His attempt to lighten her spirits brought a brief smile to her face, but the weight of sadness and the anxiety of what was about to happen forced it from her lips as soon as it arrived.

Erno displayed more compassion by leading her through a back corridor to reach Malin's office. The alternative was making the walk of shame down the main hallway where she was guaranteed to meet dozens of her colleagues.

He nodded to her just outside Malin's door.

'Good luck.'

He knocked, pushed the door open and nudged Stella over the threshold before retreating to his subterranean territory.

Stella was breathing shallowly and much too fast. She felt lightheaded and her eyes were full of white sparks that wormed and twinkled everywhere she looked. She swayed and for a horrifying moment thought she was going to faint.

Malin saved her.

'Come and sit down, Stella,' she said from her seat at the round conference table.

Her voice was firm. Not angry, or not so Stella could tell. But that was the thing with Malin. Why she was such an effective leader.

Whereas other senior officers would blare and bluster, believing that volume equated to authority, Malin was more like a headmistress you desperately wanted to please. When you failed her, the mood was one of profound disappointment. The lowered voice somehow ten times more devastating that the loudest yell.

Stella sat.

'Malin, I—'

Malin held up a hand.

'Wait. I've asked someone else to join us.'

Stella whirled round in her chair.

'It's not Nik, is it? You can't have him here. He's got it in for me.'

Malin's response was eloquent and yet understated. She arched one eyebrow.

'*He's* got it in for *you*? The way he explained it to me, he was engaging you in conversation and the next thing he knew you'd drawn your service weapon.'

'I can explain.'

'I'm sure you can. But since Nik was both the victim and the arresting officer, I want him here.'

She depressed a button on the sleek wooden intercom unit on her desk.

'Sofia, would you call Nik and ask him to join us, please.'

Clearly, Nik had been primed and waiting. He entered the office less than a minute later.

He glanced down at Stella before drawing up a chair and sitting opposite her. He looked every inch the victor in the simmering war between them. Nothing as overt as a smirk now. Not in front of Malin. Nik had his emotions well under control. But she sensed it. Something about his posture, which was maybe just a shade more relaxed than normal, as if he already knew he'd won.

Malin clasped her hands in front of her, on top of a single

sheet of paper – a typed-up arrest form. She looked first at Nik, then at Stella.

'I have called this meeting because of the unusual circumstances. Nik, you know I feel I should have been called as soon as you arrested Stella. I have read your report. Now I want to hear both of you tell me in your own words what happened.'

Stella opened her mouth. Malin held up a hand again.

'Nik first. Then you'll have your chance to explain yourself.'

Nik leaned forwards, his elbows on the table, his fingers interlaced under his chin, an unusually coquettish pose for such a morally rigid police officer.

'I thought I would offer a colleague my congratulations on the case she had just solved. Well, she and her team, of course. I noticed she had been drinking—'

'It was a wrap-up party!' Stella jerked forwards, causing Nik to recoil, somewhat theatrically. 'Of course I was drinking!'

'Stella, please,' Malin said, more sharply now.

Nik looked at Malin as if to say, *You see what I mean. Out of control, as usual.*

'I noticed she had been drinking heavily. She was flushed. Slurring. Out of nowhere, she drew her service weapon, as I said in my report, and pointed it directly at me.' He stared at Stella as he continued speaking. A look of smug confidence infused his features. 'This is clearly an offence under Section 5 of the Swedish penal code. Specifically—'

'Thank you, Nik, I know the code. I don't need you quoting the law at me,' Malin said.

But the head of the Rat Squad wasn't to be put off. Now it was his turn to hold up an admonitory hand, like an overzealous traffic cop.

'Stella made an unlawful threat, putting me in fear for the safety of my person. Since she employed a weapon, specifically a firearm, the offence was, in legal terms, gross. Thankfully, Jonna Carlsson, with no regard for her own safety, intervened and was able to disarm Stella, at which point I arrested her.'

Malin had been making notes as Nik spoke. Now she turned to Stella.

'How do you respond to Nik's account?'

Stella's chest was heaving. She'd been struggling to maintain her cool as Nik's lies dripped from his lips. She inhaled deeply and let the air out in a hiss.

'Parts of Nik's story are true,' she began, angry that her voice was still trembling. 'Yes, I had been drinking. Yes, he did come over to talk to me. And yes, I did pick up a pistol. And I am ashamed to say that I did point it at him.'

'I told you,' Nik said.

'But, Nik's account is inaccurate on a number of material points.' Stella tapped the table. 'One, I had not been drinking heavily. Just a few cans of Oppigårds. They took my blood alcohol level last night. You can check the results.

'Two, Nik didn't offer me or my team congratulations. I guess thanking honest cops for their hard work would have stuck in his throat. Instead what he did was first to insinuate I was drunk. Then he threatened me with these wild accusations of supposed misconduct when I was at the Met. He was invading my personal space and making *me* feel unsafe so I pushed him away from me.'

Stella had her breathing under control again. And the look in Nik's eyes told her she was landing punches.

'Finally, and not for the first time, he referred in derogatory terms to the effect the deaths of my husband and my baby daughter had on me. He also made reference to my medical records, which, as you know, are confidential under British and Swedish law, so I have no idea how he got hold of them. That's when I picked up my service weapon. I didn't draw it, by the way; it was on my desk.'

'Which in itself was dangerous,' Nik said.

'No, it wasn't. It was unloaded.'

Nik pounced. 'Really? Because as you ought to know, Stella, the 2012 regulations change required Swedish police officers to carry their pistols loaded with a round in the chamber.'

'No, Nik, the regs *permit*, they don't *require*. In any case, I personally prefer not to take any kind of risks. So I always unload my pistol and put the magazine in my desk drawer.'

Malin held up a hand for silence.

'We are not here to discuss SPA firearms regulations. Now, you, Nik, have made serious allegations against Stella. But she has directly contradicted some of your testimony. Were there any witnesses to what was said between you?'

'No,' Nik said.

'He made sure of it,' Stella said.

'Quiet, please, Stella. Shit-the-devil, do I have to get a talking stick from the creche to keep you two under control?'

The image of Nik bouncing in his seat, holding up his hand to be given a gaily painted wooden stick allowing him to talk was too much. Stella laughed, then, wide-eyed with shock, clapped a hand over her mouth.

'I am sorry, are you finding all this funny?' Malin asked. 'Because I am not. You are under arrest because you pointed your service weapon at Nik. This is no laughing matter.'

'No. I know. I'm sorry, Malin. And...' She cleared her throat, then forced an unwilling head to rotate until she was looking directly at her accuser. 'And, Nik, I'm sorry for what I did. It must have been a terrible fright.'

He inclined his head. 'It was. But please don't imagine an apology is going to change the substance of this matter. Malin, I want to talk to the prosecutor about having Stella charged.'

Stella felt a disorientating sense of vertigo. Everything she'd worked for was dangling over a precipice, kept aloft by the thinnest of threads, around which Nik was closing a pair of razor-sharp shears.

'Hold on, Nik. Let's put the bridle on the horse before we send it out to race,' Malin said, employing a Swedish saying Stella hadn't heard before. 'Did you threaten to investigate Stella over things she is supposed to have done while in England?'

Nik couldn't meet her eye. 'Well, I—'

'And did you also refer to confidential health matters contained in Stella's medical records?'

'Look, Malin, this isn't the issue. She pointed—'

' — an unloaded pistol at you. Yes, and she has admitted that. So?'

'So, what?'

'Did you, or did you not, refer to Stella's confidential medical records?'

'Look, I really don't see what this has to do with the charge of making gross unlawful threats.'

Malin eyed him beadily, her lips a thin line. 'At the moment, there are no charges. Did you talk about Stella's family?'

He hesitated. And in that moment, Stella felt the ground firming beneath her feet. It was going to be OK. Malin believed her.

Nik shook his head.

'No. Absolutely not. I wouldn't. I know how traumatic her loss was. I wouldn't be so insensitive.'

Stella jumped to her feet.

'Liar!' she shouted. She pointed a finger at him and this time, if it had been curled around a SIG Sauer's trigger, there was no doubt in her mind what she would have done. 'You fucking liar!'

'Stella! Please. Sit down.'

Malin's eyes were flashing dangerously. Stella complied, her chest feeling light and fluttery.

Nik smiled. 'You see, Malin. As I said, she is unstable and clearly has anger-management issues. And when she is off the force, perhaps she can arrange for some therapy. Or maybe the SPA itself can help an ex-officer with what is evidently a serious mental health issue.'

Malin placed her palms flat on the table. She looked at the sheet of notes in front of her, then back at Stella. Then at Nik.

She opened her mouth to speak.

'In view of the seriousness—'

There was a knock at the door and then Jonna strode into the office, her heart-shaped face pale but with a flash of defiance in her eyes.

'Malin, I have something to say. I know this is supposed to be a private meeting but I believe Assistant Commissioner Olsson may be making false testimony.'

Nik was on his feet.

'This is outrageous! Yes, Inspector Carlsson, this is indeed a private meeting. You have no right barging in. I suggest you leave at once before your actions result in unpleasant consequences.'

Jonna didn't move. She folded her arms across her chest. In the shadow of her jawline, a blood vessel pulsed. Stella counted the beats. Jonna's pulse was racing.

'Malin, please. I had to come. You have to listen to me.'

Malin said nothing for a full minute. To Stella it might have been an hour. Then she inclined her head, just as Nik had done a few minutes earlier. She pointed to the third chair at the table.

3

Jonna gave Stella the briefest of glances, then faced Malin. Waiting to be invited to speak.

Stella admired her friend's self-control. Felt keenly her own lack in this department. What was Jonna going to say? How could she possibly pull Stella's chestnuts out of the fire? Right now, she needed more than a character witness.

Malin smiled at her subordinate.

'You'd better tell us what was so important you gate-crashed a private meeting.'

Jonna nodded and gasped in a short breath.

'Last night, I was dancing with Micki. Then, after the track ended, I went over to offer to fetch Stella another beer. But it was clear she and Nik were having some sort of argument. I hung back a little, but I could still hear everything, even though I don't think either of them was aware I was still there. Then he said something super-provocative and that was when Stella,' she glanced sideways at Stella, 'well, that was when she picked up her pistol.'

Stella felt a surge of love for Jonna. She'd heard it all. She looked at Nik. His face had paled. He was chewing his lower lip.

'Did you hear what he said, Jonna?' Malin asked. 'And I mean, exactly what he said?'

The room went totally silent for a count of five. Jonna stared at Nik.

'Yes.'

'Then please tell us what you heard.'

Jonna cleared her throat. 'First of all I want to say that it was so outrageous, I went and wrote it down straight afterwards. After Nik arrested Stella, I mean.' She pulled a notebook from her pocket and opened it. In her hyper-alert state, Stella could see the herringbone pattern of the woven tape bookmark. 'He said, "losing your husband and baby daughter to a hit and run would be enough to turn anyone away from righteousness. I suppose we should be grateful that this time it's only alcohol you're abusing, and not pills".'

Jonna closed the notebook.

Her face an unreadable mask, Malin turned to her right.

'Nik?'

He shrugged, folded his arms, then uncrossed them and locked his fingers together in front of him. His jaw muscles were bunching under the close-shaved skin of his cheeks, but his mouth was a straight line. Finally, he worked his lips loose.

'Yes, well, my memory is hazy. The stress, you know. Maybe I did mention Stella's family.'

'Though a moment ago your memory seemed quite clear when you denied it. And you referred to confidential details of her medical history. Meaning, presumably, that you *did* find a way to access her medical records.'

His face screwed up as if his guts were griping.

'Look, none of this is relevant,' he blurted. 'She pointed a Goddamn pistol in my face. I could have been killed!'

'With an unloaded gun?'

'All right, I *believed* I could have been killed.'

Malin turned to Jonna.

'Thank you, Jonna. That will be all.' As Jonna got up, Malin held out her hand. 'Leave the notebook, please.'

Playing the Devil's Music

Once it was only the three of them in Malin's office again, she spoke.

'Well, what do I do now? Nik, you lied to my face about your encounter with Stella. But, Stella, you still drew down on a fellow officer. That was unforgivable.'

'Exactly!' said Nik, 'Which is why I—'

Malin's temper, tamped down throughout the entire meeting, finally flared up.

'For the devil in hell, Nik, shut up! Stella, I am releasing you from custody.' Nik opened his mouth, unwisely, in Stella's opinion. Malin cut him off. 'If a single syllable comes out of your mouth, I will shoot you myself. It's clear to me that you deliberately provoked Stella. If all she'd done was give you a bloody nose or knocked a tooth loose, we wouldn't even be having this meeting. But the fact that you, Stella, pulled a gun on him makes this impossible to ignore. I'm putting you on administrative leave – without pay – for a week, while I figure out what the hell I'm going to do. Get changed, collect your things and go home. And do *not* speak to anyone on your way out. Especially not Jonna. Nik, I hear you loud and clear and I will take appropriate action to punish Stella. That's it.'

Nik shot to his feet, two spots of colour blooming high on his angular cheekbones.

'You can't do this. I'll take it to Agnes.'

Now both of Malin's neatly plucked eyebrows ascended towards her hairline.

'Really? You'd bother the National Police Chief with this? I'd say it would be a fifty-fifty call on who she'd throw the book at. But do what you think you have to.' Malin began shuffling her papers together into a neat pile. 'Now, if you will both excuse me, I have some actual work to do, maintaining at least a semblance of law and order in Stockholm.'

Stella thanked Malin and skirted the table to leave the office before Nik. He was bluffing about going to the chief. He'd committed at least one offence himself and she knew what it would cost him to be exposed as a liar. His entire image was built on being a pillar of moral rectitude.

Doing as she'd been ordered, she collected a few things from her desk and went home.

Inside her apartment, she poured a glass of wine then caught sight of the time – 10:15 a.m. – and immediately tipped it down the sink. Instead, she headed for the bathroom, stripped off her clothes and stepped under a scalding hot shower where she stayed until the water ran cold.

Five minutes later, she was running down to the waterside, ignoring her muscles' plea to take it easy until her heart and lungs had adjusted, pushing herself harder and harder until she was flying alongside the river, the wind pulling water from the corners of her eyes and then immediately drying them.

What the hell had she done? And what kind of punishment would Malin impose? She was neither a sadist, nor a dictator. But she was going to have to do something serious, if for no other reason than to buy off Nik Olsson.

A sarcastic voice in her head piped up.

Maybe you should get fitted for a traffic uniform over the weekend, babe.

She blanked it out. It was only her subconscious adopting that hated persona to make her feel worse.

That's what she told herself.

4

The weekend passed in a slow-moving parade of dull domestic tasks Stella floated through as if semi-conscious. By Monday, she resolved to shake herself out of the torpor into which she'd sunken. No way was she going to let this drag her any further down.

Stella had just finished loading her breakfast things into the dishwasher when the doorbell rang.

She pressed the intercom button.

'Hello?'

'Stella, it's Malin.'

Her stomach knotting, Stella thumbed the door-release button. She put the kettle on and began spooning ground coffee into her cafetière. The first scoopful caught on the edge of the glass container and scattered the fine brown powder over the work surface. She swore and reached for a cloth. Caught her shirt sleeve on the tap and heard the rip as she tore the cuff.

She sighed out a breath and tried again. Finally, with the coffee made and her cuff rolled back on itself, she was just setting out some crispbreads and marmalade when Malin rapped on the door.

The expression on her boss's face was unreadable.

'Hey, Malin,' Stella said. 'Come in. I made coffee.'

Seated facing each other across Stella's kitchen table, sipping coffee and, in Malin's case, nibbling crispbread, the two women might have been old friends discussing a book they'd both finished. But old friends didn't make each other feel nauseous, anxious that they were about to lose everything they'd worked so hard for.

Malin placed the half-eaten crispbread down on the white side plate. She looked at it for a second, then poked an index finger at a corner and rotated it by a few degrees. Stella was almost crying with nervousness. She wanted to scream at her boss to just get it over with, but at the same time, to prolong the moment before she had to confront the end of her police career.

Malin sighed.

Stella blinked.

Malin spoke.

'You are the best homicide investigator I have ever met.'

'Malin, please, I—'

' – tenacious, brave. Brilliant, actually. You have impressed me from day one. But you have a dark side, Stella. And you let it get the better of you last Thursday night.'

She looked into Stella's eyes. A much more piercing gaze than that of the kindly Alyssa, the SPA psychologist she'd been seeing on and off.

'Just tell me, Malin,' Stella blurted. 'Are you firing me?'

Malin held Stella's gaze. Stella realised she'd never wanted anything so much as, right now, she wanted to keep her job at the SPA.

Then she shook her head.

'No. I am not firing you. Although part of me thinks maybe I should. But in any case, it's not that simple. All those Organisation and People procedures to go through, you'd still be here at Midsummer.'

She offered a half-smile. Stella realised it was her boss's

attempt at a joke. She tried to reciprocate, but her own lips were frozen into a taut line.

'Then what? Will I be charged like Nik wants?'

Malin sighed. 'No. Nik and I had several long conversations over the weekend. I persuaded him to let me handle it.'

That was weird, even for the Queen of Weirdness. Nik was not the sort of man to back down.

'How though? He hates me. I could see it in his eyes when he arrested me.'

'It doesn't matter. But I had to offer him something ... substantial. He will lose face as it is.'

'Just tell me, Malin. Please. I can't bear this,' Stella pleaded.

'How much do you know about ketamine, coke, meth, all that?' Malin asked.

Stella blinked.

'You're not transferring me to the drugs squad, are you?'

'No. I'm putting you in charge of the drugs outreach and education programme. You'll be delivering talks to school children.'

Stella's heart sank. But she could handle a brief retreat from front-line policing.

'For how long? A week? Two?'

'Six months.'

Stella's jaw flopped open. Six months? Standing in front of bored teenagers trying to instil in them a terror of drugs they'd never had and never would?

She could only repeat the length of her sentence.

'Six months?'

Malin nodded. 'You start today. Go to see Dirk Jansson in Community Policing. He'll take you through all his materials,' she said. 'PowerPoints, props, scripts, leaflets. He'll give you the list of schools and colleges on your patch, too.'

'Malin, *please*. You can't.'

The bang as Malin's palm smacked down onto the table made Stella jump. Gone was the calm expression her boss managed even during the most stressful moments. Gone was the half-smile.

In their place, something filled with a teeth-bared fury so rare Stella felt genuinely terrified.

'*I* can't? How about *you*, Stella? How about what *you* can't do? You can't pull a gun on a senior officer and expect to walk away without a scratch. If you don't like the sound of it, I could always let Nik have his way.'

Stella knew she should stop protesting. Take her punishment. Suck it up. And six months wasn't so long. It seemed her mouth disagreed.

'But, I'm a *murder* detective. It's what I do. It's *all* I do!'

'Stella, let me explain something to you,' Malin said, in a tired-sounding voice. 'You *used* to be a murder detective. If Nik had got his way, even without you facing assault charges, you would now be an assistant exhibits room clerk in Uppsala. It's in the basement. And it smells of dried blood, mouldy clothes and stale semen. I had to negotiate hard with Nik to get you bumped *up* to this job.'

She should apologise. Thank Malin. Go quietly. Take her medicine. Villains had a saying, after all. 'If you can't do the time, don't do the crime.'

'But six months! I'll go crazy,' she said instead. 'And what about my live cases? Who'll handle them?'

'Oskar is more than capable. Jonna can act up. Micki is keen. They'll be fine.'

'But—'

'No!' Malin barked. 'You're a senior officer, Stella. You let Nik get to you and you left yourself exposed.'

'You heard what Jonna said. Nik provoked me. And my gun wasn't even loaded.'

'That's not the point!' Malin snapped, her voice rising to a dangerous pitch again. 'A conviction for assault would have ended your career overnight. Maybe six months teaching kids about the horrors of drugs will give you some perspective.' Then her voice softened. 'Nik's a humourless zealot, OK? We all know that. But you shouldn't have risen to the bait.'

Maybe it was the sudden diminution of anger in Malin's voice that did it. But suddenly all the fight went out of Stella. She was beaten, and it sounded like Malin had fought pretty hard to get Nik to back away from the criminal charges. She owed her.

'I'm sorry it's come to this and I'm sorry for failing you, Malin. I'll go and see Dirk. And I'll talk those bloody kids out of trying anything too heinous.'

She'd been hoping for a smile. But Malin's expression was stony.

'There's one more thing. As of today, I'm demoting you from Inspector, Group Chief to plain Inspector, with a concomitant reduction in salary.'

Stella swallowed. It wasn't the money. It was the pride. In Met terms she'd just been busted two ranks, from DI to DC. A detective constable. Oh, her title remained the same. They were all *kriminalinspektörs*. She could still introduce herself as Detective Inspector Cole. But everyone in the department would know. Once again, tears pricked at her eyes and she had to clear her throat to prevent them overspilling her lids.

She clamped her lips. Nodded. Managed a brief, quiet, 'OK.'

Malin stood, stuck her arm out stiffly. They shook hands. And then she was gone.

Stella turned around a full circle in her empty kitchen.

She swore, loudly.

5

That Friday, at the end of a week spent familiarising herself with Fred's PowerPoint presentations and other teaching materials, Stella answered the door to Jonna.

Jonna held up a bottle of white wine and a huge bag of crisps.

'Hey, you,' she said, stepping across the threshold and enveloping Stella in an awkward hug, punctuated by the crackling of the crisp bag. 'Fancy some company?'

'Oh, Jonna, thank you. And yes, absolutely. I don't know how I'm going to survive this.'

Jonna poured them both some wine and tipped the crisps into a large orange plastic bowl. She pointed to the sofa.

'Sit down, drink some wine and tell me everything.'

Once they were comfortable, facing each other from opposite ends of the sofa, legs tucked underneath, Stella raised her glass.

'Cheers.'

'Cheers.'

They drank and then Stella sighed.

'Tell you everything? Honestly? It's so boring I think you'd get up and leave. Tell me what's going on in the office instead. Have I missed anything juicy?'

Jonna pursed her lips.

'It's weird without you. Micki's still learning the ropes, bouncing around like a puppy who isn't housetrained yet. Oskar's in an even grumpier mood than usual. And it can't be little Gustav because I spoke to Hedda last week and she said he's being good as gold. It's probably because of Malin.'

'What about her? He can't be mad at her for suspending me, surely? I mean, now I've had some time to think, she had no other option. I mean, I did pull a gun on Nik.'

'Which he totally deserved. But no. Not exactly. You see…' Jonna reached for her glass. 'Well, the thing is she made me promise not to tell you.'

'Tell me what? You can't just dangle that in front of me and then clam up, Jonna. Tell me!'

'OK. But you have to swear you won't tell anybody you know. Or if you do,' she smiled, 'at least don't tell them it was me.'

'God, just spill it before I force you.'

'Well, you know she had to negotiate with Nik to get him not to take the whole thing to Jan Harkin?'

Stella pictured the prosecutor's face, the way he always had the ghost of a smile playing on his lips. Normally a friend, she wondered how he'd have reacted if he'd had to charge Stella.

'Yes. Hence my suspension. And demotion.'

Jonna's gaze flittered away from Stella's just for a second.

'It's not just that. The Stockholm Police Master's job is going to be vacant when Carl Bergdahl retires at the end of next month, yes? Well, Malin was going to apply. Nik said he'd agree to leave you alone only if she withdrew her candidacy.'

Stella was shocked. 'Why? What does he have to gain?'

'He wants one of his own to get the job. Malin's a much stronger candidate but if she pulls out, it's all but certain Nik's guy will get the job.'

Stella was struggling to process the news that Malin had sacrificed massive progress in her career to save Stella's. She took a big mouthful of the wine and swallowed. Then she emptied her glass.

'Jesus. That's terrible. I mean, of course I'm grateful. I would have been toast otherwise. But why?'

'I asked her. She invited me out for coffee. I think she just needed to talk to someone. She said, and I quote, "Stella's too good to lose. Sweden's a safer place with her on the team". End quote.'

Stella leaned back against the cushions. Malin thought that about her? Her eyes pricked and she had to cough suddenly to clear the lump that had formed in her throat.

'I have to see her. To thank her. To promise her nothing like that will ever happen again.'

Jonna's eyes popped wide. 'No! You can't. She'll know I told you, dummy. What did I just say? You can't tell her.'

'Then I have to get through my suspension and then prove her right.' She refilled their glasses and this time took a more measured sip of the wine. 'This is good. Pass the crisps.'

Jonna handed her the orange plastic bowl and then, as she sat back, a frown flitted across her features. Not for long. A here-and-then-gone expression. Stella caught it all the same.

'What?' she mumbled through a mouthful of salty, crunchy slivers.

'It was when you said about being demoted. You and Malin aren't the only ones with career changes.'

Stella swallowed hastily and sat up, leaning towards Jonna.

'What? Why? You're not leaving the force, are you?'

Jonna shook her head, offered Stella a nervous smile.

'No. Nothing like that. Actually, I've applied for a new job, too. Please don't be mad at me.'

Stella smiled. 'Of course I'm not mad. What's the job? Tell me.'

'You know I used to work in Financial Crime? Well, my old boss is leaving and the new chief has asked for me to apply to be her deputy. I'll have to go through the interview process, but she hinted the job's as good as mine. It's a big step up. I'll be Deputy Section Chief.'

Stella felt a sudden mix of emotions swirling through her.

Sadness that Jonna would be leaving Homicide. But joy for her friend.

'Jonna, that's amazing. I'm so happy for you. Come here.'

She hugged Jonna tightly.

'I'm proud of you. Just, tell me though. Is it me? You don't like working for the "Queen of Weirdness". I know I get a lot of media attention, but I wish I didn't. You know that, right?'

'Of course I do. And no. I love working for you. It's actually the job. When I started in Homicide, it felt so much more real than fincrime. All those spreadsheets and paper trails felt cold compared to the real-world stuff you and Oskar do. But these last few cases, and especially what happened with Tilde, I just don't think I'm cut out to do it long term. You're really OK with it?'

'Of course. And I do get it, Jonna, believe me. Sometimes I wonder if there's something wrong with me. The way I can rock up to each new crime scene and just get stuck in.'

'I don't think there's anything wrong with you. You're great. I could never be half as good an investigator as you.'

Stella grinned. 'Quick, pour more wine before this turns into a mutual love-fest.'

Jonna smiled shyly. 'Would that be so bad?'

'No. But I think the rest of them might get jealous.'

'Who cares about them?' Jonna said, taking another mouthful of the wine. 'Hey, are we going to eat? This stuff's going straight to my head.'

'Fish OK for you? I bought some salmon today. It's quite nice having the time to go to the market mid-morning. Did you know some people actually go shopping in the daylight hours?'

'Really?' Jonna said, faking amazement. 'Are you sure they weren't actors?'

'No, I'm sure they're real Stockholmers. They talk about stuff like the weather and whether AIK are going to win the championship cup, instead of how you'd glue a swan's wing onto a dead person's arm.'

Jonna shook her head. 'No. I don't buy it. Sounds ridiculous. They *must* be actors.'

Laughing, the two women went through to the kitchen where Stella skinned the salmon fillets and pulled the pin bones out with a pair of pliers.

After the meal, during which they finished the first bottle and began on a second, Stella sprawled on the sofa, Jonna next to her. Both of them with their feet up on leather pouffes.

Stella picked up the TV remote.

'Movie?'

Jonna took a swig of her wine.

'Movie. Nothing soppy. Maybe a horror film. Vampires, werewolves, something nice and scary.'

'Said the woman making a move back into spreadsheet-land.'

'Hey!' She elbowed Stella in the ribs. 'I bet you're the one who ends up hiding behind a cushion.'

As the credits rolled, and a full moon illuminated a wood populated entirely by spiky, bare-branched trees like clutching hands, Stella relaxed against the back of the sofa, hip-to-hip with Jonna.

The new gig was going to be a pain, but maybe she could use the time to regroup mentally. Book some appointments with Alyssa. Work through some of her anger issues. She could still hang out with Jonna and their friendship would certainly be easier now she didn't report into Stella.

And then she screamed.

The young hiker, her face white in the moonlight, way off the path but still cheerfully oblivious to the skeletal trees that practically screamed, 'Danger!', was attacked by a hideous creature.

The monster had a man's torso but it was twisted horribly with ropy muscles and pulsing blood vessels just beneath the skin. Its head was like a peeled skull. No cheesy sideburns and dog-like snout: more like something she'd see on Henrik Brodin's dissection table. Yellow fangs dripped with slime.

Stella snatched up the cushion in her lap and clapped it to her face. Beside her, Jonna screeched with laughter.

'Thirty seconds! I told you.'

Heart pumping, Stella gingerly lowered the cushion. The director allowed her to settle for a full five minutes before hitting her with another jump-scare, but by now the wine was starting to have an effect and she felt her eyelids drooping.

She woke with her head lolling onto Jonna's left shoulder, her right hand clasping Jonna's left. White names, thousands of them, scrolled upwards on a black screen.

'Oh, sorry. I missed it all.'

Jonna turned her face towards Stella.

'It's fine. I dozed off myself.'

Stella struggled to focus. Jonna's face was too close.

'Time is it?' she mumbled.

'Late. Midnight, nearly.'

'Oh. Do you want to stay? You can't drive.'

'Probably best. I can take the sofa.'

'No, no,' Stella said pushing herself upright. 'You can share with me. You don't snore, do you?'

Jonna smiled. 'Nobody's told me I do. Why, do you?'

Stella shrugged.

'Just roll me over if I do.'

* * *

The next morning, Stella awoke with a throbbing head to find Jonna already gone. She'd left a note on the kitchen table beside a cafetière ready-prepped with ground coffee and a packet of ibuprofen.

Got called into the office. Body floating in river. Thanks for last night. Xx

Stella pressed a couple of painkillers out of the blister pack and swallowed them with a mouthful of cold water straight from the tap. She filled the kettle and switched it on then strolled across to the window.

Somewhere out there, Jonna was probably suited up and standing over a waterlogged body. Would it be her last case before moving back to white-collar crime where the worst people did to each other was measured in ones and zeroes in hidden bank accounts?

She shook her head, then immediately wished she hadn't as a shower of sharp-edged bolts and screws rattled loose inside her skull.

The image of the bloody monster from the previous night's movie flashed into her mind's eye. Why did lone female hikers always take the wrong path? Didn't they know any better?

6

NINE WEEKS LATER, AXBERG, 161 KM WEST OF STOCKHOLM

He checks his watch. Five to midnight. He tugs the zip on his bomber jacket up as high as it will go, and pulls the ear flaps down on his hat. A stiff breeze is blowing off the water. It's cold for the first day of May.

Where the hell is the man he's supposed to be meeting? And what's with the stupid code-name he gave him over the phone? Baffömett, was it? Idiot.

If the meeting was so urgent, why the hell isn't he here as promised? Some stupid power play, probably. Reminding him who's boss. Except Baffömett isn't the boss, either, is he? He just has delusions of grandeur. He's stayed alive long enough, done enough bad things, greased up to the right people often enough to rise upwards. Like shit in a septic tank.

In the distance, a dog barks. Something big, deep-chested. A rottweiler maybe, or a German shepherd. When he retires, which all being well will be end of January next year, he intends to get a dog himself. He fancies a French bulldog. Or maybe one of those ugly-looking sons of bitches – Ha, ha, literally! – an English bull terrier. Head like a melted wax model and those slitty, triangular eyes.

The dog is going crazy. The barking takes on a frenzied air. He shakes his head. Grins. Shit-the-devil, some kid breaking into a house for drug-money is going to get the shock of his life.

He smiles to himself as he imagines some skinny-arsed teenaged pill-head getting a mauling from some farmer's guard dog. 'Shouldn't have broken in, then, should you,' he says into the cold night air, his breath pluming in front of him.

The barking ascends in pitch. The dog sounds panicky more than angry. A loud, plaintive squeal tears through the air and is choked off on a rising note. Then … nothing.

All the hairs on the back of his neck stand on end.

He spins round, but he is alone. Still.

'Come on, man, I'm freezing my balls off out here.'

He pats his hip. The gun feels comforting under his jacket. He doesn't believe in boogeymen, trolls, ogres or ghosts. The only people he worries about are flesh-and-blood, and then not much. He's put a couple down when they've made the wrong move. So, basically, they can go to hell.

Five more minutes pass. The wind stiffens. In the moonlight, the nearby birches sway, their slender branches curving like whips. Their new leaves rustle and whisper. A car speeds along the distant road, window open, music blaring from the radio.

He catches the sound of footsteps and turns, hand coming up to the butt of his pistol.

Then he sighs, smiled. Relaxes. Baffömett is here at last.

'What took you so long? I've been waiting for twenty minutes.'

'My watch stopped.'

'Stopped? What, the battery died, you mean?'

'No. Like, it stopped. I forgot to wind it.'

'You've got a clockwork watch? What is this, the seventies?'

'I like it. It's old school.'

'Yeah, and it stopped. That's real old school.'

'I'm here now, aren't I?'

He sighs.

'Yeah, you are. So, what was so urgent we had to meet in the middle of the night?'

'I need you to look at something for me,' the man calling himself Baffömett says, reaching into his jeans pocket.

If Baffömett had gone for a jacket pocket, he would have had his pistol on the way out of its holster, but the guy's jeans are a snug fit. No way he has a concealed weapon. OK, maybe a flick-knife, but why would he?

When the hand emerges it is curled round a piece of white cloth. What the hell?

'What's that?' he asks, peering closer at the upraised hand.

Baffömett snaps his other hand out and grabs the back of his head, dragging him forward and down. He staggers as he struggles to keep his balance, then the cloth is clamped against his nose and mouth.

He gasps and the first wisps of vapour enter his nostrils. Waxy, oily, lemony. He coughs, staggers, tries to breathe. Takes a lungful this time. Nausea overwhelms him. His stomach rolls over. His vision greys out, then everything turns black.

* * *

He opens his eyes. He feels sick. Tries to turn his head but finds, with a sense of disbelief, that it is immobile. He frowns. What the hell happened? He smells cowshit and, floating lightly over the top, diesel. He is in some kind of farm building. A barn? A vehicle store? Above his head, a single bulb hangs on a long, off-white cable, looped among the rafters.

He tries to move his hands but they are pinioned to his sides. His feet next, but they, too, are fixed in place What the fuck?

Is he tied down? Or taped? A nightmarish vision presents itself. Those horror films he likes to watch after the pub. Some dipshit hiker off the path, hunted down by backwoods cannibals. Turned into a bloody *smörgåsbord*.

Panicky and lightheaded, he draws in as deep a breath as his rackety lungs will let him and screams for help. His terror echoes back at him off the corrugated-iron walls.

Footsteps.

'You're awake.'

'Yes, I'm fucking awake. What is this? You're pissed off, I get it. But you've got to let me go.'

Baffömett hoves into view, behind where his head is strapped down so he has to roll his eyes upwards in their sockets. From this angle, Baffömett looks ominously like the trolls and giants he doesn't believe in.

He spots what Baffömet holds in his right hand and screams again.

'Scream all you like. Nobody'll hear you. There's nobody *to* hear you.'

Then he does something terrifying. He throws back his own head and bays up at the roof. A deep, moaning, fiendish howl that gathers volume and then rises to become an unearthly scream that sets the very metal of the walls ringing in sympathy.

The curved blade he is holding ends in a sharp point. Light from the overhead bulb glints off the mirror-polished steel.

'Please, no,' he says, feeling his bladder let go and smelling the acrid stink of his own urine as the knife slides under the neck of his shirt.

The knife slips down, all the way to his navel, parting the brushed cotton of his shirt and exposing his bare torso. His bowels loosen. He clenches his buttocks together, as hard as he can. No way is he going to allow Baffömett to scare him into shitting himself. This is all a bluff. He'll stop at any moment and explain what he really wants.

Baffömett smiles. Upside down, it looks wrong.

'This is going to hurt.'

'What? No! Don't. You can't!'

And then the cutting starts.

Joel screams for a while, then passes out when the pain overwhelms him. He dreams of devils prodding him with pitchforks, jabbing them into his unprotected flesh as they drive him towards a fiery pit in which more red-skinned demons cavort.

When he awakens, the pain from his chest is like burning hot wires dragged tight across his skin.

Baffömett is waiting. He holds up a mirror, like a barber anxious to make sure his client likes his new haircut. Only the angle at which he holds it means the client can see his own breastbone. He screams again.

His breath comes in rapid, fluttering spasms. His terror deepens to something so primal he wants to simply hide somewhere dark, his arms over his head until the danger has passed.

Baffömett nods down at him. Then he produces something that at first he can't identify. A dirty creamy-white, twisting and ridged, with a wicked point. Then, when he does recognise it, he screams for the third time.

The weapon upraised, Baffömett chants something gibberish. It sounds like it might be Norwegian or one of those bastard languages they speak up in the far north where the Sàmi people herd reindeer.

'Please, no,' he moans. Then begs. 'I'll do anything. Just don't—'

Gripping the weapon in both hands, Baffömett drives it down towards his chest. It breaks through his ribcage with a sound like crackling logs on a fire.

As it punctures his heart, the last thought that flits through his darkening mind is that he won't be getting that dog after all.

7

OLOF PALME HIGH SCHOOL, ÖREBRO

The mottled female corpse with the syringe dangling from the crook of the left elbow below a tied-off length of brown rubber didn't belong in the sunlit classroom.

Which was precisely why Stella had projected the photograph onto the screen behind her. The government's latest line on drugs education (there had been many) was much more hard-line than the previous attempt to prevent the flower of Swedish youth from succumbing. The minister had gone on record as saying she wanted children to be confronted with 'the shocking reality of drug addiction'.

The slouching teenagers ranged in front of her moaned in feigned, or actual, disgust.

'I'm shook,' a boy drawled.

Beside Stella and slightly to her rear, an attractive woman in her late forties sat on a table swinging slim legs clad in expensively shabby jeans. She wore a white linen shirt and lots of chunky amber jewellery and she smiled at Stella as she caught her eye. She ran a hand through her tousled, dirty-blonde hair.

Stella clicked onto the next slide, a syringe of heroin, beside a little conical pile of brown powder. As she delivered the lines she knew off by heart, her mind wandered, as it usually did at about this point in the drugs talk.

She was daydreaming about riding her new motorbike through the Swedish forests when a voice interrupted her spectral journey among the towering pines.

'Stella?' a girl asked.

She frowned. Snapped back to the present. She had no recollection of the last five minutes. She supposed she must have finished the talk.

'Yes?'

'Have *you* ever done drugs?'

Giggles rippled through the classroom. Stella looked at her questioner; slender, bespectacled, pimple-studded forehead. She wasn't smirking. No half-raised eyebrow or sideways glance at her classmates.

When he'd handed over all his materials at their first meeting back in March, Dirk had given her stock answers for all the Smart-Alec questions kids thought they were the first to come up with. She deployed one now.

'I had some brilliant diamorphine once,' she deadpanned. 'That's clinical-grade heroin, essentially. Trouble was, I couldn't afford the street price once the hospital discharged me.'

Her questioner looked unimpressed.

'But seriously, Stella. Have you?'

She shook her head.

'No. Sorry. Alcohol's my poison, which, as I made clear right at the beginning, *is* a drug, but it happens to be legal. And that's the big difference.'

The blonde woman slid off the table and came to join Stella at the front of the classroom.

'Remember, you can get loads of information from the Frankie Miller Foundation website and get confidential answers to your questions from the official sites, as well.'

The young female teacher joined them at the front of the classroom. She smiled at Stella and then turned to face her students.

'Let's thank Frankie, whose foundation is sponsoring this drugs education programme, and also Stella, for sharing some of her experience and knowledge with us.'

The applause was ragged and, Stella thought, ironic. Something about the pace and volume of the clapping suggested the group of fifteen- and sixteen-year-olds had heard it all before and had long ago done their own research online.

After receiving a private statement of gratitude from the teacher, Stella and Frankie left.

Outside, Stella smiled at the sight of her new bike, a Triumph Speed Twin. It was a warm, bright day and she was looking forward to riding home. Frankie's ride was altogether more luxurious. A metallic bronze Porsche Cayenne SUV with privacy glass.

She came to stand beside Stella, stretching out manicured fingers to stroke the gleaming petrol tank.

'Very stylish. And so cool for a cop. I'd have thought they want you driving something serious and Swedish like a Volvo.'

Stella shrugged as she fastened up her treasured leather jacket with the orange stripe, enjoying the snug sensation as she clipped the press stud home at her throat.

'For work, yes. But as this is my private transport, I drive what I like.'

Frankie laughed. 'Isn't this work?'

Stella rolled her eyes. 'I suppose so. I meant real work.'

Frankie checked her watch. 'Do you have time for a coffee? We're actually only a few kilometres from my house if you want to follow me?'

'Sure. I'd like that.'

In truth, what Stella would have liked more was to power east along the E18 back to Stockholm and blow the classroom dust out of her head. But in her current situation, she needed all the friends she could get. And in Frankie Miller, she'd discovered a kindred spirit who was also influential and connected.

8

JACOBSSON FARM, AXBERG

Kim Jacobsson loved driving the big, charcoal-grey Valtra N Series. For a tractor, it was pretty comfortable. Air con in the summer, a decent heater in the winter. Multi-sprung seat that was more comfortable than the sofa in the house. His favourite tracks playing through a sound system tons better than the one in Dad's Subaru.

As he made the turn by the corner of the wood bordering the big field, he craned his neck to get a better look. Something – no, somebody – was hanging around by the Devil Tree. What in hell's name was he doing? Was he? He was! The damned idiot was wearing antlers.

The story was that, back in the seventeenth century, they burned a witch and buried her body in the wood. An oak tree grew from an acorn she had in a pouch on her belt. The tree would grant favours to anyone brave enough to offer a sacrifice.

Nowadays the only people who believed all that nonsense were the wiccans and the pagans. Mostly posh kids from the city who had the money to indulge such stupid beliefs. They'd come up here at the solstices or just when there was a full moon. Performing their so-called rituals. It was trespassing. But Dad just said 'Oh, let them be, Kim, it's harmless enough'.

Kim was too busy working on the farm for it. If it were up to him, he'd have cut the bloody thing down and sold the lumber to a sawmill, but the county authorities had slapped a preservation order on the tree. Now it stood there, on their land, festooned with ribbons, glass ornaments, naked Barbie dolls, pentagrams woven from twigs, all kinds of crap.

He circled back to get a closer look at the new age idiot trespassing on their land.

He dropped the side window, ready to yell out a warning. The words died in his throat.

The guy by the tree wasn't standing there hammering a five krona coin into the bark, or tying a rainbow ribbon onto a lower branch.

He was dead.

Kim was in no doubt. It was pretty obvious.

The whole front of the man's chest was a mess of blood. The dark crater of some kind of stab wound blared out of the gore. His antlered head hung down onto his chest. He'd been roped under his arms and tied to the trunk. His knees were bent. Clearly, only the rope was preventing him from flopping to the ground, as much life in him as one of the dolls those private-school idiots left as 'offerings'.

Kim turned off the Valtra's engine. It died with a deep grunt.

He pulled his phone out and called the police.

* * *

Staring at the corpse, *Kriminalinspektör, Befäl* Sven Petersson was delighted.

Eight years on the job and this was unlike anything he'd ever seen. Or not in real life, anyway. Only in pictures. He knew what he was seeing, but for now decided to keep it to himself.

He stood back while the forensics guys took photos and scoured the leaf mould around the tree for physical evidence. At thirty-two, he was the youngest detective inspector commander ever at Bergslagen region homicide squad, and he was trying hard not to smile.

He'd spent his entire time in homicide so far 'solving' murders that were no more difficult than changing the sparkplug on his motocross bike.

Domestic homicides where you just went and found the husband in the pub, blood still speckling his hands, wailing like a newborn and confessing to his wife's murder before you'd even got him in the car.

Or drug stuff. Some low-level dealer battered to death, lying in his own filth in some scuzzy squat. Well, it was either a rival dealer, or someone higher up the chain.

Once he'd had a real puzzler. An Örebro city councillor had been found in a park, throat cut, her skirt pulled up and her panties ripped off, bra yanked up to expose her breasts. Everybody thought it was a sex killer. But Sven took a more back-to-basics approach.

He spent the weekend digging into her background and found an unwise, not to say unhealthy, association with a local gangster. Money for influence sort of thing. A new country house and in return planning permission for some deathtrap social housing projects in the south end, where immigrants could be housed on the cheap by unscrupulous landlords.

The councillor got cold feet about the whole thing, tried to back out. The gangster didn't like it. The councillor threatened to go to the cops. The gangster tied off the loose end and then, in a bid to throw everyone off the scent, did all the weird stuff.

But *this*.

This was different.

This was the real deal.

The brutal cavern gouged through the chest wall. Sven knew

exactly what the weapon was, but he'd keep it back until revealing it, no, *deducing* it. More of a coup that way.

Then there was the carved-up breastbone. Not the random slashings of an out-of-control druggie, either. A symbol he'd explain the significance of to whichever cute journalist he could get somewhere for a quiet drink.

Finally there were the deer antlers duct-taped to the guy's head. All in all, it screamed that single word that every homicide cop lived for. *Seriemördare*. He, Sven Johannes Petersson, had landed his first serial killer.

Sven watched as a CSI tweezed something out of the leaf litter and dropped it into a little clear plastic debris pot before screwing on the red lid and labelling it.

He was finally going to get to have some fun solving a case.

Footsteps beside him.

He turned.

Kriminalinspektör Lucy Magnusson, his partner, nodded at the corpse, which, having been photographed, was now being cut down and laid at the foot of the tree.

'What the hell is that?'

He smiled as he lit a cigarette.

'That, Lucy, is our path to promotion.'

Her rather lovely smooth forehead, the result of youth not Botox, furrowed.

'What do you mean?'

'It's a serial, isn't it?'

'Is it? What happened to "Look for the obvious first"?'

Now it was his turn to screw his features up.

'You're being serious right now? Tell me what you see.'

She turned and looked in the corpse's direction. Wrinkled her cute button nose that he fantasised about kissing.

'I see a middle-aged man, dead from massive sharp trauma to the chest, with a five-pointed star carved onto his sternum and antlers tied to his head. What is that, duct tape?'

Sven knew all the details. In advance of the post mortem. In advance of the investigation. It was just, he had to keep them to himself. For now. Just until he could use them for maximum advantage. Sven was playing the long game.

'I think so. And that's not just a five-pointed star, is it? Look at it. It's upside down. It's a pentagram. You know, a Satanic symbol.'

She shrugged.

'Still doesn't make it a serial, does it? We need three for that.'

'Sure, sure. That's what the rulebook says. What the *textbook* says. But what does your *gut* say? Because mine is going crazy right now, like before a first date.' He looked in what he hoped was a meaningful way at her, but she was still staring at the corpse. 'And what it's saying is, "Hey, Sven. Gear up. Because this is only his first. There's more to come unless you stop him." Mind you, we probably won't. Not till we've figured out the pattern. The victim type. The trophies he's taking. All that.'

Now Lucy did pull her eyes away from the corpse. Her mouth quirked into a kind of half-smile. He loved the expression.

'Oh my God,' she said. 'You're enjoying this, aren't you?'

The voice of their boss, *Kriminalinspektör, Chef för Grupp*, Kersten Sandén cut across their banter.

'Enjoying what?'

They turned in unison.

'Nothing, boss,' Sven said. 'We were just discussing our initial impressions.'

Kersten brushed a strand of her long black hair behind an ear. Focused her narrow-set eyes on him.

'Which are?'

'You've got a dead male. Early forties. Sharp-force trauma to the left side of the chest. Mutilation to the epidermis over the sternum. Deer antlers taped to the head. Tied to an oak known locally as the Devil Tree. Beyond that, I think it's best to follow the evidence. See where it takes us.'

Beside him, Lucy had turned to look at him, eyes wide. He knew what she was thinking.

'How about you, Lucy?' Kersten said. 'Thoughts?'

'Obviously, at first sight, there are aspects of the murd—' She stopped herself. 'Aspects of the *death* that suggest a connection to Satanism. But I think it's much too early to speculate,' she finished, shooting Sven a warning glance. 'However, whatever he was stabbed with, it was big, and I can't see it near the tree. So I don't think it was a suicide.'

'What about the symbol on his chest?'

'More evidence pointing away from suicide. Although we know people in extreme mental distress can do all kinds of things to themselves, I don't believe he could have carved that symbol into his own skin before killing himself. The lines are too precise. He would have been in so much pain. This further adds to a conclusion of homicide.'

Kersten nodded, already moving away from them, pulling out her phone.

'OK, then. Sven, you're leading this one. Keep me posted, yes?'

And she was gone.

Lucy turned to Sven. Her eyes flashing pure indignation.

'"Follow the evidence? See where it takes us?" Hell, Sven, you were all gung-ho on our first serial killer hunt. Then the alpha bitch turns up and you go all Mr By-the-Book. I don't get it.'

Sven grinned.

'Don't you? Try this on for size then. We go shooting off our mouths—' He caught his partner's warning look. 'OK, *I* go shooting off *my* mouth and she gives us the lecture about looking in all the obvious places first, money troubles, all that. It'd only slow us down.'

'And you don't think we need to do all that?'

'Sure we do. All I'm saying is, we're not going to find some wife fed up with his controlling behaviour or a druggie robbing him to get his next fix. It's weird, and the person we catch will be a weapons-grade weirdo. End of.'

Lucy fixed him with an off-kilter smile. Like she could see a massive hole in his argument. Or even his pants.

'What?' he said, having to fight down the urge to check his flies.

'All this talk of weirdos, you want to be careful or we'll have Stella Cole swanning in from Stockholm taking it over.'

Now it was Sven's turn to smirk.

'Haven't you heard? She's in the shit. Neck deep. Apparently she threatened to shoot the head of the Rat Squad dead. She's been busted back to basic inspector and spends her days telling schoolkids not to do drugs.'

Lucy's eyes widened.

'Really? But she's, like, "the British Super-Cop",' she said, switching to English for Stella's nickname. 'She's untouchable.'

He shrugged.

'Not now, she isn't.' He nodded to the far side of the crime scene where a youngish man with oversized tortoiseshell glasses was striding across the field towards the body, medical bag gripped in his left hand. 'Look, it's the pathologist. Let's go and say hello.'

As they passed the corpse, Sven looked down. Swallowed hard as he took in the details at close range. Told himself that they'd need at least two more like that if this case was going to make their careers.

9

MILLER RESIDENCE, ÖREBRO

Since moving to Sweden, Stella had encountered a couple of rich, powerful women. But their meetings had always been in either workplaces – theirs or hers – or restaurants and bars. This was the first time she had been invited inside the domestic space of one of Sweden's elite.

She followed Frankie's Cayenne down a gravelled track flanked by towering laurel bushes, their glossy dark-green leaves blocking out any sight of her neighbours' properties.

Arriving at the front of the house, she rolled the Triumph to a stop at the edge of a gravelled parking area she judged to be larger than the entire floor area of her apartment.

It was big enough to hold, with space to spare, four extremely expensive vehicles. Frankie's oversized Porsche SUV. A chunky pickup truck riding on huge knobbly tyres and decked out in a menacing matt-black paintjob. A low-slung silver BMW sportscar. And beneath an oak-framed carport, a sensuously curved Mercedes coupe that looked like it had come either from the future or the jazz age. Swooping silver bodywork that appeared to have been poured rather than riveted, and, as she peered inside, her gloved hand cutting out reflections, rich-red leather upholstery. She could almost smell it.

Frankie joined her, leaning close enough beside her that Stella caught a trace of her perfume. Something tasteful, yet expensive. Woody, yet floral.

'You like her?'

'She's beautiful. What is she? I can see the Mercedes badge but cars aren't really my thing.'

'She's a 1955 300 SL Gullwing. Not mine, my husband's. Come inside and meet him.' Frankie winked. 'He'll happily bore you till midnight with details of her history.'

Inside, the house radiated good taste. Bright woven rugs interrupted polished, bare-wood floors. Modern art hung on the beige and pale teal walls. And, visible through an entire wall of bifold glass doors, an expanse of wild-looking garden that surely must have cost a fortune to create and maintain.

Birch trees studded a rolling area of grass that was more meadow than lawn. Beyond them, sun glinted off a wind-ruffled lake. A spreading oak tree stood proudly in the centre of the view. A rope swing wide enough for two moved gently in the breeze. It had been slung from a branch so massive it had curved down to the grass under its own weight before elbowing up again like the arm of an ancient folk-giant.

'David? It's me. We have a guest,' Frankie shouted. 'Come and say hello.' She turned back to Stella. 'Coffee?'

'Please.'

While she prepared the coffee, Frankie spoke over her shoulder.

'How are you finding the outreach work?'

'Oh. Well, it's very rewarding. Helping kids get the information they need and hopefully avoid the worst of what drugs can do.'

Frankie laughed.

Playing the Devil's Music

'Did you learn that from the manual, too? Come on, Stella, I've read your file. Up until nine weeks ago you were putting serial killers behind bars. Now, you're sitting with some yoga bimbo, lecturing frankly bored teenagers about the evils of weed. I'd have thought you were hating it.'

Stella thought of Malin. Her sacrifice.

'Not at all. It's different.'

Frankie snorted, forcing Stella to backtrack. A little. 'OK, obviously it's different. But it's a change, you know? I'm getting to see a different side of life here. And I'd hardly call you a yoga bimbo.'

Frankie's husband entered the big open-plan kitchen.

'Nor would she, unless she was talking to somebody she trusted.' He offered his hand. 'Hi, I'm Davey Miller.'

As she shook his hand, she tried to place the good-looking but grizzled fifty-something smiling at her. He was English.

(*Like Jamie*, an unwelcome voice piped up between her ears. She ignored it.)

She could picture a poster somewhere. Some rock venue in London. His dark hair was speckled with silver and cut short. She imagined it longer, wilder. Then she had it.

'You're *the* Davey Miller. The guitarist with Black Death Rattle.'

He held his hands up, grinning.

'Guilty as charged, officer. You were a fan?' He looked sceptical. 'I wouldn't have thought thrash metal was…' He faltered. 'I mean, not that there's any reason why a woman shouldn't, but you're what, forty?'

'Davey!'

Stella smiled. Thought maybe it was time to let him off the hook.

'Since you ask, I'm forty-five. And sorry, but I wasn't a fan. A friend's son was, though. You were massive.'

'I know. Until my bandmates decided they wanted to change musical direction. There was a parting of the ways.'

Frankie joined him and put her hand around his admirably trim waist.

'Yes, but not before my clever husband had made sure he had full ownership of the song copyrights.'

He shrugged. 'I wrote them. They were mine all along.'

Frankie smiled at Stella.

'Sorry. We do tend to start riffing, no pun intended, on this subject.'

'No, I'm interested. So how did you two meet? I mean a yoga clothes entrepreneur and a heavy metal guitarist isn't an obvious pairing.'

'Drugs,' Davey said, flatly.

'Oh. I'm sorry,' Stella said, thinking rehab, private facilities, paparazzi hanging around outside tall iron gates deep in the countryside.

They laughed again.

'He's being naughty,' Frankie said. 'Davey was always outspoken about drugs. Obviously in that scene they're everywhere, but you were more of a beer and vodka guy, weren't you, darling?'

'Until I got sober, yes.' He turned to Stella. 'Along with the change in direction, the rest of the band got into hard drugs. Coke first, then heroin. I didn't want any part of that. Gradually, then all at once, they made it clear I wasn't wanted.'

Frankie handed Stella a mug of coffee. She took a sip. Delicious.

'What direction did they take? From my memory, you were pretty dark. Did they go into pop? Jazz?' She shuddered theatrically. 'Disco?'

'Death metal. It was getting huge over here at the time. Paganism, the occult, Satanism, all that. I just didn't get it. And there were some really bad elements, especially in Norway. I wanted to make it in America. They basically said "F" America.'

Frankie took up the story in what looked to Stella like a well-rehearsed routine with her husband.

'I was over in England researching the yoga market. I met

Davey at a party. Our eyes met across a crowded room, as they say. And after that we were inseparable.'

Davey put a hand on his wife's shoulder.

'I provided some seed capital for the clothing business and because she liked my name she called it Frankie Miller.'

Frankie laughed, shook out her mane of tousled blonde hair.

'Well, Frankie Gustafsdotter was a bit of a mouthful. Anyway, when the business started doing well—'

' – she's being modest,' Davey said. 'It's massive. They were the youngest-ever company to get a listing on the Swedish stock market.'

'So,' she said, punching him lightly on the arm, 'that's when I decided to start a charitable foundation. We decided to focus on drugs outreach. Prisons, refuges, homeless shelters, but mainly schools and colleges.'

'Well, it's brilliant that you do it,' Stella said, finding unexpectedly that she meant it. 'Maybe it wasn't my first choice for a mid-career break. But I really do enjoy meeting those kids.'

'Even if they give you the old death stare?'

Stella laughed.

'Yes. Even then.'

Frankie glanced at Stella's ring finger where she still wore a plain gold band.

'What does your husband think of your career move?'

Stella had got used to explaining about Richard, but it never seemed to get easier. She spoke around the lump in her throat. Knowing that if she didn't explain about Lola, too, there'd only be a follow-up question.

'He's dead. He was murdered. A hit and run. My daughter, too.'

Frankie gasped and covered her mouth with her hand.

'Oh God, Stella. How terrible. I am so sorry.'

Davey looked to be in pain, too. His eyes screwing into a wince.

'Me, too. Did they ever catch the person who did it?'

She nodded. Drifted to another time, another place.

A burning purple Bentley. A High Court judge trapped inside. Tortured. Then shot. His corpse burning to ashes.

She snapped back to the present. Banished the horrific image.

'He's dead now.'

'Good.'

Stella sucked in a breath, trying to expand her lungs against the steel band constricting her chest.

'How about you two? Do you have children?'

'We do,' Davey said. 'Magnus is twenty-six and Sofia is twenty-two. He's in a band. Sofia wants to save the world. She's doing climate science research at Lund University.'

Frankie smiled. 'Another Greta Thunberg.'

'Good for her. How about Magnus? What kind of music does he play?'

Davey frowned. And for the first time since they'd been speaking, she saw a glimmer of, what, disapproval? Unhappiness?

'Black metal.'

Stella frowned. 'Like your old band.'

He shook his head. 'Not really. I won't bore you with the details, but Magnus's band is on the darker side, still. You know, they call themselves Satanists, use pentagrams, all that dipshit iconography. And the lyrics! It's all torture and mutilation.' He wrinkled his nose.

'Come on, darling, you're starting to sound like an old fart,' Frankie said. 'I bet that's what they said about Black Death Rattle back in the day.'

He shrugged. Grinned. There it was again, that boyish charm Stella could quite imagine sweeping the younger version of Frankie away.

'Maybe.'

Frankie checked her watch. A rose-gold Apple with a square face.

'Do you mind if I turn on the TV? I'm a bit of a news junkie.' She blushed prettily. 'Oops! Sorry.'

The small flatscreen in the kitchen flickered and brightened. The SVT1 news had just started. The presenter, a serious redheaded woman called Luisa Hedin whose low voice Stella liked, wore a serious expression. Bad news, then.

'We are getting reports that Örebro police are at the scene of a suspicious death at a farm in Axberg. Now we go live to our reporter Britt-Marie Jansson. Britt-Marie, what can you tell us?'

In a scarlet trench coat over a cream roll-neck sweater, the petite blonde reporter had to keep brushing her flyaway hair out of her eyes as the wind whipped it about her head.

Frankie tutted beside Stella.

'Wear a hairband, for God's sake.'

The reporter clutched the mic tight against her mouth.

'I'm at the Jacobsson farm just outside Axberg, Luisa. The farmer's son discovered the body of a man earlier this morning. Now, the police are not releasing details but I have spoken to a witness. I apologise to viewers who may find these facts shocking in the SVT lunchtime bulletin, but this witness told me the victim had been stabbed and his body mutilated. I saw for myself, Luisa, and one of the most disturbing details in an already disturbing murder is that the victim, who is as yet unidentified, was, well, I don't think "adorned" is the right word, but he was basically wearing antlers.'

Beyond details guaranteed to have the average Swede shaking their heads and reaching for the off button, Britt-Marie had nothing else of substance to impart.

The camera returned to Luisa Hedin, who looked pale. Stella wondered what she'd look like without the skilfully applied professional makeup. Like a corpse herself, probably.

Frankie snapped off the TV.

'Sounds like your sort of thing, Stella,' she said. 'They call you the Queen of Weirdness, don't they?'

Stella nodded. Was there anyone in Sweden who didn't know her unofficial nickname? Every fibre of her being was screaming for her to call in. Blag a copy of the file. Start reviewing the details. And then, once again, she thought of Malin.

'It was. But the Örebro police will be perfectly able to handle it. It could just be a one-off. Someone with a grudge against the victim. Ninety-nine times out of a hundred, the obvious answer – someone known to the victim, an intimate partner, usually – is the right answer.'

Her outer voice might have convinced Frankie and Davey Miller, though to judge from Davey's troubled expression, she doubted it. But her inner voice dismissed her reasoning out of hand.

Of course it's not an 'intimate partner'! That's a nutter right there. And you need to catch them.

10

LINKÖPING

That afternoon, Stella had a talk to deliver to another school in Western Sweden. While she struggled, yet again, to connect with thirty more uninterested teenagers, RMV pathologist Henrik Brodin stood at the centre of a small group of people in a gleaming white-tiled and stainless-steel dissection room.

The *Rättsmedicinalverket*, or National Board of Forensic Medicine, had several facilities situated across the southern half of the country. Nearest to the crime scene was Linköping, a two-hour drive due south down *Riksväg* 50.

Henrik pushed his tortoiseshell glasses higher on his nose then settled the hinged plastic visor over his face. Blood spatter. An occupational hazard.

Surrounding Henrik in the dissection room were his assistant, a photographer, the Örebro prosecutor, two CSIs and two detectives. He'd memorised everyone's names. It was something he liked to do.

Given everybody's face was hidden behind a surgical mask, he invented little cues to keep them separate in his head. The male detective, Sven, a little over-excited in Henrik's view, he pictured with a bouncing toy Tigger on his head. The female, Lucy, studious, he imagined standing beneath a cartoon library SILENCE sign.

He switched on the ceiling mic and began to enumerate the visible wounds on the body.

'Finally, a pair of antlers has been duct-taped to the victim's head.'

'They'll be calling him the Deer Hunter,' Sven said, his voice muffled by his mask but still betraying what Henrik still regarded as an unseemly level of pleasure. An audible smirk.

Henrik was one of a group of young pathologists at the RMV known as the 'Young Turks'. Collectively, they had a reputation for occasional flippancy and a willingness to offer opinions in advance of the full results of the post mortem they were conducting. But Henrik, at least, still had boundaries where the dead were concerned. Treating them with respect came top of his list. He frowned at the detective. The detective shrugged. Tigger held his white hands out wide. *What?*

Shaking his head, Henrik asked for a pair of trauma shears. Settling his fingers inside the red-plastic coated grips, he began to cut away what was left of the man's shirt.

When the clothes had been bagged and tagged by the CSI responsible for dry items, he resumed his commentary.

'The victim is a male of white European appearance.' He prodded the skin on the right cheek, stretching it a little and letting it relax. Eased the lips apart and examined the teeth. 'He appears to be aged between forty-five and fifty-five. In overall good physical health. Apart from his injuries he has no gross physical trauma evident on his body, although there is an old scar on the side of his neck. Ligature marks on the wrists, from where his were tied to the tree, and traces of what appears to be adhesive. It is possible that he was restrained with more duct tape before being killed.' He leaned closer. 'He has a single tattoo. Left deltoid. Roughly eight by five centimetres. Black lettering. It reads, "Hunter Killers 03". Army, maybe?'

He focused on the stab wound. It was deep, wide-mouthed, and clearly not the product of a regular-bladed weapon. No carving knives or hunting knives for this murderer. Something had been driven with great force through the chest muscles, the ribcage and deep into the chest cavity.

'As to the principal wound, which appears very likely to be the cause of death, further forensic analysis will be necessary to determine the precise nature of the weapon. Whatever it was, it was four to six centimetres in diameter. A sharpened piece of wood, perhaps. Or a broad-bladed stabbing weapon. A pike, a lance, something of that nature.'

'Shall I take samples now, Henrik?' the CSI responsible for biological samples asked.

He nodded and she methodically took scrapings from beneath the fingernails, tapping the stainless-steel tool into a plastic debris pot. Hairs followed. Then swabs from inside the mouth, around the genitals, and the anus.

'OK,' he said, once she'd finished. 'Let's open him up, shall we? I think we will start with these.' He took a broad-bladed scalpel and started slitting the duct tape holding the antlers in place. He lifted them clear and the CSI on artefacts bagged them.

'What the hell?' the male cop said. 'Did someone start the autopsy already?'

Beneath the duct tape, a crude red cut encircled the dead man's head. Staples had been punched through the skin every six or seven centimetres, closing the cut as effectively as sutures. The tape had smeared blood across the wound as Henrik removed it.

'No. This is not the work of a pathologist,' he said, peering closer.

'You mean the killer did it? Hell. He's a twisted bastard all right,' the detective said.

There it was again. That note of prurient delight in his voice.

Henrik referenced the details of the cut into the mic, then turned to his assistant.

'Do we have any needle-nosed pliers, Lottie?'

She nodded. 'I'll fetch them.'

She returned a few minutes later and handed Henrik a pair of blue-and-grey-handled pliers, their slender jaws angled at the tip.

He thanked her and settled the jaws around the staple directly above the man's nose. He pulled. The staple came free with a tiny screech. It must have been pushed hard enough against the skin to penetrate the periosteum, the fibrous layer of collagen, nerves and blood vessels protecting the skull from damage. A staple gun.

He tapped the staple into the stainless-steel kidney bowl his assistant held ready. He repeated the process seven more times. Removing the eighth staple, he pushed down on the top of the man's head. He heard the male officer retch, then swallow noisily. *Not so cocky now, are you?*

'Normally, at this stage, I would remove the skin from the head using a transparietal incision.' He glanced at the cops. 'Ear-to-ear. But as the murderer has already performed this service for us, I will proceed to removing the skull cap.'

The mortuary assistant handed him a T-shaped stainless-steel chisel with a wide, flat blade, and a wooden-handled rubber mallet. He inserted the tip of the blade into the incised wound in the forehead. A quick tap with the mallet and the first centimetre of the chisel tip disappeared. Gripping the T-handle firmly in his right hand, Henrik gave it a sharp twist. With a sucking sound, the top of the skull separated from the lower half and plopped into his waiting left palm.

In the first second after he exposed the brain cavity, his brain failed to process what his eyes were seeing. Next to him, his assistant screamed. In the slowed-down time as he recoiled from the —

(horror)

— of the scene before him, he reflected that this was most unlike her.

The cops had fled to the far side of the room. The CSIs, panicking, tripped over each other. One fell to the floor with a crash. The prosecutor swore colourfully before retreating to the door, hand over his mouth.

The photographer, alone among them calm enough to do her job, was snapping pictures, the digital shutter whirring like a cloud of flies over a five-day-old corpse.

From the bowl of the dead man's skull swarmed a mess of crawling, wriggling, scuttling, and – oh, shit-the-devil, jumping! – creatures.

Six legs. Eight. Ten. Devil take him, hundreds! Tawny, black, yellow, mud-brown, ebony. Red legs with yellow stripes, creamy spots. Emerald-green wing cases fluttering open and closed with a noise like playing cards pegged against a kid's bike wheel spokes. Shiny. Rough. Horned. Hairy. Antennae waving like whips, jaws opening and closing. Monstrous fangs. Serrated jaws.

They swarmed out of the skull, down what remained of the head, over the stainless-steel lip of the dissection table and then tumbled to the floor, some taking flight, whirring and fluttering around the heads of the horrified onlookers.

Everyone was shouting at once.

'Kill them!'

'Get out of my way!'

'What the fuck!'

The male detective had his boot raised high. Staring, wide-eyed, at a spider the size of a sparrow.

'NO!' Henrik bellowed. The cop froze, mid-stomp, as if caught attempting a new yoga pose. 'Nobody move. They're evidence. Catch them.'

For ten minutes the eight humans chased, harried, cornered, and, finally, with a yell of triumph – 'Got you, you little bastard!' – captured the creepy crawlies.

The dissection room was alive as it had never been alive before. Two dozen assorted insects, spiders, centipedes and, to the terror of the CSI who caught it, a large, black scorpion. Thankfully, the non-human creatures were now safely contained in everything from small cylindrical debris pots to Tupperware boxes and a large blue plastic bucket, normally used for the temporary storage of organs.

The sound of panting filled the room. Then someone giggled. The next moment, all eight were shrieking hysterically, before Henrik raised his hands and called them back from whatever psychological refuge they'd fled to.

'Well, that was unexpected.'

This set them off again. The door opened and another pathologist poked her head round to see what the noise was. Frowning at the convulsed law officers, she withdrew.

Henrik cleared his throat.

'OK, people. Anyone get the faintest idea what that was all about?'

'One for the Queen of Weirdness, I'd have thought,' the prosecutor said.

'Haven't you heard? She's been transferred out of Stockholm Homicide,' the male detective said. 'We can handle this. Let's get on with it, doc, shall we? We're losing precious time here.'

Henrik shrugged. The cop was right. Praying that the murderer hadn't left any more surprises inside the torso, he went back to work.

* * *

Pleading pressure of time, Sven excused himself and Lucy from the autopsy room. Time to reveal the source of his certainty about the case.

'You know what this means, don't you?' he asked her as he pulled onto the 50 on the way back to Örebro. 'It's Ulrik Ahlgren. Except it can't be.'

'Sorry, what? Who's Ulrik Ahlgren?'

'Who's— Don't you read anything? Ulrik Ahlgren! The Brain Surgeon?'

'A surgeon?'

'No, you idiot! A serial killer. *The* serial killer. Only he's locked up in Kumla Bunker with all the other nutcases. He must have a disciple. It's the classic pattern. The master goes to prison, but he's already trained up, or, you know, maybe he sort of attracts one.'

'Attracts what? Jesus, Sven, slow down, you sound like you're on coke or something.'

He huffed a breath in and blew it out through flapping lips.

'Sorry. Let me start again. In 2003, right? There's this string of really gruesome murders. Young girls are found in upside-down crucifixion poses. Deer antlers tied to their heads, stabbed by a sharpened ram's horn, pentagram carved into their chests and, get this, because this was, like, his signature. Their brains removed—'

'— hence the nickname.'

'— and replaced with a couple of handfuls of bugs. Just like our guy.'

'So you're saying it's a copycat?'

'No. Try and keep up. I'm saying what we're looking at here is a genuine master–disciple relationship between two serial killers. I told you. We've got ourselves a genuine serial killer.' His pulse was still jumpy from the episode in the dissection room. 'Better buy ourselves some new threads. There'll be national TV all over this. Probably international, too. Sky. BBC. Al Jazeera. CNN.'

She turned to him, still trying to shake the image of that room full of those *disgusting* creatures. She shuddered violently.

'You're enjoying this, aren't you?'

'Aren't you?'

'A man was murdered, Sven. Horribly.'

'I know. And obviously that's sad, and when we find next of kin you should give it the full sympathetic act.'

'Me?'

'I'm the senior officer.'

'You only joined two months before me!'

'Which gives me precedence. So, you express our condolences and then we get to work catching this fucker. And, as I think I may have said before, when we *do* catch him, we will be on every front page. All over social media. The telly. I wouldn't be surprised if we get a Commissioner's Commendation.'

She shook her head. 'You're weird. Maybe we should get Stella Cole to take a look at *you*.'

'Nobody's getting her to look at anything,' he snapped. 'Hell, it's like there weren't any decent homicide cops in Sweden until she turned up.'

'Touchy, are we?'

'No, I'm not touchy! I'm just saying if the SPA gives every juicy murder case to her it doesn't say much about their faith in actual Swedish officers.'

Lucy shook her head. When Sven got into one of his moods, she preferred to think about something else. Like maybe getting partnered with someone who was more focused on policework and less on turbocharging his own career.

Glory hound.

11

STOCKHOLM

Back home after her second talk of the day, Stella's head was buzzing.

Partly, it was the deep thrum of the Triumph's engine on the ride back to Stockholm.

Mostly, it was the shocking news from Axberg.

What had she gleaned from the sanitised report offered up by Britt-Marie Jansson? A middle-aged man had been murdered and his body left for a farmer to find out in the boondocks.

She poured herself a glass of wine and fetched a little blue bowl of green olives with basil and garlic from the fridge. Took them out to the balcony. The evening was warmer than the day had been. The turn of the seasons. She looked forward to running along the waterfront without her legs stinging from the cold.

'*Mutilated.*'

That was the first keyword in Britt-Marie's windblown testimony from the crime scene. The second, '*antlers*'.

And the body had been displayed. Not hidden. Although Britt-Marie had been coy when pressed by 'Luisa-in-the-studio', the implication was clear. He'd been crucified on a tree.

A domestic murder? A jealous spouse? Unlikely. Those murders tended to happen in the home. And if the perpetrator didn't immediately give themselves up, ringing the cops while still covered in blood and sobbing out their confession to a startled call-handler? Then there was only the most rudimentary of efforts to hide the body. Maybe rolled into an old carpet and dumped in woods. Or half-burnt inside an oil drum on an abandoned industrial estate.

Depending on the victim's perceived offence against their killer, there could be mutilation. Women were known to castrate their cheating husbands on occasion. But, antlers? No. No way.

Drugs, then?

It was a possibility. Gangs liked to make examples of people who tried a little freelance dealing on the side. Or who set up in direct competition with their former employers. A warning to others considering a move into the entrepreneurial side of the trade. 'This is what we do to traitors.' That sort of thing.

But then why leave the body out in the sticks? On a farm for God's sake? The usual MO was a more urban affair. Gun the man down in the street, or in a club, and never mind the innocent civilians who got caught in the crossfire. Or take him somewhere nice and quiet, torture him for a bit, have him kneel for the ritual round to the back of the skull and then dump the body somewhere very public.

That left a third possibility.

The possibility homicide cops secretly hoped for, even as they protested volubly that the idea was abhorrent.

The possibility that might offer her a way out of her current predicament.

She called Henrik Brodin. The voice on the other end was warm, and she could hear the smile in it.

'Hey, Stella. How are you liking life as a teacher?'

'Funny. No better than the last time we talked. How are you? Busy?'

'Aren't I always?'

'I meant on anything specific?'

'Why do I get the feeling you know I am?'

'I saw the lunchtime news. Sounded pretty strange to me.'

'Yeah,' he drawled. 'I guess "strange" would cover it. Just.'

'So come on, then. Tell me.'

'You're working homicide investigation into your drug talks now, are you?'

Stella clutched her phone tighter.

'Please, Henrik, stop torturing me! Maybe I can help catch the twisted sonofabitch.'

'You know, Malin would have kittens if she found out you were investigating a homicide. Plus I haven't even finished my report yet.'

'I'm not "investigating". I'm just…'

'Curious?'

'Yes! Exactly. I'm curious.'

'OK, sorry. I was just teasing you. Do you have your crown on? Because this one is right up your street.' Henrik cleared his throat. When he spoke again, all trace of the humorous tone had vanished. 'In increasing order of weirdness, we have the following artefacts. One, the victim was stabbed with something big. Sharp, but not edged. Nearest I could guess would be some sort of wooden stake, but not regular like a fence post. More like a sharpened tree branch. I found white debris in the wound. I sent it off for analysis. Two, he had a pentagram incised over his sternum. Three, he had a pair of antlers duct-taped around his head. And four—'

'Wait! You're saying that isn't the weirdest part?'

'Oh, you are going to love this. The killer had already performed a craniotomy. I lifted the skull cap off and there was no brain. And, in its place, there were twenty-three assorted arthropods.'

'What? You mean bugs?'

'I mean spiders, insects, centipedes, a millipede and a scorpion the size of a hamster.'

'Shit the devil!'

'Honestly, Stella, it was like a fucking madhouse in there. I mean you've got cops, CSIs, me and Lukas my assistant, and we're all rushing around with debris pots and cadaver sheets, anything we could find, really, chasing down these bloody creepy crawlies.'

Stella shook her head, trying and failing to imagine the chaos that must have ensued when Henrik removed the top of the skull.

'Did they find the brain at the scene?'

'No. It's gone.'

'Was the symbol done ante or post mortem?'

'Very much ante, I'm afraid. He would have been in extraordinary pain before he died.'

Stella took a deep breath. If this was a one-off, then she'd volunteer to stay on the drugs outreach programme until her retirement.

'Was that it?' she deadpanned.

Henrik laughed. 'What? That's not enough for you? The guy looked like something out of a horror film. Actually, yes, though. There was one more thing. Not weird, not as such. His fingers were all broken.'

'How? By hand?'

'No. I think probably a hammer. The bones were splintered.'

'Anything that might help us, I mean them, identify the victim?'

'He had a tattoo. Just the one. Left shoulder blade. It reads "Hunter Killers '03". You think he could be a paedo hunter?'

'It doesn't sound quite right. In the UK they might give someone a beating, but they usually just hand them over to the police. But it's ringing a bell.'

'Maybe he was in the military. But, anyway, that's it, really. The guy was in basically good shape for a middle-aged smoker. Not a heavy drinker. No organic disease lurking in any of the major organs.'

'How about toxicology?'

'The lab's snowed under at the moment. A couple of people left last month. Plus the latest round of cuts. Could be weeks before they get back with their findings.'

She thanked him for his candour. Went back to staring out over the rooftops.

A Satanic symbol.

A pair of antlers. Not horns, which would have been more Satanic, but still. They fit with the whole Wiccan, folk-religion-cum-paganism side of things, which was starting to get big in Sweden.

A skull full of bugs.

The corpse crucified on a tree.

Well, if it *was* a jealous lover, he must've fucked the very devil behind her back to get the treatment she'd meted out.

12

ÖREBRO

When Henrik's report dropped into Sven's inbox late the next afternoon, he skim-read it. What he wanted at this point was a positive ID for the victim. They'd got fingerprints and tissue samples, so in the fullness of time, they'd get results back from the national databases. But unlike those dumbass cop shows where everyone had test results in thirty seconds, in real-world Sweden, things took time. Like, days. Weeks, sometimes.

Henrik had sketched the design the killer cut into the victim's chest.

He'd described it accurately. For a maths nerd, anyway. Pentagram. But it made a hell of a lot more sense, or at least it did if you had Sven's specialist knowledge, to describe it as a *pentacle*. It was a Satanic symbol. OK, so the wiccans and all those freaky-deaky neo-pagans liked it too. But the Satanists got there first. And, more to the point, so did the Brain Surgeon, AKA Sweden's most notorious serial killer, Mr Ulrik Ahlgren himself.

Finishing the report, Sven went to find Kersten. Time to begin the series of reveals that would elevate him in her estimation from workmanlike detective to brilliant homicide investigator. Queen of Weirdness? Ha! How about 'King of the Killers'? No. That sounded wrong. Like *he* was a killer. Scratch that. He shook his head. Something to work on over a couple of beers at home.

Kersten was in her office, poring over some report or other. It was the only aspect of climbing the ladder Sven wasn't keen on. The paperwork. He already had more than he cared for. Sometimes he'd deliberately skimp on his reports just because it was more fun on the street.

He *could* write. In fact, his teacher at school had always said he should have been a journalist. He just had that natural gift, he supposed. But be honest, who built a career out of being the best report-writer? Nobody, that's who. It was a necessary evil. A bit like serial killers. Funny.

Playing the Devil's Music

'Come in, Sven,' she said, pointing to the visitor chair. 'You have something?'

He sat, leaned forward.

'I know who the killer is.'

She straightened.

'That was fast. Who is it? Can we start planning an arrest?'

He realised he'd overplayed his hand. Not much. But he needed to back up. Just a little.

'I don't know his exact identity, but listen, Kersten,' he hurried on, as she puffed air out in a sigh of clear exasperation, 'the MO is identical to that of Ulrik Ahlgren. He was—'

' — the Brain Surgeon, yes, I know, Sven. I didn't arrive yesterday.'

'So what I'm saying is, Ahlgren is clearly behind this. Connected at least.'

He cursed inwardly. On the short walk to Kersten's office his theory had seemed so much more solid. Now he was saying it out loud it was stretching, thinning, drifting, like cigarette smoke blown into the cold Swedish night.

'Have you checked with the prison?' she asked. 'He hasn't escaped?'

He nodded.

'I spoke to the director: Lina Stormare. Ahlgren's still enjoying the cosy hospitality of Kumla Bunker. She even sent a warder to check on him.'

'So it's a copycat?'

He stifled the sigh that threatened to hiss from between his lips.

'I suppose technically, yes, that's what we've got. But my theory is that we're dealing with more of a disciple. We need to interview Ahlgren, find out if he's been getting letters from anyone who might be a possibility. See if he's sending messages to somebody. Even see if he's got any insights into the case.'

'And do you have any idea who I should send in?'

Kersten raised an eyebrow. It was a pretty good bit of body language. Supposed to put you on the defensive. Make you feel small. Sven had been practising it at home in the bathroom mirror after shaving every morning and evening. He nearly had it, although the right was loads better than the left.

He shrugged. 'Well, I've done the legwork so far. Made the connection to Ahlgren. So me, basically.'

'You don't think this is a bit of a jump up for you, Sven? I mean, no offence, but so far your cases have been pretty straightforward.'

He bit back his frustration. He knew what Kersten was thinking. She wanted to kick it up to the big boys – and girls – over in Stockholm. He needed to forestall it quickly.

'Look, you're right. I get it. Örebro isn't Stockholm, and, thank God, Stockholm isn't London, or Berlin or New York. But I'm ready for this, Kersten. I've got a great clearance rate. I'm smart, I'm dogged, I'm—'

' – modest?'

He blushed. But Kersten was grinning. 'Sorry, Sven. Go, go. Call Lina and make an appointment. If you get any pushback, have her call me. We were at university together.'

He left her office at a trot, already pulling his phone out.

13

STOCKHOLM

It was 11:00 a.m., the day after Stella had spoken to Henrik. She was ensconced in a tiny, acoustically dead room with Janik Forstrüm, the presenter of *The Issue*, Radio P1's regular live show devoted to contemporary cultural trends.

A mic encased in a spindly black metal cage was suspended directly in front of her mouth.

'Speak at your normal volume and keep close to the mic,' Janik said with an encouraging smile. 'Other than that, just talk like normal. Two friends discussing stuff in the pub, OK?'

'I think I can do that,' Stella said, pulse racing, fighting down the urge to run from the studio and burst free onto *Oxenstiernsgatan*.

His eyes slid away from hers for a second, presumably as his producer spoke into his earpiece. He nodded, flashed Stella another toothy grin.

'Good morning. I am Janik Forstrüm and this is *The Issue*. Kids and drugs. That's what we're discussing today. Who takes them?

Why do they take them? What do they take? And what, if anything, can – or should – society do about it? To discuss these and other questions, including yours, I have in the studio with me today Detective Inspector Stella Cole.'

He paused. Winked at Stella. Presumably another bit of gee-ing up for the rookie. It made her feel sick.

'Stella arrived on our shores a few years back and has been making waves ever since. Not least for speaking Swedish better than some of our own citizens manage.' He winked again. It was starting to look like a nervous tic. 'But she is currently on sabbatical from the business of catching serial killers to promote the government's message on drugs. Stella, welcome to *The Issue*.'

She stared at him, her eyes apparently unable to blink. Lightheaded. Why was he frowning at her? Was a shirt button undone? She looked down. No. Everything was OK. Back at Janik. He was nodding and pointing at the mic. Oh.

'Thanks, Janik,' she choked out. Her throat felt like she'd emptied a spoonful of dust into it. 'Happy to be here.'

'And we're happy to have you.' He nodded. Smiled. Mouthed, *Good*. 'So, what's your impression of the Swedish attitude to drugs? Do the kids take in your message? That drugs are dangerous?'

She leaned closer to the mic. Tried to formulate a sentence that was honest and diplomatic. And in line with the policy she was supposed to be promoting. Without sounding like a hypocrite. No pressure.

'Well, Janik, Sweden is no different from a lot of countries, the UK included. We know young people experiment with drugs. You could argue it's part of growing up. And yes, they are illegal. But I think any parent will tell you that forbidding a teenager to do something is only going to make them want to do it more. If you say it's risky, or dangerous, well, that's just going to make them want it twice as much.'

Chin cupped in the palm of his right hand, elbow supported in the other, Janik nodded, as if she'd just delivered the most searing philosophical insight of the twenty-first century.

'True, true. So, what's your message? You visit schools, right?'

Playing the Devil's Music

'And colleges, yes. I give them information. I explain about the law and how my colleagues treat drug offenders. I talk about the effects on their health.'

'And you work with the Frankie Miller Foundation, that's right, isn't it?'

'Yes, we do. Frankie has a great rapport with kids and I think she's truly an asset to the programme.'

'Let's take some calls,' Janik said. 'Then we'll circle back to some of the issues we'll discuss in the next part of the programme.' He straightened his shoulders. His eyes went momentarily out of focus as he touched the earpiece again. 'You're listening to *The Issue*, with me, Janik Forström, and today's special guest, Detective Inspector Stella Cole. We have Marj on the line. Hey, Marj, what's your question?'

A middle-aged woman's thin, querulous voice filled the studio.

'What I want to know is why the police don't throw them all in prison? I walk my little dog, Olof, after the prime minister, the one who was assassinated, I mean, not the new one, bloody woman. Anyway…' Marj seemed to lose her thread. Then picked it up again. 'I walk Olof every evening in Stockholm, down by Berzelii park, and they're all there. Arabs. Blacks. Syrians or whatever. You know, immigrants. They sell drugs to our kids. Well, the police should go down there and arrest them all. Lock them up. Or send them back to wherever they came from. The buyers, too, for that matter.'

Janik nodded as if agreeing with every word Marj was saying. He cut her off with a smooth, 'Thanks for that interesting opinion, Marj. Stella, how would you respond to Marj's point that anyone with half an eye can see drugs being dealt openly on our streets. Why *don't* the police do more?'

She felt on firmer ground here. She took a breath.

'Obviously, we could arrest street dealers. We could assemble a taskforce of ten or twenty or a hundred officers and pick up everyone we could find with a wrap of cocaine, a bottle of pills or a little bag of weed on them. And within twenty-four hours, they'd all be back on the street. That's the Swedish justice system.'

'Is that a criticism?'

'Not at all. But it's a fact that there simply aren't the resources to prosecute everyone. On the subject of deportation. Swedish human rights law does not permit the police to deport people suspected of minor drugs offences. And we have to remember that they may well be Swedish citizens. But, even if it did, I can guarantee that there would simply be a fresh crop of dealers taking their places the very next night Marj took her little dog for a walk.'

'So you're saying the problem is systemic. Endemic, even.'

Trying not to be distracted by her attempts to mentally define the two rhyming words, Stella said, 'I'm saying if you arrested every single person in Sweden who either bought or sold drugs, you might find you needed to build more prisons.'

He nodded. As if he believed every word Stella was saying. Maybe he was just a nodder.

'Let's take another caller. We have Ronnie on the line. Hey, Ronnie, what's your question?'

'Yeah, hi, Janik.' The caller's voice was deep, muffled as if he had a bad cold. 'I have a question for Stella. What did you think of my handiwork over in Axberg?'

Stella felt suddenly cold. Her stomach flipped.

Janik smiled. Puzzled.

'Handiwork, Ronnie? Are you a drug user yourself? A dealer, perhaps?'

'Stella knows who I am. While you're sitting there discussing the minor sin of smoking weed, I am doing my Lord's work. Stella likes to hunt people like me. But she will never catch me. I have protection.'

Janik was touching his earpiece again. He nodded.

'OK, thanks for that, Ronnie. Let's take—'

He was going to cut the caller off. She couldn't let him.

'No!' she said sharply, holding her hand up palm outwards. 'Ronnie, what do you mean about Axberg?'

'Clever. You are testing me. I mean that sinner I left on the Jacobsson farm.'

Was he a crank? It was entirely possible. But there was something in his voice. A lack of emotion. A note of superiority. Of arrogance. She'd spoken to people before who sounded exactly the same. She needed to test him further.

'The antlers. The pentagram. That's what you mean, isn't it?'

'You know perfectly well what I mean, Stella,' he said. 'Let's just say he had plenty of company when he died.'

He was talking about the bugs. Had to be.

'You said you're doing your Lord's work. Is God telling you to kill?'

'God? That old fraud? No. The one I serve is far more powerful.'

'Tell me his name.'

'"For I am an angel fallen among sinners, yet I will rise up and lead them. My father will feel my wrath when I burn his city down into smoke and ashes".'

The line went dead.

Janik's tanned face had turned a sickly beige. Sweat beaded his upper lip. His eyes were wide and he was staring at Stella, his mouth opening and closing like a fish.

She had to do something. Dead air was stretching out. Janik touched his earpiece. Left his finger there.

Stella leaned forwards.

'Well, maybe Ronnie has taken something he shouldn't have. Religious delusions are one of the serious side-effects of LSD, a topic I speak about in my talks with young people.' She stared through the window into the control room, where the young female producer was rolling her hand in the air: *Keep going.* Then she mimed picking up a phone.

'I think we have another question,' Stella said.

* * *

Somehow, they got the programme back on track. Janik pulled himself out of his panic attack while Stella vamped about drug policy in response to the questioner.

Thirty minutes after it had started, he signed off with a serious-sounding, 'Thank you for listening to *The Issue*. Next week, institutional racism in Swedish business.'

'We're clear,' the producer's voice announced over the speakers.

Janik leaned back and ran a hand over his high forehead, which looked as though he'd lost more hair from it since Ronnie's unfortunate intervention in his show.

'Fuck!' he said in English. 'Thanks, Stella. You saved my life. Was that him, then? The actual murderer of that guy over in Axberg?'

She nodded. She was sure of it. And now she'd spoken to him, she was sure of one thing.

He was going to do it again.

14

VETLANDA, JÖNKÖPING COUNTY

Ever since the body had been found on the farm, Barbro Ekblad had been on high alert.

Poor guy. Tortured, and all that shit Ahlgren used to do. She'd rushed to the bathroom and retched until her stomach was knotted so painfully she'd wept with it.

It had been a while since she'd carried a pistol. Once you made senior management, a working knowledge of Excel was more valuable than how to operate a SIG Sauer P225.

Even so.

She'd retrieved her pistol and taken it straight down to the range. Earned a few looks from the other officers down there in that echoing space that stank of burnt gunpowder. Some questioning, others impressed.

Asked the armourer for a box of bullets and spent an hour down there blasting away at paper targets until her index finger cramped.

She was ready.

And then she wasn't.

She awoke in the middle of the night.

Beside her, Erik snored raggedly. He sounded different. Normally if he woke her in the night, the noise of his clogged breathing was clearer. More … consistent, somehow. A logger way out in the forest cutting down fir trees.

A shadow loomed over her side of the bed.

A huge, paw-like hand clamped over her nose and mouth.

She struggled, flailing arms and legs. Why wasn't Erik waking?

A cloth soaked in something that smelled a bit like the wax polish they used on their treasured hardwood floor. She struggled. Gasped. Everything went swimmy. Then, darkness.

Oh, no. Erik. I'm so sorry my l—

* * *

Muammad al-Huq woke up from his own sleep four hours later. He'd been sleeping rough ever since crossing into Sweden.

The mornings were cold, but no worse than those in Syria. And at least now there weren't snipers ready to snuff you out if they caught you on the street after the curfew just because you were trying to track down a loaf of bread.

His plan was to join his cousin, Aisha, in Stockholm. Get a flat. A job. Tell the authorities about himself. A qualified pharmacist. A shop in Aleppo. Gone now. Reduced to so much brick dust and shards of glass and burning medication packets.

One problem.

He was illegal. Undocumented.

He wandered down to the stream to wash and then to pray.

As he raised his head from the mat he'd brought rolled up and wrapped in waxed paper, he blinked as sunlight hit him straight in the face. What was that? In God's name, what *was* it?

He shaded his eyes with his hand, prayers forgotten for now. Because now he could see what it was that appeared to be watching him from a nearby tree.

He'd seen similar. Not like this. But close enough. In Syria.

Nearer to, he could make out features. A woman. The blonde hair every Swedish girl seemed to have. He chided himself. She was well past the age when one would call her a girl.

Her head hung down. Dead.

And tortured.

Memories swam up from the place where he'd locked them away. Broken bodies turning up in the streets of Aleppo after the secret police had taken them from their homes in the middle of the night. Injuries their families couldn't bear to see, yet had to. Peeping through slitted fingers.

Antlers taped to the sides of her head.

A gaping bloody wound over her heart.

Between her exposed breasts, a crude five-pointed star.

He offered a prayer for her soul. Drew the cut sides of her nightgown together over her chest as best he could.

He sat at her feet. His mind reeled. Because now what? A dilemma. But worse than those he'd studied at the university in Damascus. Philosophy. He'd come a long way. Problems, in which trolley cars full of passengers raced towards abandoned babies. Switch the points, save the infant, kill the passengers? Or leave them be, save the adults at the cost of a single child?

Muammad's dilemma was starker. For being real. And immediate.

A monster was on the loose. Killing women. Torturing them.

As his mind worked on the puzzle, he giggled out of sheer anxiety as a name presented itself.

Not 'The Trolley Problem', but 'Death and Deportation'.

Muammad was devout. The Quran was clear. Murder was an evil act. He had a duty to report it.

So should he call the police – and be deported? Back to his old life, his old identity? And everything that awaited him?

Or ignore a monstrous crime, and the Prophet's teachings – and stay in Sweden to restart his life.

Quietly, as if he might wake the dead woman, he walked away.

15

ÖREBRO

The next morning, Sven was in early. He wanted to beat Lucy to the office.

Once she'd arrived, made herself a coffee and logged on to the SPA system, he dropped his bombshell. Lucy's eyes flashbulbed. Sven was gratified at his partner's surprise. She had a lot to learn about him.

'You're going *where?*'

'I'm going down to Kumla prison. The Bunker, actually. To interview Ulrik Ahlgren. Just have to clear it with the director.'

'And Kersten was cool with that?'

'Totally. I went to see her yesterday afternoon. She actually said it was a great idea. Told me she was impressed with my work.'

'Wow. Do you want me to come with you?'

He shook his head.

'I'm not being funny, but check yourself out in a mirror in the ladies. You're exactly his type. Well, a bit older, but you know what

I mean. Classic beautiful Swedish girl. He'd just be perving over you the whole time.'

She folded her arms.

'I think there might have been a compliment buried under all that patriarchal bullshit, so thanks. But seriously, let me come, OK? I've never met a real serial killer before.'

Sven shook his head. On the one hand it would be cool to have her with him. Someone to record how he dealt with Sweden's most dangerous serial killer. But then there was always the risk he'd have to share the glory.

'Let me handle it. But we still need to ID the victim. Why don't you stay on that?'

Leaving her to fume, her gaze so hot he felt it burning through his jacket, he went to call Lina Stormare again.

The voice on the other end of the line was cultured. Definitely upper middle class. Like one of those Östermalm types who were always popping up on the late-night news shows.

Sven introduced himself and explained the reason for his call.

'Ulrik Ahlgren has refused to speak to detectives or reporters since taking up residence here,' she said. 'Actually that's not quite true. He did agree to speak to one criminologist. She bore certain physical similarities to his victims. God knows why it was allowed. I was on sabbatical at the time. But she suffered a panic attack after something he said. Our doctor had to sedate her. So I doubt very much he'd agree to see you.'

She wasn't saying any of this unkindly, Sven thought. As she saw it, she was just stating the facts. But he had a fact he thought would trump hers.

'I get that Lina, really, I do,' he said, striving to kick his own less bourgeois accent up a notch or two. 'But the homicide I'm investigating bears an uncanny, in fact, you could say, a direct correspondence to his own crimes.'

He heard the shrug in her voice as she said, 'I'll ask him. If he agrees I'll call you back.'

'When would you be able to do that, please? Time is of the

essence here. I need to catch this new killer before he murders anybody else.'

'Give me an hour. I have a meeting to attend. I can do it after that.'

Sven wanted to yell down the phone, *'Don't you get it? There's a nutcase out there rigging his victims up like crucified deer. I need to know now!'*

Wanted. But he prided himself on his excellent impulse control. *Unlike psychopaths, haha!* So he contended himself with a meek, 'Thank you. I'll await your call.'

While he waited, he reread the reports by the psychiatrists who'd assessed Ahlgren back in 2003. His stomach ignited in a fizz of excitement, mixed with a little anxiety. Ahlgren was the real deal. A genuine, certifiable, gold-plated crazy. The only thing he hadn't done was eat his victims. Or not that anybody could prove: their brains had never been found.

In the passage he was currently reading, Ahlgren patiently explained to an eminent psychiatrist that only by purging one young woman of her sinful thoughts – by replacing her brain with bugs – could he hope to force Sweden as a nation to confront the evil in its soul. Sven shook his head. Loony.

His phone rang. He jumped. Swore. Checked his watch.

Lina was as good as her word. Seventy-one minutes had passed.

'Ulrik must be feeling generous. He says come to see him this afternoon.'

'Thank you, Lina. I appreciate this. Tell me, is there anything Ulrik likes?'

'I'm sorry, likes?'

'Yes. You know, something that he finds pleasurable.'

'Apart from ritually slaughtering young women, you mean?'

He smiled. The director had a sense of humour. Unusual among the bleeding-heart 'it's all society's fault' types who ran most of Sweden's penal facilities.

'I was thinking more like biscuits. Or candies.'

'Bribing him might not be a bad idea. Most people just want

to come and stick a microphone under his nose. He spends his allowance on Annas ginger thins in the prison commissary.'

'And I'd be allowed to bring those in?'

'Might be easier than buying them here. They often run out. We'll have to X-ray them, of course. But no, other than the usual security checks, you're fine.'

* * *

On the twenty-minute drive from Örebro down to Kumla, Sven's pulse ticked along at an elevated, but not unpleasant, rate. He did have to keep wiping his palms on his trousers, though; they were slipping on the steering wheel.

He pulled in at a minimarket and took a packet of Annas-brand ginger thins off the shelf. Made for the till wondering whether it was worth asking for a receipt so he could claim the eleven krone back on expenses. Then he tutted, spun round and replaced it, reaching instead for the 300g gift box. That cost thirty-five and he was absolutely claiming for that.

He reached Kumla and slowed for some women pushing strollers across the road at the crossway where *Sörbyvägen* crossed *Stenevägen* to become *Viagatan*. So far, so middle-of-nowhere smalltown Sweden. Family cars, Falun Red *mamma och pop butiks* with wooden clapboard fronts. A bar called The Cowboy Grill – *why?* – a Navet charity shop, also Falun, but this time faced with aluminium sidings instead of traditional timber.

Across the junction, a simple white wooden church raised its spire above the low roofs of its neighbours. He wondered, briefly, whether Ahlgren had genuinely believed he was doing God's work. Or the Devil's. Or whether it was all an act. Maybe he'd ask him.

The women reached the far pavement and he accelerated away, anxious now to get on with it.

He drove down the dead-straight *Viagatan*, on the final approach to the prison. A grassy plain stretched away on both sides to distant woodland. Opposite the prison was a custard-yellow factory owned by Orkla Foods Sweden. Its boxlike structure, forbidding stacks of chimneys and windowless front would have made a half-decent prison itself.

Orkla was a bit of an institution in Örebro county, producing Ekström's blueberry soup, which Sven, personally, couldn't stand. Far too sweet. But his three sisters all loved it, and insisted he try their home-made recipes every time he visited. Which, and not only for that reason, wasn't very often.

Orkla had been there since 1948. He wondered what they thought about having a category one penal institution built right opposite them in '65. Unchuffed, he thought it was fair to say.

He wondered if Orkla also made Annas ginger thins. Glanced at the box beside him on the passenger seat and peered at the tiny white writing. Lotus Bakeries. Fucking Belgians!

The roar of multiple airhorns jerked him upright and facing front. Heart-pounding against his ribs, he wrenched the wheel over to bring his silver Toyota back to his side of the road.

The Orkla truck thundered past, its blaring airhorns sliding down a tone as they doppler-shifted.

Shaking, he gripped the wheel and took the car the last five hundred metres to the prison at a sedate 40 kph.

After navigating the various levels of security, he waited in a small room for Lina to come and escort him to meet Ahlgren. She arrived not sixty seconds later, a tall, severe-looking woman in chunky black boots and a boxy black suit that had to have cost a fortune to look that good on her bony frame.

'Sven?'

'Lina. Thanks again for arranging the meet.'

'Yes, well, if it helps stop another Ulrik Ahlgren, I'm all for it.' She looked at the package in his hand. 'You've gone all-in, I see.'

He grinned.

'I was just wondering how to phrase it on my expenses claim.'

'What, you think, "Bribe to notorious Satanic serial killer" might not cut it with your finance department?'

Was that a hint of sarcasm? He checked her expression. Her

grey eyes crinkled at the corners. Yes, he decided. Definitely bone-dry and pretty black sense of humour.

'They'd probably reject it, saying they only disburse money for Lutheran serial killers.'

This brought forth a proper laugh from the director. Sven felt unaccountably pleased with himself. She was at least ten if not twenty years older than him, but there was something nice about a powerful, attractive woman laughing at his jokes.

'Come on,' she said. 'Let's introduce you to Ulrik.'

On the long walk from the reception area, through General Population to Kumla Bunker, Sven felt his anxiety levels increasing.

He'd been inside prisons before, of course, but only to interview regular criminals. Burglars, muggers and, yes, murderers on occasion. But they were regular guys. There-but-for-the-grace-of-God types.

Ahlgren was different. He was in the Bunker, one of Sweden's three secluded maximum security units for extremely high-risk prisoners.

His cohabitees in the Bunker were as unpleasant a bunch of men as it was possible to find. Among them, Jon-Anders Johansson, the neo-Nazi who'd murdered two police officers. Rami Namdar, the Islamist terrorist who'd driven a bus into a crowded marketplace in Uppsala and killed nine people. Tommy Malenius, your basic psycho who'd been denied entry to a bar, gone home in a taxi, fetched an AK-47 which, apparently, he'd just had lying around, went back and emptied the magazine through the front window, killing five and wounding another eleven. Nutters.

Kersten nodded to a burly warder with a bunch of shiny keys on a large ring at his waist. He unlocked the heavy, cream-painted door, protruding rivet-heads giving a clue as to its function, and let them through into the prison-within-a-prison that constituted Kumla Bunker.

Sven inhaled sharply. This was it.

He was going to meet his first serial killer.

16

VETLANDA

Muammad stood up.

The Swedish police were here.

He'd rolled and repacked his prayer mat. His destiny would be taken out of his hands now. In Allah's. And the cops'.

These two were in uniform. A man with red hair cut short like a soldier's. And a woman. Watchful eyes.

He'd supposed that they would send detectives. Maybe he'd seen too many TV shows. They hadn't drawn their guns, but they kept their hands on the butts poking out of the black holsters.

They emerged from the scrubby bushes, looked at him inquiringly.

'She is there,' he said, in English, since he hadn't mastered more than a few words of Swedish.

He pointed.

The cops turned in unison. The woman hissed out a couple of

short words. Muammad supposed she was swearing. It sounded like it.

The male cop turned to him, consulted his phone.

'You are Muammad al-Huq?' he asked in English.

'Yes, sir. I reported it.'

'When did you find the body?'

'Earlier this morning. I woke up and, after washing, I saw her.'

'What time was this?'

'Seven o'clock. I have an alarm on my phone.'

The man checked his watch.

'You only called it in at nine. Why did you not call us immediately?'

The woman was on the phone. She glanced over at Muammad. He saw no animosity in her gaze. Just a frank, appraising stare. Maybe this would be OK. He could claim asylum. It could work. The Swedes were supposed to be a soft touch.

One thing he knew. He was not going back.

'Officer, I have no papers. Only my Syrian passport. I am in your country illegally. I thought if I called the authorities, I would be deported. I prayed for guidance.'

The officer sniffed.

'OK, well you did the right thing. I need you to come with us to the police station to make a statement. Get your stuff together.'

'But what will happen to me?'

'Once we're done with you, we'll call the Swedish Migration Agency. They'll send someone down to talk to you. After that, it's down to them. It's not a police matter.'

'I want to help Sweden,' Muammad blurted. 'I am a professional person. I am educated. I have a degree. I could be of use. I am already learning to speak Swedish.'

The police officer shrugged his broad shoulders as if resettling a heavy weight.

'Great. But it's still not our call.'

Muammad could only nod. He packed away his thin-walled

nylon tent, his copy of the Quran and his few other meagre possessions. Maybe they would let him call Aisha.

He stared at the dead woman.

At least *her* cares in this life were at an end.

17

KUMLA

Lina turned to Sven.

'You're meeting him in a secure room,' she said. 'I won't be there but you'll have a guard in with you. There's a panic button on your side of the table, although he'll be in restraints and also handcuffed to the table.'

Sven nodded. Swallowed. Why did the director's words of reassurance produce the opposite effect?

Inside the stark, empty room, Sven took a seat opposite Ahlgren. In the flesh he was so much less... Sven searched for the right word ... well, just so much *less* than he'd seemed in all the books and websites and news reports.

Ahlgren wasn't tall, or bulky. Maybe 170 cm, 175 if he had long legs. And slim-built. His hair was thinning, and mostly grey. He wore glasses with clear plastic frames that magnified his watery blue eyes and gave them a slightly amphibian appearance. The resemblance to some slippery aquatic creature was enhanced by his fleshy, colourless lips.

His bony wrists were encased in rigid steel cuffs. A length of chain ran inside the cuffs and through a thick eye-bolt secured to the metal-topped table.

Sven smiled at him. Brought out the box of biscuits and pushed them across the table.

'I hear you like these,' he said.

Ahlgren reached for the biscuits, but the chain snapped tight against the eye-bolt, preventing him from reaching the packet.

'Would you mind?' he said, in a soft, cultured voice, with a hint of the far north in it.

Sven reached for the packet.

Behind him, the guard shouted.

'No! Stop!'

Sven froze. Saw that his hand was within a few centimetres of Ahlgren's.

Ahlgren looked disappointed. His fleshy lips were downturned. Almost pouting.

'Sit back, Ulrik, please,' the guard said.

Smiling, Ahlgren complied, pulling the chain tight so its links rattled unpleasantly through the eye-bolt.

'Of course, Tim. Anything you say.'

The guard approached the table. Using a long baton, which, Sven noticed, was looped around his wrist in the approved manner so it couldn't be snatched away, he pushed the box of biscuits over to Ahlgren's side of the table.

Having accomplished this manoeuvre, he retreated to the shadows, but not before murmuring in Sven's ear, 'Careful.'

Heart racing, Sven tried to compose himself.

'Ulrik, I don't know how much news you get in here, but there's been a murder up in Axberg that bears a strong resemblance to your, er—'

Ahlgren leaned forwards. Drew the box of biscuits into his lap and began tearing the cardboard open.

'It's all right, you can say it. You mean my crimes. I won't be

Playing the Devil's Music

angry with you, Sven. After all, you did bring me my favourite treats.'

He tore through the thin cellophane on the inside of the box and extracted a single ginger thin, which he placed between his teeth and nibbled off one of the little scalloped petals on the edge.

Ahlgren closed his eyes in either genuine, or feigned, ecstasy, Sven couldn't tell which. Sven shuddered. How had Ahlgren got hold of his first name? Surely Kersten would have just said a detective wanted to speak to him?

Ahlgren opened his salamander eyes again.

'They're very good. Have one?'

He nudged the box towards Sven. He shook his head. More violently than he'd meant to.

'No, thank you. I'm good.'

Ahlgren shrugged. 'Your loss.'

'Listen, Ulrik,' Sven said, trying to regain control of the conversation. 'The thing is, obviously you couldn't have committed this murder.'

A sympathetic smile. 'Obviously.'

'So I'm thinking there's a copycat out there. Or maybe a super-fan.' He paused, aiming for maximum impact. 'A disciple, even. What do you think?'

Ahlgren eyed him for the longest time. Sven fought down the urge to fill the silence. The wall clock ticked. The gaps between the seconds expanded until each took a minute all on its own.

Finally, Ahlgren spoke.

'Are you sure you won't have a biscuit? They're made by a Belgian firm now, which is a shame. Lotus Bakeries. They bought Annas Pepparkakor out in 2008. They used to be better when they were made here in Sweden. The company was originally based in Tyresö. Do you know it?'

'No, I don't. Look, Ulrik. I'm here because—'

'You should go. It's only fifteen kilometres southeast of Stockholm. Such a pretty town. Trees everywhere.'

'I'll plan a trip.'

'I killed my fifth victim in Tyresö. Her name was Isabel

Röndström. A slut, obviously. Dripping with sin. Putrescent with it, you could say, the Devil take her.'

'Look, I didn't come here to discuss your record, Ahlgren,' Sven snapped.

Ahlgren's lips pooched out in a *moue* of disappointment.

'No more "Ulrik", Sven?'

'Tell me about your disciple. I know you've got one.'

'I'm tired. Tim, I want to go back to my accommodation, please.'

Sven twisted round in his seat. Held up a hand.

'No. Wait.'

He turned back to Ahlgren.

'Help me and I'll help you.'

Ahlgren smiled, a loathsome expression making him look like one of those weird slimy things that lived in the dark and had their gills or lungs or whatever the hell they were outside their bodies.

'Will you get me moved back into Gen Pop, Sven? Restore my privileges? Get me transferred to somewhere with a decent view?'

'You know I can't. I can get you more ginger thins, though. Just help me out here—' He swallowed. ' – Ulrik.'

This time there was no delay. Ahlgren leaned forward, and, very deliberately, hocked up phlegm from somewhere deep in his nasal passageways and spat the mess out onto the open box of biscuits.

'Send Stella. I'll talk to her. Nobody else.'

'Pardon?'

'You heard me. Tim! I said I was tired. Take me back to my cell. Now, please.'

The guard moved into Sven's eyeline. 'Told you,' he murmured as he passed.

As he was leaving the white-painted room, Ahlgren called out.

'Sven?'

Sven turned. Had he had a last-second change of heart? Was it all a monstrous bluff?

'What?'

'I hope we meet again.'

'We won't.'

Ahlgren smiled.

'Never say never!'

Ten minutes later, scowling so deeply the gate guard shot him an inquiring, *What did I do?* look back at him, Sven passed from the prison into the outside world again.

As he turned right onto Viagatan, he jammed his foot down so hard on the accelerator he got an immediate cramp. He held it there, grinding his teeth as his arch locked in an agonising muscular spasm. With acrid blue smoke billowing up from the screeching tyres he inhaled deeply, dragging the acrid burnt-rubber smell deep into his nostrils.

'Fuck!' he screamed into the empty cabin.

His mood was only marginally lifted when Lucy announced as soon as he'd got back to the station that she'd got an ID for their victim.

His name was Joel Varela.

And he was a cop.

18

STOCKHOLM

The following Monday, Stella was preparing for a talk when her phone rang. Malin.

'What are you doing this morning, Stella?' she asked after the briefest of pleasantries.

'A talk down in Norrköping, why?'

'Cancel it. Get yourself into headquarters. My office. As soon as you can, please.'

Stella frowned. 'What's this all about?'

'I'll explain when you get here.'

The line went dead.

Fifteen minutes later, having arranged for another drugs outreach team member to deliver the presentation, Stella headed in to Kungsholmsgatan. She nodded to a few people she knew as she made her way to Malin's office.

She knocked and entered, to find Malin with two more plain-clothes officers. The woman, older, fiftyish, maybe, but well preserved. Athletic build, a skier maybe. The man, much younger, maybe late twenties. Not happy to be there to judge from the scowl he was doing a poor job of hiding.

Malin gestured for her to sit.

'Stella, I'd like to introduce you to Detective Inspector, Group Chief, Kersten Sandén and Detective Inspector, Commander, Sven Petersson. Sven is the lead investigator on a murder in Axberg. Sven, could you explain to Stella what you told me, please?'

The young – *and obviously successful, Stel* – male detective looked about as happy as a man waiting for his dentist to do a root canal.

'I don't know if you've heard about the case?' he began.

From his expression it was clear to Stella he suspected she knew at least as much as he did. She felt a twinge of guilt for having called Henrik. Time for some diplomacy.

'Only what the average citizen picks up from the news.'

He inclined his head.

'Well, then. Bloke's found crucified on a tree. Pentagram carved into his chest, stabbed with something big and improvised, antlers taped to his head and when the pathologist did the autopsy, his brain was missing and replaced with a shit-ton of bugs.'

'Just like Ulrik Ahlgren's victims,' she said, figuring he'd think it odd if she didn't at least know the basics of Ahlgren's hideous crimes.

'Exactly. Anyway, now a second body's turned up. Same MO. I went to see Ahlgren in Kumla. Thought maybe he'd groomed a successor or something. He wouldn't tell me anything. But he said he *would* talk to you.'

Now Stella understood. A guy who'd climbed the greasy pole to a command position before his thirtieth birthday. Lands the biggest case of his career to date. And then his boss orders him to hand it over to the Queen of Weirdness. *She'd* be pissed off if it happened to her, and she wasn't a native-born Swedish male copper with his eyes on the prize.

Kersten turned in her chair so she was directly facing Stella.

'We'd like your help, Stella. You have experience we just don't have in Örebro. Maybe in Sweden,' she added, with a glance at Malin, who nodded. 'We need to stop this new killer before he does it again.'

Stella looked at Malin. She couldn't think of anything she'd like better than to shrug on the homicide investigator's harness again and get to work. But there was the small business of her suspension. For which Malin had sacrificed her next career move.

Penance. It weighed heavy on her.

'Obviously, I'd like to offer Örebro police whatever help I can, but I'm currently, er…'

Kersten spared her blushes.

'On suspension. Yes, Malin told us. I understand it stems from an altercation between you and Nik Olsson?'

Stella tugged on her ponytail.

'You could call it that, yes.'

Had Malin kept the details back? It sounded like she had. More to be grateful to her boss for.

'This may surprise you, then, Stella, but when I spoke to Nik and explained what I wanted, he was amenable to the idea of your re-joining Homicide.'

'What?' She turned to Malin. 'Is this true?'

She nodded. 'I spoke to him myself. He said that there were times when bigger issues were at stake than internal discipline.'

That sounded so unlike something Nik would say that Stella wondered if the three of them were playing a practical joke on her.

'Not to be rude, Malin, but Nik *lives* for internal discipline. I mean it's *literally* his job.'

Malin shrugged. 'Go and see him yourself if you like. After this briefing. As of now, you're back on the team.'

'Permanently?'

'Let's get this case solved before he kills anyone else, shall we? Then we can discuss your future.'

Well that was pretty clear. Get a result, get your old job back. Not quite blackmail, but not far off.

Stella nodded. She could work with that. She looked at Sven.

'I'll need to see everything you've got.'

'We've got an incident room set up at Örebro. I've found a desk for you.'

If he'd been running a restaurant, she had no doubt she'd have been seated just by the toilets.

19

Having spent most of the previous night, until 2:00 a.m., reading up on the two murders, Stella needed fresh air and the sun on her skin. She wheeled the Triumph out from its covered parking spot into a patch of sunshine at the rear of her apartment block. The chromed parts sparkled like a wind-ruffled sea somewhere hot. Portugal. Greece. Malta.

Their honeymoon had been in Sicily.

She put the bucket of hot, soapy water down with a clunk that sent a litre or two slopping over the lip to wet her boots.

A tear welled in the corner of her eye. They'd been so happy. As newlyweds should be. They'd talked about the future.

'What would you say if I told you I was pregnant?' she'd asked Richard, as they strolled, arm in arm, down a narrow street lined with bright-purple bougainvillea.

He turned to her, a lazy, lunchtime-wine smile crinkling his eyes.

'Are you?'

'No. But what would you say? *If* I was?'

He frowned. Stopped walking. Turned to face her and wrapped his arms around her waist.

'I would say,' he kissed her, 'that it would be the start of a very exciting adventure.'

They'd had Lola two years later. Stella thought she'd known love before that moment. She'd loved her parents. Then Richard. But, as the midwife placed Lola in her arms, her heart was vaporised in a supernova of emotion. *This.* This exact, precise, overwhelming feeling. This moment that divided her whole existence in two. Before. After. *This* was love.

She didn't love her husband any less. But as she cradled the squalling, angry, scarlet-faced bundle against her aching breast, she knew that she had discovered the universe's hugest message.

You are a mother. She is yours.

Stella sank to a crouch beside the bike, plunged her hands into the water. Squeezed her fists around the sponge until her knuckles cracked. Ducked her head to each shoulder to scrub away the tears.

'Hey, Stella. Washing your pride and joy?'

She looked up. Her neighbour. Nils. He'd moved in the previous year and always insisted on speaking English with her.

He ran the kitchen in a nearby Lebanese restaurant. She'd eaten there with Jonna a couple of times. The first time, Nils had recommended they try *Batata Harra*. After one mouthful of the spicy potatoes, their tastebuds pinging with flavours of garlic, sumac and fresh coriander, they'd asked their waiter for a second plateful.

'I've been doing a lot of motorway miles.' She sniffed. 'He's not looking his best.'

Nils frowned. 'You're not, either. What's wrong?'

She got to her feet, not enjoying the cracks from both knees. Was she getting old? God forbid.

Should she tell him? He was a friend. Not close, like Jonna, or even Oskar, and Hedda, his long-suffering wife. But they'd been for coffee in each other's apartments once or twice. That they both worked unconventional hours meant they'd often be awake when others were asleep.

The problem was always the same. She was frightened. What if she started crying and wasn't able to stop? Mostly these days, she limited herself to keeping her journal. She'd let Jonna in, of course. But for the most part, the grief felt like an old wound. OK as long as you didn't prod it too hard. She rubbed her left bicep, over the spot where Mim Robey had smashed down her machete, leaving an ugly ridge of scar tissue.

'I was thinking about my family.'

'In England?'

'Kind of. They're...' It was coming. Her mouth had made the decision for her. 'They're buried there.'

Nils lowered his thick black eyebrows. Pursed his lips.

'"They." Your partner? But children, too? I'm so sorry.'

She nodded. Sighed. No tears. Not that it mattered. He wouldn't mind. It was her own fear of letting the emotions out that concerned her. Other people's reactions were their business.

'My husband. His name was Richard. And our daughter. Lola. She was only a baby.'

Nils nodded. Held eye contact. Didn't look away, like he was wishing he'd never asked. Or check his phone, hoping a social media message might offer him an exit from an uncomfortable silence.

'I was going to get breakfast. Do you want to come? Wash your bike later?'

She drew in a deep breath. Felt the tension leave her chest.

'Yes. I'd like that.'

* * *

The cafe had tables looking out over *Riddarfjärden*'s sapphire-blue water. Pleasure boats meandered in graceful curves, their skippers skilfully avoiding the larger ferries and tourist boats plying their trade between the islands. A smiling couple in their sixties paddle-boarded directly beneath their table. The woman looked up and smiled, waved with a free hand.

The waitress brought their coffees. Plus a croissant for Nils.

He took a bite of the flaky, buttery pastry. Best Croissants in Stockholm! according to the chalkboard outside the front door.

'You can always talk to me, Stella. If I'm in, I'm available. You know that, right?'

'I do. And thanks. Mostly it's fine. It was a long time ago now.'

'But things like that never leave us, do they?'

She sipped her coffee.

'No. But they get easier to bear. Have you lost someone, too?'

He nodded.

'Ghasif. We were married for three years. His parents came here from Lebanon in the nineties. They had a restaurant in Beirut. They started again here with nothing. It's how we met.'

'What happened?'

'Three of those Reborn Sweden thugs ambushed us one night after work. Put us both in the emergency room. Ghasif died the next day of his injuries.'

Stella stretched out a hand and covered Nils's.

'That is so awful. Did they catch them?'

She knew the answer in advance. Of course not. Stockholm had seen a dramatic upsurge in street crimes, especially violent crimes, in recent years. The uniform branch was stretched too thin to maintain order and the CID were constantly being reshuffled or presented with new targets.

His answer surprised her.

'They did. Inside a week. They're in prison now. Not for long enough, but that's the Swedish legal system for you. I wish they were dead.' He looked across the table at her. 'Reborn Sweden. That reminds me. Their old leader, Jenny Freivalds. She was killed by that serial killer up in Söderbärke, wasn't she? You caught him.'

'I did.'

'I almost wish you hadn't.'

'You don't mean that.'

Nils sighed. Finished his coffee and signalled for another, raising his eyebrows at Stella. She nodded. He held up two fingers for the waitress.

'I guess not. *Så vem är du i sikte nu, Fru Cole?*'

His sudden switch into Swedish – 'So, who's in your sights now, Mrs Cole?' – made her laugh.

'Well, if you'd asked me the day before yesterday I'd have said teenaged tokers. They had me on Drugs Outreach.' His eyebrows jumped again, like two over-excited little rodents. Shrews, would they be? Voles? 'It's a long story. But now I'm back on Homicide. The two weird murders over in Axberg and Vetlanda.'

His eyes widened. 'Yeah. I read about it on Facebook. It's some guy repeating the Brain Surgeon's crimes. Antlers and pentagrams. All that Satanic shit.'

'It's his MO, certainly. Beyond that, I'm keeping an open mind. Maybe it's just a jealous lover.'

Nils nodded sagely, as if he were Sweden's leading criminologist.

'Yes, yes. Good point. It could just be a love triangle.'

'A two-timing Satanist. That would be a first for me.'

* * *

After washing her bike, Stella went inside and entered the spare bedroom she used as her home office. She'd screwed a large whiteboard to one wall and had already started scrawling up notes. Lines of enquiry. Potential interviewees. Wild ideas. To which she now added in orange dry-wipe marker: 'Jealous lover?'

Shaking her head, she went to rub it out, then put the cloth back down. Why not? It was an age-old motive for murder. Just ask Othello.

The killer clearly had a screw loose when it came to religion. Although, unlike those nutcases who thought they were doing God's work, this guy had gone below ground for inspiration.

She Googled, 'Jealous husbands in the Bible.'

Proverbs 6:34 told her, 'For jealousy is a husband's fury. Therefore he will not spare in the day of vengeance.'

On a whim, she tried again, substituting 'wife' for 'husband'.

The same verses as before.

'How surprising,' she said to the empty room. 'Not.'

She checked her watch. Jonna was due round at seven for dinner. They wouldn't be seeing much of each other until Stella's case was over.

20

ÖREBRO

Jonna drove over with her on Sunday, bringing Stella's suitcase and murder bag. That meant Stella could ride behind on the freshly washed-and-polished Triumph. Jonna was in her usual not-a-kilometre-over-the-limit mode, so Stella delighted in zipping past her then falling back before repeating the whole manoeuvre.

On the way they overtook a stream of bikers on Harley Davidsons.

Some owners of the big American bikes tended to the cliché of the paunchy accountant having a mid-life crisis.

These looked altogether more authentic. Either shaven-headed or sporting long manes of wild hair, much of it greying. Plus beefy, heavily tattooed arms protruding from cut-off leather jackets and sleeveless denim waistcoats that biker gangs adopted as a uniform.

More than one wasn't wearing a helmet. Stella could only

imagine Jonna's face inside the Volvo and her burning desire to call it in.

Each biker looked sideways at her as she rode past. Eyes unreadable behind wraparound shades. A couple nodded appreciatively at the big-engined British motorcycle. Most scowled or gave her a grim-lipped stare she supposed they thought was intimidating.

Stella spent the remainder of her weekend trying to make the little two-room flat in the apartment-hotel they'd found for her feel like home. Unsuccessful in the main, but it had a kitchenette and she'd managed to find time to buy some basic groceries.

Her first Monday at work in Örebro passed in a deluge of briefings, team meet-ups, and reading. Lots of reading.

By Tuesday morning, after five hours' sleep, she was ready to hit the road and start wearing out a little shoe leather. Tyre rubber, anyway.

She arrived at Kumla prison a little before 9:00 a.m., having agreed with the director that they should meet first to discuss how best to conduct the interview with Ulrik Ahlgren. She handed over her service weapon on arrival. The female guard waved her through without passing the metal detector wand over her.

'I think we can trust the Queen of Weirdness,' she said with a smile. Then leaned closer and murmured, 'Pity we didn't have you here years ago. Half this lot wouldn't have got as far as they did.'

In her spacious office, Lina poured them both coffee and offered a packet of ginger thins, which Stella declined.

'Ulrik can be very charming when he wants to be,' Lina said, snapping one of the crisp little biscuits in half and releasing the scent of cinnamon and ginger. 'But be in no doubt. He was, and, in my opinion and that of our resident psychological team, remains an extremely dangerous man.'

Stella nodded. 'Noted.'

She'd met more than her fair share of such creatures. The glib charm of a daytime TV presenter behind which lurked monsters ready to rend and tear, manipulate, torture and destroy, all for their own warped sense of pleasure.

'Have your psych team ever suggested any areas of weakness?'

'Ulrik is very fond of these.' Lina pointed to the red biscuit package. 'Your colleague Sven tried to, well, ingratiate himself by bringing a box.'

'How did that go?'

'Not well.'

'Psychopaths tend to be hyper-aware of the varieties of manipulative behaviour. It's their stock-in-trade after all.'

'There was one thing we discussed. He was always rather proud of his status as one of Sweden's very few serial killers to have functioned in a high-profile role within society.'

'Managing Sepülkå.'

'Yes.'

'That's helpful. Maybe I can try to get him angry that someone's stealing his limelight.'

Lina frowned.

'But wouldn't a disciple be flattering to a man like Ulrik?'

'Not if I paint him as a successor, rather than a disciple.'

'Just be careful, yes? And don't get within his reach. A journalist lost a finger ten years ago.'

'He bit it?'

Lina shook her head. Popped the other half of the ginger thin into her mouth.

'I think the medical term is "avulsion". He pulled it off. He is strong for his size.'

With Lina's warning, and her information about Ahlgren – Stella couldn't bring herself to think of him as 'Ulrik' – buzzing around her brain, she followed a custody officer through the main prison and the inner cordon.

The corridor leading to the Bunker was decorated with a mural that stretched over its entire thirty-metre length: distorted human faces in sad blues and underwater greens seemed to be calling out of the painting to the viewer. Stella found it profoundly unsettling and wondered why the prison authorities had allowed it. Presumably as a harmless way for the inmates to vent emotions that might otherwise be channelled into less acceptable activities. *Avulsion*. She shuddered.

After passing through ten locked doors and two security checkpoints, they arrived at the complex within a prison: the notorious Fenix wards, overseen by a central guardhouse.

Finally, the warder unlocked a door and ushered Stella into a glaring white room where the Brain Surgeon was waiting for her.

As she neared the plain metal table to which he was shackled, he half-rose from his chair. With a pinging series of metallic *chinks*, his leg restraints, and the chain looped around a thick eyebolt in the table, stopped him.

She came to a stop on the other side of the table. 'Please don't get up.'

She drew the basic utility chair out and sat facing one of the most sadistic murderers Sweden – or Stella – had ever seen.

'Hello, Mr Ahlgren. My name is Detective Inspector Stella Cole.'

He pooched out his fleshy lower lip and tugged on it. He had very long, though immaculately manicured, fingernails.

When he spoke, it was in American-accented English.

'"Mr Ahlgren"? So formal. You must call me Ulrik. And I shall call you Stella. How would that be?'

'You've tired of your nickname, then.'

His froggy gape widened.

'The Brain Surgeon? A cheap trick by the media and, forgive me, your colleagues in Stockholm Homicide, too. I should have thought, given the end-point of my surgery, The Entomologist would have been more appropriate.'

'You said you'd talk to me. What about?'

'Isn't it obvious? The killings in Axberg and Vetlanda. You will want my help apprehending this butcher, yes?'

'Why do you call him a butcher? Isn't he doing exactly what you were doing back in 2003?'

'But he isn't, is he? You've seen the difference, haven't you? Why do you think he's made that simple error?'

'What error?'

Playing the Devil's Music

His grin widened. He moistened the lower lip so that it glistened under the harsh light of the neon tubes above their heads.

'Come and see me when you spot it. Until then, perhaps you have some questions for me?'

'How does it feel to be put in the shade by a butcher? The public have short memories and shorter attention spans these days. Yes, the Brain Surgeon was famous for a while, but wait until the media give this new guy a nickname of his own. Son of Satan's pretty catchy. Who'll remember you then?'

His nostrils flared, the wings whitening. That was the only sign he let slip that she'd landed a blow.

He sighed. Shook his head. Stella reminded herself, as if she needed to, that the man facing her was a madman. Evil, yes. Just, mad, too.

'What I did, I did not to be remembered. I did it because they needed to be cleansed.'

'And you figured out cockroaches kill ninety-nine percent of all known germs. Is that it?'

Without warning, he lurched across the table. Stella had been expecting the move. She sat calmly as Ahlgren's wrists jerked against the chain. She hoped it hurt.

Behind her, the guard shifted his weight. Shoe soles scraping over the disinfectant-smelling linoleum.

'Sit back, please, Ulrik,' he said. The tone cautionary. A verbal equivalent of a levelled Taser.

Ahlgren complied, smiling over Stella's shoulder.

'Certainly, Tim. My apologies.'

He looked at Stella. His eyes were remarkable. So pale they were almost white, like a Husky's. Magnified by the thick lenses of his spectacles, they looked diseased, as though strong sunlight might burn them.

'And to you, too, Stella. Please, let's continue.'

She nodded. She felt calm. Not just because Ahlgren was properly restrained. Nor that Tim weighed at least eighteen stone and carried a long black baton.

Her main source of reassurance was the subcompact pistol strapped to her ankle inside the bootcut jeans she'd put on that morning. Strictly against regulations, but still. Who'd go for a chat with a Satanic serial killer without some good old-fashioned lead prayer beads? Not hollow-point, though. These were 9mm full metal jacket rounds. She'd bought them from a gun shop and hollow points weren't on sale to the general public in Sweden. If the friendly female guard on the door had found it, Stella had planned to acknowledge her mistake and surrender it.

'Do you think it's a copy-cat?' she asked Ahlgren. 'Or have you been grooming someone to act in your stead? You know, a willing little acolyte?'

'I really don't know what he is. Or she. We must be inclusive, mustn't we? This is 2023 after all. But as for acolytes, disciples, all that? I read, Stella, you know? Not online. Sadly, Lina feels that privilege is not suitable for one such as I. But I am allowed books and magazines. So I know all about the academic theories surrounding serial murderers, trite though much of it is. You see, *I* am the disciple.'

'And who is your master? Satan?'

'Who else? The prime minister?'

Stella swallowed. She had her own problems with prime ministers. Though not Florence Kintsson, Sweden's current PM. Stella's *bête noire* was Gemma Dowding, the British prime minister. The woman behind the conspiracy that had murdered Richard and Lola. Dowding had exiled Stella to Sweden in return for a promise not to hurt her brother- and sister-in-law and their two teenaged daughters.

'Are you quite all right, Stella? You look a little pale.'

She blinked. Damn! She'd allowed her concentration to wander. Given Ahlgren an advantage, however slight. That was never part of her plan. Never answer the suspect's questions. Counter with a question of your own.

She checked her watch. Time to up the stakes.

'Look, Ulrik. You wanted to see me, yes?'

He inclined his head. Smiled. Believing he had the whip hand. She allowed him to believe it for a few seconds more.

'I believe that's what I told young Sven, yes.'

'Well, I have two brutal murders to solve, which for all I know have fuck-all to do with you. So far you've just sat there on your bony arse, throwing out "I don't know"s and coy little puzzles you think I have time to solve. As for the "Satan is my master" bit? That got old at your trial, so please don't waste your breath giving it to me now. Either you have something I need or you don't. If you do, let's hear it. Otherwise, I'm gone and welcome to the rest of your two-by-three-metre, prison-catered, internet-free, stainless-steel-lavatory, clanking-chains-when-you-need-to-see-the-prison-doctor, miserable, shitty little life.'

She got up to go. But didn't wait for him to throw her a bone. Instead, she strode straight for the door.

'Open it, please, Tim.'

The burly guard moved on quiet feet towards the door.

'Wait!'

She turned.

Ahlgren had risen to a crouch, as straight as his restraints would permit.

'I do want to help you, Stella. Please come back.'

She resumed her seat. Faced Ahlgren. While she waited for him to speak, she conjured up a memory of her, Richard and Lola on the beach in Cornwall. Screeching with startled laughter as a sudden hail storm blew up out of nowhere, stinging their exposed skin as they rushed for the shelter of their little nylon beach tent, Lola enclosed inside Stella's protective arms.

'Why are you smiling?' Ahlgren asked.

She refocused. 'None of your business. What can you tell me?'

He sighed.

'Check the pentagram. It's the wrong way up. If I *did* have a follower, I would, of course, have schooled him in my methods.'

'How do you know about that?'

He smiled his most unpleasant smile yet. Moistened his lower lip again.

'I am like a journalist, Stella. I never reveal my sources.'

She resisted the urge to look over her shoulder. Was the big fellow, Tim, a little too cosy with his charge? All that first-name business worked on a person. It was hard to avoid the easy familiarity that came with the Swedish custom of addressing everyone from a road-sweeper to the king by their given name.

'One last question for you, Ulrik, then I have to go. Why?'

His high, smooth forehead furrowed. 'Why?'

'Yes. Why? Why offer to help me? If it's nothing to do with you, then why bother helping the police?'

'Oh, well, that's easy. If it were just "the police", I probably wouldn't have bothered. But you're different, Stella. Special. The Queen of Weirdness, that's what they call you, isn't it? I suppose I just thought that I should reach out. Given how alike we are.'

Cold insects crawled down her spine from the nape of her neck to her sacrum. Their icy, clawed limbs scratched and pricked, and the hairs on the back of her neck, and her forearms, rose in mute protest.

She shook her head.

'You and I are nothing alike.'

She got up a second time. This time there would be no turning back.

Outside, in the crisp spring air, she inhaled deeply, then had to fight down a sudden urge to laugh – as sudden and unwelcome as an uprush of vomit.

21

Back in the office, Stella called up all the old records on Ulrik Ahlgren's crimes. One by one, she opened the images from the seven autopsies. Tears pricked at her eyes.

Such pretty girls. You could see that, despite the ravages he'd wrought on their bodies, naked under the harsh, unforgiving light of the RMV photographer's flashgun. Blonde hair. Peach-soft complexions. Slender figures. Even a little puppy fat on two of them.

Trying to ignore the monstrous, gaping stab wounds over their hearts, she zoomed in on the pentagrams. Ahlgren had cut them in with a knife he'd bought in an occult shop in Stockholm. Black wrought-iron handle surmounted with a goat's head pommel, and a long, narrow blade onto which the smith had etched a Latin phrase so it stood out silver against the black steel of the blade:

FAC QUOD VIS TOTA LEGE

It translated as *Do what thou wilt shall be the whole of the law*. That turned out to be a quote from a nineteenth-century English occultist named Aleister Crowley. Another idiot with delusions of grandeur, was her take on him.

She frowned. Davey Miller had mentioned Crowley when she'd had coffee with Frankie. His old bandmates in Black Death Rattle were into occultism, Satanism. What had he said about pentagrams?

She closed her eyes and called the kitchen to mind. Pictured the central kitchen island against which Davey was leaning. Yes. '...all that dipshit iconography'.

She made a note.

Black Death Rattle-occult-Sepülkå-Ulrik Ahlgren-new killer. Linked?

Back to the pentagrams. Ahlgren had said his non-disciple had got it wrong. She arranged the seven images along the top half of her screen. The cropped segments resembled a particularly grotesque set of playing cards.

Something about them wasn't right. She rolled her eyes. *What, apart from the fact they're sliced into human flesh, you mean?*

'No,' she murmured. 'Aren't they upside down?'

She searched online. Plenty of companies had five-pointed stars in their logos. Plenty of countries employed them on their flags. And in every single case, from the US to China, the EU to Ghana, every single one had a single point facing upwards and two pointing down.

Ahlgren had placed his pentagrams upside down. The single point aiming down towards the belly, the two aiming up at the throat.

He'd said 'the butcher' had got it wrong. Trying to remember what she'd seen over the weekend in the autopsy photos, she opened, cropped and scaled the corresponding images from the two latest killings, placing them below the original seven.

As she'd thought, this new guy had carved his obscene 'handiwork' the right way up, single point below the notch in the collar bone.

Why?

He'd got every other detail correct. Right down to the single fact they'd always held back from the media. The skull full of insects. That pointed to either a leak or the fact that the new killer was working inside law enforcement. Surely there couldn't be another cop-as-serial? Not so soon after Tilde Enström? No. The stats were against it.

'How did you do it, then?' she muttered, staring at the gruesome images until they became seven blurry red stars.

She pictured Ahlgren, after having killed a girl, probably swathed in some ridiculous blood-red hooded robe, or else stark-bollock naked with a joke shop devil mask over his fat-lipped face.

He pulls out the knife, chants some Latin gibberish about the Devil and then bends lower. Makes the first cut. It's upside down because every-day occult symbols are just a bit too ordinary for Ahlgren, who sees himself as reporting directly in to Satan himself. So he has a brainwave. Or what passes for one in that diseased mass of jelly between his ears. He inverts it.

New guy knows all about Ahlgren's crimes. But maybe he never saw a photo. Maybe he just knew, or heard, about the pentagrams. *They're upside down*, he says to himself. *Better do the same.*

Then why did he *not* do it?

The answer, when it came, was so obvious.

'You're joking,' she said to the screen.

She rotated the image of Joel Varela's bloody chest through 180 degrees. The tip of his chin was just visible at the bottom of the image.

And the pentagram matched the original seven.

The killer had been standing at Joel's head, looking down at him. Probably off his face on meth or acid, or just the enormity of his own actions. Blood rushing, adrenaline making him distant from reality, he got to work and forgot which way round he was working. Idiot.

But then that went for a lot of murderers. They thought they were so smart, but they did dumb things all the time. Left their fingerprints in their victims' blood. Took a shit at the scene of the crime not realising it contained DNA. Boasted online. Really! Numpties.

At this point, Stella wasn't sure what it signified about the killer she was hunting, except that, in all likelihood, he wasn't directly connected to Ahlgren.

Then why copy his methods? If he was a genuine serial killer – *wait, Stel, you mean there's some sort of hierarchy?* – if he was a genuine serial killer, surely he'd have his own twisted psychosexual pathology that would determine his MO?

She bit her lip. Once upon a time there was someone she'd have called to solicit a quick expert opinion. Not anymore. She shoved the thought down.

* * *

That afternoon, Kersten called a meeting for the team investigating the murders.

Slouching in office chairs, perching on tables around the edge or, in Kersten's case, standing at the front before a screen, were half a dozen detectives, a handful of uniformed officers, the chief CSI and the assistant prosecutor for Örebro county.

Steel jugs of coffee occupied the centre of the table. Between them, a transparent plastic tray on which sat half a doughnut and a flattened croissant.

Kersten looked at Stella and smiled.

'As we have a guest, we'll conduct this meeting in English.'

'There's really no need,' Stella said in Swedish. 'Please. Guests should make the effort to learn their new hosts' language. I hope my Swedish is OK.'

'It is excellent.' Kersten grinned. 'Although when you say "guests" you sound like an Östermalmer.'

Laughter rippled round the classroom-sized space.

'From Stockholm *and* posh,' one cop said to more appreciative chuckles.

'No, no.' This was Lucy, Sven's assistant. 'Stella doesn't drive an Audi or a Tesla. She came on a motorbike.'

'Really?' This was Roger Amundsen, an incomer like Stella, only in his case, from across the border in Norway. With his bushy silver beard and heavy build he resembled the bikers she'd passed on the way over at the weekend. 'What do you ride?'

'Triumph Speed Twin 900. You?'

'Indian Chief Dark Horse.'

From the front, Kersten cleared her throat.

'Perhaps our resident bikers could leave their discussion for after work?'

More good-natured laughter. Stella smiled at Roger. He was quite good-looking under all the wild-man facial hair. Nice eyes.

'Sorry, Kersten,' she said.

Kersten smiled briefly. 'Now, before we begin, I want to remind everyone that *three* people are dead. It looks as though Erik Ekblad was murdered because he was in the way, rather than as part of this person's overall plan. But he is still a murder victim and he still deserves our compassion and diligence.'

Murmurs of agreement.

Kersten tapped the table lightly. 'What do we know? Sven? Bring us up to speed, please.'

Sven rose from his chair and rounded the table to stand beside the screen. Chest thrust forward. Chin raised. Smart jacket and a dress shirt. A man clearly on a mission. And not just to solve homicides.

'We now know that the two victims were both serving SPA officers. Joel Varela in the drug squad over in Stockholm. Barbro Ekblad the deputy head of Bergslagen Region.'

He clicked the remote control and pictures of Joel Varela and Barbro Ekblad, the two victims, appeared on screen. Thankfully from their SPA ID photos and not their corpses.

A second click. Indrawn breaths. Stella saw at least one cop wince. She did not. Was that bad? Had she become inured to the darkness at the core of the job? She hoped not. She'd known more than one homicide detective who'd burned out as their souls fried under the relentless horrors of the job.

Sven displayed two crime scene photos side by side.

'Both murdered in exactly the same way. No ID, phones or

wallets, so he's taking his trophies. Now, we all know what this particular MO signifies. Anyone?'

Stella wrinkled her nose. That was a bit obvious. Treating a roomful of experienced homicide investigators like a class full of kids. She decided to step in. Save anyone else the trouble of satisfying Sven's little power trip.

'It's pretty much the same as Ulrik Ahlgren's.'

He nodded, obviously pleased one of his students had given the correct answer.

'It's *exactly* the same as Ulrik Ahlgren's. Which means we have a classic master-disciple scenario, people. Our killer is going to be younger than Ahlgren, let's say by ten to twenty years, but, based on my research into serial murderers, older than eighteen. Now, Ahlgren is forty-nine so that gives us the following initial profile.'

Sven turned to the whiteboard and scrawled a few bullet points with a red marker. Stella had to give him full marks for jumping in with both feet. A male, aged 18–39. Physically strong. White. So far, so hundreds of thousands of Swedish men, including Sven himself.

When he started adding his thoughts about an obsession with devil worship and/or black magic, she tuned out. It was going to take more than some amateur profiler with his eye on a promotion to catch this one. Stella was sure of it.

Kersten brought the meeting to a close with a single emphatic instruction. Nobody was to say anything about the two victims' background as cops. Joel's widow, Carol, had asked that they not make it public and Kersten had agreed, for now.

22

RMV FORENSIC MEDICINE FACILITY, LINKÖPING

Barbro Ekblad's autopsy took place the following day.

The initial stage involved the visual inspection of the body. Stella pointed to the tattoo on the corpse's right shoulder blade.

'Hunter Killers '03. Looks like he's got his victim profile.'

From a safe distance, she observed the preliminaries – clothes removed, bagged and labelled, visual examination completed, swabs and fingernail scrapings taken, antlers – God *help us!* – removed. Then she found out what Henrik had meant when he told her ahead of the autopsy that he'd be 'better prepared this time'.

He asked his assistant for a large, heavy-duty, clear plastic bag. Normally they were used for disposing of biological waste. Today he had a different purpose in mind. And he'd modified the bag earlier that morning.

'What is that?' Stella asked, peering at the curious assemblage of plastic and blue rubber gloves.

'My own version of an infection-control hood. Watch.'

With his assistant holding the bag up and manoeuvring the gloves from the inside, Henrik pushed his hands into them so that they were on the inside of the bag. He picked up a pair of pliers and laid them on the table beside the head. Then a T-shaped chisel and rubber mallet. His assistant fitted the bag over the corpse's head and down onto the shoulders. There it was taped with micropore surgical tape.

Stella nodded. It made sense. No way Henrik would want his dissection room full of flying and crawling creatures for a second time. Once and he'd be forgiven. Twice and he'd earn himself a nickname as the bug man. A Swedish word she must have heard Oskar or Hedda say to Gustav popped into her head. *Småkryp*. It worked better in English. Creepy crawlie. Maybe *Bugmannen Brodin* would stick, though. Same alliteration. She smiled behind her mask.

'Ready?' Henrik said, to the room at large, Stella thought. Or maybe to himself, knowing what was to come.

The room fell silent. Henrik prised the staples out with the pliers. He swapped the pliers for the other tools.

Tap-tap, crack.

Henrik drove the T-chisel into the crudely sutured incision around Barbro Ekblad's skull and twisted it. Despite knowing what was to come, Stella couldn't help leaning forwards, craning to get a look at what Ulrik Ahlgren's acolyte had done. Hardly able to believe he'd have done it twice.

Henrik gripped the skull cap and pulled it away from the rest of the head.

'The devil in hell!' someone exclaimed as the polythene waste bag filled with fluttering motion. Its sides crackled and shivered as the multifarious creatures inside panicked, and flew or hurled themselves against its pliable but unyielding sides.

'Now, please, Anders,' Henrik said, calmly.

Stella looked at him with renewed admiration. The Young Turk was truly unbothered by the facts his hands were sharing a very small space with a couple of dozen biting, stinging and nipping critters. Or he had pre-loaded with an industrial dose of Xanax.'

Anders the assistant approached his boss from the left side and deftly untaped the bag from the body. Taking great care not to let a single bug escape, he slid it free until he could twist and then tape the open end shut.

Someone hissed out a held breath. Another swore. A third giggled nervously as they all observed the bag full of creatures that had no business being inside a human body, let alone its decerebrated skull cavity.

As she looked at the bag and its jerking, flittering occupants, Stella frowned.

'How the hell did he get them in there?'

'What do you mean?' the prosecutor asked.

'I can see how he might get the first one in, but every time he wanted to put another one in, wouldn't the first ones just jump out?'

Henrik nodded.

'Although we're still waiting for the toxicology results from Joel Varela to come back, I have a theory. I think he knocked him out with chloroform or another incapacitant. I didn't find any puncture marks. Well, apart from the rather large one in his chest.'

Stella looked at him carefully. His eyes were crinkling at the corners. Was he grinning behind that surgical mask?

'So he didn't inject him with anything to knock him out.'

'No. But I did find some tiny abrasions around the lips and nostrils. I believe the killer clamped a rag soaked in chloroform over the nose and mouth.'

'You think he could have knocked the bugs out the same way?'

'Probably not individually, but in a killing jar like butterfly collectors use.'

'Wouldn't he have to know the dose? Not to kill them, I mean?'

Henrik shrugged. 'He probably used trial and error. This is not a man overly concerned with the sanctity of life, after all.'

Stella rolled her eyes. Of course! Their serial killer would probably have grown up killing small creatures for fun.

The rest of the autopsy confirmed that this was the same MO as Joel Varela's killer had used, and therefore, almost certainly – 'Ninety-nine percent,' Henrik opined – the same killer.

Barbro Ekblad had been mutilated with a pentagram. Interestingly, this one was the 'right' way up. One-eighty degrees to that incised into Joel Varela's chest. To Stella it seemed obvious why. The killer had approached his second victim from her waist. He'd stove in her chest with a large-diameter stabbing weapon, penetrating her heart and causing the fatal wound, leading to death by blood-loss.

'I know we have to wait for a third victim before we officially label him a serial killer, but I'm calling this one now,' Sven said, not bothering to conceal the note of triumph in his voice.

'I don't disagree,' Stella said, aiming for the most diplomatic tone of voice she could muster. 'But the MO *isn't* identical.'

Everyone turned to her.

'Meaning?' Sven demanded. 'And don't say it's because the pentacle's the wrong way round. No judge is going to bother with a tiny detail like that. He probably just felt like inverting it to confuse us.'

Stella shook her head. The others hadn't noticed. Maybe it was because their gaze had been fixed on the other artefacts on the body. The antlers. The *skalle småkryp* – 'skull critters' – as she'd heard one of the CSIs mutter to her colleague. The gaping stab wound. The pentagram. But Stella had been methodical. And she'd seen what *wasn't* present, not just what was.

'Her fingers. Look. They're intact. Joel's were mangled.'

'So he got careless,' Sven said dismissively. 'The point is it's the same guy.'

Stella caught Henrik's eye. They hadn't worked together for that many years, but each time she'd felt the relationship strengthen. Both were willing and able to think in unorthodox ways for their chosen professions. A pathologist willing to speculate beyond the narrow scientific realm his job demanded. A homicide detective able to think her way inside the mind of a killer.

She hoped he'd pick up her reluctance to get into it with her new colleague in front of so many witnesses. Because although she was convinced she was right, she didn't want to show off her experience and risk alienating him.

Henrik returned her stare, and nodded minutely.

'Let's maybe save the theorising until after I've conducted the autopsy,' he said.

Stella was only too happy to comply. Sven shot her a look that was very easy to interpret. *Remember who's the lead investigator on this case. And who now outranks you.*

* * *

At Örebro copshop, Sven found her in the kitchen.

'Look, about the autopsy,' he began, spooning ground coffee into a jug.

'I'm sorry. I was out of line.'

'Well, yes, you were. We all know about your reputation, Stella. Jesus, sometimes it seems like you only have to turn on the TV and there you are outside SPA headquarters with a mic shoved under your nose. But we do know how to investigate murders out here in the sticks, you know.'

So that was how he wanted to play it. He didn't even have the grace to accept her apology. Fair enough. Time to set out her ground rules, too.

'I think the broken fingers matter. And, for the record? Serial killers never get careless.'

'Bundy did. Nilsen did. The Wests did. Even Will Andersson did in the end. Otherwise how did you catch him?'

Stella bit back a sharp retort. 'What I was *going* to say was that they never get careless when it comes to their MO. Their signature. The trophies they take. The way they display the bodies. Each detail matters to them. It means something. So if he broke Joel Varela's fingers, it meant something to him. Probably something to do with his psychosexual drives. So my question is, why didn't he break Barbro's?' Sven cupped his chin and nodded. 'It wasn't a rhetorical question, Sven. Why didn't he break her fingers?'

Sven huffed out a breath. Threw his arms out to the side.

'How should I know? I'm not a shrink, am I?' His eyes brightened. 'Speaking of which, we should get a profiler in.'

Stella shook her head.

'Let me save you the trouble. And Kersten the money she almost certainly doesn't have after the latest round of government cuts. Your profiler will be a criminology or psychology academic with zero field experience. They'll demand all the files, all the witness statements, all the crime scene photos and autopsy records. And here's what they'll say. "The killer is a white male, aged between 18 and 49. From the brutal nature of the killings, he will be of lower than average intelligence and working, if at all, in a manual occupation. The Satanic symbol indicates a fascination with the occult. The killer is almost certainly a loner with access to somewhere secluded to perform his ante mortem mutilations. Maybe he has a workshop, a basement, or a farm, or a unit on an industrial estate or even a lockup. He may work in an environment where access to bugs is possible such as a zoo, pet shop or even in pest control." See what I mean?'

Sven was scowling. But she could see the light of understanding dawning in his eyes anyway.

'You're saying they'll give us a mixture of statements of the obvious, sweeping generalisations and enough wiggle room that when we catch the killer they can say, "See, I told you so".'

She nodded. 'Exactly. You've already narrowed the likely age down. And we can tell a lot about his preoccupations from the way he left the bodies.'

'So how do you propose we go about catching him?'

'The same way we catch any murderer. We look for forensic evidence he left at the scenes. Security video from around the locations where he left the bodies. ANPR from nearby national or county roads, because he must have transported the bodies to the deposition sites in a van of some kind. But mostly by finding out the significance of the Hunter Killers tattoos worn by both victims.'

He nodded. She saw she'd got through to him. Maybe she could forge a decent partnership with him after all. They needed to before anyone else got killed.

Sven was hot for it to be officially declared multiple linked homicides. He thought it would make his career. Stella would do anything to prevent that coming true.

23

CHARLOTTENBERG, WESTERN SWEDEN

Fredrika Rudbeck hadn't expected much from her first book.

Her husband, a lecturer in Swedish Literature at Gothenburg University, had been the one to suggest she write a novel based on her time in the SPA. She'd laughed and batted Rolf's suggestion away. But it had taken hold, catching in her mind like a burr snagging on her favourite corduroy trousers on a walk in the forest bordering their property.

With the team's capture of Ulrik Ahlgren still fresh in everyone's minds, especially the officers who'd cornered him at the remote farmhouse – poor Nik! – she found her story straightaway.

Initially writing it late at night, then early mornings too, then in literally every spare moment, Fredrika had completed the first draft of *Från Ett Mörkt Sinne – From A Dark Mind* – in six months. She'd submitted it to a few agents, not expecting anything bar rejection letters. Two had immediately expressed an interest and one had clinched the deal by bringing her an informal offer for a

500,000 krone advance from Sweden's largest publisher of crime novels.

She'd earned out her advance in six weeks. The book went into a second printing a month after that. And her editor had begged her to write a second book. That had been ten years ago. She'd quit her job with the SPA and now occupied her time writing and walking her two elderly English setters, Rebus and Bosch.

Fredrika and Rolf liked to maintain their privacy, so she turned down most invitations to speak at conferences or give interviews, much to her publisher's chagrin. But the latest blogger had been so persistent, he'd eventually worn her down and she'd agreed to chat to him. He was one of those obsessive fans who seemed to know more about her career, both before and since quitting the police, than she did. But he'd been charming both in his emails and on the phone.

The doorbell rang. She checked her watch. Ten to eleven. He was early. But not embarrassingly so. She smiled to herself. It was of a piece with this almost puppyish eagerness to learn 'about your process' as he'd put it in his final call. Really, what he expected to learn, she had no idea. Any 'process' she might have had was as much a mystery to her as it was to him. She just sat at her desk, inhaled deeply, and began. Characters appeared before her and she merely wrote down what they did and said.

Rolf shouted from downstairs.

'I'll get it. Must be your super-fan!'

Smiling, Fredrika pushed her chair back from her desk, rolled her head on her neck, wincing as her neck vertebrae crackled like bubble-wrap, and got to her feet.

She was at the top of the stairs, when Rolf's voice, raised both in pitch and volume made her stop.

'What the hell d'you think you're doing? Wait! No!'

The blast was enormously loud in their wood-panelled hallway. Her first, horrified, thought was that Rolf had shot the blogger with his hunting rifle.

Something heavy – *A man's body*! her inner voice screamed – hit the polished floorboards with a clump.

'Rolf,' she shouted, taking the stairs two at a time, 'what the hell did you do? It's just—'

Her heel slipped off the third to last step and she landed painfully on her coccyx on the next one down. It meant she caught her first sight of her husband's corpse from a seated position. The top of his head was missing, and blood and brain tissue had been sprayed onto the walls and ceiling. Her mouth worked, but no scream emerged, just a gasp of rapidly expelled air.

The … the… her cop-brain, dormant for so long, kicked back into life and supplied the right word – *the shooter* – stepped over the threshold, sawn-off shotgun held casually over one shoulder. Kicked the front door closed with a booted heel. Moved towards Fredrika, grinning.

'I am a massive fan, it's true. But not of you. Of my master. Ulrik Ahlgren.'

The dogs pattered in from the kitchen, low growls rumbling from back in their throats. But the shooter just knelt down and extended a hand, knuckles uppermost.

'Hey, guys. You're too smart to get in the middle of this.' He pointed at the body. 'Get lost, yes?'

After sniffing his hand, their growls subsided, replaced by thready whines. Fredrika felt the last vestiges of hope leave her like the tide going out. As if directed by the same remote control, Rebus and Bosch turned as one dog and slunk back into the kitchen.

She was hyperventilating, and she knew that if she didn't move fast her life was over just as surely as Rolf's. Sparks flew around in her vision, obscuring the shooter's features. Casually, as if putting down a briefcase, he placed the gun on the narrow console table where Fredrika and Rolf left the post, and their keys. She pushed herself up on her elbows but then a rag appeared from somewhere and was clamped over her mouth and nose.

'No,' she gasped out, trying to wriggle her head free. Then she took a breath – had to or else pass out from suffocation – and everything became swimmy. Nauseous, she struggled for breath but that only made things worse. As her brain filled with a lemony, waxy, oily stink, she gazed imploringly into those ice-blue eyes. 'Please,' she whimpered. 'Don't…'

Blackness.

* * *

The local police in Charlottenberg were called to the Rudbecks' house by a concerned neighbour who'd reported hearing gunfire. 'It was a shotgun,' he'd confidently asserted. 'Being a hunter myself, I recognised the sound quite clearly.'

The front door had been left open, so it was *Polisassistent* Janik Andresson, a rookie fresh out of police college, who found Rolf Rudbeck's body lying in a lake of blood, half his head splattered up the off-white walls. Janik staggered back outside and threw up in a flowerbed before yelling for his colleague. She was older by ten years and far more experienced. She glanced inside then radioed for detectives and crime scene investigators.

'Come on, Janik,' she said, not unkindly, but with steel in her voice. 'We'll check round the back. We need to find Fredrika.'

All the local cops knew Fredrika, or 'Fred' as she insisted they call her. They were proud that one of their own had parlayed her experience into a job as a best-selling novelist and would often invite her into the station for *fika* when things were quiet.

So Janik accompanied *Polisinspektör* Annifrid Jonsson as, gun drawn, she crept around the side of the house, keeping tight against its Falun Red clapboarded walls.

No way was she going to present the killer with another cop-target. She mentally ticked herself off. Who was to say Fredrika was a target at all? Maybe Rolf had been the gunman's chosen victim all along. Or was it just a robbery gone wrong?

She was getting ahead of herself. Stilling her racing thoughts with a deep breath, she rounded the corner of the house and emerged into the spacious back yard with its red-painted Japanese bridge over an ornamental stream.

'Shit and send the devil back to hell!'

'What is it?' Janik asked, from six feet behind her.

'Well, it's not a robbery, botched or otherwise,' Annifrid said, scratching her nose, which had started itching furiously. 'Cover me.'

Annifrid left Janik in the lee of the house, his service pistol drawn and aimed into the woods at the bottom of the garden. She advanced across the grass to the graceful, red-leaved Acer that stood in its own circle of bark chippings in the centre of the garden.

Her own pistol she kept raised, pointed skyward just a little out from her right cheek. Head flicking left and right, ready to level her SIG should she catch even the suspicion of movement, she reached the tree.

Bound to it by blue polypropylene rope, head dropped to her chest, arms extended along a bundle of bamboo canes lashed together with green garden twine, was Fredrika Rudbeck. Antlers had been duct-taped to her head and her shirt had been slashed open, revealing a crudely cut pentagram in the space between her breasts. Lower still, on the right side, a bloody rent in the pale blue cotton, the fabric beneath it soaked a deep scarlet.

Heart thumping against her ribs, Annifrid crouched in front of the body. She knew this was a homicide. The latest in a series that had started over in Örebro County. But a small sliver of hope remained.

'Fred?' she said, then again, louder, 'Fred?'

She straightened and pushed a finger into the soft place behind the angle of Fred's jaw. Closed her eyes. Searched desperately for a pulse. But Fred's heart had stopped beating some time ago. She knew it.

'It is safe?'

She jerked upright. Janik! She'd forgotten about him.

'Yes. Come over.'

He trotted over the grass and came to a standstill beside her. She holstered her pistol and gestured for him to do the same.

'Jesus! It's only my second week,' he said, peering at Fred's mutilated body.

'You going to throw up again? Because if you are, do it far away from here or the CSIs will go crazy.'

He shook his head.

'I'm fine. Sorry about before. It's just, I've never actually seen a dead body before.'

Anni smiled at him, grimly. 'Let's hope you don't see another one for a while, hey? These two should keep you going for at least a year.'

24

ÖREBRO

The call had come in ninety minutes earlier. The local cops over in Charlottenberg had requested assistance. A homicide, they said. Same MO as the two in Örebro County, they said. Totally out of our fucking depth, they hadn't said. Not out loud, at any rate. But the meaning was, according to Sven, 'clear as crystal'.

Lucy, his usual assistant, was out of the office, so, as he replaced his black desk phone in its cradle, he turned to Stella.

'Fancy a trip to the borderlands? Our boy's just officially become a serial killer.'

'Shit! Where?'

'Charlottenberg. About a three-hour drive. We can do it in less with the lights on. Bring a warm coat. They're having some unseasonably cold weather.'

Sven had the keys to a metallic burgundy Volvo. 'Fastest in the pool,' he grinned as he swung himself behind the steering wheel.

Tyres screeching on the smooth surface of the underground carpark, he spun the wheel this way and that before exiting the ramp, blues and twos signalling to other traffic they'd better damn well get out of his way.

Stella caught a rainbow shimmer against the black tarmac. A truck must have spilled some diesel on the road. As a biker she'd got used to looking out for the telltale slicks. Fail and you'd learn the hard way that diesel and bike tyres didn't mix. She'd learned the hard way as a twentysomething novice biker in London when her newly acquired Kawasaki had slid from under her and dumped her on her bottom in the middle of Piccadilly Circus.

Sven was too intent on demonstrating his stunt driving skills to notice. He hit the slick at 30 kph. Not fast enough to cause problems if he'd been driving in a straight line. But as he powered into the turn that would take them out to the E18 and on to Charlottenberg, he was too busy applying opposite lock to bring the Volvo's shimmying back end into line.

'Christ!' he yelled as the car hit the patch of recently spilled truck fuel and executed a full three-sixty. Horns blared from all around them. Stella heard the crunch of metal and glass. Mercifully, it wasn't theirs. She swung round in her seat to see a cute little pea-green hatchback French-kissing a black estate.

Sven spun the wheel back the other way and the car lurched as all four wheels found traction. He floored the accelerator, leaving the scene with the alacrity of a getaway driver.

'What the fuck, Sven! You could have got us killed. Or somebody else. It's carnage back there.'

His face was pale. But his lips were drawn back and after a second Stella realised he was grinning fiercer than ever.

'This is a homicide investigation, *Inspector* Cole. They can get in line to complain about the police like everybody else.'

Siren whooping, Sven ran nine red lights before he reached the E18. Thankfully causing no further collisions, though Stella reckoned at least a couple of commuters would be hitting the bars earlier than usual today.

They drove in silence for another thirty minutes. Finally Sven cracked. He emitted a sigh.

'Maybe I got a little over-excited back there. But think about it, Stella, we're on the trail of a serial killer!' He spun his left hand in the air between them. 'OK, in your case *another* serial killer. This kind of case can make careers.'

She turned her head. Was this arrogant young cop for real? People were being sadistically mutilated and killed, and all he saw was a step on the promotion ladder?

What, and you never did? a sardonic inner voice piped up.

She pursed her lips. That was a fair point. But even so, she felt she needed to say something that would get Sven to see the full horror of what was going on around them.

'Look, Sven. You're right. Catching a serial killer? It does make you into the golden boy—'

' – or girl,' he interrupted, glancing across at her and grinning.

'Or girl. But I've also seen cops driven to the point of obsession, sometimes beyond, by cases that never broke. Let's just focus on solving these murders. And maybe try to remember that three people have been killed. People with families, friends, colleagues. We don't want to go marching into their lives like we see their loss as some career-development challenge. This is *real*.'

Sven's lips tightened.

'I know that! I'm not completely new to policework, Stella. Anyway, it's not as if I'm the one with the cool nickname, is it? Queen of Weirdness. How does having a personal brand fit in with all your talk of compassion for victims?'

Stella felt her cheeks heating up. Her pulse was thudding in her throat. No way did she want to fall out with Sven, but neither was she going to let him accuse her of being a glory hunter

'Right, for a start, I didn't ask for that stupid name. I got stuck with it.' *Although I do kind of like it, but I'm not going to tell you that.* 'Second, it's not a personal brand. If anything, I'm known for kicking against the pricks. And lastly,' she said, counting off the final point on her finger, 'I don't "talk" of compassion for victims of crime. I actually do feel it...' She sucked in a shuddering breath. 'Given that my husband and baby daughter were murdered.'

Tears were running down her cheeks. She hadn't meant to tell Sven about Richard and Lola. Hadn't known it was going to happen. It just had. She sat back in the padded seat, head turned away so she could stare out of the window at the countryside flashing past. Fields as far as the eye could see. Distant tractors like shiny green and red beetles labouring among the crops. Seagulls flocking behind them, diving for whatever creatures the tractors had disturbed.

'Jesus, I'm sorry, Stella,' Sven said after a minute of silence. 'I had no idea. What happened?'

'Hit and run,' she said. 'The guilty were punished. But I learned what it felt like to be the one left behind that day. So let's be professional, OK? Let's be respectful and most of all let's catch this twisted fucker before he kills anybody else.'

Sven nodded. 'Absolutely.'

Ten minutes later, Stella's phone rang. Jamie. What the hell? This was something she could do without.

She answered nonetheless. She could let it go to voicemail but he'd keep trying until he got through. Jamie was persistent. At one time she'd admired it in him.

'Hi, Jamie.'

'Hi, Stella. How are you?'

'On my way to a crime scene, actually.'

She could hear the shortness in her tone. Regretted it. But couldn't find a way to soften it. After the bruising way they'd parted, she'd realised they really didn't have a future together. He was too needy, for one thing, and he knew too much about her. And, of course, there was the whole arresting him as a suspect in multiple homicides thing. It took more resolve – and love – to get past something like that than Stella had to offer.

'Is it another Satanic murder?'

Inwardly, she cursed the internet. Jamie had followed her last case online. He'd admitted to stalking her via the web before rocking up unexpectedly on her doorstep outside her apartment building on *Mariebergsgatan*.

But there was no point denying it. Especially not to Jamie. Forensic psychiatrist or not, he could easily read any Swedish newspaper's website and discover what she'd been doing.

'Looks that way.'

'Three's the charm,' he said, a smile evident in his voice.

'I know. And there's nothing charming about it, believe me,' she added, irritated that here was another man who seemed to find ritualistic slaughter funny.

'Of course not. But this makes it a serial killer.'

Stella frowned. Did he think she didn't know?

'Was there anything in particular? Only we're almost there.' She caught Sven's puzzled glance; they were still an hour away from Charlottenberg. She shook her head at him.

'I wasn't calling to offer my help, if that's what you're thinking…?'

'I think, after the way our last bit of international cooperation panned out, that would probably not be wise.'

'Indeed. But anyway, Stella, that's not the reason. I was thinking, well, hoping really, now that some time has elapsed, you know, maybe we could try again?'

She frowned. What was he on about? She'd just said trying again would be a bad idea And now he was… Oh. Christ. He meant try the relationship again.

'Look, Jamie…'

'I know, I know. I disappeared in a huff last time. And I don't mind admitting, I *was* furious with you. Well, not just you. Your colleagues, Malin, the SPA in general, actually. I mean, I volunteered to help. Worked pro bono and all I got in return was a pair of steel bracelets and Sweden's shittiest Airbnb.'

Stella's heartrate sped up faster than Sven's screeching exit from the Örebro copshop carpark. What the hell? Jamie was playing the victim card? She didn't want to have a full-blown row here. Not in a speeding car with Sven at the wheel. Thought she could steer the conversation onto neutral ground.

'So, what are *you* doing at the moment? Have you got a new job?'

'No. I'm considering my options. My publisher is very pleased with my book. They want me to write another. But please don't try to distract me, Stella. Mind-games are rather my area of expertise. So, what do you think?'

'Think?'

'Er, hello? Yes, think! About you and me? I thought you could take some leave. I know you. You're always working. I bet you've racked up lots of holiday entitlement since moving to Sweden. You could just grab a flight. No need to book accommodation, you could stay with me.'

What the hell? This was going from bad to worse. No way could she afford to take time off now. And even if she could, flying back to England to stay with Jamie? Why? If anything, she'd go on a long-talked-of skiing trip with Jonna, up north. She sighed. If – when – Jonna got her new job-slash-promotion, would they still have time to spend together? Jamie interrupted her thoughts.

'I'm waiting.'

He drew out the final syllable into a singsong cadence that sounded like an impatient teacher.

'Jamie, it's impossible. I'm right—'

' – in the middle of a murder investigation. Well, three. I know, darling. I meant after that, obviously.'

She had to force her jaw to unclench. Had Jamie always interrupted her this much? She didn't think so. But now, everything he said made her feel like swearing down the line at him.

'Look, Jamie, I don't think that's a good idea.'

She glanced guiltily to her left. Sven was doing a marvellous job of acting like the world's most-focused driver. Eyes locked straight ahead. Serious expression. Hands at ten-to-two on the wheel.

No point in lowering her voice. Short of stuffing wax plugs into Sven's ears, he was going to hear it all anyway.

'Am I permitted to ask why not?'

Something in Jamie's tone had the fine hairs on the back of her neck prickling. *Am I permitted...? God*, he sounded so cold.

'I, we, it's not...' She sipped in a quick breath. 'I just don't feel—'

'Oh, spit it out for fuck's sake, Stel. You sound like a nun trying to give a sex-ed talk to a bunch of horny adolescents.'

That did it. Any lingering anxiety about hurting Jamie's feelings evaporated. Anger flashed through her as the words tumbled out.

'Spit it out? OK. I don't love you anymore, Jamie. I *don't* want to give it another try. I *don't* want to see if we can make it work. I *don't* want to "just grab a flight" and I *especially* don't want to stay with you. How's that?'

She took the phone from her ear and stabbed the red icon. Breathing heavily, she thrust it into a pocket then folded her arms across her chest.

Sven spoke into the silence, which had thickened in the car like cooling molasses.

'So I'm guessing I don't need to buy a new suit for the wedding, then?'

The remark was so outrageous that Stella burst out laughing. Sven's dead-straight face set her off again into wilder peals.

'Sorry about that,' she said, once the paroxysm had passed. 'I guess that would feature under over-sharing, no?'

Sven shrugged eloquently.

'It's not like my own love-life is anything to write home about. My last girlfriend dumped me over my hours. Said she saw the postman more than she saw me. Last I heard, she was with a personal trainer. A *female* personal trainer.'

'Well, if we're going to be partners, I guess sharing a little bit of personal stuff isn't the end of the world.'

Sven nodded at an upcoming road sign.

'Fifteen kilometres to go. Look, I know I've been acting like a bit of a dick, but I really do want to bring this guy to justice, Stella. And I know you've caught plenty of murderers.' She looked over at him. He was blushing. 'What I'm trying to say is, if you've got any tips, or, you know, insights, I'd be really grateful if you'd share them.'

It was a big admission from the ambitious young man sitting behind the wheel. And he did sound genuine.

'Fair enough. The thing that's bothering me, and maybe when we get to the crime scene, my intuition will be confirmed or disproved, is that there's something not right about the MO.'

'You mean the little variations?'

'Yeah. And the thing is, to us they're little variations. But to a genuine psychopathic serial killer... I mean one who derives a perverse sexual thrill from his kills, those variations are huge. I mean, it just doesn't happen.' She huffed out a breath in frustration with the way her own logic seemed to support two contradictory hypotheses at the same time. 'Do I think it's one killer? Yes. Is he following a classic serial killer's trajectory? To a degree although we've not seen any escalation.'

'Sorry, escalation?'

'Ramping up one or more aspects of the violence. Either adding in sexual assaults, or more torture, or multiple fatal blows or the way the corpses are displayed.'

'But he's only done three so far. Maybe it's too early for that.'

'Maybe. And like I said, we need to see victim number three first. But it's as if someone was trying to kill like a serial killer without actually being one. If that makes any sense.'

Sven frowned. 'Kind of. But, if someone kills three people the same way, what's the difference between acting like a serial killer and just, you know, being one?'

'That, my friend, is the sixty-four thousand krone question. And right now, I don't have an answer.'

Twenty minutes later, Sven swung the Volvo off the highway, followed a country road – *Varggatan* – for half a kilometre and then parked a few metres back from a marked police car. A white forensics van sat beneath a pine tree, its rear doors open, revealing racks of specialist equipment.

Blue-and-white crime scene tape entirely cordoned off the house at the end of the cul de sac.

Stella climbed out, easing the muscles in her back. The Volvo's seats were well padded but the tension on the drive over, heightened by the breakup-by-phone with Jamie had put a kink into her spine.

She knuckled the knotty muscles as she and Sven walked over to the uniformed cop guarding the property.

25

CHARLOTTENBERG

Stella and Sven introduced themselves and she added their names and badge numbers to her log.

'She's round the back. CSIs are still here and the pathologist is there, too.'

Stella and Sven donned booties and overalls before ducking under the tape and making their way to the rear of the house.

Other white-suited figures, hooded and gloved, were busy all over the garden. Crouching or kneeling, taking samples, photographing the scene and making trips inside the house from time to time.

Stella spotted Henrik Brodin over in a corner, deep in conversation with a detective in a brown suit. He looked up and smiled, raised a hand in greeting. The detective followed his gaze and when he saw who had come to visit his crime scene, said something to Henrik and then strode across the lawn to join them.

He held out his hand.

'Inspector Lars Enquist. Thanks for coming.'

'I'm Inspector Sven Petersson and this is—'

' — Stella Cole,' Lars said with a smile, shaking her hand warmly. 'It's an honour. I would say a pleasure, but—' He jerked his chin in the direction of the corpse tied to the tree not ten metres away, 'it doesn't quite seem appropriate.'

Stella caught the twist to Sven's lips, as if he'd bitten down on a lemon wedge. No matter how loudly she protested about not having a personal brand, it was clear she did possess, even if she didn't enjoy it, a certain reputation in Swedish law enforcement circles. She smiled back at Lars.

'Sven's the lead investigator. He caught the first murder in Axberg and the one in Vetlanda.' She turned to him. 'Maybe you should fill Lars in. I'll go and say hello to Henrik.'

Leaving the two men to exchange ideas and get each other up to speed, Stella walked over to where Henrik was writing notes on a tablet with a sleek grey stylus.

'New kit?' she asked as she arrived beside him.

He smiled. 'Hey, Stella. Got it yesterday, actually. It's brilliant! Like writing on paper, only it's digital.'

She pulled out her own notebook.

'I'm still at the actual paper stage, I'm afraid.'

'Whatever works for you. Do you want to see the body? I can talk you through what I've found if you like?'

He led her to the corpse and asked the CSI taking photos to give them some space for a couple of minutes.

She performed a slow circuit of the tree, burdened with its grotesque fruit. Squatted to look up into the dead woman's face. In death, like every corpse Stella had ever seen, she looked peaceful. Staring eyes and twisted mouths were strictly for horror films. All skeletal muscles went slack on death. Eyelids closed, therefore. Lips and jaw soft.

'Do we have an ID? I'm assuming since she was murdered at home…'

Henrik nodded. 'Fredrika Rudbeck. Her husband was murdered, too. Rolf was shot in the head in the hallway. A sawn-off shotgun would be my guess, though the ballistics experts will be able to tell you for sure.'

She nodded thoughtfully. Picturing the sequence of events. Killer rings the doorbell. Husband answers. Killer shoots him dead. Maybe waits for wife to arrive then chloroforms her, kills and mutilates her. Crucifies her on the tree and makes his getaway. It would do for now, though questions were multiplying in her mind like the flies currently swarming around the body.

'Same MO?' she asked.

Henrik pointed at the pentagram incised into Fredrika Rudbeck's skin. Rivulets of dark dried blood descended to her waist.

'He did it while she was vertical. Presumably tied to the tree. The track in the chest wound descends at an angle of about thirty degrees.'

'So he stabbed her while she was tied to the tree as well.'

'That's what it looks like. The wounds in the other two victims were more or less vertical.' Henrik mimed stabbing straight downwards. 'He had them laid out in front of him, supine, and killed them where they lay before mounting them on the trees.'

'Chloroform?'

'We'll need a toxicological report to be certain, but I sniffed the area around her nose and mouth and yes, I did detect the characteristic odour.'

Stella gestured at the antlers crudely duct-taped to the dead woman's head.

'Think he did his trick with the bugs on her, too? That would have been hard to manage with her vertical, I'd have thought.'

Henrik narrowed his eyes behind his tortoiseshell spectacles. Tilted his head on one side.

'I don't know.'

'I guess you'll find out at the autopsy.'

'You'll be there?'

'Try and keep me away.'

Sven joined them, pausing on his way to examine, from a respectful distance, the corpse.

'She's an ex-cop,' he said.

'So I hear,' Stella replied.

'Quite a famous one, actually. Fredrika was a member of the Stockholm Homicide team that caught Ulrik Ahlgren.'

Stella's eyes widened as she digested the shocking news. The story behind the killings came into sharp focus.

'And the others? Were they on the team, too?'

'I called Lucy. Asked her to check our first two victims,' Sven said. 'Joel and Barbro were also members of the squad. It's what the tattoo means. "Hunter Killers '03" is the name they gave themselves. They all got it done in celebration of putting Ahlgren behind bars.'

'Was it just those three? No, of course not, it couldn't have been.'

'They were part of the core team. There were five of them in total.'

'Do we have names for the other two?'

He nodded. 'The fourth member is a guy called Sören Roos. He's retired now. But you're never going to believe who was number five.'

'Just tell me. Sven, please. It's not a bloody pub quiz.'

A sly smile crept across Sven's face as he identified the fifth member of the Hunter Killers.

Stella blinked as she mentally translated the Swedish nickname, '*Kung Råtta*'.

'King Rat? Who the hell's that?'

Sven looked at her as if she were stupid. 'The head of the Rat Squad, of course! It's only Nikodemus-bloody-Olsson, isn't it? The poor guy must be shitting his pants.'

For many years after that precise moment, Stella would wonder at her immediate and, thankfully, unvoiced reaction. *Would it be so bad if Nik became the final victim?*

She immediately banished the thought as both unworthy and unhelpful.

What mattered was that there was a serving officer and one

apparently retired and living way up north, who were both in extreme danger of being murdered.

She excused herself and marched off to a quiet part of the garden. She called SPA headquarters on Kungsholmsgatan and asked to be put through to Nik Olsson.

He picked up on the first ring. First half-a-ring, actually.

'Stella. I assume you're calling about the latest murder.'

'You've heard then,' she asked unnecessarily.

'We all set up alerts with all our names. Ever since we arrested Ahlgren. Anyone of us died, the other four would get to hear about it immediately.'

'So you knew about Joel Varela and Barbro Ekblad?'

'I did.'

'And you didn't think to contact the investigation in Örebro?'

'And say what?'

'That you believed someone was after the members of your team. The cops who put Ahlgren in Kumla Bunker.'

'I checked in and satisfied myself that the lead investigator, what's his name, Petersson? That he'd already made the link to Ahlgren.'

'You're in danger, Nik. So is the other member of your team from back then. Sören Roos. We need to get you both into protective custody.'

'No. Not going to happen. It would be prohibitively expensive given the latest budget cuts and there's no guarantee it would work either. This guy's cunning. Sly.'

'You can't be serious? This is bigger than bloody budgets, Nik.'

'Come and see me and I'll explain. Maybe even give you some leads you haven't found yet.'

'Can't you tell me over the phone? It's a five-hour round trip to Stockholm and time's tight. You know what murder investigations are like.'

'Come and see me, Stella,' he repeated. 'Tomorrow.'

The line went dead.

26

STOCKHOLM

Arriving at SPA headquarters at 9:00 a.m., Stella went to find Nik. He was not in his office. The spartan cube was devoid of ornament apart from a family photo on his desk, itself so clean it might have been delivered by IKEA that morning.

'He's gone out for a cigarette.'

Stella turned. A young female officer was smiling at her from a desk just across the clear strip of carpet from Nik's office door.

'I didn't know Nik smoked.'

The young woman nodded. 'He just started. Or maybe restarted. I don't know. I only joined two weeks ago.'

'Any idea where he went?'

'The roof is popular.' She frowned and bit her lip. 'I only heard a couple of people talking. I don't smoke myself.'

Stella smiled.

'It's fine. I don't think even Sweden would dare to ban it completely. Thanks. I'm Stella.'

'Oona.'

'That's a lovely name.'

'Thank you. My mum named me after Charlie Chaplin's granddaughter. She and Dad are, like, these massive fans. That's a bit odd, don't you think?'

'Not really. I'm named for a British actress myself. I think my dad had a crush on her.'

Oona grinned. 'Parents!'

After thanking Oona, Stella made her way to the roof. She saw Nik immediately, standing by a brick hutch that presumably led to some of the building's utilities.

He was leaning on a rail, a cigarette between his lips, smoke drifting away from him, out towards the waterfront. In other circumstances, Stella might have paused to admire the view. The pastel-coloured apartment buildings lining *Pilgatan*: pistachio, peach and baby-blue. The trees and mini pagodas of *Norr Mälarstrand*'s Playground. And the sparkling waters of *Riddarfjärden*, alive at this time of day with pleasure crafts of all shapes and sizes from little sailing dinghies to glass-sided tourists boats crammed with trippers in rainbow-coloured windcheaters.

'Nik,' she said as she approached, not wanting to startle him.

'Good morning,' he said, without turning.

His gaunt cheeks hollowed as he sucked more smoke into his lungs.

'Those things'll kill you, you know,' she said, joining him at the rail.

She rested her forearms on the metal, still cold from winter despite the spring sunshine irradiating the roof and raising the smell of warm bitumen from its gritty surface.

'I see you've absorbed our government's well-meaning but tedious line on nicotine.'

She frowned. Nik the cynic? This was a new facet of his persona.

'Nik, listen, I know there's been bad blood between us. But I really think you should listen to me and get some protection sorted out. I can't believe budget will be a problem given the unusual circumstances.'

Now, finally, Nik did turn his head to look at her. His eyes were red-rimmed and he hadn't shaved that morning. Dark circles shadowed his eyes. Another drag on the cigarette then he flicked the butt out into the air and watched it spiral down to the road. He fished out a crumpled pack of Camels from his jacket pocket and lit a new one. Pulled a lungful of smoke down so hard the tip glowed scarlet even in the bright sunshine. He exhaled with a sound like the groan of a dying man.

'You remember early on in our relationship, I showed you a scar on my chest?'

Stella flashed on the memory. Nik, shirt unbuttoned to the waist, a long, pink scar carving diagonally from his left shoulder across his heart and towards his belly.

'I do. We were comparing war wounds.'

'And do you remember, I said it was a serial killer who was torturing and killing farmers.'

'I remember.'

'Only half of the story was true. We *were* hunting a serial killer. But the victims weren't farmers. They were young girls.' Nik pinched his lips around the cigarette and drew in more smoke. 'We *did* corner him on a farm and he *did* attack me. I just couldn't bring myself ever to mention him because people always want to know all the horrific details. I tell people about the farmers because it helps me cope.'

'I know that the team members were Joel, Barbro, Fredrika, you and Sören Roos. It looks like someone's avenging him by killing the detectives who put him in Kumla.'

'A reasonable hypothesis.'

'The tattoo. Hunter Killers '03. Did you all get them done?'

It was a mark of Nik's palpable fear that he didn't even question how she knew about the ink on all three corpses.

'It was a bonding thing. You could call it a celebration, if you like, but we all carried a grain of fear in our souls. We just felt he wouldn't give up just because he was behind bars.' He sucked on the cigarette like it was delivering oxygen, not tobacco smoke. 'He is a truly evil man, Stella. I mean that. And no amount of good old Swedish social democratic, liberal compassion for criminals is going to change that. We all agreed we'd keep an eye on each other. Wherever we moved on to. If anyone should die in suspicious circumstances, we'd know and we'd do something about it.'

'Do you have Sören's address?'

'He retired two years ago. He lives up in Norrbotten County. Luleå. I'll send you his address.'

'Thanks, Nik. So, about protective custody?'

He snorted. 'You think that would do any good? Joel was an experienced cop. OK, so he was in the drug squad not Homicide, but he could handle himself. Never went anywhere without his pistol. Barb was the same, and she was a karate black belt. She competed for Sweden in the bloody Olympics, for fuck's sake!'

'It wouldn't hurt, Nik.'

He reached under his jacket and pulled out his own service weapon.

'Ahlgren nearly killed me before. If he tries a second time, even through an accomplice, I'll be ready. And there'll be no arrests this time.'

He was rattled. Badly. The most morally uncompromising man in the SPA had just admitted to her that he would shoot to kill rather than follow procedure if he was contacted by the serial murderer hunting down his master's captors.

'I still think we should arrange protection.'

'Fine!' he barked, startling her, and a couple of pigeons who'd waddled foolishly close in search of scraps. They flapped airborne, wings clapping out half-hearted applause. 'Do what you like. I don't care! Just catch this bastard, Stella. Because I'm not going to lose another friend to Ahlgren. This has to stop!'

'You know I'll do my best, Nik. You *know* that. Is there anything else you can tell me about Ahlgren or his crimes?'

'Everything's in the files. His MO, his psychiatric evaluation, all the witnesses, the members of his band, everything.'

'What band?'

'As you'll discover when you start work, Ahlgren managed a rock band in the late nineties and early noughties. Right up to the moment we caught the bastard. They were called Sepülkå. They were into really dark stuff. They call it extreme death metal. Satanism, torture, autopsies.' Nik screwed up his features as if he'd bitten down on the sourest of all pickled herrings. 'My God, the lyrics were abhorrent. And *they* were hardly any better. The lead singer used to goad the crowds at their concerts to chant Satanic curses. He was arrested several times for incitement to violence and causing public disorder.'

'Were any of them ever suspected of involvement in Ahlgren's crimes?'

'We looked hard at the singer. He called himself Norn but his real name was Björn Lyngstad. He seemed to find the whole thing funny. Maybe even titillating. I mean, his manager was slicing up young girls and he just sat in the interview and smirked like it was a big joke.'

'But there was no hard evidence.'

'A lot of circumstantial stuff, but in the end the prosecutor felt we should focus entirely on Ahlgren. There was a risk the whole case could get muddied if they tried to build a case against Lyngstad.'

Stella made another note. She had her first person of interest.

Before she left Nik to his third cigarette, which he'd just lit, there was the delicate matter of his complaint against her and the deal he'd struck with Malin.

'Listen, about my suspension…'

'I understand Malin has temporarily reinstated you so you can pursue this maniac. Obviously, given I'm in his sights, I'm fine with that.'

Nik smiled grimly. An undertaker telling himself an unfunny joke about death to lighten his own spirits. He leaned closer, even though, bar the pigeons, they were alone on the roof, and dropped his voice to a murmur, forcing her to lean in if she wanted to hear his words.

'I'm guessing if you catch him, that'll be the end of your stewardship of the drugs outreach programme. But listen to me carefully, Inspector Cole. There's something about you that I don't like.'

He pushed his face into hers and sniffed, like a dog.

'I can smell it on you. Maybe I did provoke you at the party, but I saw the look in your eye when you pointed your service weapon at me. I've seen that look before. I saw it in Ulrik Ahlgren's eyes that day he cut me. There's a darkness in your soul and at some point you let it rule you. I think Roisin Griffin knew it and, although I'll never be able to prove it, I think that's why she died.'

Stella pulled away. She swallowed. Because Nik was right. In every single point of his diagnosis. He was looking into her eyes but it felt like he was looking directly into her heart. Or even her soul, where he claimed, rightly, a darkness resided.

His bloodless lips stretched into a corpse-smile.

'I see I'm right.'

'No. You're wrong.'

He shrugged. 'Catch this killer, Stella. Put that darkness to good use.'

* * *

Her way out took her through Major Crimes. Jonna was at her desk, repeatedly stabbing a pencil through the messy bun she'd gathered her hair into at the back of her head.

Stella waved from across the room. Jonna's face lit up and a grin split her face. She hurried over and hugged Stella, giving a kiss on each cheek.

'Hey! I thought you were over in Örebro.'

'I was. Am, I mean. I had to come back to see Nik Olsson.'

'Really?' Jonna's forehead creased as she drew her eyebrows together. 'He's not making more trouble for you, is he?'

'Just the opposite, actually. Got time for a coffee?'

Jonna smiled. 'Sure! My paperwork can wait.'

'Can't it always?'

Laughing they left the office, heading for a little coffee stand in the small park opposite the building's front entrance.

27

Stella and Jonna took their coffees and flaky cinnamon pastries to a nearby bench in the centre of a group of young pear trees, their slender branches fluffy with delicate white blossom. A faint, sweetish smell drifted down to their table on the breeze.

'It's good to see you,' Jonna said with a smile before sipping her coffee.

Sunlight slanted across her face, catching the amber flecks in her blue irises.

'You too. I miss you and Oskar over there in Örebro. How's Micki settling in?'

Jonna rolled her eyes. 'Oh, God, Stel. He's like this, sort of, super-excitable puppy. Don't get me wrong, he's very good at what he does, which is mostly internet research, but I wish he'd calm down a bit.'

Stella nodded, thinking about how the new boy had been dancing with Jonna at the party that had led to her suspension.

'Is he still making a play for you or have you put him out of his misery yet?' she asked with a grin.

'I told him I was gay. You should have seen his face. Poor guy. I thought he was going to burst into tears.' She blushed. 'I mean, not because I'm such a great catch or anything. I just think he was embarrassed.'

'Don't sell yourself short. You're a great catch!'

Jonna sighed out a breath. 'It's a pity the ones I like don't seem to think so.'

'It's either that, or the ones we don't like don't seem to get the message.'

Jonna looked worried. 'You don't mean that time when I came on to you on the case in Söderbärke?'

Stella laughed. 'Don't be silly! That was fine. No, I'm talking about my ex.'

'Jamie?'

'For a forensic psychiatrist, he's being incredibly obtuse. And rude, actually. I can't believe he's the same guy I fell for back in England.'

'He's been in contact?'

Stella put her cup down on the table. The memory of Jamie's tone when they'd argued on the phone produced a surge of anger that washed through her.

'He called me, yes. And, honestly, Jonna, it was like he'd had some sort of total personality transplant. He was really patronising. You know, mansplaining my own job to me. Aggressive, too. He actually said, and I can't believe I've committed all this to memory, but I was trying to let him down gently, he said, "Oh, spit it out for fuck's sake, Stel. You sound like a nun trying to give a sex-ed talk to a bunch of horny adolescents".'

She was shaking. And the caffeine wasn't helping. Tears overran her eyelids and rolled down her cheeks before she scrubbed them away with the back of her hand.

Jonna's mouth had dropped open and now she hurried round the bench to sit beside Stella, putting a protective arm around her shoulders.

'Bastard!'

'I know! I think being arrested did something to him. He's so used to being the expert, always in control.'

Playing the Devil's Music

'I don't care!' Jonna snapped. 'Sorry, but he doesn't get to have excuses made for him. You had no choice after Tilde planted his DNA on the body. And anyway, that remark shows so much hostility.'

Stella sniffed away more tears and smiled. Jonna let her arm drop, but Stella took her hand.

'Thanks, mate. I guess it upset me more than I thought it had. I really thought Jamie was special. But it turns out he was another dick.'

Jonna smiled. 'Talking of dicks, why did you have to come back to speak to Nik? Is he dropping his charges against you?'

'Not exactly. It's the case. Have you been following it?'

Jonna looked down. Her cheeks flushed again.

'I've been a bit busy on my own cases. Sorry, I know how much it means to you to be back on a homicide investigation.'

'It's fine, really.'

Stella explained about the connection between the three victims and Nik Olsson. During the telling, Jonna's eyes saucered and she was shaking her head like a metronome.

'My God, that's unbelievable. So Ulrik Ahlgren has some kind of, what, super-fan serial killer hunting down the Hunter Killers?'

'That's what it looks like. Nik gave me a good lead, though. The lead singer in the band Ahlgren was managing back when he was killing. A guy called Björn Lyngstad. I also need to go up north to see Sören Roos. Nik's been in touch but I want to talk to him face to face. See if he can think of any other names apart from Lyngstad.'

Jonna checked her watch. Her face fell.

'Oh. I have a meeting in five.'

Stella got to her feet. 'Is it with Malin by any chance? I need to see her while I'm here.'

'Jan Harkin. He wants to discuss charges in a case we closed last month.'

They walked back together, taking the lift up to Homicide. As the doors opened, Stella remembered about Jonna's interview for the role at Financial Crime.

'How's your job application going? I forgot to ask back there.'

Jonna smiled. 'I had a first interview and it went super well. Basically they told me the job's mine if I want it. They just need to follow HR protocol so all the boxes are ticked.'

'That's brilliant. Although I'll probably have to salute next time I see you. You'll be so many ranks above me.'

Jonna laughed. 'Yeah. I'll make you bring me tea in—' She flushed scarlet. '…I mean to my office. OK, look I have to go. Call me!'

And she was gone, practically running down the corridor to the conference room.

Shaking her head, Stella made her way to Malin's office. Tea in … what? Bed? Her stomach fluttered.

Malin was at her desk, head cradled in her hands as she stared at a pile of reports in front of her. Feeling the big boss's pain – what cop enjoyed paperwork? – Stella knocked softly, went in and closed the door behind her.

'Hey, Stella. How is the investigation going?'

So, no small-talk then. Just straight down to business. Maybe Malin was feeling the heat from the higher-ups. Big boss or no, she had her own superiors. And the more removed you got from the frontline, the less you cared about things like fruitless searches and impossible-to-track-down witnesses. Everything became a number on a page. A 'metric', to use Stella's least-favourite word in the cop lexicon.

'We've got a couple of leads, but it's early days. My working hypothesis is that Ulrik Ahlgren has a disciple who's after the cops who put him in Kumla back in '03.'

'Any suspects?'

'I just went to see Nik. He pointed me to the lead singer in the band Ahlgren managed. One Björn Lyngstad. I asked Nik about protection for him and Sören Roos.'

'Sören Roos?'

'He and Nik are the only surviving members of the team. Nik seems,' Stella shrugged, 'fatalistic about it. Said he's got his service weapon and that's what he's putting his faith in. I don't know about Sören. I'm going to see him next.'

Malin raised an eyebrow.'

'Ironic that you should be concerned to see Nik Olsson getting protection from a serial killer.'

Wow. That was dark. Even from Malin. She must really be under the cosh.

'He's a cop, Malin. In fact, scratch that. He's a human being. Whatever bad feeling there is between me and him, I still don't want to have to watch his post mortem.'

Malin ran a hand over her forehead. 'Sorry, Stella. That was in poor taste. And I didn't mean to suggest that you'd enjoy seeing him dead. I'm just…'

A huge sigh escaped her lips.

'Under pressure from the brass?'

Malin smiled weakly. 'The brass I could cope with. No, the Minister for Justice is making all kinds of noises about the SPA having lost its focus. She says, and I quote, "the SPA is paying too much attention to diversity and inclusion and protecting the rights of illegal immigrants, and not enough to putting criminals behind bars".'

'That's bullshit! Is this about that protest last month in Gothenburg?'

Malin rolled her eyes. 'You mean when a bunch of far-right thugs threw Molotov cocktails at an asylum-seekers' hostel? Yeah, that one.'

Stella nodded. Even though Jenny Frievalds was dead, her party, Reborn Sweden, had gained strength from her murder, and a couple of ministers in the new coalition government. Some were still peddling the false narrative that her killer was an immigrant and not a native-born Swede.

'But you're getting back-up from the fifth floor, aren't you?' Stella asked, referring to the suite of offices where the National Police Chief and his deputies and assistants worked.

'Up to a point. But when the minister shouts, they jump. And when their highly polished shoes hit the carpet again, they come down here and make me clear the bar, too. They take the landing-pad away, as well.'

It was an unusually vivid image for Malin, who in Stella's experience tended to speak in plain, unadorned language.

'And by "landing-pad", they mean...'

'I mean there've been veiled threats about a wholesale shakeup of the SPA. Current units disbanded. Command structures reviewed. Which,' she sighed again, 'is SPA code for shifting experienced officers like me over into administrative roles and putting younger, more ambitious officers in place instead.'

'Shit. And all so they can turn round to the minister and say, "Yes, ma'am, we're on the case"?'

Another shrug. 'Well, it's a little more nuanced than that, but basically, yes. That.'

'So a result in Örebro would be a help?'

Malin smiled tiredly. 'Typical British understatement. I think we can safely assume that, yes. And in case you're wondering, I spoke to Nik about you. Once news of Joel Varela's murder broke. He knows as well as I do that we have to secure some big wins in Homicide and Major Crimes. His job is as much under review as mine.'

Stella nodded. Now she understood why Nik hadn't raised any objections about her being reinstated, on whatever basis. Yes, he was scared of the Devil of Axberg. But, in typical Nik fashion, it was the threat to his role as the *Kung Råtta* that bothered him more. And a service pistol would be no match for the fifth floor.

Stella bit her lip. She wanted to thank Malin for standing aside, so Nik's man could have a clear path to the big job they both wanted. But in light of what she'd just been told, was that even relevant anymore? It didn't matter. What counted was that Malin had made the offer.

She inhaled quickly, started speaking before she changed her mind. Believing it was the right thing to do.

'Malin, there's something I wanted to say to you. About when I was suspended. Well, transferred anyway.' She swallowed, her mouth suddenly dry. 'I know about the deal you struck with Nik. I want to say that I'm just so incredibly grateful. And I feel so bad that you had to do that for me. I won't let you down again. Not over this case, not ever again.'

Malin pursed her lips. 'I'm guessing it was Jonna who told you? Don't worry, I won't hold it against her. I know you two are close. And thank you. If I'm honest, it was always a fifty-fifty decision on whether I would have applied. It would have been a significant promotion, but it would have been the end of my involvement with frontline policing.' She ran a hand through her hair and then smoothed the ruffled layers out again. 'Even now, with my nice office and my PA, I can, just, get involved in the day-to-day running of cases if I want to. But on the fifth floor? No. I'd be another senior manager. I'd spend all my time in meetings, writing reports and answering emails from the Justice ministry.'

Stella tried to imagine a working day where the closest she came to real crime was entering numbers onto a spreadsheet. Or, more likely, trying to justify numbers in a report based on some crime analyst's spreadsheet. She could see why Malin had felt conflicted.

'So you're saying my pulling a gun on Nik gave you an escape route?'

Malin's eyes flashbulbed and her mouth dropped open. She laughed loudly. 'My God, you've got a nerve! Well, I would hardly put it like that, but who knows. Maybe I will come to see that little episode in your career as the one that actually saved mine. Now, if you'll forgive me, sadly I really do have a meeting with a bunch of MoJ officials.'

Stella got to her feet. 'Thanks again, Malin. I'll keep you posted.'

In the ground-floor reception area, Stella called Sven to tell him she was on her way up north to see Sören Roos.

After that she checked in with the man himself. He knew all about the murders and, in none too cryptic language, let Stella know he had taken measures to protect himself.

As she mounted the Triumph and headed for Arlanda airport, she hoped they'd be enough.

28

LULEÅ, NORRBOTTEN COUNTY, NORTHERN SWEDEN

Stella climbed into the back of the silver Toyota Prius waiting at the front of the taxi rank at Kallax Airport.

'Where to, please, Mrs?' the driver asked. He was a recent arrival from the Middle East to judge from his appearance and heavily accented Swedish. Stella glanced at the ID card taped to the back of his seat. Akram Hosseini.

She gave him Sören's address. He nodded, put the car into drive and pulled away. Immediately he began speaking.

'You are Swedish, Mrs?'

'English. You?'

He switched to English, which he spoke fluently.

'I am a proud Afghan. I was an interpreter for the Swedish army. The NATO Resolute Support Mission. Did you know Sweden had troops in ISAF?'

'I did not,' she said with a smile, amused at his friendly but direct line of questioning. He'd make a good interviewer, she thought.

'Not the fiercest. But loyal to their staff. My captain helped me and my family get exit papers.'

'I'm happy for you, Akram. Sweden must be quite a change from Afghanistan, though.'

He signalled right out of the airport and shrugged at the same time.

'It was not safe there anymore for us. And I love Sweden. You work hard, you get on; there is democracy, law and order, safety.'

She wondered if news of the Gothenburg protests had reached Luleå. She decided to match his candid approach and asked him straight out.

'Do you get much racial violence up here? There were protests down in Gothenburg.'

He caught her eye in the rear-view mirror. He was smiling.

'Those southerners! Up here, we're a bit more laidback. I get the odd idiot in my taxi. But when I say I was with the Swedish army, they are usually more interested in whether I killed any Taliban than my skin colour or religion. So, what brings you all the way from Stockholm to Luleå? Are you with the SPA?'

That took her by surprise. She leaned forwards.

'How on earth did you guess that?'

Another smile for her in the rear-view.

'I can tell you're not military. But there's something about cops and soldiers that sets them apart. Plus, I know Sören.'

'You do?'

'He always asks for me if he needs a taxi. Is he in some sort of trouble?'

What, like being on some Satanic nutjob's kill-list you mean?

'No, nothing like that. I just need to ask his opinion on a couple of things.'

'Like the Devil of Axberg, for example?' Akram asked slyly.

'You've heard about that, then?'

'It is hard not to. TV, social media: he's everywhere isn't he? You think Sören may be a target?'

'I can't comment on an open case, I'm afraid.'

'Of course.' He flicked on the signal to change lanes. 'Sören does.'

'Think he's a target?'

'Last time he called me, it was to go into town to buy a new rifle. He said, "If that bastard comes for me he's going to get more than he bargained for". End quote.'

'Have you seen any strangers in Luleå over the last few weeks? Maybe picked someone up from the airport?'

'Aha! You think maybe the Devil is already here. Casing the joint. I pick up so many people it is hard to say for sure.' He scratched his beard, producing a raspy sound in the near-silent cabin. 'But yes, there was this one guy. Maybe early forties? Said he wanted me to drop him off at the Facebook datacentre. But honestly, he did not look like an IT guy to me. More of a rocker, you know? Long hair. Tattoos. Lots of silver chains and stuff.'

Stella's pulse quickened. Was she really going to get a description of the Devil of Axberg from her cab driver?

'What's this datacentre?'

'We're going to go straight past it. The access road, anyway. I'll tell you when we're there. But it's a big server-farm. Where they process all those images and people's posts about their kids' cello recitals.'

Stella had precisely zero experience of the IT industry. The nearest she'd ever got was a suspect in a murder investigation who'd been stalking his victims online. As such, she had no idea what was standard dress code for Facebook employees. Was rocker gear too out there? Didn't they all lounge about on multicoloured bean bags and get around the office on electric scooters? Or was that advertising agencies? Akram struck her as a man with more than the usual level of skill in observation and character assessment: probably vital for someone perceived by many of his former countrymen as a traitor.

But her thoughts were leading in another direction. Because Ulrik Ahlgren had managed a rock band, hadn't he? Literally while committing his heinous crimes. And Nik Olsson had pointed a nicotine-stained finger straight at its lead singer. Had Björn Lyngstad flown up to Luleå to research his next victim?

She Googled him and selected the Images tab.

Here was Lyngstad gurning at the camera, long tongue curling from his mouth and coated in what, presumably, the viewer was supposed to believe was blood. Heavy white makeup with smudgy, kohl-rimmed eyes, so that it was impossible to discern his true appearance. But he did have several heavy silver chains around his neck and long, jet-black hair. She selected another picture, minus the blood. All the photos showed Lyngstad in full performance makeup, though.

She stretched her arm between the front seats and held the phone up.

'Your passenger? Could it have been this man, do you think?'

Akram glanced quickly at the phone, then back at the road ahead. He shrugged.

'Maybe. Same physical type but behind all the makeup, who knows? Yes? No?'

He pointed ahead and to the left. They'd entered a forest thickly planted with rows of Scots pine and Norway spruce. A dirt track curved away from the main road. No signpost. No tarmac. Nothing to indicate that somewhere down that uninviting lane lay an outpost of one of the world's most valuable social media companies.

'The datacentre is down there. Not that you'd know it.'

'Why don't they signpost it?'

'Maybe they don't want to advertise their presence to eco-terrorists. Plenty of people here were against the idea.'

'Why? Doesn't it create jobs?'

Akram shook his head. 'Not many. Most of the professional staff come from elsewhere. Stockholm, Malmö, or overseas. Facebook rotates people in and out. There are a few jobs for locals but they are all low-level, menial. Cleaners, catering, drivers, that sort of thing, yes?'

'Has there ever been any trouble?'

'Not really. Maybe I was being a little over-dramatic talking about terrorists. I think really it is just that the only people who go there know exactly where it is. It is why I was suspicious about the man who hired me. Facebook people usually just ask to be taken to "The Farm". That's the local nickname for it. This guy gave the full title. You know? "The Facebook Data Centre", like it was on a big signboard outside the main gate.'

It did sound suspicious. But there was always the chance the visitor would have an entirely innocent reason for being there. And maybe he just didn't know the nickname.

'Did you see him again?'

'No. It does not mean anything. There are plenty of other taxis in Luleå.'

Five minutes later, Akram took a left off a country road and bumbled the Prius down a rutted and stony lane barely wide enough for the not-overly-large hybrid.

He drew up in the front yard of a pretty wooden house. For once painted in a colour scheme other than the white-plus-Falun look that Swedes seemed to have collectively fallen in love with. A soft sage green for the wooden walls and the roof. Contrasting chestnut-brown eaves, window frames and railings around the veranda.

Stella paid Akram and took a card from him, promising to call him when she was ready to go back to the airport.

She slammed the door behind her and strode across the soft, pine needle-strewn ground to the steps leading up to the front door. Akram executed a neat circular three-point turn and waved as the Prius hummed away from the house, leaving Stella alone. She turned a full circle, taking in the towering fir trees and, in a gap where two rows intersected, the sparkling waters of a nearby lake.

Sören was clearly a man who enjoyed solitude. A loud crack off to her left startled her. She chided herself. *Don't be a city-slicker, Stel. It's just a deadfall or some woodland animal out for its morning constitutional.* She stared hard in the approximate direction the sound had come from. Was that a movement? A flash of brown amongst the green? It was impossible to tell. Could have been a deer or, this far north, even a wolf.

Shaking her head and repeating the mantra every city dweller had drummed into them by country folk: 'they're more scared of you than you are of them', she mounted the steps to the veranda and approached the front door.

Her index finger was stretched out in front of her, almost touching the bell push, when a deep-throated growling had her whirling round, hand instinctively going for the gun on her right hip.

The dog wasn't huge. No towering mastiff or Great Dane. A medium-sized German shepherd, its shaggy coat the shade of blackish-grey favoured by the Met's dog-handlers. Not those whose animals were used for crowd-control. The less-well-known teams whose dogs were trained for a single job, attacking dangerous suspects and disabling them.

It was stalking towards her on stiff legs, jaw hanging open a little, revealing long yellow teeth. The saw-edged sound it was producing way back in its throat had the hairs on the back of her neck standing as stiffy erect as the bristles on a yard brush. The reaction was so primal she could no more have controlled it than she could have stopped the sense of fear threatening to overwhelm her.

She took her hand off the butt of her pistol. *Hi, I'm Stella and I just shot your dog*, was hardly the sort of introduction likely to get him onside with her investigation.

Instead, she stood perfectly still, struggling to keep her breathing regular. Something one of her former colleagues in the dog unit had told her came to mind. *Don't look him in the eye, DI Cole. He'll take it as a threat. Makes him jumpy.*

By 'jumpy' she'd taken him to mean, 'more likely to rip your face off and take it somewhere quiet to enjoy'.

Stella looked at the ground at a spot about halfway between her and the advancing canine. If it came to it, she'd defend herself. But not with her SIG.

The dog stopped five feet in front of her. The growling hadn't ceased, but it hadn't increased in volume either. Stella took that to be a good sign.

Christ! Where was Sören? He ought to be out here by now, having heard his personal bodyguard spring into action. Calming the dog with a kind word and a scratch behind its tufty black ear and sending it inside and its bed by the kitchen stove.

She hadn't seen a car. Was he out? Oh, great! This was going from bad to worse. Was she going to be standing here all day like a character in a Stephen King novel?

She didn't have the time, nor the inclination to find out. So, painfully slowly, she descended the steps, placing both feet on each narrow wooden tread before taking the next one. She dropped her hips to minimise her height and was relieved to see that the dog was making no attempt to come any closer.

Reaching the pine needle-strewn ground, she squatted, trying to ignore the clanging alarm bells vibrating in every nerve fibre in her body.

'Hello,' she said softly, startled at how pathetic her voice sounded. Quavering, insubstantial, thready, like someone had their hands round her neck. She cleared her throat and tried again. 'Hi, boy. Are you a boy? You could be a girl, I suppose. I'm Stella.'

She extended a quivering hand, knuckles uppermost. That was what you were supposed to do, wasn't it?

The dog barked once, loud enough to set Stella's ears ringing. Shit the devil! She'd made a wrong call. Visions of spurting finger-stumps crowded her mind, making thought impossible.

The dog barked again and advanced a half-step.

Straighten and run? No, not a chance it would work. She readied herself to grapple with the dog when it leapt. She'd tackle it in mid-air. It was a quadruped designed for land-travel; airborne it would be helpless. All she had to do was avoid the front end.

A third bark. She bunched her muscles, preparing to rear up and meet it halfway.

29

The dog advanced on Stella, head lowered, a soft whine issuing from its throat, and sniffed her hand. Oh, God, she'd nearly wet herself in fear. She clenched the muscles of her pelvic floor as the dog, close enough to touch now, proceeded to lick the back of her hand.

'Fucking hell,' she crooned to the now docile dog, behind whose left ear she was mechanically scratching, much to its obvious delight to judge from the soft grunts it was making. 'I thought you were sizing me up for your next meal but you're just a big softie, aren't you?'

In answer, the dog pushed the side of its head against Stella's scratching hand, turning it sideways to give her better access to the ear. She laughed, out of sheer relief and scrunched a handful of fur at the scruff of its neck with her other hand.

'I see you've met Astrid.'

The voice was high-pitched, wheezy. She pictured a skinny, pale asthmatic clutching an inhaler, his illness having robbed him of his vitality.

She risked turning her head to be greeted by the sight of a

very fat, ruddy-faced man with a bushy red beard and twinkling blue eyes the colour of old china.

'Sören Roos?'

He placed a chubby hand on the front of his voluminous red and black plaid hunting shirt.

'In the flesh, rather too much of it according to my doctors, but what the fuck do they know? And you would be Stella.'

'Am I OK to stand, do you think? Astrid and I didn't exactly hit it off when we met.'

'Oh, she's fine. You found her weakness. The only risk now is she might not let you leave.'

He was smiling, but the image of a King-esque canine monster keeping her captive in a remote woodland cabin still seemed like a very real possibility. She forced out a laugh. She patted her pistol. 'I could always fight my way out.'

The man frowned. The dog growled. Stella raised her hands.

'Oops. Sorry. Bad joke.'

She bent at the knee and resumed scratching Astrid behind her ear again. Calm ensued once more.

'Come on,' Sören said. 'Let's go inside. 'I've got coffee brewing. I put it on before I went to feed the livestock.'

'What animals do you keep?' Stella asked as she followed Sören down the pine-panelled hallway.

'Gotland Sheep. Imported them to the mainland myself. I make cheese from the milk.'

He cleared his throat loudly, which produced a wheezing fit. He grabbed an inhaler from the breast pocket of his shirt and took several greedy pulls from its narrow blue mouth.

Stella pointed at the inhaler. 'Asthma?'

He shook his shaggy head, reminding her once again of Astrid.

'COPD. Turns out smoking twenty a day for thirty-odd years isn't good for you.' He hoisted his shoulders and grinned. 'Who knew?'

'You seem pretty happy for a man with an incurable disease.'

Playing the Devil's Music

'I like you. Brave, from what I hear, *and* plain-spoken. I'm not bothered too much, to be honest.' He patted his corpulent belly. 'I think the Type 2 will carry me off first.'

He brought two mugs of steaming coffee to the table, returning a moment later with a blue-and-white enamel plate loaded with cookies.

'Coconut and white chocolate. Baked them myself.'

She took one out of genuine hunger. She'd missed breakfast and the no-frills airline which ran flights between Arlanda and Kallax hadn't bothered with refreshments on the hour-and-twenty flight.

'It's delicious,' she mumbled.

Sören nodded his thanks. 'My wife's recipe.'

Stella looked around the kitchen. There were a few decorative elements that could fall under the heading: 'a woman's touch'. Some yellow-and-blue bunting tacked to the front of a pine dresser. A watercolour painting of some woodland flowers. But something about Sören himself and his body language suggested he lived here alone.

'Is she out today? I didn't see a car.'

Sören wouldn't meet her enquiring gaze. Looked out of the window instead.

'Leonora died last year. Breast cancer. I took it hard, raised my drinking – and my stupidity – to new levels. I got banned from driving in January, so I sold the car. Akram's pretty much my personal chauffeur.'

'I'm sorry.'

Sören said nothing. Nodded. Scratched his beard again.

'Life's a bitch,' he pronounced finally.

'Sören, what do you think about the Devil of Axberg? You know it looks very likely that you and Nik are on his kill-list.'

Sören took a mouthful of coffee, swallowed noisily. Finished his cookie in one enormous bite and selected another. If he was scared, he was doing a brilliant job of hiding it. Although she wondered whether the drinking and over-eating was some sort of death wish after his wife had died. Maybe that's why he wasn't bothered about a serial killer coming after him.

'I saw the news when Joel bought it. Called Nik, asked him what he thought. He said to sit tight. Might be something, might be nothing. Then Barb, and Fred. Well, OK, so it's some nutcase with a hard-on for Ahlgren trying to balance the scales or whatever the fuck justification he's cooked up for himself.'

'Any idea who?'

Sören shrugged. Bit his second cookie in half and washed it down with a mouthful of coffee.

'At the time, we wondered about the lead singer, did Nik tell you that?' Stella nodded. 'OK, but there were all kinds of weirdos hanging round the band back then. Groupies, dealers, hangers-on generally. And then there were these weird super-fans: "the Acolytes". They had a club with its own merchandise, everything. They followed the band all over Sweden. Saw them hundreds of times. Christ knows where they got the money.

'Anyway, the fan club, because that's all it was, despite their pretentious crap about being slaves of Satan or whatever the fuck they believed...' He shook his head. 'Sorry, rambling here. The fan club was run by this woman. Called herself Lilith. She was lost in it, you know? Had herself scarified. I had to look the word up first time I heard it. Anyway, it means ritually cut.'

Sudden interest flared in Stella's breast. 'A pentagram?'

'Yep. Right between her t—' The visible portions of his cheeks reddened. 'Sorry, been living on my own too long.'

Stella grinned. 'It's OK. So she had the pentagram right between her tits. Like where the Devil is cutting his victims.'

Sören smiled back and the blush receded. 'Exactly.'

'Does she have a second name?'

Sören shrugged. 'I'm not even sure Lilith is her real first name. You could check if the fan club's still going. Or maybe there's a Facebook group. That's what all the bands have these days, isn't it?'

'Anyone else strike you at the time as maybe being a little too interested in what Ahlgren got up to?'

Sören shook his head. 'Believe me, I've been wracking my brains since the news about Joel came out.'

'This is still a great lead, Sören. Thank you. Look, about protection. I could—'

He held up a hand.

'Forget it. Astrid's a better bet than some goon from the Tactical Support Squad. Who, by the way, I really don't want to share living space with. Plus, I'm not exactly unprepared. There's a sporting goods shop in town that does very nicely out of me.'

'I can't persuade you, can I?' Stella asked, smiling.

'He's in a three-way race with the COPD and the diabetes to finish me off, and I'm not sure he's fast enough to win. Let's just leave it at that.'

'Keep a gun on you at all times, then, yes?'

Sören lifted the hem of his shirt to reveal the butt of a pistol. He smiled.

'If a skinny little fuck like Akram could deal with three AK-toting Talibans, I think I should be OK facing off against a lone nutjob armed with a carving knife.'

* * *

While she waited for her flight back to Arlanda, Stella's phone buzzed with a message from the head CSI on the investigation.

DNA results in from fragments left in wound to Joel Varela's chest. Murder weapon is horn of Gotland Sheep. Probably sharpened.

Stella glanced over her shoulder, suddenly possessed by an irrational fear that the Devil of Axberg would be right behind her. But there was nobody racing towards her with a chloroform-soaked rag and a ridged and twisted stabbing weapon. Just a couple of young girls who might have been students, chatting to each other while scrolling on their phones.

She was on edge suddenly, because from never having heard of that particular sheep species in her life before, she'd now heard it twice in an hour.

30

ÖREBRO

Sven strutted to the front of the conference room at the following morning's briefing.

'So, what have we got?' He nodded to his assistant. 'Lucy?'

Lucy nodded back, cleared her throat.

'I've been reviewing all the security video I could find from the latest crime scene. One of the Rudbecks' neighbours has a doorbell cam and they picked up this individual at 8:45 a.m. walking down the centre of the street.'

She clicked a button on the remote she was holding and a grainy video still appeared on the back wall of the room.

'According to our anthropometry expert at the university, he or she is about 1.5 to 1.7 metres tall. Weight between 65 and 80 kilos.'

One of the male detectives rose from his chair and walked up to the screen, peering at the image.

'Pretty crappy doorbell cam. Can't be one of the new models.

It's so pixelated you can barely make out any details. I need my glasses. Looks like a guy, though.' He pointed at a hand. 'And he's white.'

'Or he's wearing a glove,' another male cop argued. 'You said yourself it's pixelated.'

'The amount you drank last night, it's you who was fucking pixelated, Jonas!' a third cop chimed in to a few low-pitched chuckles.

'People! Come on. Really? We've got three dead ex-cops on our hands so I'm not seeing any reason for laughter,' Sven said. 'And there are two more members of the Hunter Killers who are *currently*,' he laid extra emphasis on that word, 'alive. But he's not going to stop unless and until we catch him.'

'Yeah, OK, Sven,' the first cop said, as he retook his seat. 'We know the details. But we have no decent leads, do we? I know this guy's a nutjob, but he's one of the smart ones isn't he?' He turned to Stella. 'You've caught enough of them, Stella. I'm right, aren't I? They come in two flavours. The smart ones who have it all planned out and the crazies who just run amok until they get caught chowing down on a human leg or whatever.'

'Thanks for that charming image, Dan,' she said, before turning to take in the rest of the room.

She couldn't fail to notice Sven's expression. Annoyance that he'd effectively been upstaged by the new girl and curiosity at what she might say. Maybe she could salve his wounded pride and provide a little Serial Killer 101 education at the same time.

'Sven's right. He's clearly targeting members of the Hunter Killers. Now, maybe in his own twisted psychology, he needs to kill all five to complete what he sees as his mission. But there's also a chance, a very real chance that, having got a taste for killing, he won't stop at those five. He'll extend his own remit, come up with some plausible – to him – reason why he needs to carry on killing.

'Maybe he imagines there are other people who *deserve*,' air quotes, 'retribution. Prosecutors, CSIs, pathologists, even judges. So, yes, I agree with Sven, time is of the essence.

'But there are a few things that are troubling me. And

something Ulrik Ahlgren told me at Kumla Bunker confirmed my misgivings.'

'What's he like?' Lucy asked. 'None of us has even seen him, except in pictures. And you've talked to him.'

'*I* saw him,' Sven said in a hurt tone of voice.

'Yeah and a fat lot of good that did us,' the short-sighted male cop named Erik, said. 'From what I hear he sent you out of there with your tail between your legs.'

Once more, Stella waded in, attempting to quell the sniping that could easily poison a working team when results were thin on the ground.

'Ulrik Ahlgren looks human on the outside, and I'm sure we could round up plenty of highly qualified academic criminologists who'd be all-too ready to talk about his early-life trauma and chaotic home-life as a child. But you know what I saw?' She scanned the room, locking eyes with each person present. 'All I saw a was a manipulative, creepy, narcissistic, smug, sadistic, homicidal little freak.'

The silence grew.

'Not a fan, then?' Erik said.

This time the laughter wasn't muted. Sven opened his mouth but Stella caught his eye and offered the tiniest of head-shakes. *Let them have a moment. It's good for team morale.* He got the message. Nodded back. Waited it out.

Finally, the laughing petered out.

'Ahlgren told me that his supposed follower or disciple had got a detail wrong. And he was right. Lucy, can you show the images of the pentagrams for me, please?'

They'd arranged this little piece of theatre between them before the meeting. Lucy double-clicked on a new folder and projected a fresh image onto the screen. It was the montage Stella had created of the two sets of victims.

Nods and mutters of understanding all round as the assembled cops and CSIs took in the difference between the upper and lower rows of grisly images.

'Now, this doesn't necessarily mean anything,' Stella said, 'but

Ahlgren claimed not to know anything about a disciple. In fact, to me, he seemed affronted that anyone would think that. However, I did manage to find two potential people of interest over the last couple of days. First, meet Björn Lyngstad.'

Lucy clicked up a new image.

'Fuck me!' someone said. 'It's the evil love-child of Marilyn Manson and Count Dracula!'

'Lyngstad was the lead singer of Sepülkå. The original team didn't pursue him because the prosecutor was worried it would damage the case against Ahlgren. Then there's Lilith.' Lucy projected a black silhouette with a white question mark centred on the head. 'She ran the band's fan club. According to Sören Roos, she was so obsessive she had a pentagram cut into the skin of her sternum.'

'In my day we just used to write the band name on our school bag,' Lucy deadpanned.

Stella smiled at her. The young cop had impeccable comic timing.

'No photos online?' someone asked.

'She's a dark horse. No images on or offline as far as I can tell.'

'So, actions.' Sven tapped on the table with his ballpoint pen, harder and harder until the fragile plastic barrel snapped and its inner workings flew apart. 'People, please? Pay attention, people. Actions.'

Sven handed out tasks which had the assembled investigators scribbling in their notebooks. Sure they had it down, they rose as he was closing the meeting and headed out. Some pulling out phones, others discussing tactics with their partners.

Stella had been tasked with tracking down Lilith and bringing her in for an urgent interview.

It suited her fine. Although she thought she might find her more quickly using old-fashioned coppering methods than farting around on Facebook for hours. She wanted to speak to Ulrik Ahlgren again.

It took another two days. She guessed Ahlgren didn't exactly have a packed calendar. But keeping a homicide cop waiting for the pleasure of his company was probably one of the few tiny elements of control left to him.

The rain that had been pattering on the windscreen at the start of the drive to Kumla had increased in ferocity by its end. Blue-white lightning flickered across the fields beyond the custard-coloured food factory, jagging down from charcoal clouds.

Thankfully the visitor spaces at the front of the prison car park were all empty. She'd been dreading the trip across the tarmac from one of the more distant bays.

As she exited the car a peal of thunder exploded, making her flinch as she rushed across the ten metres between her and the front door of the prison. Closer she may have been, but her black jeans were soaked by the time she reached the door and was buzzed in.

The guard who checked her in was the same stocky young woman Stella had met on her last visit. She offered Stella a sympathetic smile as she took in the puddles forming around her boots.

'Hi, Hanna. I seem to have got a little damp,' Stella said, shaking droplets of rainwater off the tips of her fingers.

The young woman looked puzzled.

'A little? But it's pouring down out there.' She frowned, then grinned. 'Oh, wait. That is British understatement, isn't it? You're famous for it. Like, Ulrik has some *unpleasant hobbies*, yes?'

Stella nodded wryly. 'Something like that, yes. It's him I'm here to see.'

The guard nodded. 'He's been telling everyone about it. He claims he's practically running the investigation.'

'Does he now?' Stella signed the visitors' book, seeing a potential angle for getting Ahlgren to cooperate.

'Oh, yes. He says that you rely on him for psychological insights into the Devil of Axberg.'

Stella straightened, handed over her sidearm. She lifted the hem of her sweatshirt. 'You need to wand me?'

The young woman smiled. She was remarkably pretty, the

severe military buzzcut throwing emphasis on her eyes, which were a startling shade of green.

She shook her head, grinning. 'It's not as if you've come here to kill him, is it?'

On the whole, Stella thought that was a shaky assumption for any prison guard to make. She glanced down, where her rain-soaked jeans were clinging, perhaps rather obviously, to the lump of metal strapped to her right ankle.

31

KUMLA BUNKER

As before, Ahlgren was waiting for Stella at the plain white table in the centre of the featureless room.

The guard was new. Perhaps Tim had the day off. Or had the director decided it was a good idea to rotate the people charged with keeping Ahlgren and his guests separate? Taller than Hanna by a head, and lean where Hanna was stocky, this woman nodded at Stella, but showed no sign of wanting to strike up a friendship.

'Remain seated at all times until you are ready to leave.' She thrust her chin in Ahlgren's direction. 'Do not place your hands on the prisoner's half of the table. Do not move around the table. Do not offer, or accept, anything from the prisoner.'

'Understood. New rules?'

'Old rules, tightened up.'

Stella pulled her notebook out of the inside pocket of her jacket. Mercifully still dry. As she strolled over to the table she flipped over the black card cover, found the latest page and consulted the notes she'd written there.

Buy bread, cheese, salad. Go for a run. Call Jonna.

As she pulled out the chair, she continued to read, head bowed. In the top of her peripheral vision, she caught the movement of Ahlgren's head as he leaned forward. But she'd angled the notebook away from him; he could see nothing.

'Good morning, Stella,' he said.

She ignored him. Flipped over to a fresh page. Took out a ballpoint pen and wrote the opening line of a song she'd heard on the radio that morning. She caught the movement as he resettled his weight in the chair.

'I said, good morning.'

The edge in his voice was unmistakeable. Good. Now Stella did look at him.

'What's our next move, then?' she asked.

He frowned. 'Our next move? Yours and mine, you mean?'

'No-o. The SPA's. I mean, since you're practically running the investigation, I thought perhaps you had some insight for me? Or perhaps a list of urgent lines of enquiry you think I should be following.'

He smiled that repulsive amphibian grin again, lips widening, stretching.

'You've been listening to prison gossip. I really advise against it. The guards are pleasant enough but with little to occupy their minds they do tend to focus on silly rumours.' He looked over Stella's shoulder. 'Don't you, Magda?'

Stella resisted the temptation to turn in her chair. The guard maintained her silence. Sound woman.

'As you're so keen to help, what can you tell me about the woman who ran the band's fan club? She went by the name of—'

'Lilith. Not very original. There is a great deal of theological debate over whether Lilith ever really existed. In fact—'

'Yeah, I don't have time to discuss Biblical scholarship, I'm afraid. In case you'd forgotten, someone who appears to be following your methods is murdering former police officers.'

Playing the Devil's Music

The interruption wasn't entirely strategic. Stella had had way too much of men interrupting her in meetings in her career. And when the latest individual was a certifiable nutcase with a string of grisly murders of young women to his name, she *really* didn't have time for it.

It worked, anyway. Ahlgren's flabby jowls quivered with obvious irritation and she enjoyed seeing the effort it took him to restrain himself from an outburst.

'What can you tell me about her?' Stella asked, turning to a clean sheet in her notebook.

'Plenty. But first I need an assurance from you, Stella.'

She fought down the shudder that rippled just below the surface when he used her first name.

'You're not really in a position to demand assurances. Either you help me or you don't. And seeing as you've been boasting about your influence on the progress of the investigation, I'd assume you do want to help. Or was I wrong?' She pushed her chair back and looked over her shoulder at the guard she now knew was named Magda.

'No, no,' Ahlgren said hurriedly. 'Not an assurance then. How about we call it a consideration? *If* I help you, there's bound to be media interest in the case and your handling of it. Your *successful* handling. Journalists, maybe documentary-makers. Who knows?' He formed that stretched-mouth smile again and this time the pink tip of his tongue flickered over the lower lip. 'I would very much like to think you would be honest in explaining to them my role.'

She stared at him in amazement. This calm, smiling creature was discussing media credits with her as though he were an academic expert in psychological profiling. And not a depraved serial murderer who had once thought nothing of removing young women's brains and substituting chloroformed bug collections.

'Your role,' she said.

He nodded enthusiastically, began speaking rapidly. 'Yes. You needed my help in understanding the Devil of Axberg, especially given his slavish devotion to my own, ah, career. Despite having nothing to gain by cooperating, I nevertheless offered my insights, helping you to apprehend the killer.' As he spoke, the corners of his mouth filled with webs of frothy white saliva. Stella's stomach heaved. 'You will take the credit, naturally. But my contribution will be there on screen for everybody to see. Maybe someone will want to write a book about me. True crime is a very popular genre these days, so I'm told.'

Somehow, Stella managed to maintain a neutral expression. Internally, however, her emotions were boiling like the storm she had driven through to get to Kumla. Shock at his reframing of his sadistic murders as some kind of 'career' as if they were listed under the 'Achievements' on his LinkedIn profile. Rage at his narcissism. Disbelief at his lack of self-awareness. And, seething below them all, a burning desire to reach down to her right ankle, release the pistol and put a couple of full metal jacket rounds into his smug, froggy face.

Breathing steadily, if heavily, she left the pistol where it was.

'I see,' she managed. 'I suppose nobody is better-placed to aid the investigation than yourself. After all, he is following your footsteps. You were the pioneer; he is merely the follower.'

Flattering him like this had her belly roiling and clammy, cold sweat breaking out inside her shirt. She swallowed. If it helped catch the killer before he got to Sören or Nik, she could handle a little nausea.

Ahlgren had been nodding throughout her little speech.

'Exactly! So do we have a deal?'

'I tell you what,' she said, leaning forward and dropping her voice a little so he could take it as a conspiratorial whisper out of Magda's earshot. 'I do know a couple of journalists quite well. One actually does some ghostwriting on the side. Let's catch this man and then, who knows, perhaps an autobiography could be on the cards.'

IN YOUR DREAMS! she wanted to scream.

He nodded, half-closed his eyes. Smiled again.

'Hmm. Yes, I can see that. People have been fed a diet of

newspaper clippings and internet research. This would be my own story, told by me.'

It seemed whatever levels of animal cunning Ahlgren possessed, he was as susceptible to flattery as most criminals Stella had interviewed over the years. The more horrendous their crimes, the more you could ladle it on. They all thought they were criminal geniuses, whereas in reality they were just twisted, degenerate, greedy, stupid or, more usually, a combination of all four.

'Lilith. Who is she?'

His watery eyes opened fully. She saw the monster behind those pale-blue irises, shifting, uncoiling, readying itself.

'Her name is Anna Eriksson. Before I had to resign as manager, she used to come to see me from time to time. To discuss merchandise, interviews, fan meet-and-greets, that sort of thing. She lived in Västerås then. In fact, isn't that where the second murder took place? I do hope Anna hasn't been taking her mythology too seriously.'

Leaving aside the obvious response that, far from 'having' to resign, Ahlgren had in fact been arrested for multiple murders, Stella was intrigued.

'That's a fairly common name. Can you describe her?'

'I can do better than that. I can show you a photo. Would you like that, Stella?'

'Very much.'

For the second time, Ahlgren looked past her to the guard.

'Magda, please will you take me back to my room for a moment? I need to retrieve my photograph album.'

This time the taunting note in his voice was absent. She had him hooked good and proper. Eager to play a starring role in the investigation that he believed would lead to some fawning ghost-writer wanting to immortalise him on the page. Well, good luck with that. She'd been very careful not to promise or assure, only to suggest, and let Ahlgren's monstrously bloated ego do the rest.

He left with the guard, and Stella was on her own in the

echoing white-walled space. She checked her phone but nobody wanted her. Nobody had texted.

She got up from the hard chair and wandered over to the barred window. It gave onto a playing field. Proper grass, not asphalt. A football match was in progress.

Two teams, one bare-chested, the other in white T-shirts, were kicking the ball about. A guard served as referee. Two more were running the lines. As she watched, the player with the ball lofted it high in the air.

All heads lifted to observe the ball's progress. It bounced high and as two players went for the header, they clashed in mid-air. A fight broke out, and all three prison guards switched seamlessly from match officials to disciplinarians, rushing towards the brawl between the two players, who were now surrounded by a ring of men, all laughing or clapping as they threw wild punches.

Something about the football match, before it had degenerated into a fight, pricked at her memory. Where had she seen such a scene before? She closed her eyes. Heard more male shouts. But happy ones this time, not the angry yelling floating up from the field below the window.

Oh, God.

It had been in Jamie's office, when he'd been on the staff at Broadmoor, back in England. She'd visited him at the secure psychiatric hospital for help catching Miriam Robey and their chat had been interrupted by shouting. Patients had been playing football in the yard beneath Jamie's office window and one of them had just scored. Hence, the shouting.

What the hell had happened to Jamie? He'd turned up outside her apartment block brimming with Hooke charm but by the end of his trip he'd left without so much as a word of goodbye.

Since then he'd changed into this sarcastic, unpleasant man who acted as if *she'd* dumped *him*. Maybe if you spent too much time hanging around with society's most depraved men, some of their pathology rubbed off on you. She shuddered. Unpleasant thought. Presumably psychiatrists in those sorts of roles had access to all kinds of counselling to ensure they avoided that fate.

A clang from the door pulled her out of her thoughts. She turned to see Ahlgren being led, in chains, back to the table. Under his arm he carried a large-format album with pale leather covers. For one horrifying moment she imagined it had been bound in human skin.

Reality asserted itself. She was fairly sure the director would have strict rules about keepsakes of that sort within the walls of her prison. Especially the Bunker.

While Magda bent over him, fastening his chains through the eye-bolt and shackling his ankles, Stella walked back to her own chair, still smiling grimly at the dark place to which her imagination had just taken her. Maybe Jamie wasn't the only one whose personality had been tainted by the company he kept.

Catching her expression, Ahlgren smiled back at her.

'Something amusing you, Stella?'

'Just an old joke,' she improvised. 'How many narcissists does it take to change a lightbulb?'

'Surprise me,' he said, raising one pale eyebrow, which she noticed was flecked with scales of dry skin.

'Just one. He holds the lightbulb while the whole world revolves around him.'

A high-pitched laugh escaped Ahlgren's fleshy lips, startling Stella more than the unbidden image of the skin-covered photo album.

'That is very good. Don't you think, Magda?'

But the guard was already walking back to her station against the wall, equidistant between the window and the heavily fortified door. Her face remained impassive. Perhaps she was laughing on the inside. Stella doubted it. She glanced at the album, on which Ahlgren was resting his hands.

'So, what do you want to show me?'

He shot her a sly look. 'You know, I would feel so much more ... comfortable if you would call me Ulrik. Everybody else here does. Even Lina, on the rare occasions when our paths cross.'

She'd managed it once before on their previous encounter. But somehow, getting that cosy with a killer as twisted as Ahlgren was proving a high hurdle for Stella to straddle. But, she thought, needs must when the devil drives. And right now, he, or at least his self-appointed representative on earth, was most definitely the one with the whip-hand.

She inhaled, pasted a small smile on her face.

'OK, then … what have you got in there, Ulrik?'

'There. That was not so hard, was it? This is my highlights album from my time with Sepülkå. There are many more, as I am sure you can imagine…' – his watery eyes flickered up to the ceiling for a moment – 'but I am severely restricted for shelf space.'

Wondering what horrors might be contained in the rest of his albums, and hoping desperately that the arresting officers had recovered and housed them securely, or preferably incinerated them, Stella leaned forwards.

Just a little.

32

Taking great care to keep her hands well back from Ahlgren's side of the table, Stella nodded at the photograph album.

'Show me.'

Ahlgren glanced up from the album at her, eyebrows raised.

'Please,' she added, fighting down another urge to draw down on him.

Let's see how fucking patronising he'd be staring down the business end of a nine.

He opened the album. Page after page filled with colour images of a much younger Ahlgren posing with members of the band. They all wore either outlandish makeup like Lyngstad, the lead singer, or grotesque masks, one with a mass of tentacles descending from the chin-piece. Must have been hellish hot to perform in.

He turned over a few more pages and then tapped a photo.

'There she is! Lilith herself. Take a look.'

He spun the album round and pushed it towards her until his chain chinked sharply against the restraining eyebolt. She reached across the table, her hands heading for Ahlgren's side. Behind her, she caught the sound of Magda's feet shuffling. And a warning cough.

'The rules, Stella.'

But Stella had anticipated Ahlgren's move. Now it was *her* turn to raise her eyebrows. With a leer spreading across his face like slime on the surface of a stagnant pond, he slid his fingers off the cover and placed his hands in his lap.

She pulled the book of photos towards her. In the photo Ahlgren had indicated, a young woman, no more than twenty or twenty-one, surrounded by the five members of Sepülkå. She was tall, that was the first thing Stella noticed. Slim build, with a striking mane of crow-black hair. It signified very little, probably dyed.

The musicians' eyes were glazed, lazy, lecherous smiles on their black-lipsticked mouths. Their long, lank hair was greasy or damp with sweat. Stella assumed the photo had been taken after a performance, although who was to know how death metal bands conducted themselves. Maybe a little light drug-taking and group sex was their way of psyching themselves up for a gig. Somehow she couldn't picture this group of devil-worshipping rockers meditating or busting out a few downward-facing dogs.

In contrast, Anna Eriksson AKA Lilith, appeared completely sober. The look she bestowed on the camera – full lips curving in a half-smile, level gaze, chin lifted just a fraction – was full of self-satisfaction. Her arms were outstretched, her palms resting on the shoulders of the two young men flanking her.

To Stella she looked like a witch among her coven. She was saying, *Look at me. I have everything I want. They think I follow them. But ask yourself who's really in control.*

'Quite a piece of work, wouldn't you agree?'

Stella pulled her eyes away from the photo. Ahlgren was leaning forwards, though he had taken care to keep his hands down.

'She is certainly very striking to look at.'

'Oh, it wasn't just her looks that were striking. Young Anna had extremely strong and I would have to say, unusual, appetites.'

Coming from a certifiably insane psychotic serial killer, this veiled remark needed careful unpicking.

Stella glanced again at the photo. 'Would you care to elaborate for me?'

'She liked the boys to cut her while they were fucking her. All at once, sometimes. Though two or three was her usual preference. I hope I haven't shocked you, Stella,' he added, a solicitous frown buckling the pallid flesh above his eyes.

'Not at all, Ulrik. Now, on the assumption you're not just making this up to arouse yourself, in which case, I can leave right now and you can forget any thoughts of a ghostwritten autobiography...' He shook his head. Good. She'd found his weak spot and could exploit it for the rest of the interview. 'Did she ask them for any specific sorts of cuts?'

He smiled, though the expression didn't reach his eyes.

'Can't you guess?'

'Why don't you tell me?'

'A pentacle. Not too deep, obviously. Not like mine.'

'Ulrik!' A sharp bark from Magda, who Stella had forgotten about, so intense was Ahlgren's gaze. 'You know the rules.'

'Sorry, Magda. My bad.'

He looked at Stella once more. 'Lina is very strict. Bunker inmates are not permitted to discuss details of their crimes except with a certified mental health professional appointed by, and reporting to, Lina herself.' He swallowed, his Adam's Apple distending his pouchy throat and making Stella think of swallowed insects. 'I don't suppose—'

'I'm not a psychiatrist, Ulrik. I'm a homicide investigator.'

She was beginning to tire of this back-and-forth. She had what she'd come for. But as she had his treasured photo album, she thought she might as well take a look at the rest of the pictures. Maybe there'd be one of Björn Lyngstad without his stage makeup.

She paged on, but only encountered more shots of the band, either playing live, horsing around in the studio or posing in graveyards or forests, among towering pine trees.

One page was taken up with a single large photo. The photographer had used a wide-angle lens, producing a curved distortion at the edges of the frame so that the outermost figures were bending surreally in to the centre.

Unlike the other images in the album, this one wasn't focused on the band. They were visible on the left of the shot, which had been taken just below the stage at an outdoor concert.

Banks of black-grilled amplifiers rose behind the band. Sunlight glinted off guitar strings. Lyngstad's face was broken up into light and dark planes by sharp shadows. Somehow she'd never imagined a band as dark as Sepülkå playing in daylight, let alone a beautiful sunny day at some sort of Swedish equivalent of Woodstock.

At the centre of the image was a young couple, both naked from the waist up. And utterly beautiful, their faces radiant. So out of keeping with the image she'd formed in her mind of the band's followers from the other photos. Regarding them with a mixture of disdain and obvious lust were three long-haired bikers, each wearing a leather jacket and a denim vest over it, festooned with patches. Much more the Sepülkå fan-demographic.

Dragging her eyes away from the young woman's perky breasts, which had clearly never experienced the changes demanded by motherhood, Stella looked up at Ahlgren.

'You've found our high priest and priestess, I see,' he said. 'Jonny and Maria Söderstad. Brother and sister, and we'd better not delve too deeply into the precise nature of *that* relationship.'

'What are they doing now?' A barely coded question. Translation: *Could they be working together as your disciples?*

'I believe Jonny runs his own accountancy practice in Uppsala. Maria sadly died of a brain haemorrhage in 2001.'

Striking both siblings from her growing list of people of interest, Stella tapped the photo.

'Who are the bikers? I notice they're not watching the band.'

'May I?' Ahlgren lifted a hand.

'Be my guest.'

He pulled the album back towards him and rotated it. Nodded.

'They weren't there to watch the band. They provided security. The boys were adamant we weren't going to pay off-duty police officers. Not really consistent with their image.' He offered a smile as if to say, 'Artists!'. 'So I hired this lot. It was a big event and the local council said they wouldn't grant our licence unless we had security.'

'And is that all they provided?' Stella asked, suspecting she already knew the answer.

Ahlgren's smile confirmed it.

'Did you ever work in the drugs squad, Stella?'

'Didn't need to. It's hardly rocket science, is it? Biker gangs deal in drugs, often. Rock bands like to party. Two plus two equals four, yes?'

'Yes. The big fellow on the left is their leader. I negotiated the contract with him personally. Klas Helander.'

'And that's his real name?'

'As far as I am aware, yes. I think he thought the band's theatrics rather childish, to be honest. But the drugs were good quality and his prices were reasonable.' Ahlgren shrugged. 'As manager, it was my job to keep the band happy. Klas was instrumental in that.'

'Who are the other men in the photo?'

'No idea. They all had that look, you know? Their uniform code was at least as strict as the SPA's.'

'What was the name of the gang?'

'The Vampires? No. The Werewolves. I mean, it's funny, really. Klas telling me my boys were childish, when he'd named his gang after some cheesy horror film character.'

Stella nodded. Klas Helander might be worth talking to as well as Anna Eriksson. She made another note. But she was tiring of having to maintain this chummy facade with Ahlgren. He seemed to have forgotten all about his demonic 'slave of Satan' act and was treating her as some sort of advance guard for his ghostwriter. Time to remind him she was a working cop.

'Could I borrow this photo? And the one of Lilith? I promise to take good care of them.'

She could just as easily take pictures with her phone, but she wanted to push him as far as she could into doing what she wanted, and not the other way around. Maybe it was a childish power play, but deep down she wanted him to know who was in control of their interactions.

He chewed his lower lip. 'Well, I suppose if you told Lina how helpful I'd been, it might go some way to restoring me to her good graces.'

'Oh, yes? Did you do something to upset her?'

Detaching a journalist's finger would have achieved that effect, Stella assumed.

'I had a visitor and I'm afraid rules were broken. Not my fault, I should add. But there you are. Once guilty, always guilty.'

Ignoring the obvious invitation to engage in a little light philosophy, Stella slid the two photos from their pages and pushed her chair back.

'Thank you for your help, Mr Ahlgren. I have to go.'

She stood and signalled for Magda to let her out.

'But you'll come back, Stella, won't you? With your journalist friend. I have so many stories that people must hear.'

His voice had taken on a new tone. Part querulous, as if he'd been a diner in a fancy restaurant and not enjoyed his main course. Part barely suppressed anger, as though the maître d' had taken a shit in his dessert.

She turned at the door. Ahlgren was eyeing her with his head cocked on one side, fleshy lips pursed. Never had his resemblance to some grotesque amphibian been more apparent.

'I'm busy catching someone who's copying your murder techniques. It doesn't leave a lot of time for acting as your literary agent.' She nodded to Magda. 'Thank you.'

Magda rolled her eyes. 'Made for an interesting change to the routine.'

'But, Stella, you can't just go like that. You can't! I forbid it.' Ahlgren was hovering above his chair, chained ankles shuffling

Playing the Devil's Music

and clinking as he attempted to stand erect. Impossible given the wrist restraints.

Stella glanced over her shoulder.

'Watch me.'

Something happened to Ahlgren then. All trace of the placid, if repulsive demeanour disappeared. His face contorted with rage, eyes popping, lips pulled back in a hideous snarl revealing small yellow teeth.

'NO!' he roared, yanking at the eyebolt so the chain rattled and clanked. 'Come back here, you filthy cunt! I'll slice you open and fill your belly with rats. I'll dig your eyeballs out and fuck the sockets. I *demand* you return here!'

As Stella left the echoing space and made her way down the corridor, Ahlgren's demented cries grew steadily fainter. She caught her reflection in a pane of newly replaced glass, still with the peel-off plastic film on its inner surface. She appeared to wink as her reflection moved over a ripple in the film.

Can't kid a kidder, eh, babe? it seemed to say.

She smiled. Her versus Ahlgren in a deserted warehouse? Choice of weapons? He wouldn't stand a chance.

She fantasised about different ways of killing him all the way back to Örebro nick.

* * *

Back at the police station, she found Sven slumped at his desk, head in hands, his palms pooching his cheeks together as he stared at a database query screen. His pose suggested a depressing picture entitled *Disconsolate Cop Confronts the Futility of Investigating Multiple Linked Homicides*.

She looked down at the full mug of coffee by his right elbow. A wrinkled skin floated on the surface.

'That bad, huh?'

He looked up at her. Eyes red-rimmed, face grey with that prison pallor she'd observed on Ahlgren's face not forty minutes earlier.

'We're running out of time, Stella.' He took his hands away from his face, revealing two rose-pink prints. 'Time, ideas, budget, and, as for suspects, well, nobody can trace Björn Lyngstad, so none.'

'Maybe I can help. I just got back from my second and almost certainly final interview with our friend Ulrik Ahlgren. I have two names. Anna Eriksson and Klas Helander. Respectively the head of the band's fan club and the leader of a biker gang Ahlgren hired to do security and supply drugs.'

Sven nodded, and mumbled. 'Yes, yes. That's good, that's good. Not suspects, not yet. But names are what we need.'

He raised a finger to his mouth and began gnawing at the nail, detaching a ragged white sliver. He hissed out a breath. 'Shit the devil!' He pulled the finger away from his teeth. Blood was flowing along the raw edge and down the side of the nail bed towards the cuticle.

'Are you OK, Sven?'

Now that she looked closer, he looked anything but. There was a tightness around his eyes that lent them a staring quality and he hadn't shaved for a day or two.

'Yeah, yeah, fine. Just, you know, it's a high-stakes case. I have a lot to prove. Yeah, yeah, a lot to prove all right.'

He was looking out the window as his voice dropped to a semi-audible mutter. Poor guy looked like he was on the brink of burning out. She laid a hand on his shoulder. The muscle was so tense it was quivering beneath the thin material of his shirt.

'When did you last eat a proper meal? Get a decent night's sleep? Have you taken any time off since this case began?'

He whirled round, startled. 'What?'

'Sven,' she said, squatting beside him and looking up into his eyes. 'Not being rude, but you look like shit.'

She glanced at his ring finger. No gold band. It didn't mean anything but she hadn't formed the impression he was married, or even living with someone. Made a decision.

'Come round to mine tonight. I'll cook you a proper meal. Do you run?'

Playing the Devil's Music

He frowned, as if she'd asked him whether he hunted whales in his pyjamas.

'Do I?'

'Run? You know. For exercise? I've found a nice five-K route that goes round the nature reserve. We could work up an appetite.'

He shook his head.

'I do but there's no time. We have to stop him before he kills the other two Hunter Killers.'

'I know, Sven. But we need to look after ourselves, too. If it makes you feel better, we can discuss the case at mine. Maybe we'll come up with some fresh angles. It's not doing you good beating yourself up like this.'

'Who's getting beaten up?'

Stella rose from her crouch, wincing as her knees popped.

Lucy had just come in and was unstrapping her service weapon and locking it in a steel cabinet beneath her desk. Maybe when Stella got back to Stockholm, she'd suggest to Malin they install a similar system in Homicide. It would have saved everyone a lot of grief.

'I was just telling Sven that cops who drive themselves too hard end up unable to function. They think they're helping the victims but all they're doing is burning themselves out.'

Lucy rolled her eyes.

'I've been telling him that every day! He won't listen.'

Sven offered a cracked grin. 'Hey! I am actually still here, ladies.'

Stella had an idea. 'Lucy, come for dinner at mine, yes? I've got loads of nice ingredients in. I was inviting Sven when you arrived. I said maybe we could go for a run first.'

Lucy's face broke into a smile.

'Great idea. I'm not much of an athlete, though.' She patted her gently out-curving belly. 'Too fond of my mum's cooking.'

'You live at home?'

'Yeah. I'm saving for a deposit on my own place, but prices are just ridiculous.'

'Great! So it's a cheap night out for you, we can burn a few calories first, and Sven will have no excuse not to come because the three of us can talk through some new approaches.'

Sven nodded. 'I guess a change of scene would be a good idea. And I defrosted my last ready meal last night. I'm down to crispbreads and some sad-looking smoked herring pâté.'

Stella finished up her notes from the day and headed out. She had some food shopping to do.

33

Stella met Lucy and Sven at the southernmost tip of the nature reserve. By the time they arrived she'd pulled off her leathers and was warming up in her shorts and running vest. The sun was low in the sky to the west of the reserve, lighting up the wetland lakes so they appeared to be composed of liquid fire.

Once the other two had changed, Stella led them off on a path that snaked between a pine forest on one side and a wide lake fringed with reeds on the other.

'Pace all right?' she called over her shoulder.

In truth she was barely jogging, but she'd been mindful of Lucy's remarks about not being a great one for exercise.

'Fine,' she called back. 'But Sven's struggling.'

Stella looked over her shoulder. But Sven was matching Lucy stride for stride, a determined look on his face.

'I'm OK,' he puffed. 'Just finding my rhythm.'

Five minutes later the cops were running in a tight group, taking it in turns, at Stella's suggestion, to set the pace in front. She pointed to a bench a hundred metres ahead.

'Sprint to the seat then a break?'

'OK,' the others chorused.

'Three, two, one, go!' she shouted.

Sven sped past her, elbows pumping. Stella permitted herself a grin. Male pride was at stake. Not to mention Sven's need to prove himself better than the 'foreign import' from Stockholm. Which was a bit rich considering she wasn't even Swedish. Or did that make it worse?

She didn't waste time considering it. Put her foot down instead, drawing level and glancing sideways. Behind her she could hear Lucy's breathing growing ragged. Should she drop back, give Sven his win, show some solidarity with Lucy? Yes. That was what she *should* do. But when had Stella Cole ever done what she was supposed to?

She lifted her chin, sighted on the bench and simply … opened up. Heart, lungs, arms, legs, core: her whole body synced up in a gloriously free feeling of total abandonment to the joy of running. She passed Sven without feeling like she was making any effort.

She simply *flowed*. That was the word that always came to mind whenever she was truly in the zone. She'd run hundreds, then thousands, of miles after Richard and Lola had been killed. First to block out the pain. Then to try and deal with it. Finally, because, somewhere along those cold, dark London streets she'd found she loved it for its own sake.

From somewhere deep down, Sven produced another burst of speed and they reached the bench neck and neck, flying past it before slowing to a trot and circling back to meet Lucy, whose face was suffused with blood.

'Your face!' Sven said. 'It matches my house.'

Stella thought that was a little unkind. No way was Lucy's colour the deep shade of Falun.

Lucy jutted her chin out. 'Want another match? Your face…' She turned and smacked her bum. 'My arse.'

They sat three abreast of the wooden slatted bench, staring out over the lake. Some kind of water birds were calling to each other across its ruffled surface, a high-pitched twittering.

As their breathing slowed, Sven leaned forwards and put his elbows on his knees.

'Does it ever bother you, Stella?'

'What?'

'How there can exist such beauty in a country, and also such evil? I mean, look at it.' He lifted his chin towards the horizon, streaked deep rose pink by the setting sun. 'It looks so peaceful, but out there the Devil of Axberg is probably planning how to kill Sören Roos right now.'

'Don't worry about Sören,' Stella said, sounding more confident than she felt. 'He's got enough firepower to annex northern Norway. If the Devil shows his face up there in Luleå he's going to get it shot off shortly afterwards.'

'I hope so. Because I don't see how else we're going to catch him.'

'Let's not get defeatist. Tell you what, we'll head back to the carpark then rendezvous at mine. I bought some steaks and a couple of good bottles of red. We'll eat them and put our heads together on the case.'

The second half of the circuit round the reserve ended in another sprint finish. This time, despite her best efforts, Stella finished five metres behind Sven, who yelped in triumph punching the air as he shot past the unofficial finish line.

* * *

At Stella's, the others took it in turns to shower and change in the bedroom while Stella used the separate bathroom. In the kitchen, she poured three glasses of the wine, a deep plum-red Barolo and raised hers.

'Cheers. To catching the Devil by the tail.'

'Cheers!' Sven and Lucy said in unison.

Whether it was the run, the change from takeaways eaten at their desks, or the chance to let their hair down, their appetites had been sharpened to a razor's edge. The steaks disappeared between sporadic bursts of general conversation. When the plates were cleared and stacked in the dishwasher, Stella produced coffee, chocolates and brandy.

Stella and Lucy fell back into the comforting embrace of a squashy leather sofa. Sven took the matching armchair, slinging one leg over the arm.

'We'll have a full team briefing in the morning,' Sven said, 'but what are we going to tell everyone?'

'Let's talk about the two names I got from Ahlgren this afternoon,' Stella said.

'How was he?' Lucy asked.

Stella thought back to the last sight she had of Ahlgren. Eyes wild, whites showing all the way round those strangely pale irises. Lips pulled wide in a snarl as he yelled obscenities at her. She shrugged.

'I think it's safe to say I'm off his Christmas list.' She fetched the photo he'd given her of the outdoor concert with the heavyset bikers front and centre. She tapped the face of the tallest of the three. 'Meet Klas Helander. According to Ahlgren, he ran a biker gang called the Werewolves. Supplied drugs to the band.'

'You think he could have been involved?' Lucy asked, leaning forwards to scrutinise the photo.

'It has to be a possibility, don't you think? He and Ahlgren dealt with each other in person about security and the drugs. We know biker gangs are often involved in criminal activity. Violent, usually, organised often. Maybe he got a taste for Ahlgren's activities on the quiet. Maybe, despite what he told me, Ahlgren was grooming him even then.'

'You said there was a woman.' This was Sven, mirroring Lucy's pose, unslinging his leg and leaning forwards. 'Anna Eriksson?'

Stella produced the second photo. 'She ran the fan club back then. Again, according to Ahlgren, she enjoyed S&M with the band, specifically having a pentagram – or he actually called it a pentacle – cut into her chest.'

'Wow, that's pretty fucked up,' Sven said, unconsciously rubbing his sternum.

Playing the Devil's Music

'So, I suggest,' Stella looked at Sven, 'if you're OK with it, that I take Klas and Lucy takes Anna. Track them down, interview them, ask for alibis, the usual.'

'With me coordinating.'

'You're the lead investigator. And there's still stacks of interviews, calls from members of the public, reports to be read and acted on, case notes, meetings with Kersten.'

'I kind of hoped I'd be playing a more active role in the investigation,' Sven said.

In truth, Stella detected relief in Sven's face. Maybe the stress really was getting to him, however much good the steak and the run had done him.

'Welcome to my world. Well, my old world.'

As she said this, Stella realised with a brief twinge of pleasure that she was really enjoying working a case as an honest-to-god detective and not trying to juggle investigative tactics with keeping the brass, politicians, the prosecutor, the media relations team and the general public happy.

'Sven's got his sights set pretty high,' Lucy said, sipping her wine. 'You're looking at a future National Police Commissioner.'

Stella snapped off a salute, sending her wine sloshing dangerously close to the rim of the glass.

'I look forward to watching your interviews on *Aktuellt*. Sir.'

'Seriously, Stella, you've caught plenty of big fish,' Sven said. 'Can a cop from Örebro make it to the top?'

Stella shrugged. 'I don't see why not. Although haven't the last two NPCs both been director general of Säpo? Maybe you ought to think about applying for a transfer to the Security Service.'

He offered a rueful smile. 'Yeah. I've actually had my application in for six months now. Kersten said she'd put in a good word for me, but apparently they're not recruiting at the moment. Budget cuts. Same old story everywhere, even for Säpo.'

He yawned so widely his jaw cracked, making Lucy laugh. 'Oh my God, Sven, do you need Stella to make you a bed on the floor or something?'

'No, but I better get back. I'll collect my car in the morning.'

'Share a taxi? I need some sleep too.'

They offered to share the clear-up, but Stella ushered them out of the door, figuring that rested colleagues were better than helpful ones.

Tomorrow was going to be a busy day.

* * *

The next day *was* busy. But also fruitless. Stella finally threw in the towel at 9:15 p.m., having failed to locate Klas Helander.

Two weeks passed and still she couldn't find him. She checked in with Nik and Sören every day until both men started barking at her to leave them in peace. Each was armed, and taking what he regarded as over-engineered precautions. In Sören's case, this extended to measures he referred to darkly as, 'stuff I learned in the military'.

Stella queried this remark with Nik, who revealed that, before joining the SPA, Sören had served with Swedish Special Forces. She pictured bear traps, spike-lined pits, spring-guns, all manner of gruesome improvised weapons that would take out the Devil of Axberg before he got within cockroach-throwing distance of Sören's secluded house.

In truth, she had started to relax. Maybe the killer was done. Maybe he'd been arrested for another, unrelated crime. It happened. But a two-week interval after three closely spaced killings again didn't fit the classic pattern of a serial murderer.

34

VÄSTERÅS

Lucy had interviewed witnesses in all kinds of dwellings, from scuzzy drug dens to fancy penthouses. But a houseboat was a first.

Tracking Anna Eriksson down had been difficult, since she'd done a reasonable job of staying off the grid. But Sweden didn't really believe in that level of nomadism, and Lucy had eventually traced her via a social services official who'd handled a benefits claim a few years earlier.

As she approached the black-painted craft, she wondered what it would be like in the depths of a proper Swedish winter. Today, with the sun shining, and weeping willows drooping their branches prettily over the river Svartån, yes, it looked idyllic. But in January? At four in the afternoon with the sun nothing but a distant memory, and thick snow clogging the riverbank?

She shivered despite the warmth. No thank you very much. She'd take her mum's nice centrally heated apartment in downtown Örebro any day.

She approached the back of the boat. Or, what did they call it, the bow? Or was that the front? Didn't matter to her. She was a land-dweller and happy to keep it that way. The steering pole-thing was highly polished brass with a handle bound in intricate knotted string. She used it to swing herself on board and then knocked at the double doors down a couple of wooden steps.

'Hello! Anyone home? Anna?'

Silence. Great. Now she'd have to start scouting around looking for her.

'She's gone into town.' The gruff male voice came from behind her.

She spun round. A middle-aged guy with a short beard and a paunch was strolling along the bank from another houseboat. This one an altogether jollier affair with straggly herbs planted in tubs on the roof, flowers and birds painted on its sides and net curtains in the windows.

'Anna, you mean?'

He nodded, smiled, revealing a winking gold tooth. 'Ran out of snus and beer, apparently. I'm her neighbour, Bernard.'

They shook hands and Lucy introduced herself with her full name and rank. 'Will she be long, do you think?'

He shrugged well-muscled shoulders. Clearly the nautical life was as good as going to the gym, despite his beer belly.

'I wouldn't have thought so. The Willys is only a twenty-minute walk and she left about half an hour ago. Want a coffee while you wait? You won't miss her, she always knocks on my roof as she passes. You know, "deer-and-a-hunter-bang-bang".' He rapped out the familiar rhythm on the side of Anna's boat.

'Sure, thank you.'

Inside, Bernard's boat was fitted out like a miniature wooden palace. Every surface was gleaming with polish, and the furniture and fittings had clearly been made with a lot of skill, and love. Brass hinges, hooks and screwheads glinted everywhere she looked.

'Did you do all this yourself, Bernard?' Lucy asked, while her host boiled water and ground coffee.

'Every panel, every screw, yes. I'm a carpenter by trade and, for once, I found the time to do something on my own account.'

He reappeared with two mugs of coffee and offered her a ginger snap, which she declined, having been watching her weight recently.

'It's very beautiful,' she said as she accepted the delicious-smelling coffee.

'Thanks. Better than all that IKEA crap anyway.'

'What's Anna like?' she asked after taking a sip of the coffee, which tasted as good as it smelled. Strong, dark and almost chocolatey.

Bernard tipped his head on one side.

'Well, she's ... different, I guess. All of us boaters are to a degree. We wouldn't be living this way if we were boring old nine-to-fivers, would we?'

Lucy nodded her agreement. Though she was uncomfortable with the notion she was a 'boring nine-to-fiver'. Mind you, with the hours they were putting in on the current case, 'seven-to-tenner' would be closer to the mark, even if a good chunk of those were spent at home, with an official SPA laptop open on the coffee table and a bottle of beer or a glass of wine by your elbow.

She loved the job, and getting a transfer to the detective branch had been her career goal, well, the first of them, anyway. But the hours pretty much put paid to any idea of a social life. And as for a boyfriend, good luck with that. Occasional hook-ups were about the closest she came to an intimate partner. And since they were usually paramedics, other cops or nurses, they ended up on conflicting rotas and never saw each other again.

She sighed. Bernard was eyeing her curiously. Crap! Had she missed something?

'Different, how?' she asked, hoping he'd take her silence for deep-level investigative cogitation.

'You know, she doesn't see things the way the rest of us do.'

That aroused Lucy's curiosity.

'Can you be a little more specific?'

'She thinks we should all live as freely as possible. That's why she has the boat.' He frowned. 'I guess we all do. But Anna, well, she takes things to extremes.'

Now Lucy was definitely interested. In the context of the investigation, the word 'extremes' had unwelcome connotations.

'Like how?'

'She says laws are for the weak-willed and the police, excuse me, but the police are just tools of a repressive state. We should all do whatever we like and that if everybody lived that way, the universe would be in perfect balance. She's always quoting this saying at me.' He switched to English. '"Do what thou wilt shall be the whole of the law". Some English philosopher or something. Crow's-beak? Cowley? Something like that anyway.' He winked. 'I mean, obviously it's all horseshit, but it's not as if she's hurting anybody, is it?'

Lucy nodded, distractedly. That all depended, didn't it? She made a note of the saying, which sounded like the kind of thing people put on Instagram with an airbrushed illustration of some witch done up like a porn star. Her breath caught. No! It was a lot closer to home than that. It was scrawled in orange whiteboard marker on the murder wall, under the photo of Ulrik Ahlgren's knife. He'd had it in Latin and Stella had written up the translation.

'Has she been here all the time over the last month or so?'

'Yeah, I think so. She does healing to pay her moorage fees and buy groceries. I think it's Reiki? Maybe aromatherapy, I'm not too sure. Could be Red Indian shamanic rituals for all I know.' He put a hand to his mouth, play-acting embarrassment. 'Oops. I don't think we're allowed to say that anymore, are we?'

'I think the approved phrase is Native American,' she said dryly.

He sighed. 'Like you can't say Laplander anymore. It's Sámi now.'

Sensing he was on the brink of uttering the immortal phrase 'it's political correctness gone mad', Lucy headed him off with another question.

'Have you discussed the recent murders at all?'

'You mean that business over in Axberg?'

'And Charlottenberg. And Västerås'

'The devil-in-hell, I had no idea there'd been one here, too.'

'I'm afraid so. *Have* you talked about it with Anna?'

His eyes narrowed.

'How's your coffee?'

'It's fine, thank you.' That was interesting. Clearly he didn't want to answer her question. It seemed to Lucy like he and Anna definitely *had* discussed it. 'So *have* you?'

His cheek twitched. 'I mean, probably. It was on the radio, I think. But we wouldn't have spent much time discussing it. We boaters like to keep ourselves separate from the world, you know? It's bad stuff like what you're talking about that drives us to choose the life in the first place.'

Lucy nodded. Offered a sympathetic smile. In fact, she'd read a piece in *Svenska Dagbladet* online about people opting out of living in houses. Vans, removals trucks, horse boxes, and, yes, boats: all were pressed into service as dwellings. For some, sure, it was a lifestyle thing. But for plenty of others, it was more to do with unaffordable rents and the lack of decent social housing. Something the right-wing parties like Reborn Sweden were happy to blame on immigration.

'So, when you discussed it –' Bernard opened his mouth to interrupt, '– *briefly*,' she added, 'what did Anna say about it? Did it fit with her views about living outside the law?'

'I can't remember,' he said. He was closing down, she could see it in his face. It happened. People could be as sweet as a *kannelbullar* when they thought they were just having a nice, friendly chat, but when the conversation turned to the matter at hand, they could get decidedly squirrelly.

'That's OK, I can always ask her myself.'

Before she could ask another question, a loud knocking filled the cabin. Just as Bernard had said: *rat-tat a-tat-tat, rat-tat.*

'I guess that will be her,' Lucy said getting to her feet. 'Thanks for the coffee.'

Bernard rose also, but by executing a neat swivel, she blocked him from getting out from behind the table, and in this way was able to precede him out on to the deck.

The woman standing on the bank was somewhere around forty. It was hard to tell under the mane of long, raven-black hair. Her outfit was throwing out weird vibes too.

Bernard wasn't wrong when he said his neighbour was different. A baggy hand-knitted jumper in fluffy mohair: red-and-black hoops like some latter-day Örebro punk. The cuffs came down past the woman's fingers. Black fishnet tights ended in thick-soled black Dr. Marten's boots embellished with red pentagrams that appeared to be hand-painted.

She looked like she belonged in some retro nightclub, or an 80s horror movie. And she also looked surprised to see Lucy. Her eyes, heavily made-up with kohl, popped wide. Behind Lucy, Bernard clambered out onto the cramped little space.

'Anna, she's a—'

' – police officer,' Lucy said, flashing her ID. 'Detective Inspector Lucy Magnusson. Are you Anna Eriksson?'

'Yes.' She folded her arms across her chest. A defensive manoeuvre.

'Can we have a chat? Maybe on your boat?'

'Am I in trouble?'

'No. Nothing like that. I'd just like to ask you a few questions, that's all. It's in connection with a murder investigation and I need your help to clarify a few things.'

Anna hoisted her arms higher. She might as well have been raising a shield.

'What if I don't want to "have a chat"?' Sarcasm dripped from her lips.

Lucy nodded, as if this was the most normal reaction in the world.

'Not too keen on the police?'

Anna shot a dirty look over Lucy's shoulder. Lucy heard Bernard retreat back inside. Anna fixed Lucy with a variant of the same look, kohled eyes narrowed to smoky slits.

'I know my rights. I don't have to talk to you if I don't want to.'

Lucy smiled. 'Well, you're half-right. You don't have to talk to me *here*, and you don't have to talk to me *now*. But, as I am investigating a series of murders of the most cruel and depraved nature, I would then arrest you and take you straight to Örebro police station for questioning. At which point, you *would* have to talk to me.' She paused. 'Naturally, you'd have the right to legal representation.'

She let Anna mull it over. The silence lengthened as the two women stared at each other. A pair of swans drifted close to the bank and hissed at Anna. It seemed to make up her mind for her.

'Fine.'

'"Fine", we can do this here, or "fine" you would like to come to Örebro with me?'

Anna jutted her chin in the direction of her own boat.

35

The interior of Anna's boat was no smaller than Bernard's, but it felt cramped.

Most of the free space was taken up with a narrow padded table on folding metal legs. Lucy assumed this was where Anna did her healing. A plastic cantilevered box of the type used by hobbyists to keep fishing lures or sewing items or model paints overspilled with tiny bottles in blue, green and brown glass. Essential oils, Lucy thought, spotting a just-legible, oil-stained label that read *Rose Otto*.

'You'd better sit, then,' Anna said dismissively, waving a hand at a bench upholstered in black vinyl that had split at various points, revealing foam the colour of pea soup.

Lucy moved a tatty crocheted throw – black, naturally – and sat in the resulting space. She looked down and caught sight of a couple of smoked-down roll-ups. Or were they joints? Was that why Bernard had been so keen to warn Anna that Lucy was a cop?

No offer of coffee. Instead, Anna sat facing Lucy, arms still folded, black fingernails poking through the open stitches of her cuffs.

'So?'

Lucy smiled. It amused her to be facing a woman old enough to have teenaged kids acting like one herself. It reminded her of her early days in uniform, trying to stop Örebro youth from hurting themselves or making themselves vulnerable by drinking too much.

She explained the purpose of her visit.

'I'm wondering what you can tell me about the band?'

Anna rolled her eyes. 'That was a long time ago.'

'I know, but you held an important position. You ran the fan club, didn't you?'

'Yeah, but so what?'

'Well, did you ever see any of them show more than the usual amount of interest in Ulrik's crimes?'

'I don't know. What is the usual amount?'

Lucy kept her breathing nice and steady. As a child she'd had to contend with the taunts of three older brothers. It had given her both a thick skin and bottomless levels of patience.

'Well, for example, did any member of the band ever talk to you – or maybe you overheard them talking – about maybe admiring what Ulrik was doing? Wanting to copy him? Anything like that?'

'No.'

'No?'

'Do you want me to say it in a different language? *Nei. Ingen. Nyet.*'

'That's impressive. Norwegian, Danish *and* Russian. Did you study modern languages at university?'

'I did and it certainly helped. Running a fan club you have to learn how to say a few things in a lot of languages. You'd be surprised how many female fans wanted nude photos of the band.'

'I suppose Björn got the most requests, being the lead singer.'

Anna pulled her hair back and flipped it over her shoulder.

'I guess.'

'Did he enjoy the attention?'

'They were young guys getting all the drink and drugs and girls they wanted. What do you think?'

'Did you ever see him with groupies?'

'I wasn't on tour with them. I wouldn't know about that.'

Lucy nodded. Anna had just made her first mistake. Second if you counted the stubbed-out roaches on the floor.

'No? Only I saw a photo taken at an outdoor festival of some kind. You were in it. Backstage.'

'I forgot, yeah. That was BeltaneFest. But I wasn't exactly touring with them. I just had a backstage pass.'

'You with a couple of bikers. Pretty scary-looking guys, actually. Do you remember them?'

Anna nodded. 'The Werewolves. Cool name, decidedly uncool people. If you want to talk about groupies, talk to them. They were like hyenas, fighting for scraps off the big boys' table.'

'Just going back to Björn for a moment, what I'm wondering is, whether you ever saw him get aggressive, maybe even violent with a groupie.'

Anna's eyes flashed white from the smoky caves of their sockets.

'He was a sweet guy, OK? No way would he have hurt one of the girls. You're not seriously suggesting he's got anything to do with these latest murders? Anyway, Ulrik was the one killing girls, and you said this current guy is killing ex-cops. Not even slightly the same victim profile.'

Lucy made a note before looking back at Anna.

'Forgive me, Anna, but that's quite a technical term, isn't it? Victim profile?'

'Is it?'

'I'd say so, yes.'

'I read, OK? About serial killers. I find it interesting. What drives people to do evil.'

'Quite a change for a woman who used to handle fan mail for an avowedly Satan-worshipping metal band.'

Anna snorted. 'Oh, please! Look, back then, the scene was super-competitive. All those bands were desperately trying to outdo each other. Who could write the most extreme lyrics, create the darkest, doomiest riffs. The stage acts were just that: an act. They didn't worship Satan. The good ones worshipped music, the rest? As long as they could party hard, they didn't really care.'

Lucy was inclined to believe Anna, especially since now they were talking, she'd dropped the sarcastic act and seemed genuinely eager to help.

'So what do you think drives them to do it? You must have spent a fair amount of time with Ulrik. Why did he do it?'

'Honestly? In his case, I just think he was – is, I mean – batshit crazy. The others, who knows? Maybe it's something in their brain. There's a theory that they have underdeveloped limbic systems.'

'Yeah, I read that, too.'

'Listen, I meant what I said about Björn. And I can't see any of the others being influenced or whatever by Ulrik. I mean, he was their manager and they trusted him to make the business decisions, but he wasn't some kind of Svengali, OK? I mean, if he'd have wanted to, like, train one of them up as his apprentice or whatever, they'd have freaked out. Probably called the cops if they'd known just how far he was taking it.'

'Then—'

Anna held up a finger.

'I haven't finished. I was going to say, if you want to focus on anyone, you should focus on that guy in the photo with me. Klas Helander, his name is. I can easily imagine him carving people up for fun.'

'Why do you say that, Anna?'

'I heard him once. At BeltaneFest. Him and this other guy. Lenny? No, Kenny. They were talking about drugs and Klas was in this total meltdown. My God, the language he used, it's why I can still remember. He said something like, "If they try anything, I'll shove a pipe through their hearts and gut them like dead elk."'

'A pipe?'

'Yes. At first I couldn't work it out. I mean, like a smoking pipe? But I think he meant something off a bike. Maybe a bit of frame, or an exhaust pipe.'

Lucy made another note. This was great. Sven would be so pleased, poor guy. The stress was really getting to him. But Anna was serving up Klas on a plate. He'd practically admitted to using the killer's MO. OK, not exactly, but elements of it. If nothing else, it showed he was a man with violent tendencies.

A man like the Devil of Axberg, then.

36

PARTILLE, NEAR GOTHENBERG, SWEDEN

After touring what felt like half the country on her bike, stopping in at biker bars and clubs all over southern Sweden, Stella finally caught a break. In a small town eight kilometres west of Gothenburg, a friendly bartender told her she might find Helander at a truckstop five kilometres up the E20.

She pulled up next to a lone bike, a Harley Davidson custom-painted to resemble neon-green crocodile skin, with a monstrously fat rear tyre, extended front forks and pulled-back handlebars. Her Triumph looked comically undersized next to the American monster.

Inside, once her eyes had acclimatised to the gloom, she spotted him immediately. A tall, silver-haired biker playing pool, apparently against himself. He wore a cut-off denim vest over a black T-shirt. The denim was festooned with enamel badges.

Holding her helmet under her arm, she approached him slowly, from the front, not wanting to start off on the wrong foot.

'Hey,' she said. 'Fancy a game?'

The biker snapped off a shot, ricocheting the target ball, a purple spot, off a cushion and into a corner pocket. He shouldered the cue and raised his eyes to hers. Slowly, he looked her up and down.

'You ride or is that how you get guys like me into bed?'

She locked eyes with him.

'Come outside and take a look.'

She turned and stalked off, pulse ticking along quite nicely, thank you, and no matter she'd just crossed swords with 180 pounds of lean, sinewy muscle plus pool cue.

With the biker's boot heels clicking on the bar's wooden floor behind her, she pushed through the doors and into sunshine so fierce it set her eyes watering. Blinking away the moisture, she turned to face him.

'That's my ride over there, beside Bikezilla.'

He grinned at the quip.

'Triumph. Nice. So, you just out for a ride?'

The look in his eyes. She'd seen it before. Wary. Calculating.

Villains had it. Terrorists had it. Serial killers had it. Oftentimes whether or not they knew they were using it. Man's natural suspicion of the unknown, ratcheted up by a life devoted to evil.

Right now, the look was telling her a story. A story about a man who hadn't survived as long as he had, in the world he'd chosen, without developing reserves of cunning that would shame a fox, and the ability to read people that would produce the same effect in a forensic psychiatrist.

No lies then.

'Not exactly. Though I've put a few thousand kilometres on the clock since I started out. I'm looking for someone.'

'You a cop?'

'Would that make a difference to whether you agree to talk to me?'

He shrugged. 'I've got nothing to hide.'

'My name's Stella.'

He held out a hand. 'Klas.'

They shook. She was prepared for a mini-trial of strength, the winner declared by the number of unbroken fingers. But he was gentlemanly about it. Firm, dry pressure, a quick release.

'I meant what I said in there,' she said. 'I can play and talk at the same time.'

He appeared to think about it. Then nodded.

'Hundred krone and a round of drinks.'

Inside, he racked up and flipped a ten-krone coin. Stella called heads. Lost. Bad omen.

Klas broke with a ferocious strike that sent spots and stripes scurrying all over the table, clacking and spinning like panicking fish fleeing a shark. Two balls rattled into pockets, one of each flavour.

'Stripes,' Klas said, already lining up a shot.

The ball slammed home dead-centre in the jaws of the pocket with a sharp, percussive crack. Stella nodded. The guy had talent.

'You used to run security for a band called Sepülkå,' she said.

'Now and then, yes. Turned out their manager was the Brain Surgeon. That kind of put an end to the gig.'

'You've seen there's someone out there replicating his crimes?'

'Plenty of twisted fuckers in the world.'

Slam. Another stripe rocketed home. Klas strode around the table eyeing up possibilities. Stella did the same, keeping two cushions between them.

'When you were working for Ahlgren, did you ever see anyone at a gig who struck you as, I don't know, odd in any way?'

He paused his assessment of the geometry problem laid out before him on the blue baize. His face cracked into a grin. White teeth. Good dentistry. Or good genes. Somehow it belied the image of the grizzled biker. She imagined they lived on takeaway pizzas and burgers. Didn't care overmuch about a proper oral hygiene regime.

'These are Sepülkå fans we're talking about. You do know that, right? I mean, "odd" was table stakes. They used to turn up with roadkill hanging from their belts, know what I mean?'

Stella smiled back. 'OK, then. Not "odd". I mean really strange. Weird, you know? I'm talking about someone, probably a guy, who was overly interested in the killings. Anyone who tried to engage you in conversation about what was going on. We're working on the theory that the current killer may be a disciple of Ahlgren's.'

Klas settled on his shot and stretched across the table. With surprising delicacy, he rolled the cue ball into a blue stripe and sent it clicking off its neighbour before dropping silently into a pocket. He straightened and rested the butt of his cue on his boot.

'Nobody like that springs to mind. It was a long time ago, though. My memory's not what it was.'

He lined up another shot. Stella tried to remember how much cash she had on her.

'What about Björn Lyngstad?'

'What about him?'

'How did he seem when the news about the killings broke?'

'You think it was him? I thought the cops back then had Ulrik in a slam—' He thunked another ball, an orange, home into a centre pocket. ' – dunk.'

'They did. I'm just looking at people who were close enough to Ahlgren to maybe get a taste for what he was doing.'

'It could be. Björn was pretty extreme. The other guys? They just played up to the image. All that Satanic bullshit, you know? But he was really into it. Kept asking me to get him a girl he could sacrifice.'

Stella, who had heard, seen and, not that she would admit it to anybody, performed all manner of heinous acts was still shocked.

'Was he serious? Or was it some kind of rockstar acting-out?'

'Oh, he was serious all right. Showed me this big fucking knife he'd had made by some folksy artistic blacksmith up in Norrbotten County. All kinds of Satanic symbols on it.'

That was interesting. Norrbotten County was in the north and its capital was Luleå, where Sören Roos had chosen for his retirement.

'You didn't...'

Klas snorted. 'Listen, Stella. Bikers have a bad rep, OK? But were we procuring virgins for some overpaid arsehole to cut up like a reindeer? No. Absolutely not.'

'But you did get drugs for them.'

He miscued his shot, and the white ball hopped on the baize, barely kissing the target ball, which shifted by perhaps three centimetres before spinning to a stop.

'Par for the course,' he said, scowling at the cue ball. 'And I'll deny it if this goes any further.'

Had she touched a nerve? Time would tell.

She nodded and rounded the table to line up her first shot. Klas got out of her way, which she appreciated, instead of standing behind her so he could check out her arse as she played. A biker and a gentleman. Unless he was a serial killer's acolyte.

She pocketed her first ball, a red. Not as cleanly as Klas, but a pocket was a pocket, even if it rattled off both leather-clad jaws before going down the throat.

Time to switch it up.

'Where were you on May first, Klas?'

'I'm a suspect?'

'I'm just trying to put names, dates and places together. Do you remember?'

He shrugged. 'Not off the top of my head. I was probably hanging out in a bar or at our clubhouse.'

She rattled off the dates when Barbro and Fredrika had been murdered. 'How about those?'

'There's guys I could check with.'

'Guys? Like who?'

'Other members. Maybe Olaf. He's our membership secretary. He and I hang out a lot.'

The phrase 'membership secretary' conjured up an image of blazered middle-class Stockholmers vetting applications to join tennis clubs or Swedish folk dancing societies, not outlaw biker gangs.

'Something funny?' Klas asked.

'Olaf who?' she countered.

'Wallin.'

'OK. And that job involves what, exactly?'

'Keeping records. Checking out applicants. Monitoring their progress.'

'Would you have records of who was a member back when you were doing the security for Sepülkå?'

'Yes. But you'll need a warrant to look at them.'

'Fair enough. I think my boss would be happy with that, given we're investigating the murders of three current or former police officers.'

Klas shrugged. 'Am I supposed to be intimidated?'

Stella pocketed another ball, a clean shot right the way down the table and into a corner pocket.

'Let me put it to you this way.' She saw an easy pot and sank it with a crack like a pistol shot. 'Imagine someone had brutally murdered three of *your* members. And you thought a police officer might be involved. Would you let anything stand in your way?'

He stroked his moustache. She could see she'd got through to him. The question was, who, or what, was lurking behind that abundant facial hair?

'Can we go and talk to Olaf now?' she asked. 'Maybe take a look at your social calendar as well as your membership records? If you've got nothing to hide, that is.'

He sniffed loudly and stared at the table.

'Let's finish the game first. But we're changing the stakes. I win, you hand over a thousand krone and a case of aquavit and I'll see you when you've got a warrant. You win, fine, we'll go and see the boys.'

Stella regarded the table. The score was five–four to Klas. Two more and the black for him to win; three more and the black for her. One of her spots was hanging right over a pocket. A child could sink it. But her other two balls were in mid-table nowomansland. Klas, on the other hand, had a stripe sitting maybe ten centimetres from a corner pocket and his final ball hard against the baulk cushion.

'Deal,' she said.

Over the next few minutes, maybe owing to the dramatically increased stakes, neither player potted a ball. Then Klas sank his penultimate stripe only to suffer a near-miss. His final ball fluttered between the jaws of a side pocket before rolling free. Finally, Stella had a clear shot and sank it cleanly. A second ball followed, leaving her with a tricky pot along a side cushion and then off Klas's remaining stripe.

Taking a long, slow breath as if she were lining up a rifle shot, she let it out and stroked the cue ball in between heartbeats. The contact was clean and the purple spot rolled straight up the cushion, kissed Klas's ball and right-turned to drop out of sight.

Stella caught the bartender's eye. He'd been watching the game avidly while polishing the same glass. He shook his head quickly. His meaning was pretty clear. Best not beat the leader of the Werewolves in a game of pool. Maybe he'd find another use for the length of varnished maple wood in his right hand.

Stella stared back defiantly. Klas wasn't the only one with a cue, and even if he was the Devil of Axberg, he'd a way to go before he could match her kill tally.

She assessed angles, distances. Checked the position of Klas's remaining ball. Then she tapped her cue on the head rail beside the right-hand corner pocket.

She bent low over the table and cued up her shot on the eight-ball. A memory swam up from her subconscious. Her and Richard playing pool against a couple of local lads on their honeymoon in a Palermo sports bar. Cheap red wine sloshed into thick-walled bistro tumblers, scratched and cloudy from much dishwashing. Richard's drunken grin as he doubled a pot off the side cushion, much to their opponents' disgust.

'Il maestro!' he'd crowed, before sending the cue ball hopping clear off the table, to general applause and laughter from the other patrons.

Her vision swam and sparkled as the bar lights refracted through sudden tears. She swiped them away. Refocused on the shot.

'Help me now, Maestro,' she muttered and pulled the cue back.

With a smart crack, she sent the white ball down the table. A second snick as the white hit the black and sent it on its journey towards the corner pocket. She held her breath.

37

To Stella, the next few seconds passed in slow motion.

The '8' on the black ball rolled round and around, coming up to greet her, blinking its double-eye. The distance to the pocket decreased. Thirty centimetres, twenty, ten, five, three...

She could hear her pulse thrum in her ears.

The ball made contact with the lefthand jaw. Crap! It was going to bounce out. Instead it began to spin on its axis, the '8' revolving on the uppermost surface, on the very lip of the pocket. Only the nap of the baize was keeping it on the playing surface.

She heard Klas's voice behind her. A deep, drawn-out, sonorous, 'Come on!'

Then the '8' began to wobble, describing erratic circles, and the ball wandered off-true by a couple of millimetres. It was enough. Having flirted with the pocket for what felt like a full minute, it dropped out of sight.

Time sped up again.

'Shit the devil!'

Klas was looking at her with a mixture of amazement and disgust, his lip curling. The barman had turned away and was replacing the now-gleaming glass on the shelf with its grimier brothers and sisters.

Stella laid her cue on the baize and rounded the table, hand stuck out in front of her.

'Good game. Thanks.'

Klas gripped her hand and this time did all he could to break her fingers. Expecting the move, Stella had slid her keys out of her pocket. Currently the jagged edges were digging into Klas's palm, causing the biker to wince before backing off on the pressure.

'Your place, then,' she said, with a smile.

* * *

Confounding her expectations, Klas didn't try any tricks on the ride to the club. He kept his speed well below the limit, cruising along on his customised Harley almost as if leading a ride-out for foreign visitors and anxious to show off the scenery. Even through the thick foam padding of her helmet, Stella could hear the throaty chug of the Harley's big V-twin engine, rendered all the more fruity by the modified exhaust system, which had had the last half-metre of chrome piping removed and swept up behind the rider's legs.

After five kilometres, Klas indicated and then swung off the highway onto a small county road and then again onto a smaller road still. The forest closed in on both sides of the road and they rode along two abreast for half a kilometre before a long, low building painted Falun Red hoved into view at the crest of a rise.

Outside, leaning on their kickstands were half a dozen bikes. Mostly Harleys like Klas's, and one or two like Roger Amundsen's Indian, another American firm that looked back to the forties for inspiration. No bikers visible, however. Inside the clubhouse, presumably.

Stella pulled up beside Klas and dismounted, heeling out the kickstand and settling the Triumph at a slight angle on the black tarmac. Helmet off, she drew in a lungful of air scented with pine sap and petrol, a potent combination.

Klas came to join her.

'Olaf's inside.' He pointed to a low-slung Harley in firetruck red. 'That's his ride.'

She followed him through the door of the clubhouse. It had been reinforced with a riveted steel plate that looked like it might stop an anti-tank missile. To each side, barred windows were curtained off, revealing nothing of the interior.

Inside, it felt pretty much like any other rural Swedish bar. Hunting and fishing trophies mounted on varnished wooden plaques dominated the walls. Behind the bar, amid the multicoloured bottles of spirits, hung a monstrous pike almost a metre in length. An elk's head with antlers twice as wide wore a lugubrious expression as if to say, *'I wandered out to get a bite to eat and now look at me!'*

'You want a drink, Stella?' Klas asked.

She shook her head. 'I'm more interested in the information, thanks.'

A few other bikers looked at her curiously. Her leathers said, *Relax, boys, I'm one of the gang*, but if Klas had pinned her as a cop just from her appearance, she guessed they probably had the same intuition. With a fluttery sensation in the pit of her stomach, she realised she had just entered the secluded base of a small organised crime gang with links to the drugs trade. How easy would it be for them to kill her and then dispose of her body out here in the Boonies where nobody would ever find it?

She shoved the thought down and stamped on the butterflies very, very hard. For a start, many people had tried variants on that approach to dealing with Stella Cole before. Yet here she was, walking among the living.

Secondly, a biker-on-biker murder might go unnoticed, depending on where and how you did it. But offing a cop would result in a huge manhunt, just like the one she was conducting right now. *Courage, Stel*, she thought.

Klas nodded to a biker with his boots up on a low coffee table. 'Olaf, a word.'

The man got to his feet, setting his beer bottle on the table.

Like Klas, his denim vest was covered in metal pins. But there, the resemblance to the media image of an outlaw biker ended. He was clean-shaven. And where Klas was physically imposing, here was a man Stella could imagine in another life teaching in a high school or running a small business. Average height, average weight, pleasant looks. Perhaps that was why he'd been given the boring-sounding job of membership secretary. He was probably the only one with the requisite skills.

'This is Stella.' Klas leaned his head in Stella's direction. 'She's a cop.'

Olaf stiffened. His eyes darted over to a door at the far end of the room. Stella pictured a stash of drugs or maybe a laptop holding the gang's accounts.

'I'm investigating three murders,' she said. 'Of cops. Current and former. I don't know anything about your business interests and I don't care. But Klas tells me you might have records of who was a member of the Werewolves around the time you were handling security for a band called Sepülkå. Were you a member then yourself?'

Olaf stuck his hands in his pockets. Shrugged. 'Joined when I was eighteen. Back in '03. So, yeah. My first job was babysitting that bunch of arseholes. Middle-class kids playing at being devil-worshippers.'

'Could you let me have a look at your membership list?'

Olaf looked pleadingly at his boss.

'That's private shit, Klas. Has she got a warrant?'

Stella spoke first.

'No, *she* hasn't got a warrant, although if you like, *she* could ride back to Örebro and get one. Of course, then *she* might also ask her colleagues in the drug squad to help her out. Probably request support from the Regional Tactical Support unit as well.' She smiled sweetly at him. 'You know, just in case things got…colourful.'

'Just show her, OK?' Klas said. He turned to Stella. 'But you're not taking anything away and we're not giving you the list. You look, and you take whatever you can remember. Any more than that and, yes, you will need a warrant and you can bring the drug dogs and the cowboys and anyone else you fucking like.'

'Works for me.'

With the sullen look of a schoolboy heading to detention, Olaf led them to the side door he'd glanced at earlier. Beyond lay a space utterly different to the hyper-masculine environment of the main room. It might have been the office of a firm of provincial lawyers. Or a small local police station, for that matter. Filing cabinets, two desks facing each other. Computers. A map of Örebro county on the wall. No windows but a bright strip of neon lights.

Olaf pulled out a wheeled office chair and sat. His slender fingers danced over the keys and then he swung the screen round to face Stella.

'There. Werewolves members, full and probationary, from January one to December thirty one, 2003.'

She dragged the other swivel chair around the pair of desks and sat beside Olaf. The first thing that struck her was how small the gang was in '03. Just seventeen members. Somehow she'd imagined a much larger grouping. At least it made it easier to scan them looking for any names she recognised.

There was Helander, K. With a note in the rightmost column of the spreadsheet: 'Pres.' On the last row, Wallin, O. His note read 'Prob.' Her eye skittered to a halt at the name directly above Olaf's on the list like a drug dog faced with a suspicious saddlebag.

Varela, K. 'Prob.'

Stella nodded and turned away from the computer monitor.

'Thanks. Nothing there that really moves things forward, but I appreciate the help all the same.'

Her mind was racing. Thank God they'd complied with Carol Varela's request not to make her husband's identity public. It meant the bikers occupying the small office with her were unaware of the possible link to one of their members. Would they have shown her the list otherwise? She strongly doubted it.

Varela wasn't the commonest of surnames in Sweden. Now

two had turned up in the same case. Could they be related? A probationary member of a biker gang. And a decorated homicide cop and then undercover operative with the drug squad. Stranger things had happened. Oh, yes. Much stranger things had happened.

And, after weeks of fruitless searching, Stella saw a glimmer of light in the bleak darkness of the investigation. Because what if this wasn't about the Hunter Killers and Ulrik Ahlgren at all?

* * *

By the time everybody had arrived at Örebro copshop the next morning, Stella had been hard at work for two hours. She'd requested the personnel files for Joel Varela, Barbro Ekblad and Fredrika Rudbeck. Received an automated reply explaining, in typical SPA officialese, that their office hours were 9:00 a.m. to 5:00 p.m. and that her request, while greatly valued, would be dealt with according to a strict queuing system.

She'd also run a search on the national police computer: 'Varela, K'. The computer had returned three hits. One was a woman, Karolina Varela, arrested in 2010 aged fifty-six for shoplifting. She'd be seventy-eight now. Strike one. One was a minor, Karl Varela, just fourteen years old. Cautioned in 2022 for a public disorder offence at a climate change school strike. Strike two. And one was a twenty-one year old. Kenneth Varela, arrested on a drugs possession charge in 2005. Occupation given as mechanic. Address given as the Werewolves clubhouse. Next of kin given as Lars Varela. A further search revealed that Joel Varela was Kenneth's cousin. Home run!

Lucy arrived next, and came straight over to Stella's desk.

'I spoke to Anna Eriksson yesterday. She struck me as a reliable witness. Bit snotty to begin with but she warmed up in the end.'

'Must have been your girlish charm,' Stella quipped.

Lucy smiled. 'Anyway, she didn't think much of the idea Björn might have actually done anything. In her words he came off as a bit of a sweetie. All the Satanic stuff was just for show. But she did point the finger, pretty firmly, actually, at Klas Helander.'

'Point it how?'

'I know it's hearsay, but she said she overheard him talk with another Werewolves member about wanting to stab and gut someone who, I'm not sure what exactly, but maybe double-crossed him in some drug deal. That sounds pretty similar to our guy, doesn't it?'

Stella wrinkled her nose. She didn't want to dampen Lucy's enthusiasm, but not only was Anna's testimony hearsay, it wasn't especially convincing. A biker making violent threats to a *rival* would be one thing. But what Klas had done was essentially boast to a friend. Not the same thing at all. And the Brain Surgeon and his latter-day disciple weren't into disembowelling, either.

'I was with him yesterday,' she said instead. 'If I'm honest, I didn't get a vibe off him. Well, not that kind anyway. I wouldn't be at all surprised if he was into some deeply shady shit, but a serial killer? I'm not seeing it. Sorry,' she added, seeing Lucy's downcast expression.

'But we should keep him on the radar anyway, yes?'

'Definitely.'

'Good. And also, one of my other leads came good yesterday. We finally got a hit on Björn Lyngstad. No wonder we couldn't find him. He changed his name ten years ago. He's now calling himself Jonas Andersson.'

'Which is, what, the commonest name in Sweden?'

'I know, right? There are thousands of them. But it doesn't matter. I got an address, too.'

'Please tell me it's closer than Luleå. I don't think I can face another flight up north just yet.'

Lucy nodded. 'Definitely closer, but it's still a bit of a trek. He bought a place on Gotland. Hope you don't get seasick.'

Stella walked over to the big map of Sweden that occupied half the wall between the doors to the CID unit and the kitchen. Sweden's largest island lay roughly ninety kilometres due east of the mainland. She checked travel times on her phone. Six hours and forty-two minutes, of which half would be taken up with a ferry journey.

She wrinkled her nose. Gotland. Where Sören Roos's sheep came from. Thoughts tumbled over themselves in an effort to be heard first.

Joel Varela and Sören Roos worked together back in the day. They were part of the team that caught Ulrik Ahlgren. Twenty years later, Joel is murdered, stabbed through the heart with a sharpened horn from the same breed now husbanded by Sören.

The lead singer of the band Ahlgren managed is now living on Gotland. He expressed an unhealthy interest in his manager's crimes. The prosecutor dropped charges against him to focus on Ahlgren. Had something happened to set the two cops against each other? She wished she'd asked to see Sören's sheep. A ram with a sawn-off horn would have been grounds for an arrest.

All that would have to wait. She and Lucy had a trip to plan.

But before they left there was someone Stella wanted to talk to. While Lucy made the travel arrangements, Stella called Kenneth Varela's father, Lars.

38

KUMLA

Lars Varela lived in a neat brick house in Kumla, half a kilometre from the prison. He looked older than his sixty-nine years, with an unkempt thatch of white hair and thick, wiry eyebrows like snowy eaves on a traditional timber house.

Sitting in his well-tended back garden with a china mug of excellent coffee, Stella looked him in the eye.

'I'm sorry for your loss. Joel was a good cop.'

His response surprised her: a *hmph* sound through his nose.

'You sure about that, are you?' he asked.

'Aren't you?'

'I think while he was in Homicide, yes. My nephew was honest. Believed in serving the public. Performed his duties with integrity. But after he transferred into the drug squad, well now, something changed.'

'Can you be more specific?' Stella asked, already suspecting she knew what was coming. Joel Varela wouldn't have been the first cop to discover that temptation was always lurking just round the corner for officers investigating organised crime.

'We weren't all that close but we'd see each other at family gatherings, that sort of thing. He started turning up in designer clothes, an expensive wristwatch, looking like a pimp, basically. Talking about his foreign holidays. One day, he came to see me and he was driving a Porsche. Can you believe it? A fucking Porsche! On a police officer's salary? I don't think so.'

'Did you ask him where he got the money?'

'Yes, I asked him! I knew, of course, but I wanted to see what he'd say.'

'And what did he say?'

'He said he'd been day trading foreign currency on his days off. As if! Joel could barely decipher his bank statements, let alone trade currency online.'

'He was on the take.'

Lars shrugged and made a noise in the back of his throat. 'I guess we'll never know.'

Stella filed this new piece of intelligence away. Her alternative theory was growing stronger with each passing day. The next question she wanted to ask him involved his son. That was always tricky territory for any parent, but especially one who was apparently a recently retired straight arrow in the prison service. She decided to soften him up a little first. Distract him with the past.

'It said in the files that you used to be a prison officer,' she said with a smile. 'At Kumla.'

He nodded, and looked skyward for a second.

'I put thirty-one years in. When I retired I couldn't see the point of moving away. Paulina's happy here, too. She's got her swimming group and her needlework club. There are prettier towns in Örebro County, but all our friends are here.'

'So you must have come into contact with Ulrik Ahlgren.'

He nodded, then stuck a finger into his ear and poked around for a bit before removing it, inspecting the glob of yellow wax on the tip and flicking it away towards the hedge.

'Him, Johansson, Namdar, Malenius, Bergdorf, Lutz, Al-Qabasi, all of them. Ahlgren wasn't the worst by a long shot. In terms of his behaviour inside, I mean. Their crimes were all pretty bad, but I always had him at the top of my weirdo-of-the-century list.'

He smiled, an avuncular expression that grooved deep crows' feet into his cheeks. 'I never really bought into the whole rehabilitation and redemption narrative the authorities are so keen on. Too many bleeding hearts in the justice system, if you ask me. You know, the same old bullshit every time some paedo murders a kid or a terrorist blows himself up at a concert. "Oh, it was his mother." Or, "He grew up in poverty". Or "He's been radicalised". I mean, fuck me, there are lots of us who had strict parents or dodgy friends, or who only got second-hand clothes when we were kids. But you don't see us chopping up young girls or torching synagogues, do you?'

Stella nodded. The older she got, and the more she came face to face with the worst human beings – some of them anyway – were willing to do to each other, the more she felt that a deep hole with inward-sloping sides would be a far more efficient and socially responsible response than any amount of group therapy or sessions with acclaimed forensic psychiatrists.

None of which she said. Not appropriate for a serving SPA officer. Especially not one currently on a very rocky path to her own redemption.

Although she'd come to talk to Lars about Kenneth, now they'd started talking about Ahlgren she wanted to probe further. After all, his original crimes had been the inspiration, if that was the right word, for what the Devil of Axberg was doing to the men and women who'd put him behind bars.

'When you were there, Lars, was there anyone who visited Ahlgren maybe an unusual number of times? I'm just trying to find out if he had the chance to school someone else in his methods.'

He shook his head, then resumed investigating his ear.

'Back then the Bunker inmates weren't allowed visitors. But I'll tell you what. He used to get a whole shitload of fan mail. Pretty much entirely from women. Can you believe it?'

Stella could. Back in the UK, it was a source of constant amazement, disgust and occasionally very black humour to cops that serial killers attracted a very particular kind of female fan. Oddly enough, the more sexually deviant their crimes, the greater the volume of fan mail.

'It's the same in Britain. I think they believe they can give them something they never got from their mothers.'

Lars's bushy white eyebrows shot upwards. If they really *had* been cloaking the eaves of a Falun Red farmhouse, they'd just have dumped snow all over the porch.

'You really believe all that psychological bullshit, Stella? You know what I think? I think those women get off on it. We had to read all his mail before he could receive it. For obvious reasons. I mean some of it was basically pornographic.

'There was this one woman. Ella Rasmusson, her name was. I'll never forget it.' He dislodged another lump of amber-coloured wax, inspected it, then flicked it towards the hedge. 'She used to write to him twice a week. Maybe she still does, for all I know. Anyway, only about one in three of her letters got through. But when she wasn't trying to fuel his wank-fantasies, she was telling him how unfair it was he'd been jailed. How the cops were all corrupt. And how, if she could only get some help, she'd take them all out, one by one.'

He paused, seemingly lost in his memories. Stella took the opportunity to circle back to her original line of questioning. Although she'd be paying a visit to Ahlgren's penpal before too long.

'Lars, I actually came to talk to you about Kenneth.'

His eyes locked onto hers. 'What about him?'

'I found him on a membership list for a biker gang. The Werewolves. Did you know about that?'

Lars wiped his forehead and puffed out his cheeks.

'I know he dropped out of college and bought himself a motorbike with the money his granny left him for his studies.'

He knew. Stella could see it in his eyes. Something too painful to admit to before a cop pulled it from you like a dentist extracting a rotting tooth.

'So he didn't tell you?' she prompted.

'Look, Stella, I was pretty mad with him at the time. We had words. Well, no, what we had was a massive argument. Things were said that probably shouldn't have been. He moved out and found himself somewhere else to kip. After that, we didn't really see each other for a few years.'

Stella nodded. 'That sounds like you do see him now.'

'Yeah, sometimes. All that was twenty years ago. We learned to tiptoe round the tricky stuff. He's married now. Got a kiddie. Another on the way.' He patted his chest and smiled. 'I'm a grandpa now!'

'So he left the gang?'

'I'm not sure. I think they have this stupid code. You know? Like, the only way you leave the gang is horizontally.'

'Do you have an address for him?'

'I'll have to get it for you. It's in the address book. I'm too old to start farting around with phones for that sort of stuff. Anyway, Paulina looks after all of that.'

He levered himself out of his lawn chair and returned five minutes later with a scrap of paper on which he'd scrawled an address in Örebro. She tucked it into her wallet. Connected the dots: at the time of his murder, Joel was on the take in the drug squad. His nephew was a member of the Werewolves, a minor organised crime group. The Werewolves supplying drugs to Sepülkå. Which was led by Björn Lyngstad, and managed by Ulrik Ahlgren, the man Joel had caught as a member of the Hunter Killers.

Had she found the killer's true motive?

She needed to do more digging on Joel Varela. Because she was becoming increasingly sure that they'd been chasing phantoms all along.

39

VISBY, GOTLAND

The man formerly known as Björn Lyngstad was opening up when the two women stepped in from the sunlit street to the gloom of the cafe.

After leaving the band, he'd drifted for a few years. Fans thought you must be loaded if you'd made a few albums and done a few tours, but death metal was never where the money was. And they'd blown most of their royalties up their noses or poured it down their throats.

But Björn had always been smarter than the others. Sure, he'd partied hard, harder, often. But he'd also got his name on the songwriting royalties contract, and he'd salted some money away like herrings in a barrel.

So, when he'd seen the cafe for sale in Visby on a long weekend trip with his then girlfriend, he'd found himself a lawyer and pulled the trigger. A few fans had tracked him down and word had spread about Cafe Valhalla.

He'd decked the place out with a few bits of memorabilia, but really the money was from the tourist trade, and they were lukewarm on the whole Satanic metal bullshit. So black guitars in scaly finishes like lizard-skin hung on the walls alongside watercolours by local artists and traditional Gotland farming tools. It was a real hotchpotch, but it seemed to work.

Or maybe it was Maddy. He'd met his wife two years after opening his doors for the first time. She'd been looking for a job and he'd taken her on to run the kitchen.

In truth, if she'd not been able to serve a plate of gravlax without burning it he'd still have been happy. Because Maddy was beautiful. Smart, too. But, my God, the woman was hot! It was her mouth, mostly. Sensuous, always on the point of smiling. Guys came in and couldn't take their eyes off her. Girls, too, come to that. He'd proposed after a year and she'd accepted straightaway.

She knew who he was, of course. In fact, the first question she asked when he'd interviewed her at an outside table over a coffee and croissant, was, 'So, were you really into all that Satanic stuff?'

And he'd smiled and shook his head, setting his mane of blonde hair waving in the breeze wafting across the square.

'It was all an act. You know, for the band's image.'

Which was true. More or less. Björn had never seen the point of all that devil worship crap. But Ulrik had been insistent that they play up the whole 'Lords of Darkness,' thing. The fans seemed to like it. And if it sold a few more records and tickets to the live shows, why not?

Then, when Ulrik got himself arrested for all those groupie-murders, well, let's be honest, that did kind of take the shine off things. Björn found himself in the frame, too. One of the cops had a real hard-on for him. What the hell was his name, Olsson? Yeah. And some weird, fucked-up Bible name, too. What the hell was it? Oh, yeah. Nikodemus.

Nikodemus 'Call-me-Nik' Olsson had decided early on that Björn knew more than he was letting on. His suspicions hardened until he started hammering him on being an accomplice. Björn had stared him out, lawyer at his side, paid for by the record company, and denied everything. In the end the prosecutor got involved and told Olsson to drop it. Apparently Ulrik was a slam-dunk and that was enough for the Swedish people.

The band fell apart pretty fast after that. Björn was distracted. Reckoned he'd got PTSD. Started doing more drugs than was strictly healthy. Missing rehearsals. Harri called him a 'fucking narcissistic psycho'. Which was a bit rich coming from a bassist who paid for a set of erectable black leather batwings out of his own fucking pocket. Jesus!

They all blamed Björn.

Björn blamed Nikodemus Olsson.

He shrugged. That was then. Except was it? Because the two women approaching him at the bar reeked of cop. The shorter of the two was pulling out her ID.

'Björn?' she asked. 'Björn Lyngstad?'

'That's me,' he said. 'Although I go by the name Jonas Andersson these days.'

He carried on doing what he was doing, taking an upended chair off a table and setting it the right-way up on the floor.

'I'm Detective Inspector Stella Cole and this is Detective Inspector Lucy Magnusson. Can we have a word?'

Björn pushed the chair underneath the table, leaning on the back rest so that its wooden feet shrieked against the rough stone floor tiles.

'I'm kind of busy, right now. We're opening up. What's this about?'

'It's about three murders,' Lucy said. 'The victims' names were Joel Varela, Barbro Ekblad and Fredrika Rudbeck. Do those names mean anything to you?'

Other police IDs flickered in Björn's mind like images back-projected at a stage show. The woman, Ekblad. She'd been the first to interview him.

He shrugged.

'Should they?' It was a clever answer. He congratulated himself. Not a denial they could prove him wrong on.

The cop called Lucy smiled. Quite pretty, really. Not in

Maddy's league, obviously. But Björn reckoned no more than one woman in a hundred even came close.

'They were members of the team that arrested your former manager for a series of sadistic murders back in 2003.'

He shook his head, then gathered his hair in his fist and pulled it into a loose ponytail before letting it go.

'I try not to think about that. It was a long time ago. And a very unpleasant period in my life.'

'Well, someone's copying him so I'm afraid there's more unpleasantness already,' Lucy said. 'Where can we talk?'

Björn stared at her. Wondering whether he needed a lawyer. But there was no need to get all official. Not yet. He called Maddy.

'Hey, babe! We got company. Can you finish opening up, please?'

* * *

Stella waited by Lucy's side, pleased with the way the younger woman had handled the initial conversation with Björn. It had given her time to get a read on him. And what she saw was not encouraging. He was wary, fair enough. He'd had dealings with the police before. And they'd tried their damnedest to get him charged as an accessory to murder.

But what she wasn't picking up was any of those subliminal cues that she was in the presence of a dangerous killer, still less a psychotic psychopath. Ulrik Ahlgren, on the other hand, despite his early attempts to be helpful, friendly, even, had reverted to type in fairly spectacular fashion.

Unlike some of the 'normal' murderers she'd spoken to, where grotesque threats were only ever that, designed to intimidate or unsettle, she had no doubt that Ahlgren would have cheerfully followed through on his.

Of course, stuffing her full of rats would have been difficult with his head missing.

Björn had called his wife, she assumed. He wore a silver band on his ring finger. Pretty funky for a wedding ring: a skull with ruby eyes.

The woman who appeared from a door with a glass porthole had startling looks. A mouth too wide to be called generous. Not the froggy gape of Ulrik Ahlgren, but unusual, nonetheless. Wide-spaced eyes, too, so that the centre of her face seemed curiously devoid of features.

She frowned when she saw Stella and Lucy.

'We only just had the hygiene board inspectors in,' she said, coming up to Björn and sliding her hand into the back pocket of his jeans.

'They're police, babe. Want to talk to me. I won't be long.'

'We'll be as long as we need to be,' Lucy corrected him, earning a scowl.

Maddy folded her arms across her chest. Glared at Stella.

'Talk to him about what? He hasn't done anything. You lot tried to ruin his life once before. I won't let you do it again.'

'We're not trying to ruin anyone's life,' Stella said, using the formal Swedish term, *Fru Lyngstad* – Mrs Lyngstad – rather than the usual first name form of address. A quiet little warning shot across her bows. She turned to Björn. 'Is there somewhere private we can talk?'

Mirroring his wife's defiant body language, he folded his considerably brawnier forearms across his chest. 'Let's talk outside. It's a warm morning.'

Stella and Lucy followed him outside, where he set out a machine-turned aluminium table and three chairs with blue and yellow plastic basket-weave seats. No offer of coffee. They'd clearly rattled him.

They'd agreed they'd get the alibis out of the way first. Depending on his answers, they'd follow up with other questions. For each of the dates Lucy read out to him he gave the same answer.

'I was here. Working, probably, or else recording music. Maddy will confirm it. But if you think a wife's word isn't good enough you can ask the customers. We have hundreds. Plus the only way off the island's via the ferry or the airport and there's security video at both. Why don't you check it? You won't find me on a single frame. I haven't been off the island since before lockdown.'

Stella glanced at Lucy. As a statement of innocence it was convincing. They probably should check it, but for now she decided to treat Björn as a friendly witness rather than as a potential suspect.

'We will in time, Björn. And I'm sorry if this visit is unwelcome. But someone is out there killing police officers and they're replicating Ulrik's crimes. So we need to speak to anyone who might have an insight into who it might be.'

This olive branch seemed to placate Björn. The arms unfolded and he turned his head to call in through the open cafe door.

'Hey, babe? Can you bring us some coffee, please?' He faced Stella again. 'Fine. I get it. So has he got the other two yet?'

Stella drew her eyebrows together. Interesting that he should know there were five members of the Hunter Killers. A minute or two ago he'd claimed not to recognise the first three names at all.

'The other two?'

'Roos and Olsson. Especially Olsson. It was him who reckoned I'd helped Ulrik kill those girls.'

'From what I've read, Nik had good reason to suspect you.'

Björn shook his head, setting his long blonde hair waving. Like he was back on a stage somewhere.

'It was all circumstantial. They couldn't prove anything. I told him, but he was obsessed. Kept dragging me out of rehearsals to ask more of his insane questions. In the end, I started doing too many drugs to cope with the stress. Drinking more, too. The band broke up because of it.'

'That must have made you very angry.'

Björn's eyes blazed. For the first time, Stella saw a flash of what felt like genuine emotion.

'Angry? Of course I was fucking angry! I lost the one thing I'd ever loved doing.'

Still a friendly witness? Stella started to have doubts. But there was the troubling issue of his apparently unshakeable alibi. Unless he was working with someone else. Hang on. Could disciples have their own disciples? Or was that getting a bit too meta? Time for a change of tack. Back to basics.

'Can I take you back to the outdoor concert you did where the Werewolves provided security?'

Lucy produced an A4 print of the shot Stella had taken from Ahlgren and laid it on the table in front of Björn. Just as she did so, Maddy arrived with three mugs of coffee and a jug of milk. She plonked a ceramic bowl of wrapped sugar cubes on top of the photo, turned on her heel and left. Stella watched her go, her curious waddling gait suggestive of a duck.

'Thanks, babe!' Björn called after her.

Stella moved the sugar bowl and tapped the photo.

'Do you recognise any of these men?'

Björn picked up the photo and squinted. Then, in a move that surprised Stella, withdrew a pair of reading glasses with narrow blue plastic frames from his shirt pocket and slipped them on. He caught her gaze.

'Getting old,' he said with a rueful smile.

She returned the smile. 'Not quite the image of a former death metal star?'

He shrugged. 'Ancient history. I'm a cafe owner now.'

Able to see properly now, he picked up the photo. He shook his head, frowning.

'God, those guys were scary. We had the dark image, OK? But that's all it was, an image. I mean, Harri kept tropical fish! And Martin used to read Moomin books on the bus. But the Werewolves, man? They were the real deal. We were terrified of them. We heard that to join you had to kill someone, yeah? Literally kill someone just to get your colours or whatever they called them.'

'Do you recognise them, though?' Lucy pressed.

He tapped the photo. 'The tall guy, the lean one, I mean. That's Klas. He was the leader. I don't know his second name.

Mean motherfucker, though. This one,' he tapped again, 'I think his name's Kenny. I don't know the other guy. Kenny was, like, our liaison or whatever.'

'Liaison?'

'Yeah. You know, artist relations.'

'Ran errands, got you to and from the stage in one piece?' Stella asked.

'Exactly.'

'Maybe brought you girls who wanted to meet the band?'

He grinned, shot a guilty look towards the interior of the cafe where they could hear Maddy ostentatiously clattering chairs and tables about.

'It happened.'

'Did he ever get you drugs?'

A guiltier look. 'What?'

'Did Kenny ever bring you drugs?' Lucy spoke slowly, and clearly, maybe turning the volume up a notch, as if addressing a young child. Or perhaps someone with dementia.

'Look, Björn, we're Homicide, OK?' Stella smiled. 'But even if we *were* the drug squad, we wouldn't be coming after you if you did a few lines or smoked some weed twenty years ago.'

'Fine. Yes, he brought us drugs.'

'Did you ever see who he got them from?'

'Nope.'

'Did you meet any other gang members? Enough to get a name?'

'Sorry.'

The rest of the interview passed with similar non-answers. But Stella formed the opinion that Björn was trying to be helpful. He just had nothing useful to tell them. As he said more than once, his memory wasn't as sharp as it could have been, in large part owing to the drugs Kenny had been tasked with bringing them.

She ended the interview with a thanks for the coffee and a business card, which he tucked into his shirt pocket along with his reading glasses.

'If you think of anything else, no matter how insignificant, please call me, OK? Any time of the day or night.'

They left him to finish opening up and strolled back across the cobbled square. All around them, tourists were stopping at food carts, buying souvenirs and taking videos of each other, posing in front of the impossibly cute mediaeval houses.

Stella sighed. They wouldn't be back in Örebro much before late afternoon. Another day gone without a positive lead. At least Björn had confirmed the drugs connection to the Werewolves. But it was thin gruel compared to the meat of a murder investigation: information on the actual killer.

They had some work to do on his alibi, too. Maybe they'd strike lucky and find his name on a passenger manifest for a private plane or a helicopter.

But top of her list was interviewing Joel Varela's cousin, Kenneth. Because Björn had identified him as the one bringing the band their drugs.

40

ÖREBRO

Kenneth Varela, who was now thirty-nine, ran a bike shop on an industrial estate on the northern outskirts of Örebro. The shop occupied a corner plot, its neighbours a wholesale butcher's and a plumbing supplies business. Stella dismounted and leaned the Triumph over on its kickstand.

She looked up at the name, which clearly drew inspiration from the owner's gang affiliation. *Fullmåne Motorcyklar*: Fullmoon Motorcycles. A skilfully painted mural to the right of the door depicted a chopper in partial silhouette against a full moon, its heavily built rider's shaggy head thrown back, bloody jaws open wide in a howl.

'You like it?'

She dropped her gaze to the horizontal. Facing her was a beast of a man who might have been the model for his shop sign. Overtopping six feet by a good four or five inches, thick ropes of muscle visible on his bare arms, a deep chest straining the fabric of a dirty white T-shirt beneath his denim vest. His beard and moustache were glossy and black, tamed in the latter case by being fed through a series of silver rings.

His deep-set eyes seemed to be all-black, about as far from the Swedish stereotype of pale blue as you could get without disappearing altogether. Yet, despite his fearsome appearance, there was something about him that Stella found reassuring. Maybe it was the half-amused smile, slouching on his lips like a biker leaning against his ride.

'It's very … dramatic. Cool name, too.'

He came over and extended a paw-like right hand, from which he'd just wiped off most of the grease with a rag that smelled strongly of white spirit. It was like shaking hands with a bear. *Or a werewolf*, an inner voice whispered.

'I'm Ken. You looking for anything in particular? I could give you a good deal on a trade for the Speed Twin? Some of my customers really dig British bikes.'

'Stella, and no. I'm happy with the bike. But I did want to ask you a few questions.'

She fished her SPA ID out of an inner pocket. The smile dropped from his face. In its place a look combining suspicion with disgust, lips curled, nostrils flaring as if he'd just smelled roadkill.

'What's this all about?'

'Can we talk somewhere private?'

He shrugged. 'You better come inside.'

The interior of the shop was divided in two. On the left, half a dozen bikes, all of them large-capacity and either American or British. A few with custom paintjobs or extensive chromework on the metal parts. On the right, racks of leathers, crash helmets, luggage sets and all the paraphernalia bikers, like members of any specialist group, seemed to need.

Kenny led her to a cramped office right at the back. He lifted a pile of papers off a rickety swivel chair before folding his sizeable frame into the leather number behind the tiny desk. He put his boots up on a two-drawer filing cabinet to one side and fixed Stella with those ink-black eyes of his.

'So, Detective Inspector Stella, what do you want to know?'

'Are you still a member of the Werewolves?'

He tapped a yellow and black enamel pin on his chest. Two interlinked Vs taken from the Swedish word *'varulv'*.

'Joining's a one-way trip, baby,' he said in English.

Stella stuck to Swedish.

'Have you heard about your cousin?'

Did you kill your cousin?

'Yeah. Bad shit, what happened to Joel.'

'I'm sorry for your loss, Ken.'

'Thanks. But honestly? We weren't that close. Our lifestyles didn't exactly gel, if you know what I mean. Him being a cop and all.'

'What did you think about how he was killed?'

'Weird. But it's a weird world, right?'

Stella had to agree. She'd be out of a job if it weren't. Or at least, back to teaching bored teenagers about drugs.

'He's killed twice more. Both ex-cops. That's the connection. We're working on the assumption that the killer is connected somehow to Ulrik Ahlgren. What do you know about him?'

'Why do you think that prick's involved?'

'The killer's MO is almost identical.'

She watched him closely, looking for a tell. If she were facing the Devil of Axberg, telling him he'd got a detail wrong would be bound to provoke some sort of reaction. But his face was impassive.

'Yeah, but you can read anything online, can't you? Charlie Manson, Bundy, Andersson, all those nutters. There's a podcast or a whole website dedicated to what they did.'

'We're pretty sure his knowledge of Ahlgren's crimes go beyond what he'd be able to find on the web.'

He shrugged. 'You're the detective.'

'Did you have much to do with Ahlgren when you were handling security for Sepülkå?'

His eyes widened. The right caught a stray sunbeam that had filtered through the lopsided Venetial blind over the window. She saw flecks of gold.

'Fuck me, that's a long time ago.' He looked upwards, running his hand over his beringed beard the way Stella did with her ponytail when she was thinking. 'Not much,' he said finally. 'Olaf did more of that side of things. He had better people skills than me.'

'What about drugs?'

'What about them?'

'Was that one of your skills? Supplying them, I mean?'

'I don't know what you're talking about.'

'Come on, Ken! I already know the Werewolves were supplying the band.'

'Maybe we were. I was only nineteen. If it *was* going on, I knew nothing about anything like that. I was just in it for the bikes.'

'Why not just join a regular club, then?'

He stared at her, breathing steadily through his nose. He was flexing his biceps, and his fingers kept curling and uncurling. She stared back, wondering whether he was about to attack her. Her pistol was inside her jacket. But it was still zipped up.

Instead, he just smiled that lazy smile again. And the charm was back, overlaying the sense of danger like a cat sheathing its claws. Or, given his gang affiliation, a wolf donning a sheep's fleece.

'Why did you join the police, Stella?'

'Are you saying the Werewolves and the police are the same?'

'Well, they're both legal organisations, aren't they? Although there's probably more corruption in the SPA than there is in biker gangs. I mean, we don't have entire departments devoted to rooting it out, do we?'

That was interesting, Ken referring to Internal Affairs.

Playing the Devil's Music

Especially given that its head was currently one of the two surviving members of the Hunter Killers. She filed it away. For now.

'You said just now that you and Joel weren't close. Any particular reason? Especially if you think cops and bikers are just two different kinds of clubs you can join?'

Ken opened a drawer and pulled out a matchbox. Extracted a match and placed it between his teeth. Started chewing methodically. Maybe he was trying to kick a snus habit. It was established fact that users of the little paper sachets of tobacco were prone to lip, cheek and tongue cancers.

'Nothing special. Like I said, we took different paths, is all. Was there anything else, only I got work to do. Bikes don't fix themselves.'

Stella got to her feet. 'Nothing else.' She reached for the door handle. 'Oh, one last thing.' She dropped her hand. 'I need to know your whereabouts on three dates.'

She recited them and waited to see how he'd respond. Few people could remember where they were on one date, let alone three. It was *how* they answered that she'd always found interesting, rather than *what* they said.

Ken just smiled. 'You need my alibi? Sounds like you think I had something to do with these murders of yours.'

'Did you, Ken?'

'No. But I can't tell you where I was off the top of my head.'

She smiled. 'That's OK. I tell you what.' She handed him a card. 'Have a look at your diary and drop me an email or call me.'

She left him in the poky little cubbyhole and went back to her bike, pausing only to admire a couple of the shiny machines parked outside.

As she rode back to the station, she was trying to pull together strands of the investigation that weren't quite knitting. Yet.

Why had Ken mentioned Internal Affairs? Did he know something about Nik? Or Joel? Was Nik investigating Joel? Had Joel confided in his cousin? But why would he? Unless he thought

Ken might have access to the kind of muscle that could warn Nik off. Ha! Fat chance! They'd have better luck trying to frighten a genuine werewolf than Nik Olsson once he got the scent of a bent cop in his nostrils.

But it did give her an idea.

41

That night, after heating a frozen pizza in the oven and consuming it at the kitchen table with a beer, Stella set to work on her new theory.

Thanks to Lucy, they now knew the Werewolves were involved in the drug trade. Perhaps not a huge revelation, but it linked to some of the other strands. Kenny Varela was Joel's cousin. Kenny had said they weren't close, owing to their respective paths through life, but Stella wondered whether there was something else. And, after a career-making collar – of the Brain Surgeon – Joel had transferred from Homicide to the drug squad.

That meant there were two lines connecting Joel to the Werewolves. His family tie to Kenny and his job investigating the drug trade. What if Joel had been murdered, not because of his membership of the Hunter Killers, but because he'd fallen foul of the Werewolves somehow?

And that led to a second question. How would a drug squad cop fall out with a biker gang involved in drug dealing?

The answer was simple. And devastating in its implications.

Because, far from working against them, he'd been working *with* them.

She hated the thought. Tried a different hypothesis. Could they have murdered him because he was getting too close to shutting down their operation? Stella desperately hoped that was the case. Maybe Klas Helander had ordered his murder to prevent that. From what Lucy had said, he wasn't averse to at least making threats to kill, even if it was just to a loyal lieutenant.

The trouble was, murdering a single cop wouldn't work, would it? It was called the drug *squad* for a reason. Short of wiping out the entire SPA, there'd always be more cops to take the places of the fallen. And however violent Klas Helander was, he wasn't stupid, as her encounter with him had proved. He'd know that murdering cops would result in all-out war with the SPA. The Werewolves would all end up in Kumla. Or dead.

But if she was right, that still left one huge, monstrous hole in her theory. What about the other two murders?

She took a pull on her beer. Tried to come up with a solution.

The answer, when it came to her, was so unpleasant she groaned out loud.

'God, please no!'

Had the killer tried to disguise Joel's murder by copying Ulrik Ahlgren, knowing that the homicide cops would eventually find the link between Joel, Kenny, the Werewolves and Ahlgren? It didn't bear thinking about. What kind of monster would…

She slammed the beer bottle down onto the tabletop. What kind of *monster*? Was she a rookie? A wet-behind-the-ears graduate who couldn't believe people would mug old ladies for their pensions or beat people up for being gay?

A human monster of course! People did all kinds of terrible shit. Sometimes for kicks. Other times for money. Pay a contract killer enough and they'd do whatever you asked them to, *ante* or *post* mortem.

What did it mean for Sören Roos and Nik Olsson? Were they still in danger? She called Sören.

'Hey, Stella, what's new? Are you calling to tell me you've caught your nutjob?'

'Sorry, Sören, no. Not yet, anyway. Listen, can I run an idea past you in confidence?'

'Sure. Go ahead.'

She wiped her free hand, suddenly damp with sweat, on her thigh.

'I'm going to lay out a theory and I want you just to listen, please. It's not pleasant, but I am honestly just trying to get to the bottom of this unholy mess, all right?'

'Sounds serious, but sure. Although I don't really see how it can be any more unpleasant than cutting people's heads open and stuffing them full of bugs.'

She took a deep breath.

'First, I'm just wondering at this stage, what if Joel was murdered because he ran foul of the Werewolves bike gang?'

'Well, he was a drug squad officer. That's kind of the day job, Stella.'

Stella bit her lip. Her nerves had caused her to flub her lines.

'Sorry, Sören, I mean like a falling-out among thieves.' She paused. Heard Sören's breathing on the line. But he was staying quiet for now. Listening, just as she'd asked him to. 'The person who kills Joel decides to hide the motive by committing more murders to make it look like a serial killer. Specifically a disciple of Ulrik Ahlgren.'

'OK,' he rumbled. The sound of a volcano deciding whether to erupt or not. 'That sounds like you're asking me whether Joel was dirty.'

She chewed her lip again. Snatched a breath. 'Was he?'

The volcano stayed dormant. Just. 'Listen to me, Stella. From what I hear, and see on the TV, you're a damned good cop. For some reason, you fetched up here in Sweden and proceeded to run around like a hellhound, slamming the door on serial killers and murderers like you were working against the clock.' The surface bubbled. A subterranean crack filled the air. 'But that does *not*' – a spout of red-hot lava jetted from the crust of greying ash – 'give you the right to sling mud at a dead cop just to make some theory of yours hold water!'

'I'm sorry, Sören. That's the last thing I want to do. And I said it was just me trying to catch this maniac. But if it *was* true, do you think he'd stop at three? Because I'm still worried he'll come after you and Nik.'

'Save your breath, Stella. And keep your worries for the case. I already told you, anyone comes for me up here, they're going to find out about death the hard way.'

He hung up. She sighed. Fair enough. She'd accused one of his team, his *brothers*, of being a bent cop. It wouldn't sit well with her either.

Roisin Griffin's accusing blue eyes flashed before her.

Didn't seem to bother you when it was me, did it?

She shook the thought away. Called Nik.

'Have you caught him?' were his first words.

'No. Not yet. But we will. Look, Nik, I just spoke to Sören and before he calls you, I need to ask you a question.'

'Sounds ominous.'

She threw caution to the wind.

'Is it possible Joel was corrupt?'

Silence.

'Nik? Are you still there?'

The silence lengthened.

'Why do you ask?'

Interesting. No blustering denial. No appeal to a sister officer to think well of the dead. Did Nik know something? Something he'd been holding back?

'He's connected to the Werewolves. I started wondering whether this isn't about Ahlgren after all. Maybe there's a more prosaic reason.'

Nik sighed. A ragged sound, like a cop putting down a heavy bag of gear at the end of a shift.

'As far as I'm aware, there was never any evidence to suggest that.'

His answer was too carefully calibrated. He sounded like a politician avoiding an uncomfortable question from a journalist getting too close to the truth.

'As far as you're *aware?*'

'Look, Stella, you must understand, my job is a complex one. There are too many complaints to investigate every single one. We have to prioritise.'

'That sounds like an admission, Nik. Just tell me. Was he involved in something?'

'Joel was a good police officer. In Homicide, we did good things together. Putting Ahlgren in Kumla was only one of them.'

Stella could hear it. Nik's struggle to hold onto the secret he was keeping buried. It was like there were two halves of his personality warring over the information she now felt sure he possessed. The old-school, former homicide cop who wanted to close ranks with his friend and former partner was locked in combat with the IA zealot who attacked corruption like an old-time knight thrusting his lance at a multi-headed dragon.

But now she'd asked the question, the morally certain part of him was fighting back.

All it needed was a little nudge from her on the butt-end of the lance.

'But?'

'But, I'd heard rumours that he was working with the Werewolves.'

'Working how?'

'The usual. Feeding them information. Steering investigations away from them and towards rival gangs.'

'I can't believe you'd not tell me, Nik. You of all people!'

He laughed. A hollow sound made all the more mirthless by the echoing quality of the line.

'It's ironic, isn't it?'

'But why? And more to the point, why weren't you investigating him? Who knows, if you'd brought him in, or had him removed from the drug squad, he might still be alive.'

'Damn-the-devil, Stella, do you think I don't know that?'

Nik sounded on the point of breaking down. His voice cracked, sending a warble down the line as if he were speaking from the back of a very long, water-filled cave. When he spoke again, it was in a flat, emotionless voice. As if he'd forced himself to ignore the turmoil he was clearly feeling.

'Remember I told you how I really got the scar on my chest?'

She saw it, then. Before Nik had a chance to tell her. How he'd survived a direct attack by the Brain Surgeon. An attack that could have ended his life back in '03.

'Was Joel there with you?'

'He was. Ahlgren was pulling his arm back for another attack. Joel shot him through the shoulder. It was risky. You know our training. Centre-mass, every time. But Joel wanted Ahlgren alive. He wanted to see him in court. And then in prison.

'He saved my life, Stella. And it almost cost him his own. As Ahlgren went down, he spun round and hurled his knife at Joel. It hit him in the neck. The doctors said a centimetre to the right and it would have severed his carotid artery. He'd have been dead in seconds.'

'And after that you felt you owed him. He told you you'd have done the same for him, but you owed him anyway. Then, one day, you heard those rumours. Maybe you even confronted him over them. He denied everything, but you knew in your heart something was crooked. To repay the debt, you looked the other way, didn't you? Maybe you even told him that that was it between you. You'd wiped the slate clean, but now he was on his own.'

'With insights like that, you'd make an excellent member of the Rat Squad,' he said grimly. 'What else can I say? Guilty as charged. Are you going to report me?'

'What good would that do, Nik? Joel's dead. And I hate dirty cops just as much as you do. We may not see eye to eye on a lot of things. But I do believe you're good at your job.'

'You're being generous, Stella. I tried to have you kicked off the force. I lied to Malin to do it.'

'Yes, well, maybe when this is all over you could talk to her. Get me reinstated. Maybe reverse my demotion, too, while you're at it.'

'I will. I promise.'

'Then let me ask you the same question I just asked Soren. Do

Playing the Devil's Music

you think, if I'm right about Joel, that this changes things? Or is the killer still a threat to the two of you?'

'You're the serial killer expert, not me. But for what it's worth, no, I don't. He's muddied the waters enough. He can disappear now and leave you and your team following a false trail.'

'You don't think he figures he should kill all five of you so the picture looks complete?'

'Maybe? But with every murder he commits, he's increasing the risk of being caught. He'll get careless, or make a mistake, or get picked up for speeding with his paraphernalia in the boot of his car. It happens, you know it does. He does, too, especially if he's not a psychopath at all, just a very cunning killer.'

Stella tugged on her ponytail. It sounded plausible. But what if Nik were wrong? Somewhere out there was a killer who'd established a story that he was telling the police, the public and the press. Maybe his need to finish it was as strong as Nik's need to protect his friend.

* * *

At the next day's morning briefing, Sven reported that Ken Varela had supplied an alibi. Plenty of witnesses and probably CCTV as well. Not a suspect, then. But a helpful witness. Lucy had visited Ella Rasmussen, Ulrik Ahlgren's favourite pen pal. And, in her opinion, she wasn't a credible suspect.

'She has agoraphobia brought on by witnessing a car crash that killed her mum. Showed me a doctor's certificate she needed to get disability benefits. I checked with the neighbours, too. They confirmed she hasn't been out of the house for five years. I checked with social services. Spoke to a carer. It's not her.'

Stella stood up in front of the team. Time to lay out her new working theory. And it was one she knew wouldn't be popular. For that reason, she'd asked Kersten to be there, too. She'd also attempted to keep Sven onside by telling him in advance what she intended to say. He'd not been happy. Tough. Her job wasn't about making other detectives feel happy. It was about catching killers. Saving lives.

'Thanks to Sven, we know Ken Varela has an alibi. But he *is* related to our first victim. They were cousins. Not close, but still family. Ken is a member of the Werewolves. I believe Ken introduced Joel to his gang-mates and either immediately, or shortly afterwards, Joel entered into a criminal relationship with them.

'If I'm right, then I suspect that at some point Joel attempted to make a move of his own. Maybe he set up a rival distribution network, or double-crossed them over a deal. But whatever happened, the Werewolves decided he had to be killed. Whoever did it saw a way to throw suspicion away from the gang by imitating Ulrik Ahlgren's MO.'

She paused. Wanting to see what kind of reaction her theory would get. These were Örebro cops, not Stockholmers. Their loyalty to Joel Varela would be of the 'all cops together' variety, rather than the intense personal connection forged between Nik and Joel in the face of a murderous attacker trying to kill them both.

'You're sure Joel was dirty?' Kersten asked.

'Not one hundred percent, no.'

'Who is this "good authority" you mentioned?'

Stella had anticipated Kersten's question. She couldn't explain without exposing Nik. Lord knew, she had good reason to, but she couldn't bring herself to do it. It would ruin him.

'A confidential informant. I can't say any more than that, I'm afraid. But I trust him implicitly. The intelligence is solid.'

Kersten frowned, fixing Stella with a probing gaze. Stella held firm.

'Very well.' Kersten steepled her fingers under her chin. 'What do you propose we do?'

'We need to be all over the Werewolves. But covertly. They'll clam up if we make a direct approach. Short of arresting every member, we'd get nowhere. Even then, I'm guessing they swear some sort of oath that says "Death before Dishonour" or some bullshit like that.'

Roger Amundsen, Stella's fellow biker among the car-driving Örebro cops, nodded.

'They'd go inside rather than rat out a fellow member. It's their code.' He turned to address the room at large. 'I used to work organised crime back in Oslo. I specialised in bikers, especially links between Norwegian and Swedish gangs. Believe me, the punishment for squealing made a stretch in Kumla look like a fortnight at your summer house.'

'So how do we find out who was dealing with Joel?' Sven asked.

Stella had her answer ready. She'd thought it up some time in the small hours the previous night, lying awake and staring at the ceiling.

'Roger and I approach another gang. We pose as journalists. Say we're doing a story on bikers. How they're demonised by Swedish society. Get them talking about other gangs. See if they'll dish the dirt on the Werewolves.'

A smile crept across Roger's craggy features. 'Fuck me, Stella, you've got balls on you, I'll say that.'

General laughter ensued. Eventually, Kersten called them to order.

'Fine. I approve the plan. But you go in armed, yes? I'm not risking two officers in the middle of the Second Great Biker War.'

Stella and Roger both shook their heads.

'We can't, Kersten,' Stella said. 'First thing they'll do is search us. They catch us with pistols, especially police-issue, and it's game over.'

'Wires, then.'

This time it was Roger who poured cold water on their boss's plan.

'Same problem, Kersten. We have to go in cold. We'll be fine. I'll sign out a nice digital SLR from forensics and Stella can be the word-jockey.'

This time, Kersten was silent for twenty seconds. The room stilled. She nodded once, a sharp-up-down bob of the head.

'You'll need press cards. Lucy, can you sort those out, please?'

Lucy nodded, made a note.

'Fake names?'

'I think that's best,' Stella said.

'I want everyone else delving deeper into Barbro and Fredrika's backgrounds. Just in case they were also somehow involved.'

'Why aren't we looking at Nikodemus Olsson?'

Everyone looked round to identify the speaker. It was an older detective, sitting at the back of the room. Bo Petersson had been brought out of retirement as a civilian investigator. Kersten lifted her head and spoke over the heads of the others.

'What do you mean, Bo?'

'Well, Stella's saying Joel was dirty and that's what got him killed. If Barbro and Fredrika were involved in his scheme, maybe that's why they got killed, too.' He looked around the room. 'Who hates dirty cops more than anyone else in the whole of the country?'

'You're not fucking serious? King Rat a serial killer?'

This was Sven, eyes wide.

'OK, people. First of all, I want you to show proper respect to APC Olsson.' Kersten glared at Sven, who blushed and dipped his head.

'Sorry, Kersten.'

'I'm sorry, Bo, but that is just a wild and, if I may say so, frivolous accusation. I'm not going to prioritise resources to investigating Nik Olsson.'

A few muttered remarks and accompanying chuckles suggested that, although nobody seriously thought Nik was the killer, Bo's suggestion was worth a laugh, at least.

After the meeting, Stella and Roger retreated to the canteen to discuss the fine details of their story. She felt nervous, but also excited. The thrill of the chase had kicked in hard.

On Roger's advice, Stella decided that a gang called the Demons were their best bet for getting intel on the Werewolves.

Over the years, there had been regular skirmishes between the Werewolves and the Demons. Their base was just outside Munktorp, a small town over in Västmanland County, two thirds of the way on a straight line from Örebro to Västerås.

She'd put in a request with the drug squad for any information on the Werewolves but the inspector she'd spoken to had come up empty-handed. Either they were clean, and her whole theory was a bust, or Joel really had been shielding them in return for payoffs. Time would tell.

Three days later, their fake IDs came through.

42

In the station carpark, Roger paused in the act of putting his helmet on as Stella emerged from the back doors.

'Well, that's a new look. It suits you.'

Stella ran a hand over her new short haircut, dyed white-blond and gelled into spikes. She'd applied makeup more in line with Anna Eriksson's goth look than her own minimalist approach.

'Thanks, partner. You didn't really need a makeover, did you? You look the part already.'

Roger stroked his silver beard. 'Remind me to show you my tattoos one day,' he said, winking.

'You ready?'

'As I'll ever be.'

They mounted up and started their bikes, filling the car park with the glorious roar of the two bike engines. Stella smiled despite the nervous energy fizzing away in the pit of her belly. Roger led the way out of the carpark and into central Örebro.

The ride was just short of seventy kilometres along the E20. Another immaculately maintained Swedish motorway with zero points of interest. As they rode west towards their appointment with the Demons, Stella ran through their cover story again. It was critical, in the absence of either wires or weapons, that it survived intact.

She was Rachel Smith, an English journalist now living in Stockholm. Roger was Greg Mortensen, a Norwegian. They'd pitched their story on outlaw bikers to *Time* magazine.

She hoped that bikers had the same egos as everyone else. In constant need of validation and bolstering. Attracting the attention of foreign journalists working for a US title even the most backwoods biker must have heard of, would surely achieve that. After that, it was down to thinking on their feet and getting the Demons talking about their Örebro County rivals.

Ten minutes later, a minor distraction. A sign for a truckstop: *Skofesta Grillen* was one kilometre ahead. A vast RV with a smiling sun painted on its side blew past Stella, mountain bikes strapped onto a rack at the rear, one untethered wheel turning lazily.

The slipstream buffeted her, and the Triumph shimmied before she brought it under control. Arsehole.

The RV passed Roger and then, without signalling, swerved sharply across the carriageway, heading for the sliproad to the truckstop.

Ahead, Roger's brake light flashed once, twice, then stayed on. The front end of the bike dipped as he hauled on the brake lever to avoid getting mashed by the lumbering RV. Stella watched, horrified, as the crash unfolded in slow motion directly in front of her.

Blue smoke puffed out from Roger's rear tyre and the rear of the bike slipped sideways. It had momentarily locked out and gone into a skid. He corrected it, but letting off the brake sent the big bike bucking under him as the conflicting forces acting on its mass battled for supremacy. With a shake like a bronco getting rid of a rodeo rider, the Indian Chief dipped its nose, kicked up its fat rear tyre and threw its rider high into the air.

Stella hit the brakes hard, desperate to avoid smashing into Roger, who was now rolling and tumbling down the road, the bike cartwheeling after him, striking sparks off the tarmac like fireworks. The RV swung off the E20 and onto the slip road, disappearing round a bend, oblivious to the carnage it had just caused.

It wasn't going to work. Stella was going too fast. In less than a second she would run over her partner. She was out of options.

She shifted her weight over to the left, pulled back on the left handlebar and sent the bike skidding beneath her onto its side. In a far more controlled slide than Roger's, she ended her journey sliding along the E20 on her side, grateful, not for the first time, for the thick layer of leather between the gritty road surface and her own, far less durable hide.

Behind and around them, traffic was braking, swerving. Horns blasted, tyres screeched. The air was full of drifting rubber smoke, its acrid smell penetrating her helmet. Thankfully, as she slid to a stop, not a single other vehicle had got involved in the accident.

Roger had tumbled into a tangled heap at the side of the road, his legs hanging over the edge of the tarmac onto the grass verge. His bike was a mess, the handlebars bent like a pretzel. He lay still, although, as she struggled to her feet, she saw his left hand moving. It took all her strength to drag the Triumph upright. It would never win a prize in a bike show, but it had only suffered cosmetic damage down its left flank. The end of the footpeg had been ground off by a centimetre or two and the tank was scraped down to the metal, but it rolled OK, the clutch and brake levers were intact, and the wheels and tyres were fine.

Waving away the slowing traffic, she leaned her bike on its kickstand and hurried over to where Roger was lying. She lifted his visor, which had a large crack running down the centre, careful not to move his head. His eyes were closed.

'Roger? Roger! Can you hear me?'

He opened his eyes.

'Yeah, I can hear you. That fucking arsehole nearly killed us both. Did you get his number?'

'Never mind that now. Listen, I need to check you over. Can you feel your toes?'

She looked over her shoulder. His black bike boots twitched

and the reinforced toecaps bent upwards a little. Good, that reduced the chances he'd suffered a spinal injury.

'Yeah, they're OK. But I think I busted something in my leg. Can you take a look?' he grunted.

His right leg was fine, lying in the approved manner, straight out from his hip. But the left was twisted, the foot rotated inwards at an unnatural angle.

'Looks like it might be broken. Hold on, I'm calling it in.'

She pulled out her phone and called for an ambulance and the police. Gave the code for an officer involved and also informed the call handler that they should send someone to the *Skofesta Grillen* and arrest the RV driver who'd caused the accident.

The ambulance arrived after ten minutes, during which time Stella managed to drag Roger's bike off the carriageway. It was a write-off.

Roger was moaning softly: the adrenaline had worn off and now the pain from his broken leg had kicked in. She spent the time talking to him, reassuring him he'd be OK and trying to give him a more thorough examination. He'd cried out when she'd gently moved his right shoulder and she apologised profusely.

His eyes were OK, though, both pupils the same size and reacting evenly when she shone the torch from her phone at them.

She unzipped his jacket and gingerly felt around on his abdomen. No more yelping, which she hoped was a good sign. No blood anywhere, either, although his leathers would need replacing. Incongruously, she remembered seeing honeymooning couples in Sicily riding hired scooters two-up in shorts, vests and flip-flops. She'd been outraged, ranting about it to Richard until, laughing, he'd told her to calm down.

Nothing we can do about it, darling, is there? It's their funeral.

Except it hadn't been, had it? Richard, her darling, careful Richard, had been the one lowered into the ground in a wooden box. She screwed her eyes shut and shook her head, forcing the unwanted thoughts out of her head by sheer effort of will.

While the paramedics began checking Roger over, Stella stood to talk to the traffic officers who'd arrived shortly after the

Playing the Devil's Music

ambulance. She gave them a full description of the RV and made them promise to keep her updated.

'We need to stay here, set up cones,' the younger one, a woman, said. 'But we called it in. If they leave before we speak to them, they'll be picked up down the road. We alerted colleagues in Västerås, too. Don't worry, they won't get far.'

While the two traffic cops began coning off the inside lane and directing traffic to keep moving, Stella went over to Roger. The paramedics had lifted him onto a stretcher.

'I'll ride behind the ambulance,' she said, squeezing his hand and smiling down at him. 'Make sure they patch you up properly.'

He shook his head, as far as the plastic neck brace would allow. Smiled lazily.

'Keep going. I'll be fine. They just gave me something for the pain. I'm feeling pretty chill, as a matter of fact.'

She shook her head. 'I can't leave you on your own. You're hurt.'

'No, Stella! There's a fucking serial killer out there. Who knows, he could be planning another one right now. I swear I'll be fine. This isn't even the worse crash I've ever had. I'm not one of your Swedish fair-weather riders.' He thumped his chest with a gloved hand. 'I am Roger Amundsen, Norwegian biker. And I say, go!'

She straightened, gave his hand another squeeze.

'You're a fucking legend, is what you are. I'll go. But I'll call you later, see how you're getting on.' She turned to the paramedics, who were waiting to carry him to the ambulance. 'Take good care of him, OK?'

They frowned simultaneously. 'Of course. We'll take him to the ER in Köping.'

She turned back to Roger and bent over him. Kissed the end of his nose.

'Take care.'

'You too.'

She watched the ambulance speed ahead, blue lights flickering, then retrieved the SLR from Roger's pannier and put it in one of her own. She climbed back onboard the Triumph, thumbed the starter button and kicked it down into first gear.

Just before the turnoff for Kungsör, Fagersta and Köping, which was overlooked by a drive-through McDonalds, she spotted the RV. Traffic cops had pulled it over, their blue lights reflecting off the chromework of the mountain bikes on the back. She glanced right and nodded her thanks to the cop who was currently noting down the driver's details in her book. He nodded back and then turned to the driver.

She rode on to Munktorp and then turned left onto an unnamed county road that wound between a redbrick single-storey school and a field on which a few dozen black sheep grazed.

The distance to the next town, Morgendal, was six kilometres, but according to Roger's hand-drawn map, the Demons' clubhouse was halfway along.

43

LULEÅ

After Stella had called him making those accusations against Joel, Sören had gone out alone with just his new rifle for company. He missed Astrid's company, but she'd gone lame the day before, coming home from a wander with her left foreleg cocked, and whimpering when he'd gently palpated it all the way from the paw to the hip. He couldn't see any thorns or find any breaks. Maybe she'd just pulled a muscle. It happened.

How could Stella, a bloody incomer, think that was a reasonable question to throw at him? Christ, Joel was as honest as the day was long. Poor sod. OK, so there'd been times when he'd arranged a bit of evidence to suit their case, but only when everyone knew the perpetrator was a guilty as sin. And there was a hell of a long road between that kind of thing and taking envelopes of cash to look the other way.

He kicked his way angrily through some nettles, slashing at them with a stick he'd picked up a few minutes earlier. Fucking

English bitch, coming to Sweden and then acting like she was some kind of celebrity just because she'd caught a couple of killers. They'd all done that, hadn't they? And none more so than the Hunter Killers. Fuck's sake, Ahlgren made the guys Stella had caught look like kindergartners.

Sören almost wished Ahlgren's disciple *would* show up in his favourite woods. Then there'd be a reckoning all right. Sören would take great pleasure in sending him for a personal appointment with the devil, courtesy of a few well-aimed rounds of Winchester.308 ammunition.

He unshouldered the rifle, a Carl Gustav M80, and aimed at the circular scar on an old oak tree where a lower branch had broken away some years earlier. Imagined it was a killer's face, grinning evilly back at him before blowing apart.

Shaking his head and smiling, he lowered the barrel.

In recent years, he'd been lax about wearing ear defenders when out hunting. Paulina had chided him. 'You'll send yourself deaf!' He'd always smiled and said if God had intended hunters to wear ear defenders he'd have just given them more hair in their lugholes. The tinnitus wasn't bad, but it had taken the edge off his hearing, that was for sure. Or maybe it was just age creeping up on him.

Anyway, as a result, he didn't hear the twig snapping behind him until it was too late. He lifted his head like Astrid did when she scented a pheasant or a rabbit. But that only made it easier for the killer to clamp the chloroform-soaked cloth over his nose and mouth.

Sören was fit, despite being in his late fifties, and he managed to rear back and deliver a half-powered headbutt. But as to unshouldering the rifle, that was never on the cards. He staggered sideways and managed to turn to face his assailant. Eyes already drooping from the chloroform, he lunged, fingers curled into claws, intending to go for the eyes. But his arms weighed as much as a dead deer apiece and merely skidded into the blurry figure's chest.

The attacker stepped smartly back, side-stepped Sören's

clumsy attempt at a bear-hug and smacked him in the side of the head with something hard. Eyes blinded with tears, Sören fell to his knees. The stinking rag descended, covering his nose and mouth once more.

As he slid into a nauseating unconsciousness that stank of lemons and the grease he used on his thornproof jacket, his last sight was of a figure grinning like the very devil.

* * *

Fuck! That did not go to plan. Roos lies there, blood leaking from the head wound, arms spread wide, fists clenched.

The head-butt was off target – no broken nose – but the point of impact, right on the cheekbone, still hurt like a bastard. A dab of a Kleenex – no blood. That was good, then. Walking into Luleå hospital's emergency room with a smashed-up face would mean some inventive lying. And who knew? Maybe there'd be some smartass doctor asking difficult questions and calling the cops.

A quick shake of the head to clear the vision, then to work. This deep in the woods there is no need to hurry. And, after all, this is the fun part. Plastic sandwich box out of the rucksack and onto the leaf litter, the bombed-out bugs still snoozing off the effects of the chloroform. Knife, horn, hacksaw laid out on a leather tool roll.

First, the death-blow. A double-handed grip, horn held high over the head like some Viking sacrifice. A grunt of effort as it comes crashing down, through the ribs and right into the heart. Now there's blood. Such a lot of it, too.

Pentagram next. Cut away the clothing. Five fast slashes, intersecting at the points. A sort of artistry to it. Probably what serial killers think when they're doing their own weird shit with their victims. People like Ahlgren.

Not so much blood, either. It just oozes out. Simple medical science. The pump's fucked, so there's no pressure.

Ha! That's a joke. No pressure?

Because it's hard work tailing these cops. Learning their routines. They're twitchy as hell. But it's amazing what you can learn from YouTube. Covert surveillance. Camouflage. Friendly body language. Different accents. It's all there, for free!

Finally the crowning glory. Another joke. Get it? Ahlgren would. Fucking idiot locked up there in Kumla. Clearly not the criminal mastermind he thought he was or he wouldn't have been caught in the first place, would he?

Off with the top of the skull. In with the right hand and the little paring knife. Cut through the brain stem then scoop it out two-handed. Like a big old jelly. Weird, really, how all that computing power they talk about on those science programmes is somehow just there, hidden in all that splodgy mess like a couple of kilos of grey-white cheesecake.

The brain chucked into the bushes, trailing pinkish slime. Food for foxes or beetles or maybe even a buzzard.

Then it's just a simple matter of pouring in the little critters and stapling the head back together. Shit! Forgot the antlers. Talk about a rookie error. A shrug. Still looks righteous horrible.

Roos was a fat bastard. No way of hoisting the body up against a tree. Oh well, drag it off the path, then. It'll be found soon enough. One way or another.

If Roos used to come out here hunting he won't be the only one. And what do hunters have? Dogs. Best sense of smell in the animal kingdom. It said so on that show on TV.

He checks the time, but his watch has stopped again.

44

MUNKTORP

Although Stella's bike had sustained plenty of cosmetic damage, she'd thought it was fine mechanically. But as she trundled down the narrow, rutted lane, its centre strip grassy and flecked with red toadstools, the engine began misfiring, sending pistol-cracks into the trees and startling huge black crows from their daytime roosts.

Great. Way to announce your arrival, Stel. Sounding like a squad from the tactical support unit.

Sure enough, as she emerged into a clearing in front of a Falun Red bungalow flying the Swedish flag and another black banner bearing a grinning red devil-face, she had a welcoming committee.

It was just that in this particularly secluded part of Sweden, the welcome consisted of several long guns sitting over brawny, tattooed forearms. A couple were pump-action shotguns, but one was a black AR-15 semi-automatic rifle with a slotted fore-end, looking every bit as menacing as its manufacturers no doubt intended.

To say the bikers were regarding her with a degree of suspicion would, she felt, have been something of an understatement. Narrowed eyes, clenched jaws, inked arms – those not cradling high-powered rifles, anyway – folded across muscular chests.

As she rolled the Triumph to a stop and removed her helmet, she caught the ratcheting double-crack as someone racked a shell into a chamber.

She held her hands up and smiled her widest smile. One she hoped said, *Hey, I'm a friendly freelance journalist, please don't kill me.* And not, *Watch your six, motherfuckers, we've come to take you out.*

'Hello!' she said in English, the goofy smile still in place, 'I come in peace!' Then again, in Swedish, deliberately messing up both the accent and the pronunciation. '*Hallå! Jag kommer i fred!*'

The guy with the AR-15, a six-footer with the lanky build that looked like he'd never put on weight however many *kannelbullar* he ate, stepped forward. He spoke in English.

'Who the fuck are you, and what the fuck do you want?'

Stella dismounted and hooked her helmet over the handlebar.

'Oh, thank God. You speak English. I thought I was going to have to muddle through in Swedish. So, my name's Rachel Smith, and I'm a journalist. Hold on.'

She made a bit of play of fumbling inside her leather jacket. She knew the action was fraught with risk, but it fitted the image she'd decided on: an overenthusiastic writer who maybe didn't quite appreciate the kind of people she was dealing with.

So it was that as she limped towards them, her press ID card held out in front of her, five muzzles pointed directly at her.

'Bloody hell! Steady there, cowboy! It's only my press card. Look. It's me in the photo.'

She held it out, straight-armed. AR-15 guy stepped forward and scrutinised the rectangle of white laminated plastic. It did the job and she silently thanked the graphics team back in Örebro. A box of doughnuts would be winging its way to them as soon as she could find a bakery.

He stepped back and, with a pat of his hand, signalled to the others to lower their weapons.

'I'll ask you again. What do you want?'

Stella delivered her cover story, telling him how she'd heard of the Demons, and how brilliant it would be if they'd agree to talk to her. He nodded as she ticked off the various points on her fingers. Finally, she was done.

'So, what do you think?' She ran a hand over her spiky blonde hair. 'I didn't get your name by the way.'

'That's because I didn't give it to you. But it's Gunnar. I'm the president.' He jutted his chin at the Triumph. 'What happened to you?'

She rolled her eyes. 'Some fucking idiot in an RV wiped me and my partner out. He was supposed to be taking photos but now he's in the ER in Köping. I think maybe a fuel line got blocked on mine. That's why I sounded like the cavalry when I arrived.'

'Yeah, well, it's not if, it's when. I'll get one of my boys to take a look at it. Leave the keys in it. Maybe we should talk inside.' He turned to his right. 'Greasegun! Take a look at this lady's ride. Maybe a blocked fuel line.'

'Sure, boss.'

While the fat biker wandered off to fetch some tools, Gunnar took Stella inside the clubhouse.

It was a variant on the Werewolves's den. A pool table, a couple of pinball machines. An old-fashioned jukebox with purple, green and yellow neon lights around the frame. Jimi Hendrix was singing 'Purple Haze'. In a corner, a couple of bikers were playing cards. They looked over, then went back to their game.

Gunnar turned to her. 'This article you're writing. What's the angle again?'

'Well, like I said outside, it's sort of a lifestyle piece combined with old fashioned reportage. Really, Roger and I wanted to chronicle a side of Swedish society that doesn't get much exposure except as lurid crime stories. We think, being bikers ourselves, that people might be interested to hear a different side of the story.'

He pursed his lips and nodded, more to himself she thought.

'I'd want approval over what you write about us.'

She frowned, prepared to protest. Not because she cared: there *was* no article. But because it's what Rachel would have done.

'That would be difficult. I have my journalistic ethics to think about. But,' she added, hastily, as he opened his mouth, 'because this is a very special interview, I'd be happy to show you the sections about the Demons. So you could see I wasn't putting words in your mouth or inventing stuff. How would that be? And I have to say that's me really chucking my journalistic ethics out the window for you, Gunnar.'

'You were going to take photos?'

'Mm-hmm. In fact, if you're OK with it, we could come back when Roger is out of the hospital. You, obviously, and some of those fabulous bikes outside. Maybe a group shot? We could discuss all that later, of course.'

The offer of photographs seemed to swing it. He relaxed visibly. The challenging stare left his eyes. And his limbs loosened, as if he'd unhooked a couple of bungee cords holding everything under tension.

'Let's do it,' he said with finality. 'You want a beer?'

'Oh God, that would be fantastic. Yes please.'

He led her to a small kitchen and cracked the tops off a couple of beers from a wheezing stainless-steel fridge.

'*Skål.*'

'Oh, right. *Skål.*'

They clinked bottles and Stella took a much-needed swig of the cold fizzy lager.

On the way out again, she paused at a row of framed photos of gang members astride their bikes – again, mostly Harleys. The card player nearest her looked up and caught her eye. He said something to his friend, put his cards down and sauntered over.

He pointed to one of the photos and then stroked a black ribbon, tied over its top-left corner.

'Know what that means?' he asked her.

The meaning was clear to Stella, but in her new persona, she decided to feign ignorance.

'I don't, sorry.'

'It means he died wearing his colours.' He pointed at other photos, all with the black ribbon. 'For Danny, Lars and Yannick, it was crashes. Mike bought it in Kosovo, running weapons into Ukraine. Angel died in the Great Biker War. Fucking Werewolf blew him up with a grenade.'

Here was her opening, and she hadn't even opened her notebook yet. Maybe it was cosmic payback for the indignity of being knocked off her bike.

'I was going to talk to the Werewolves next. So I'm guessing there's no love lost between you?'

He glared at her, before returning to his card game.

Gunnar murmured, 'Don't mind Håkan, he's not the most sociable of guys. Let's go over there and sit.'

Once they were seated on a battered brown leather sofa, Gunnar answered her question himself.

'The Werewolves are renegades. They've shat on every peace treaty, every deal, every arrangement over territory. Their boss is a guy called Klas Helander. Fucking psychopath. Have you heard about the murders round here?'

'No. We were in Oslo until a couple of days ago. What murders? Is it a biker thing?'

He shook his head. 'Not really. But there's a link to the Werewolves.'

'Really?' The wide-eyed innocent look was playing hell with Stella's cheek muscles. One had developed a tic she was sure Gunnar could see. It felt like her whole face was jumping every few seconds.

'Three cops have been killed. Slaughtered just like this fucked-up serial killer was doing back in '03. He's locked up now, but it's pretty obvious he's got a follower.'

'And you think it could be this Klas guy?'

He shrugged. 'Why not? Like I said, guy's a psycho.'

It sounded less like a solid lead and more like intra-gang shit-stirring. But she kept playing the role of the inquisitive journalist.

'I heard they're into drug-dealing.'

He narrowed his eyes.

'Who from?'

'Lee-Anne Park She's our researcher at head office. In New York? She did some background digging for me and Roger.' She paused and knuckled her right eye as if a tear might be emerging. 'Sorry. I'm just worried about him.'

He swigged from the beer bottle.

'Not enough to stay with him in the ER, though.'

'I wanted to! He said the story was more important. He told me to go. He's actually senior to me.'

'They're pretty good at Köping. Most of us have been in there at one time or another.'

He held out his left arm, rolled it over to expose the soft skin on the inside. A scar ran from the crook of his elbow to his wrist.

'Ouch! That looks painful.'

'Some entitled prick thought he bought the E20 along with his Ferrari.'

She nodded. Drank more beer. Belched loudly. 'Wanker.'

Gunnar laughed. 'You're not what I'd imagine a British journalist would be like.'

She smiled. 'You're *exactly* what I imagined the boss of a Swedish biker gang would be like.'

'What would that be, then?'

She shrugged. Swigged more beer. 'Tough. Air of authority.' She gestured at her own left eyebrow. 'Couple of battle scars. Lots of ink. The leathers and denim.'

'Good-looking?'

Christ! Was he actually flirting with her? Oh, well, in for a penny…

'In a rough side of town way, obviously, but yes.'

He nodded, apparently satisfied.

'So, how does this work, then?'

She asked his permission to record their conversation, then spent twenty minutes interviewing him about gang life, the initiation process, how he thought they were misunderstood by wider Swedish society.

After a while she began to enjoy herself. Could even imagine writing the article for real. But she had a job to do. Roger would never forgive her if she returned with the light of journalistic endeavour burning brightly in her eyes but no concrete intel.

'Talking about your rivalry with the Werewolves, did you ever hear anything about their involvement in organised crime?'

She'd blithely accepted his self-painted portrait of the Demons as somewhere between a men's consciousness-raising group and a hobby club for fans of American iron. Hopefully that meant the opportunity to strike a blow at his hated opponents would be too hard to resist. She resisted the temptation to hold her breath. Didn't want to seem too keen.

He glanced sharply at her.

'I thought you said this was all about how biker gangs *aren't* all outlaws and lowlifes.'

She was losing him. Panicking, she thought fast.

'It is! Of course it is. I didn't mean they were or anything. It's just, maybe people round here, the police even, go after you because of, I don't know, maybe they have informers or something?'

She smiled and ruffled her blonde spikes up.

The vagueness and waffly phrasing were part of her act. She couldn't afford to seem too knowledgeable: it would be fatal. And not just to her investigation. She had no doubt people like Gunnar wouldn't hesitate to off an undercover cop posing as a journalist and then dispose of her remains deep in the forest.

'Yeah, well.' He finished his own beer. 'As it happens, you've hit on something that bugs the fuck out of me. You see, Rachel,' he leaned towards her, fixing her with an ice-cold stare, 'the SPA *never* go after the Werewolves. This cop who got murdered, Joel

Varela? He was on the take from them. Maybe you should put *that* in your article.'

He sat back, folded his arms. Stella nodded, as she took in the significance of what Gunnar had just told her. This was it. He'd taken the bait.

Internally, she was rejoicing. She'd be able to tell Roger his trip to Köping ER wasn't in vain after all. But that still left the question of why the killer had murdered Barbro and Frederika.

Before she could respond to Gunnar's suggestion, the card player was back, strolling the length of the club-house and then bending to whisper in Gunnar's ear. His narrowed eyes flicked to Stella a couple of times. Gunnar nodded, but kept his own gaze down where Stella couldn't read it.

Her adrenaline spiked. The card player who'd looked over when she'd walked into the clubhouse must have seen through her disguise and recognised her. Or maybe he had a friend on the force and he'd got them to run her bike's licence plate.

She shifted her weight forwards, just a little, and winced, rubbing her back as if the crash was starting to trouble her. Managed to bring her heels under her thighs, so she could move faster if the situation went sideways, which, regrettably, it looked as if it was doing.

Gunnar raised his head and stared into her eyes. Beyond the retinas, it felt like, and straight into her soul. She felt he could read her thoughts, chief among which was the blaring klaxon saying, 'RUN!'

Gunnar nodded at the biker, who straightened, shot Stella a look of the purest evil, and then strolled outside.

Her pulse jacked up. Thudding in her chest. Her right leg had developed a twitch and was trembling. Was it visible? She glanced down. Oh, Christ!

'Everything OK?' she asked, her voice light, but also quavery.

Her plan to go undercover, so sensible in the warmth and order of the Örebro CID office, now felt like an act of the most brazen recklessness.

Gunnar smiled. 'Sure.'

Playing the Devil's Music

He wasn't going for a concealed weapon, for which she was grateful. Maybe it really was just some internal gang business. Yes, that could be it. The card player just didn't want a stranger witnessing whatever it was he had to impart to his boss.

She tilted her head towards the door.

'Trouble.'

'Not really. Remi just told me he recognised you from the TV. He's a massive news nerd. No idea why, really, but we all have our passions, don't we? Stella.'

'Look, Gunnar, I can explain. This isn't about the Demons. I—'

He held up a hand.

'I for one, love my bike. I expect you love yours, too. What was it, a Speed Twin?'

Shit! That use of the past tense was anything but accidental. She turned her head all the way to the door. Just in time to rear back as an ear-splitting bang rattled the windows. Through the glass, flames – bright orange and yellow – blossomed.

With Gunnar's mocking laughter ringing in her ears, she raced outside.

The Triumph lay on its side, several metres from where she'd left it. Fire was busy consuming it from the tail-light to the front forks. The petrol tank had burst open like an over-ripe fruit. Greasy black smoke coiled up into the trees. The stink of burning fuel, rubber and the padding from the saddle filled her nostrils, making her retch.

Off to one side, the card player stood, regarding her with a glare that would have stripped paint. Over his arm, a pump-action shotgun, into which he was slotting home cartridges, one after the other. The rest of the gang were standing off to one side of the charred wreckage of her bike. The rifles were back. And so were knives, machetes and an ominous length of blue polypropylene rope.

Time to act. Not to think.

Stella didn't have a gun, not even a knife, nor a leather roll filled with pound coins. But she still had her street-fighting skills and was as fit as she'd ever been thanks to her daily runs with Jonna.

A path led away from the clubhouse into the forest. It was that or the road. But Harleys could use the road. In the trees, they'd be useless. The Demons would have to come after her on foot.

She ran straight at the card player. Eyes wide, he raised the shotgun. But she charged into him before the barrel was anywhere near level. A handful of clawed fingers to the face and, over his scream, she ran for the pines.

A glance back over her shoulder as she entered the trees, just to see how many were coming after her. Odd. Not one.

Eyes front. No sense tripping. And Gunnar appeared in front of her, swinging a baseball bat.

The explosion was louder than when her bike went up. Blinding white light. A percussive bang between her ears. A roaring that sounded like hell itself opening up in the Swedish forests. Agony that spread from the centre of her head and radiated to every part of her body, along nerves screeching with pain.

Then blackness.

45

Stella opened her eyes.

Or the right one, at least. The left was stuck shut. Without the benefits of binocular vision, the scene in front of her looked flat. Unreal. If only.

Seven men. Gunnar at the centre. Each armed with a knife or a gun, a bat or a heavy wrench.

Shit-the-devil, her head hurt. No, strike that. Hurting she could have dealt with. Her head was ... wrong, somehow. A deep well of pain had erupted somewhere behind her eyes and spewed molten agony into every corner of her brain. Her arms were burning, too. A searing sensation in her armpits as if devils were trying to pull her apart.

She raised her head, and the act of tipping it back set off an explosion at the back of her skull.

Dark curtains swung shut over her vision, permitting her a final glimpse of her hands, bound at the wrist with blue rope and tethered to a branch.

Months passed, years... She was drowning. Icy Swedish seas lashing her from side to side, turning her over and over in the waves. Freezing water poured into her nose. Deep down below her, in the dark, sinuous creatures with needle teeth and eyes like jade marbles grinned up at her. She retched.

And opened her eyes. Both of them this time. Her face was wet and her vision was stained pink. She looked up, wincing at the lancing pain that speared from one temple to the other. Her wrists were tied individually, the rope between them slung over a broken-off stub of a branch.

Gunnar stood in front of her. A steel pail dangling from his left hand. Her head was still bad, but at least now she could think. She looked down. Her jacket was gone. And her shirt had been cut open right down to her navel.

Fuck.

Gunnar slung the pail away. It hit a pine tree with a clank and fell into the thick carpet of needles deposited over many seasons. In his other hand he held a knife. The narrow silver blade glittered in the sun slanting down through the trees.

He stepped closer. She could smell him. Sweat. Grease. Beer. Her stomach rolled over.

He sneered.

'Fucking cop. Thought you could just invade my territory? My world? Did you?'

'Wait. You don't want to do this.'

'Don't I? Seems to me like I do. It's just you and me now, Stella.'

He turned a full circle. The others were gone. He'd sent them away. Why? Did he not want witnesses? Her dread increased. Not a regular beating, then. Something more private? More personal? Oh, shit! She was face to face with the Devil of Axberg. How had she miscalculated so badly?

The blade extended towards her breastbone. She drew back until her spine was pressed tight against the rough barked trunk. He slid the tip under the band of her bra and pulled it out until the elastic parted under the edge of the knife.

'Yes, I'm a cop, Gunnar,' she said, summoning every last grain of self-possession to inject some steel into her voice. 'People know I'm here. You hurt me, they'll know and they'll come for you.

You'll spend the rest of your life in Kumla Bunker. At least you'll get to hang out with your master, Ulrik Ahlgren.'

He curled his lip. 'That freak? I don't think so. Once I've finished with you, we'll make you disappear. Let the cops come. They won't find anything. No bike. No body. Nothing. They won't be able to prove you were ever here.'

'Don't be so sure. You think we'd mount an operation like this without full back up? Of course they know I'm here.' She improvised. 'My bike was fitted with a tracker.'

'So let's talk about why you *are* here.'

'Untie me first.'

He stuck the point of the knife into the skin over her sternum, hard enough to draw blood. 'I watch the news, you know. That serial killer you're after? I know what he does. So unless you want to end up as victim number four, you better tell me why you came out here.'

She looked down. The bead of blood, bright red against the pale skin, rolled slowly down her belly. Untied, she'd stand a chance. Had put down bigger, harder men than Gunnar. With or without a weapon. But like this, all she had was her skills as a negotiator.

'I think it's one of the Werewolves. I think Joel Varela was taking money to look the other way. He double-crossed them and they murdered him for it. I needed evidence to support my theory. That's why I came to see you. I knew there was history between the Demons and the Werewolves. I swear to you, Gunnar, that's the truth. Nobody's looking at you or your club. Not for the murders anyway. Anything else going on is way outside my case. You probably know more about that than I do. Now, please, before this goes too far, untie me. I'll go and I promise I won't report this.'

He'd been nodding as she gabbled out her explanation. The knife had dropped from her breastbone, too. He was weighing up the pros and cons, she could see it in the furrows grooved into his forehead, the way his eyes kept flicking away from hers. Her honesty had worked. She'd broken a few SPA rules on discussing active investigations, but even Nik Olsson would forgive her this transgression, given the circumstances.

'It's a great story, I'll give you that,' he said. 'And to be honest you've half-convinced me.'

'Great. So can you please let me go? My arms are on fire and my head hurts like the devil took a shit in it.'

The corners of his mouth pulled down.

'That's the trouble, though, isn't it, Stella? I believe you're hunting some psycho from the 'wolves. I wouldn't put it past them. But the other bit? You leaving us in peace?' He spread his hands and the knife's silver blade sparkled as it caught another sunbeam. 'How's that going to work? We attacked a cop. Fucked up her wheels.' He described circles in front of her face with the tip of the knife before prodding her breastbone again. 'Threatened all kinds of nasty things. I let you go and that's us finished.'

Suddenly, Stella's pulse rate dived. She felt weirdly calm. Because now that the talking was done, and it had failed, only one course of action remained. A course laden with risk and with minimal chance of success. She closed her eyes, searched inside her mind, ignoring the throbbing pain in her head and the hot needles driven deep into her armpits. *Where are you? I need you. Please! I can't do this on my own.*

And, from somewhere deep in her psyche, a place she'd thought cleansed by drugs, therapy and healthy living, notwithstanding the odd drunken night out with Jonna, a voice grew steadily louder.

I wondered when you'd come calling, babe. Leave it to me.

* * *

Other Stella opened her eyes.

Other Stella smiled at the ugly sonofabitch in front of her. So close she could smell his rank stench.

'You should have untied me when I asked nicely.'

Other Stella contracted her stomach muscles and lashed her right foot out into his balls. His eyes flashbulbed and his mouth opened in an 'O'. He had no chance to scream, though. She kicked him again, driving her left heel into his solar plexus. His diaphragm paralysed, Gunnar collapsed against her. She bucked him off and he fell sideways into the bed of pine needles.

It would have been better for him if his head had fallen further from the tree trunk he'd tethered her to. But Lady Luck never smiled for too long on anyone who went up against Other Stella. She'd already suffered all the bad fortune she was ever going to.

Crushing skulls was only for horror films. You could break a bone in your foot trying. So she stood on his throat and let her weight sag. After a while, she brought her boot heel off his neck. The knife was still clutched in his right hand. Useless to her anyway, unless she could get her boots and socks off unaided and then develop Paralympian levels of foot dexterity.

She looked up. Assessed the angle and length of the sharp stub of branch supporting her. Nodded. Yes, that could work.

She tensed her stomach muscles and hoisted her legs up from her hips, bringing her knees in close to her body. Teeth gritted against the pain from her arms, she raised her knees higher then straightened her legs until she was almost inverted. Something to be said for core strength after all.

Now for the tricky bit. She needed to separate her wrists enough to get her boots between them. Joints cracking like eggs being stamped on, she parted her wrists just enough and thrust her boots into the narrow gap she'd created. In the distance, she heard laughter. Men calling for Gunnar. Asking when it was their turn.

With the rope wedged against the soles of her boots, she strained against her own weight, trying to straighten her legs. The rope started to creak over the branch. A centimetre. Then a jerk. Two more. She pushed harder, feeling her buttocks, her thighs, her calves flowing with blood as she summoned up every last ounce of strength. The rope jerked again and shifted five centimetres towards the broken end of the stub.

She screamed and imagined kicking the dead biker all the way to hell. The rope slipped off the end of the branch and she crashed down into the pine needles. She grabbed the knife and slit the rope at both wrists, shaking it off and then running into the dense tree cover.

'Hey, Gunnar, did you kill her?' someone shouted. She recognised the voice. Card player. 'No fair before we got to play!'

More laughter.

She began circling back.

They'd left the clubhouse unattended. The bikes, too. She could take one and leave. Nobody any the wiser. OK, Gunnar was probably dead, but they'd hardly go to the police, would they? Not exactly on-brand, was it?

The trouble was, they'd been going to rape her and kill her. Mess up her corpse so she looked like another victim. And there was every chance they'd come after her. What if they caught her before she reached Monktorp? Even if they didn't, they'd made her. She wouldn't be safe, even in Stockholm.

Plus, they started it.

Other Stella turned back towards the forest.

46

Screams.

No, not screams. Sirens.

Stella jerked awake. She was lying on the ground in front of the Demons' clubhouse.

The pain from the head wound had transmuted from a rusty spearpoint jabbed into the back of her eyeballs to a pounding ache like a two-bottle hangover. She could work with that. But her chest felt as though someone had made free with a blowtorch.

She raised herself on her elbows and looked down. Frowned. Hadn't Gunnar stopped once he'd jabbed her with the point of his flick-knife? Now a cut extended down from the original penetration wound for five centimetres. Black blood had clotted the wound but it still looked nasty and it hurt like hell.

She rolled sideways and managed to raise herself up onto her hands and knees.

But her head swam and she had to sink down onto her elbows, resting her throbbing forehead on the cool earth. Her forearms bore shallow cuts, too. Nothing serious, but puzzling all the same.

A familiar voice shouted from some distance away.

'I see her!'

It was Lucy. Running footsteps. Then Lucy was crouching at her side.

'Stella, are you OK? Can you hear me? Oh, shit, what the fuck did they do to you?'

Cautiously, Stella lifted her head. Swivelled round until she could sit on the ground. She took in her surroundings. She was outside the clubhouse. The bikes were still there but of the Demons there was no sign.

'I'm fine. I think. A little groggy. One of them recognised me. They tied me up. They were going to kill me. Eventually,' she added.

'Oh, Jesus. Thank God you got away.'

Sven appeared and he, too, knelt by Stella's side.

'Hey, Stella. Let's get you up. An ambulance is on its way.' Sven and Lucy took an arm each and between the three of them managed to get Stella standing. Her head went swimmy again and white stars sparkled around the edges of her vision. Where the fuck were the Demons?

And why did she have a horrible queasy sense of foreboding?

The two cops led her to a marked Volvo estate with the hatch up, and helped her sit on the back bumper.

'Get a first-aid kit, Sven,' Lucy said sharply. 'I'll stay with Stella.'

Once he'd gone, Lucy pulled a silver thermal blanket out from the boot space and draped it over Stella's shoulders. Solicitously, she drew the front edges together over her exposed breasts. 'There. That's better. Sven couldn't get his eyes back in their sockets. I'm afraid that cut's going to need stitches.' Her eyes widened. 'It wasn't one of them, was it? The Devil of Axberg?'

Stella shook her head. Then, as pain bloomed like a black toadstool between her ears, wished she hadn't. The pain made her nauseous and she had to swallow hard to stop herself vomiting.

'I don't think so. How did you know to come for me?'

Lucy smiled. 'It was Roger. He called in as soon as he was out of trouble at the ER. Said he'd told you to go in alone and now he was regretting it.'

Stella had to smile. She hadn't expected gallantry from the bearded biker-cop.

'Well, he didn't tell me exactly. It was a joint decision. And he was off his face on morphine. But I'm glad you're here.'

'Not just me and Sven,' Lucy said. 'Look.'

Gingerly, Stella turned her head in the direction Lucy was pointing. Four uniformed cops carrying automatic rifles were patrolling the area in front of the club house. Two more emerged from the front door, shaking their heads.

'Place is empty,' one called over.

'Can you remember anything before you were knocked out?' Lucy asked.

That was a good question. Because as Stella racked her brain for a memory, all she found was a blank. She'd been tied to a pine tree. Gunnar had threatened her with the knife and dug it into her skin. She'd closed her eyes, and … what? The memory just ended.

'Their leader smacked me in the head with a baseball bat. He tied me up and cut me and then it's just a blank, Lucy. I can't remember anything. I just woke up here. I must have fought my way free somehow, then blacked out.'

Lucy nodded. Her focus shifted to a point above Stella's eyes.

'That's a pretty big goose-egg you've got on your forehead. You might have a concussion. They'll probably want to keep you in overnight at Köping just in case.'

Normally Stella would have protested. But the way she felt, the thought of a night somewhere cool and safe, with painkillers on tap, held a certain appeal. And Gunnar had confirmed her suspicions about Joel Varela, which meant she could at least share the intel with Sven and Lucy.

'Detectives! Over here!'

Lucy looked over to where one of the uniformed cops had walked into the forest.

'I'd better go. Are you all right here for a minute?'

'I'll be fine. Go.'

Lucy hurried away in the direction of the shouting. Stella lay back until her head was resting on the kit bag at the rear of the load space. She closed her eyes. You weren't supposed to fall asleep if you had concussion, that's what the doctors all said. But she was so very tired. Suddenly she felt as though she'd gone ten rounds with Mike Tyson.

Even her knuckles hurt.

47

Lucy ran through the pines down the curving track, which narrowed at one point to the width of her hips. She emerged into a clearing maybe thirty metres in diameter, and gasped. The uniform, Aaron his name was, was standing open-mouthed on the far side of the roughly circular space.

Seven bodies lay scattered on the thick carpet of pine needles. Flies were buzzing everywhere, drawn especially to the blood, which was spilled everywhere in scarlet splotches.

These were clearly members of the Demons. Each body wore the denim cut-off emblazoned with their patch; a flaming horned skull with blazing red eyes. Above, the word 'DEMONS'; below, 'MC'.

They had slaughtered each other. It was the only explanation that made any sense.

One held a sawn-off shotgun. The hand wrapped around the cut-down wooden stock was bloody with back-spatter. Lying a metre away, the remains of another man, the top of his head down to his lower jaw entirely obliterated.

Another lay on his back, the handle of a hunting knife protruding from his black T-shirt. It bore the name, Sepülkå, in spiky Gothic capitals. His right hand gripped a wrench that must have been forty-five centimetres long. Its chromed jaws glistened with blood, where they weren't sullied with greyish pink clots of tissue. The source of the mess wasn't hard to find. A third man lay on his side, the side of his head disfigured by a crater large enough to push a fist into.

Lucy scanned the other bodies. More gunshot wounds. A throat slashed open like an envelope from ear to ear. A narrow-bladed flick knife with a bone handle embedded in an eye socket. Utter carnage. The metallic stink of the blood made her gag. Above the furious buzzing of the flies, she spoke to Aaron.

'What the hell happened here?'

He shrugged. 'Maybe they fell out over who was going to kill Stella. Does it matter? From what Roger said, this is a result for us.'

'Well of course it matters! Look around you. Seven dead bodies.'

'Yeah, but they killed each other, didn't they? Oh no, wait!' He slapped the front of his head. 'Despite being knocked cold and suffering severe injuries, Stella singlehandedly took out a Hells Angels seven-a-side team. Yeah, that'll be it.'

He was right. Nothing else made any sense.

'You'd better secure the scene anyway. The pathologist will need to see this. Forensics, too.'

'Fine. But Kersten's not going to be happy about having to spend her precious budget investigating seven biker-on-biker killings. Not when the vics and the perps are the same people.'

Lucy shook her head and left him to it, directing two more uniforms to the scene as she passed them on the path.

Back at the Volvo, two paramedics were tending to Stella. One was shining a torch into her eyes, left, then right, then left again. The other was applying a dressing to the laceration on her breastbone. She'd kept the thermal blanket in place to protect Stella's modesty, for which Lucy was grateful. It was bad enough getting slashed by a murderous thug without having every male cop ogling your tits.

Playing the Devil's Music

Stella's hands rested on her knees while the paramedics worked. Nasty red weals encircled her wrists like bloody handcuffs. The skin was broken in places, and they were weeping blood. She had defensive wounds on her arms, too. Poor woman.

'Did you say they tied you up?' Lucy asked, frowning.

Stella looked up at her. 'What?'

'You were tied up. How did you get free?'

'It's really fuzzy. I was trying to pull myself off the branch they'd hung me from. I think I got loose and undid the knots with my teeth.'

'My God, Stella, you're a tough one. I just came from a clearing in the forest. It must be where they took you. It's a bloodbath.'

She told Stella about the mayhem she'd witnessed, to Stella's obvious shock.

'What happened?' Stella asked.

'Your guess is as good as mine. While you were out cold it looks like they had some kind of massive argument. Things kicked off and now we've got seven corpses.'

The paramedic dressing Stella's wound straightened and pulled off her gloves.

'Right. That will hold until they can stitch you up at Köping. Let's get you in the ambulance and we'll be off.'

Lucy walked alongside Stella until she was safely inside the ambulance and lying on the folded gurney.

'I have to stay here and coordinate things with Sven, but we'll come to the hospital as soon as we're done.'

Stella smiled. 'Thanks, Lucy. You're a lifesaver.'

As the ambulance turned a full circle, clipping one of the motorcycles, which crashed over onto its side, Lucy waved, even though she knew Stella couldn't see her. She wasn't really a lifesaver. The danger had passed by the time she and Sven and the cowboy squad arrived. But it was nice of her to offer praise like that when she was half-unconscious from a head wound.

She was lucky to be alive. She must have fought like a tiger.

48

KÖPING

The morning after the Monktorp Massacre, as everyone at the Örebro copshop was calling it, Stella was sitting in the dayroom at Köping Hospital, a magazine lying open but unread on her lap.

The same thought, though dressed in many disguises, chased itself round and round inside her head.

Just what, exactly, had happened out there in the forest?

For the hundredth time, she closed her eyes and willed herself back there. Her stomach churned as the vivid memory of being strung up from the pine tree filled her memories.

She smelled Gunnar Halvorsson's sweaty stink. Saw the glint in his eyes as he swung his blade in front of her. He'd cut her, she was sure of that, at least.

But then, nothing.

Her next memory was of coming round outside the clubhouse, woken by police sirens, her head splitting and her chest burning.

Was Gunnar the Devil of Axberg? He'd known about the pentagrams, but he'd also said he'd seen it on the TV. She tried calling Sören but his phone went straight to voicemail. She called Nik. He picked up on the first ring, which answered her question. He, at least, was still alive.

A nurse came by to ask her how she was feeling. Ten minutes later, a doctor arrived. She took Stella's temperature and blood pressure, asked a few questions about her mental state and then said she was free to go once they could get the discharge nurse to sign off on the paperwork.

Stella's phone rang. She reached for it and, when she saw the Caller ID, smiled widely.

'Vicky! How the fuck are you? It's been too long.'

'I'm fine, lovely. Really good. How are you?'

'You want the Instagram answer or the truth?'

Vicky laughed. 'Been in the wars again?'

'I was undercover with a gang of outlaw bikers hunting a Satanic serial killer but they made me. I got whacked with a baseball bat and was almost raped and murdered. But lucky for me, I passed out with concussion and while I was unconscious they all killed each other.' A beat. 'So, how's your week been?'

'Stella Cole, you are shitting me.'

'Vicky Riley, I shit you not.'

'Jesus, mate, when you go for it, you really go for it, don't you?'

'Listen, until a couple of weeks ago I was doing drugs talks to Swedish teenagers.'

'Really? That doesn't sound like your usual beat. What happened?'

'It's a long, and very boring story. Seriously, though, how have you been? How's married life treating you?'

'That's why I'm calling, actually.'

Vicky's tone changed. Became more serious. Oh, God. The marriage was on the rocks.

'If Damien's been playing around, I will come back to England and cut his cock off.'

Vicky laughed. 'No, no, it's nothing like that. Although that sounded scarily authentic.'

'What, then?'

'I'm pregnant.'

'Oh my God, Vicky, that's fantastic! When are you due?'

'Not till January. We just went for our twelve-week scan. I wanted you to be one of the first to know.'

'I'm so pleased for you and Damien. And I'm really sorry for threatening to castrate him. Especially since he's obviously good with it.'

More laughter from Vicky. 'So, listen. Damien and I were discussing things, you know, about after it's born and I totally want you to say no if it's not right for you, you know if it's too ... well, too painful, but the thing is,' Vicky sucked in a breath loudly, 'well, we'd love you to be Godmother. There. I've said it. What do you think? No, don't answer that. Look, have a think OK? No pressure. Just let me know whenever you can. I'd totally understand if you—'

Stella couldn't remember feeling this happy in a long while.

'Can you just shut up for a second? Of course I'll be Godmother! I'll be the best bloody Godmother ever. I'll do the drugs talk, the sex talk. I'll take them to unsuitable movies, buy them make-up, I'll—'

' – let's start with renouncing Satan and all his works and then maybe move on to reading bedtime stories for now, yes?'

The mention of Satan dragged Stella's mind back to darker thoughts. Not the killer stalking Sweden's finest. A very different threat from Stella's past, and the reason she was sitting in a Swedish hospital and not an English one.

'January, you said?'

'Yes. I don't know the exact date, but it's early days and those calculations are a bit bloody random, aren't they? But you can get some time off for the christening, can't you? It's partly why I wanted to tell you so soon. I know how the job gets all-consuming. I used to feel the same way about journalism until this business.'

'It's not that.' *I'll just need to sneak into Britain incognito and hope the prime minister doesn't have me on some terrorism watch list.* 'I'll, er, yes. It's fine. I'll sort it out. Get some leave. Lord knows, I have enough owing.'

* * *

Stella had never told Vicky about the real reason she'd decamped to Sweden. As far as her best friend knew, like Stella's former colleagues in the Met, it was an officer swap that had worked out so well, she'd applied to have it made permanent.

Keeping quiet had, not surprisingly, been one of the prime minister's conditions. But Gemma Dowding had been as good as her word, and no harm had come to Stella's brother- and sister-in-law or their two daughters.

But now, as she waited for the discharge nurse to release her from the confines of the hospital, Stella realised she would need to find a way to communicate with Dowding. To beg for a hall pass that would allow her to attend the christening.

While she worked at the puzzle, a nurse in salmon-pink scrubs arrived and, after getting Stella to sign a couple of forms, added her own signature and then brightly told her she was good to go.

49

ÖREBRO

Kersten re-read the report from the forensics team who'd processed the scene at the biker gang's little outlaw hideout. How could such a small group of people cause her so much trouble? Although, looking on the bright side, at least the small group was now even smaller.

Stella's memory had failed to release any more details. The doctors at Köping had warned her that amnesia was a frequent and entirely expected side-effect of concussion, which Stella had indeed sustained.

The blow to her head had left splinters of wood embedded deep in her epidermis along with fragments of paint and varnish, all of which had been matched to a bat found near the corpse of one Gunnar Halvorsson, the self-styled president of the Demons' Motorcycle Club. It bore his fingerprints.

Scrapings from Stella's fingernails yielded tissue matched to several of the bikers, who it appeared had attacked her en masse.

She also suffered several defensive wounds to her forearms, though luckily the cuts, where they had penetrated her sturdy leather jacket, were shallow.

The cut to her chest was more serious and the doctors had prescribed a course of antibiotics. Kersten had arranged an appointment for Stella with a reconstructive plastic surgeon at Karolinska University Hospital in Stockholm.

Given the bizarre nature of the murders, she had recommended to the chief prosecutor for Örebro County that the case be opened and closed summarily. Her budgets being just as squeezed as Kersten's, the prosecutor had agreed at once.

It was perhaps the only bright spot in a day of dark thoughts.

But at least Kersten could save on the hundreds of thousands it would otherwise have cost her to order a full pathology and forensics work-up on seven corpses. Not to mention a primary crime scene that was literally crawling with wildlife, from beetles to badgers.

With nobody left alive to prosecute for the assault on Stella, there was nothing more she could do, bar recommend her for a Commissioner's Commendation for bravery. Stella had tried to wave it off as just part of the job, but Kersten was determined.

And now, just two days after being almost killed, Stella was back on it, putting the local team to shame.

Idly, Kersten wondered whether there was anything she could do to tempt Stella away from the big city.

50

LULEÅ

The mortuary at Sunderby Hospital in Luleå was chilly.

Stella shivered, despite the extra jumper she'd put on that morning. Beside her, Henrik Brodin shook his head as he snapped on his gloves. Owing to the need to produce fast results, he'd decided to conduct the post mortem in the town rather than have the body transported to the nearest RMV facility in Umeå.

Lying on the cold steel dissection table in front of them was the body of Sören Roos. He'd been murdered in virtually the same way as his three former colleagues and fellow members of the Hunter Killers.

The body had been discovered by hunters. It had lain unnoticed for a couple of days. In that time, it had been badly disturbed by scavengers.

Wolves, was Henrik's best guess. They had partially disarticulated the body before stripping most of the flesh from the face and torso.

As a result, the local cops hadn't immediately recognised the similarities with the investigation down south. Definitely a case of cock-up rather than conspiracy, but it had cost Stella valuable time.

The remaining visible artefacts on the body were clearly the work of the Devil of Axberg, from the bottom corner of the pentagram to the infestation of bugs inside the hollowed-out skull. But there were glaring inconsistencies, too.

Most obviously, no antlers. But also no attempt to display or pose the body. It appeared the killer had attacked Sören on the path and then dragged the body into the undergrowth. Stella's initial suggestion that the wolves might have done it was scotched when Forensics identified a set of boot prints partially obscured by drag marks.

'What does it mean?' Henrik asked as they stood, side-by-side, staring at what was left of Sören Roos.

'Two theories. Either he's coming apart under the stress. What the psychologists call decompensating. Or he's getting bored and or sloppy.'

Henrik nodded, regarding her owlishly through his round tortoiseshell glasses.

'Which do you favour?'

'Number two. I don't think he's a classic psychopathic serial killer at all. Our boy's got a taste for murder, but he doesn't have that inner compulsion to repeat and perfect his kills.'

'That would be my conclusion, too. Let's make a start, shall we?'

The cops in the cold white room stood back to give him room. As he worked, the mortuary assistant moved around him, passing him tools and taking tissue samples to be weighed or examined further.

Henrik picked up the left hand. It was clenched into a fist so tight that the knuckles had turned bone white.

He turned to the small audience watching him and held up the arm by the wrist.

'Cadaveric spasm of the hand. This is a not uncommon

phenomenon in violent deaths. And it works independently of the onset and dissipation of rigor mortis. Observe.'

He laid the arm down again and tried forcing the fingers apart with his own. Even though the muscles of the arm were soft and pliable, the fist remained a tight ball of bone and sinew. Using a pair of sturdy cutters, Henrik snipped through the tendons holding the hand closed as tight as a clam. Each parted with a snap like a pencil breaking.

Gently, he uncurled each digit. Stella peered at the small colourful object clenched into the palm.

'Can I see that, please?'

Henrik tried to pick up the metal disc but couldn't move it.

'Needle-nose pliers, please,' he said.

The gleaming stainless-steel tool was already on its way to Henrik's waiting palm, proffered by the apparently psychic mortuary assistant.

Henrik worked the narrow nose of the pliers under the edge of the disc and pried it free. Dead centre in the white circle of exposed skin was a tiny red puncture wound. Henrik turned the disc over to reveal a short spike impressed a couple of millimetres from its sharpened tip by two dents.

He dropped it into Stella's gloved hand.

'It appears to be a badge of some kind. The clip is missing.'

Stella frowned as she regarded the enamelled pin. She'd seen the design somewhere before. A black W formed from two interlocking Vs on a red background. The whole surrounded by a white circle. It reminded her of the logo of Reborn Sweden, with its fascistic overtones. But that wasn't it.

She closed her eyes. Where had she seen it? If only her memory hadn't been knocked several degrees off centre by Gunnar Halvorsson's home-run smack with the baseball bat.

That was it! She snapped her eyes open.

'It's a Werewolves badge! The biker gang down in Örebro. We've got them. I have to go. Email me your report, yes.'

Henrik nodded. Stella thanked the local cops and the assistant and photographer and then left for the airport.

By the time her plane had touched down on the tarmac, Stella had received an email communicating even better news than the presence of the Werewolves badge on Sören's body.

A CSO at the primary crime scene had found a bloodstained piece of glass bearing a single fingerprint. The results had come back from the national database with a twenty-one-point match to an individual with a string of convictions for violence, theft and possession of drugs.

One Klas Helander.

51

PARTILLE

Given the suspect's occupation, Kersten had authorised a full arrest team.

That meant the entire CID team, plus half a dozen uniformed inspectors from Örebro. Plus eight black-clad members of the 'cowboy squad' armed with an array of automatic weapons alongside the standard-issue pistols.

The Regional Tactical Support team, as they were properly known, were under the command of a black-bearded former army officer named William Brink.

The Örebro cops were under Sven's command. Privately he'd let Stella know he was happy for her to lead on any tactical decisions when the moment to put the cuffs on Helander neared.

At the briefing, William had asked Stella for an assessment of the threat level from the Werewolves.

'High. We have to assume they'll be armed. If the Demons

were a reliable guide, expect rifles at the very least. Maybe submachine guns.'

'Should we go in covert, do you think?'

She'd shaken her head.

'The terrain's all wrong. I'd suggest we go in fast and hard. They won't be expecting us so we have the element of surprise. By the time they realise what's happening, you and your team can have them all on the ground staring up the barrels of your Uzis or whatever you guys favour these days.'

That had drawn grins from the tactical squad, whose Kevlar-reinforced outfits creaked and rustled when one of them shifted in their chair or raised a mug of coffee to their lips.

'That would be the LWRC M6 assault rifle,' William said with a small smile. 'SPA variant in tactical black livery.'

'Don't forget the tear gas, boss,' a young female team member called out. 'We'll have those bikers crying for their mamas if they try anything funny.'

More laughter. But Stella could sense it: the high-stakes anxiety beneath the bravado and the banter.

And now it was time. Three plain grey Transit vans bumbled down the narrowing lane towards the Werewolves' clubhouse. Leading them, a black Volvo T5 driven by Sven with Stella literally riding shotgun. In the back seats, Lucy and another detective named Robert Nysgård, a twenty-year veteran. All four wore body armour.

Behind the Transits, four marked Volvos stuffed with uniformed inspectors, also armoured up, and bristling with pistols, Heckler & Koch MP5 submachine guns, SIG Sauer pistols and Tasers.

In all, thirty heavily armed police officers against a gang whose total estimated membership, excluding those in prison or overseas, as researched by the intelligence team, was nineteen. Whether all would be present at the clubhouse was doubtful, but as Kersten had said before sending them out, 'I do not want any unpleasant surprises. I believe the military doctrine is "overwhelming force".'

Playing the Devil's Music

'It's actually "Rapid Dominance",' William had said gravely. 'AKA "Shock and Awe".'

As the convoy sped down the lane, Stella, pulse racing, reflected that the Werewolves were about to experience a considerable amount of both emotions.

Sven slewed the T5 to a stop in the far side of the parking area in front of the Falun Red clubhouse. The move, like everything else about the arrest, had been brainstormed and planned down to the last detail back at Örebro. Whiteboards bore masses of curving multi-coloured arrows that resembled playbooks for football games.

As he, Stella, Lucy and Robert jumped out, pistols drawn, the tactical Transit vans raced in behind them. At once the rear doors banged wide and the 'cowboy squad' jumped out, assault rifles held ready to fire. Finally, the marked cars pulled in, disgorging their uniformed inspectors.

Several Werewolves were lounging in deckchairs on the wooden veranda built along the front of the clubhouse. They scrambled to extricate themselves from the chairs but by the time they'd made it to the vertical, armed officers were aiming machine guns at their heads and screaming for them to move straight to the horizontal.

More bikers ran over from a workshop on the far side of the compound, some already pulling pistols from the waistbands of their grimy jeans. But faced with a platoon of SPA officers screaming 'Armed police!' while pointing all manner of lethal firepower at them, they laid their weapons down and joined their fellows, face-down in the dirt, hands interlaced on the backs of their heads.

That left the clubhouse itself.

Stella pointed at the steel-reinforced door and shouted to Marc Andriesson, the inspector in charge of the forced-entry team.

'Break it down!'

As he beckoned the two-man team over, one carrying the

heavy steel ram known informally as *sprängaren* – 'the blaster' – the sound of breaking glass penetrated the shouting.

'Everybody take cover!' William roared as gun barrels were thrust through the shattered windows.

The remaining Werewolves opened fire, sending bullets ricocheting off the vehicles or punching holes through the bodywork. Under William's strict pre-mission orders, not one of his team returned fire.

Kersten had stipulated that she did not want a gun battle unless there was no other option. She'd avoided using the word 'optics', although Stella had felt it was a close call. But her meaning was clear all the same.

In Social Democratic Sweden, one did not simply spray bullets into a building, whether or not it contained outlaw bikers wanted for multiple murders.

Instead, one cowboy, the young female who'd quipped out the tear gas back at the copshop, levelled a launcher and sent an olive-green canister hissing its way through a window. Two more followed.

'Hold your fire!' William yelled. 'Wait.'

The Werewolves didn't emerge at once. As the seconds ticked by, Stella wondered whether they had breathing apparatus back there. But after half a minute, having burst out through the door, staggering blindly into the sun, every one of them was immobilised on the ground, his hands cuffed behind his back, retching and choking as the fiery pepper-based gas wreaked havoc on the mucus membranes lining their nostrils and eyelids.

She pointed out Klas Helander to Sven. 'That's him.'

Pistol drawn, Sven marched over and squatted beside the prone biker.

'Klas Helander, you are under arrest for murder.'

In the circumstances, they had no option but to arrest the other bikers. The charges would relate to possession and discharge of firearms, although everyone had agreed beforehand that unless any officers were hurt, the most efficient course of legal action would be to confiscate the weapons and release them with the charges left on file.

In all, the arrested bikers numbered eleven: Klas Helander himself, Lukas Ström, Elias Lindgren, Ludvig Rönnbäck, Mats Kjellson, Stefan Swansson, Egil Berglund, Karl Persson, Leif Andersson, Sten Andersson and Alex Johansson.

The station at Örebro didn't have any spare cells so apart from Klas himself, the arrested men were driven to a purpose-built SPA detention centre for violent criminals at Linköping.

* * *

Klas asserted his right to a lawyer, and it wasn't until 10:00 a.m. the following day that he sat, accompanied by *Advokat* Elsa Wiklund, facing Stella and Sven.

Accused and lawyer made an odd couple. He, still in his biker gear, wild-haired and even wilder-eyed, glaring at the two detectives as if he was about to transform into his gang's namesake. She, severe, groomed into a sleek, polished example of professional Swedish womanhood, in an olive-green trouser suit, snowy-white blouse and thin-rimmed spectacles.

Once the recorder had been turned on and introductions given, *Advokat* Wiklund opened the burgundy leather portfolio in front of her and withdrew a single typed sheet on her firm's letterhead. She slid it across the table to Stella.

'We are making a formal complaint against the arresting officers individually, and the SPA corporately for the brutal and illegal nature of the arrest of my client and his fellow club-members,' she said in clipped diction a world away from the soft burr of the Örebro accent heard throughout the county.

Rather than pick up the letter, Stella looked at Elsa. Where had a greaseball like Helander found such a high-toned lawyer? And, more to the point, how could he afford her? She hadn't read the letter, but she recognised the logo in the top-left corner. TSC & Partners were a top law firm headquartered in Stockholm, but with branches in every Swedish county.

The answer presented itself with an ironic salute and an eye-roll. *Well, Detective Inspector Cole, where do you* think *he got the money? Selling girl scout cookies?*

Drugs. Of course.

Stella smiled at her. She was attractive, with straw-blonde hair and skin that owed its glow and clarity to good genes and plenty of outdoor exercise, rather than anything purchased at a cosmetics counter. Jonna was just the same.

Oh God, it would be good to go for a run sometime very soon when this dreadful business was behind her. Maybe she could get Kersten to write a report for Malin back in Stockholm that would speed Stella's replacement on the homicide squad.

Time to get going then, and make it a reality.

52

Stella looked Klas in the eye.

'Tell me, Klas, why did you and your fellow members barricade yourselves in your clubhouse and then open fire with automatic weapons?'

'We sincerely believed we were being attacked by another motorcycle club. The Demons, if you want to make a note,' he said to Sven. 'Fearing for our lives, we took shelter in our club house and, on hearing gunfire, felt we had no other option but to defend ourselves as best we could.'

She heard, in Klas's precise phrases, the meticulous wording of an expensive lawyer. Like the one sitting next to him.

'With automatic weapons, which are illegal for civilians to own in Sweden.'

Elsa Wiklund leaned forwards. 'My client believed he was permitted to own the weapons as they were used purely on club-owned land.'

'Well, as your client could have found out, and you, *Advokat* Wiklund, most definitely *should* know, that is incorrect. However, we are not here to discuss illegal firearms charges.'

Sven leaned forwards.

'Not yet, anyway.'

Stella smiled, first at him, then the lawyer, then at Klas.

'Indeed. Not yet.'

'My client also wishes to state, for the record, that since no verbal warnings were given, he and his friends were justified in their response. However, in the cold light of day, he realises they may have over-reacted.'

'Yeah.' Klas leaned back and folded his hands behind his head. 'And I'm sorry.'

Stella nodded. 'Thank you for your apology, Klas. I'm sure the prosecutor will take your contrition into account. Although I would recommend you see an SPA audiologist as soon as possible, since verbal warnings *were* given, very loudly. Body-worn video will confirm this fact.' She smiled at Elsa. 'Perhaps you might like to make a note of my offer of medical assistance. Now, by some miracle, or perhaps your gang members' appalling marksmanship, Klas, not a single one of the rounds they fired hit an officer. Which is just as well.'

Elsa wasn't finished with her interruptions, which Stella was beginning to find tiresome. Although, to be fair, the young and clearly effective lawyer was only doing her job.

'My client further wishes to clarify that the Werewolves are not a gang, but a legally constituted club.'

'Really?' Stella deadpanned. 'In other circumstances, I would love to discuss exactly how that would sit with the many criminal convictions racked up by its members.' She held up a hand as Elsa opened her mouth again. 'But, as we are here to discuss multiple murders in which your *client* is a suspect, I think we'll move on to the matter at hand.'

At the word 'murder' Klas jerked in his chair as if electrocuted. His eyes widened until the whites were visible all the way around the ice-blue irises.

'Murder? Wait a minute! I didn't murder anybody. None of us did.'

'Where were you on Friday of last week, Klas?' Sven asked.

Playing the Devil's Music

The biker's head swung round as if he'd forgotten he was being interviewed by two officers.

'Friday? How the fuck should I know?'

'Well, it was only three days ago. Can't you remember?'

Klas swiped a hand across his face.

'OK, yeah, yeah, of course I can remember. I was riding.'

'Riding where?'

'Around.'

'Sorry, Klas,' Stella said, taking the invisible baton Sven had passed her. 'I'm afraid "around" really won't cut it as an alibi. Around where? Luleå?'

'Don't be stupid! That's the other end of the fucking country! I've never been there. It's a shithole.'

He was breathing heavily. Stella felt sure he had something to hide.

'How do you know?'

'How do I know what?'

'That it's a shithole? If you've never visited? I myself have been. I had to when Sören's mutilated body was found.'

'I meant the north generally,' he muttered.

'Leaving your next TripAdvisor review to one side, why don't you tell us where you *were* riding?'

'Up the road from Partille. I went to the lake to fish.'

'Which lake?'

'Aspen.'

'Catch anything?'

'A pike. Couple of perch.'

Sven nodded. 'Nice. Who were you fishing with?'

Klas scowled at him. 'Nobody. Look, I know how this works. But just because I don't have an alibi, that doesn't mean shit. I didn't murder anyone.'

'Inspectors, do you have any evidence to present to us?' Elsa asked. 'Because without it, I suspect you are engaged in a, forgive the joke, fishing expedition. But unlike my client, you are going to go away empty-handed.'

Stella nodded.

'You're right.' As Elsa closed her leather portfolio with a soft leathery slap and half-rose from her chair, Stella shook her head. 'I'm sorry. I meant you were right that unless we had some evidence we would be leaving with nothing. So it's fortunate that we do have evidence. Meaning your client, forgive the joke, is still on the hook.'

She turned to Sven, who handed her an evidence bag containing the shard of glass.

'For the tape, I am showing Mr Helander Exhibit SR/KH1.' She pushed the bag across to Klas, who stared at it as if she'd just handed him a piece of an alien spacecraft. 'Exhibit SR/KH1 is a piece of broken glass bearing smears of blood identified by DNA analysis as coming from Sören Roos, a former police officer murdered in Luleå on Friday June second, 2023. The glass also bears a fingerprint identified as belonging to Mr Helander.

'Klas, would you like to explain to us how your fingerprint got onto a piece of bloodstained glass found in close proximity to a dead man, in a place you claim never to have visited?'

'It's obvious. You lot planted it there.' He turned to Elsa. 'They're trying to frame me. Do something.'

Stung into action, Elsa reopened her portfolio and stared at the last page of notes. Then she looked up at Stella. Stella met her gaze and repelled it. Lawyers loved picking holes in circumstantial evidence. It was a lot harder to dismiss a fingerprint. Ideally Stella would have liked the print to be of the plastic type, actually pressed *into* the blood. But *beside* the blood was only a hair less convincing.

'Fingerprints can be smeared. How many points of comparison exist between the print on the glass and my client's? As you should know, under Swedish law, anything fewer than fourteen is of extremely limited evidential value.'

Stella could afford to indulge herself in a dramatic pause. She counted to five.

'Twenty-one. It's his, Elsa.'

Elsa eyes widened. She glanced at her notes as if a cue might magically appear there to help her formulate a response. Stella didn't allow her any more time.

'We have a second piece of evidence, Klas.'

From the beige card folder in front of her, she withdrew a second evidence bag. It contained the enamel pin Henrik had prised from Sören's palm.

'For the record, I am showing the suspect Exhibit SR/KH2.' She pushed the bag across the table towards Klas. 'Exhibit SR/KH2 is an enamel badge. Klas, could you describe the badge to me, please?'

He picked it up and examined it, turning it over in his hand.

'Fuck me,' he muttered.

'Would you like some time?' Stella asked solicitously. 'The plastic does make it a little difficult to make out the details.'

'No!' he snapped. 'It's a Werewolves badge.'

'How can you be so sure?'

He stared at her, a red-rimmed gaze she found hard to decode. He looked angry, but not with her. Yet he also looked strangely calm. If he was a psychopath, she could have found a ready explanation, but throughout the interview his emotions had fluctuated like any ordinary Swede hauled in for questioning about a brutal murder. In short, he didn't look, or act, like a wrong 'un.

'The design is two interlocking Vs. They are the first and last letters of our name. And they form a W, which we picked because it's the English way to spell Werewolf.'

'If I tell you that the pin was removed from the body of Sören Roos by RMV pathologist Henrik Brodin at the official post mortem, Klas, how would you react to that?'

'I would react by telling you I'm not your guy.'

'Despite your fingerprint being found at the crime scene and your gang's...' Stella smiled at Elsa. 'I beg your pardon, your *club's* badge being found literally spiked into a murder victim's palm?'

'Yes.'

'Can you explain that for us, Klas?'

He leaned back and folded his arms.

'That's not my badge. Check my denim. They took it off me when I was booked in. My badge is yellow and black. That one's red, black and white.'

Stella frowned. For the first time since starting the interview the ground beneath her feet felt less than rock-solid. She could picture the badge now, and he was right. The Werewolves all wore yellow and black pins. The first time Stella had met him, she'd thought it resembled a wasp in its colour scheme and wondered why they hadn't adopted that as their name.

'Whose badge is it, then?' she asked.

'Nobody's.'

'Sorry, Klas. I don't understand. You just confirmed that it's a Werewolves badge, but now you're also claiming it doesn't belong to one of your members. So, who does it belong to?'

'Nobody. Yet.' He rubbed his nose. 'Our existing badge, the yellow-and-black one? It got counterfeited. They're, like sacred. But some dipshit lost his and now you can buy replicas on eBay for a hundred krone. We had to get a new design done. That's a prototype in the bag.'

'How many people know about this?'

'The company making them. Me, and the other members.'

'OK, let me be more specific. How many people *have* one of the new design?'

Klas remained silent, biting his lip as if he could physically prevent himself from opening his mouth and answering with the truth.

And she saw it then. All this talk about legally constituted clubs and sacred badge designs. Like all gangs, they had an honour code. Probably including a clause about not ratting out fellow members on pain of death. Roger had talked about it. Klas knew *exactly* whose badge this was.

'Klas, I need to make something clear to you. At the moment, whether or not that badge is your personal property, you have identified it as belonging to the biker club of which you are the president. It was found on a murder victim's body. We also found your fingerprint at the scene.

Playing the Devil's Music

'The judge isn't going to need long to find you guilty of murder. Grossly cruel murder at that. And if the judge decides you murdered Sören, you're going to get convicted of three more extremely violent and sadistic murders as well. Two of which were of serving SPA officers. You don't need me to tell you how that's going to go down. You're looking at life inside Kumla, Klas. No parole. Ever. You'll die in there.'

Stella paused. Took a breath. Switched tone.

'Look, Klas, I understand. You have your code of honour that you live by. But don't you think we're a little bit past that? I know you know whose that badge is. Just tell me and we'll forget about the murder charge. You'll still be facing firearms charges, but I am sure with Elsa's help you can live to fight another day. It would be a shame to let Bikezilla go unridden until she rusts away.'

Maybe it was her recitation of the facts of his future that loosened his lips. But she leaned towards the empathy she'd shown him as a fellow biker.

The pause stretched out. The clock on the wall ticked. Beside her, Stella could hear Sven's breathing. Nice and steady.

Klas cleared his throat.

'It's Olaf's.'

She nodded. Beside her Sven noted down the name. 'This would be Olaf Wallin, your membership secretary?'

'Yes. He's the only one with a physical badge. We didn't want to risk the prototype getting lost as well.'

'I see. Could he have got a glass with your fingerprint on it?'

He shrugged. 'I guess so. He could have just taken one from the club house.'

A horrible thought occurred to Stella.

'Where is Olaf now, Klas?'

'How the fuck should I know?'

'Because he's your membership secretary?'

'I am not my brother's keeper.' A smirk.

'Great. Well, leaving aside the Bible quotes for now, if he's on his way to attack another police officer and you don't tell us where, you'll be facing charges of conspiracy to murder. Back to Kumla you go.'

Klas flung his arms wide. 'I'm telling you the truth!' He turned to Elsa. 'Make her understand.'

Elsa nodded to Stella. 'My client has answered your question. Please move on.'

'Do you have his number?'

'It's in my phone.'

Stella nodded. She had somewhere she needed to be. Urgently. She turned to Sven.

'Can we have a word outside?'

He nodded and suspended the interview.

Outside, he raised his eyebrows. 'What's going on?'

'I need to get to Nik Olsson. The last surviving member of the Hunter Killers. I thought arresting Klas meant he was safe but if it's Olaf, then Nik's in deadly danger.'

'What do you think we should do with Klas?'

She flicked her eyes at the closed door to the interview room. 'Him? Tell him we're charging him with illegal possession of automatic weapons, assaulting police officers, drug-dealing, resisting arrest, whatever you think will stick. Then put him back in holding.'

Leaving Sven to conclude the interview, Stella raced down to the custody suite and retrieved Klas's mobile phone. She took it back to the interview room and had him unlock it and show her Olaf Wallin's contact details.

Then she found a quiet place to make a call.

Stella pushed her phone hard against her ear.

Some strange illusion in her brain meant the gap between the second and third rings seemed to go on much longer than the first. Was he picking up? She drew in a quick breath. Then it rang again. And again.

'This is Nik Olsson. I'm not available to take your call right now. Please leave me a concise message including your number and I'll get back to you as soon as I am able. Thank you.'

'Nik, it's Stella. The murderer is Olaf Wallin. He's a member of the Werewolves biker gang and he's in the wind. I'm going after him but I need you to take steps to protect yourself. We've arrested the rest of his gang. He's going to find out we're onto him.'

She stabbed the red icon and, heart racing, called a second number.

It belonged to Olaf Wallin.

53

While she waited for the serial killer to answer his phone, Stella briefly wondered whether this was wise.

But what choice did she have? The element of surprise was already gone after the raid on the Werewolves clubhouse. No knowing whether one of them might have called him before being handcuffed.

'Who is this?'

'Olaf?'

'Is that you, super-cop? I wondered how long it would take you to catch on.'

'It's over. We've got evidence linking you to the murder of Sören Roos.'

'Oh, shit. Well, I guess you'd better arrest me. Oh, wait. You can't.' He laughed. An unpleasantly high-pitched giggle that set Stella's teeth on edge. 'Because you don't know where the fuck I am, do you?'

'Give yourself up now, Olaf, while you still can. We've got a whole squad of armed response officers coming for you.'

'Really! Coming for *me*? Come on then, super-bitch. Tell me where they're coming *to*?'

She was bluffing. And he knew it. And after all, what cards did she hold? He'd know that after brutally murdering four people including two serving police officers, there'd be no chance of release if he was caught. She had nothing to offer him.

Almost nothing.

She summoned the bad part of her. The part with a kill tally that dwarfed his. Lowered her voice.

'You have two choices, Olaf Wallin. You tell me where you are and you stay put until I find you. You'll get a fair trial and whatever comforts the Swedish justice system thinks appropriate. Or, you carry on the way you have been. And I'll come for you. When I find you, I will kill you. No Satanic props. No ritual. No stupid masturbatory fantasies. I'm just going to shoot you dead. Three seconds. One. Two—'

' – I'm at Nikodemus Olsson's summer house. I've been watching him for a while now. I thought I was going to have to do him in Stockholm, but then he made my life a whole lot easier by taking some time off and coming out here. Maybe I'll wait for you before I kill him. You can watch me in action. Then I'll kill you, too. But before I kill you, I'll—'

Stella cut him off.

She called SPA headquarters in Stockholm. As soon as the switchboard connected her to the Internal Affairs office, the phone was answered by a woman. Stella didn't recognise her voice.

'This is Detective Inspector Stella Cole. I need the address of Nik Olsson's summer house. It's urgent.'

'I'm not sure I should—'

' – I believe his life is in danger. *Imminent* danger. I need that address. Now!'

That did the trick. Although flustered, the woman found the address, actually GPS coordinates – 'It's very remote' – and texted it to Stella.

She entered it into her mapping app. It was closer to Örebro than Stockholm. A small blessing.

Playing the Devil's Music

Next, Stella called Malin. Same story but with a few more details. 'We need to get a firearms team up there.'

'I'll start things moving, but it will take a little while, Stella. They've had some personnel reductions recently and I know there's been a lot of activity in the city over the last shift.'

'They need to get over there, Malin! This biker, Olaf Wallin, he's the Devil of Axberg. He's going to kill Nik.'

'Leave it with me,' Malin said in her infuriatingly calm voice. 'What are you going to do?'

'I'm going up there.'

'Alone?'

'Our team is over-committed as it is. Örebro has even less resource than you do.'

She knew Malin would do her best. But sometimes cuts were just too deep to be stitched over, no matter how important the job or how vulnerable the potential victim.

At least Nik was forewarned, and forearmed. He'd be expecting trouble. Perhaps that was why he'd decamped to his summer house. He'd know the terrain better than Olaf and maybe he'd rigged up some additional security. Images of tripwires and high-intensity searchlights flitted across Stella's inner eye. She prayed it would be enough.

Sitting astride a liveried BMW 800cc bike she'd taken from the motor pool, Stella checked the route one last time. The journey would take less than thirty minutes.

She thumbed the starter button and twisted the throttle grip. The bike's motor coughed, then roared. She toed the gear lever down into first with a clunk and took off, the back wheel screeching as she fed it more power than the rubber could cope with.

Traffic was heavy and Stella swore as she was repeatedly blocked by slow-moving commuters or families in SUVs and estates. On a clear stretch of road she opened the throttle wide and swung out into the opposite carriageway, tearing down the line of virtually stationary vehicles, straight towards an oncoming truck. Its bank of headlights flashing on high-beam and its airhorns bellowing like an enraged elk, it bore down on her. The front car in the traffic queue on her side was still a hundred metres ahead. She wouldn't make it in time.

The truck was braking, although the driver still had the time or the bloody-mindedness to keep his hand wedged down on the horn button.

Almost blinded by his high beams, Stella shrieked at him and swung left, shooting into a gap just centimetres wider than the bike's handlebars. She had to fight to maintain control as the trucks boiling slipstream buffeted her.

The road opened up ahead of the temporary traffic lights that had been holding up the traffic.

The needle flickered upwards, crossing the hundred kph mark and surging on round the dial until it maxed out at 216 kph. Stella had to lean into the wind as she tore northwards towards the forest.

An unearthly calm descended on her as she rode towards her appointment with the Devil of Axberg. The thrum of the bike engine seemed to meld with her heartbeat, and at this speed the vibrations from the thrashing pistons died away until she was left at the centre of the storm.

Why, out of all the officers in the SPA, out of all the citizens of Sweden, did Olaf Wallin have to pick the one man who probably hated her more than anyone else?

And why, despite that, was she racing to try to save his life?

'Because I'm a cop!' she yelled into the foam-padded chin guard of her helmet. 'I *have* to.'

The storm gathered.

54

SPA HEADQUARTERS, STOCKHOLM

Tactical Support Group inspector Peter Sanger looked down at the receiver now purring softly in his hand.

So, Nik Olsson had got himself in a spot of bother, had he? Peter shook his head. Maybe the Devil of Axberg was going to give every cop in Kungsholmsgatan an early Christmas present.

Right up to January 2020, Peter's career had been on a steady upward trajectory, like a round fired from a rifle at a forty-five degree angle. *Säpo*, the Swedish Security Service, was supposed to have been his next posting. A vital stepping stone for anyone with his eye on the ultimate prize.

Until his run-in with Olsson and his sharp-teethed little colleagues in the Rat Squad, that is.

Then the bullet hit turbulence, veered off-course and plummeted earthwards. All thanks to an ill-advised investment in a property scheme that turned out to be financed with money from organised crime. Oh, boy, had Olsson had fun with that one.

Despite being entirely blameless, Peter had been made to walk the plank. Pushed off at the point of Olsson's cutlass and offered a choice. Retirement or a transfer.

He'd requested the TSG and been accepted, thanks to his military background. But it had been made clear to him that there he was based, and there he would remain.

He put the phone down.

He was short-staffed anyway, and thanks to some nutcase in Östermalm armed with a machete and wailing on about Allah or something, his entire squad were over there right now trying to prevent a bloodbath.

He'd make the call. See if he could pull a team out.

But first, coffee.

55

JÄGARASEN, VÄSTMANLAND COUNTY

Stella rode the BMW fast along the south bank of a lake named *Grågåsvatten*.

True to its name, greylag geese in their hundreds floated on its mirror-smooth surface. Honking, squabbling and occasionally flapping their way off the water, trailing diamonds of water from their webbed feet as they struggled to get airborne.

In any other circumstances, she might have stopped to admire the scene. But the need to rescue a colleague from a serial killer dampened any interest in Swedish wildlife she might have felt.

With five hundred metres to go, Stella slowed the bike to walking pace and pulled off the narrow track leading through the birch woods. She couldn't risk Olaf hearing the engine. Even if he were expecting her, she saw no need to advertise her arrival.

She heeled out the kickstand and leaned the bike over. Since arriving at the lakeshore, she hadn't seen another soul. In England a body of water this picturesque would have attracted trippers by the score, but this was Sweden. It probably wouldn't even make the top thousand prettiest lakes in central Sweden.

She drew her service weapon and checked the magazine. Nodding to herself, she headed into the woods, her boots crackling on the dry bracken and leaf litter left over from the previous autumn.

Nik's summerhouse faced the lake. Would Olaf be inside with Nik, waiting for her? It seemed the most likely scenario. Why tell her where he was, if not to lure her out there? The sun was hot on the top of her head. Sweat gathered in her armpits and trickled down her ribcage inside her leather bike jacket.

Finally, over a low ridge smothered with yellow wildflowers that smelled of honey, she saw it. A pretty wooden house, one storey, painted in, what else, Falun Red, with white eaves, window and door frames and a pretty veranda. A long dock extended out over the lake. At the far end, a rowing boat was tied up by its painter, rocking gently on the water.

As she circled around, a boat house came into view, painted to match the summerhouse.

Stella crouched behind a birch tree and closed her eyes. Strained to catch a sound, however small, that might give her a clue as to where Olaf might be holding Nik. Because that's what he'd be doing, she was sure of it.

She could picture it. Nik, restrained somehow, Olaf in a rocking chair or leaning nonchalantly against one of the wooden walls, pointing a shotgun or a handgun at Nik and boasting of what he intended to do to him.

Would Nik be pleading for his life? If he'd been a lifelong bureaucrat, Stella could easily imagine it. But Nik hadn't always headed the Rat Squad. He'd been a homicide cop. And a damned good one, too. He had steel in his soul; she'd seen it for herself. On balance, she thought he'd be keeping his thoughts to himself.

She pricked her ears.

Nothing.

Just the distant honking of the geese, fighting over mates, or just gossiping like Swedish market-goers wrangling with stallholders and exchanging the day's news.

She crept up to the rear of the house. Service weapon held up by her cheek, the smell of gun oil coiling into her nostrils, she slid under a window and then straightened her knees until she could peer over the sill and inside.

Specks of dust floated in the shafts of sunlight. Comfortable pine furniture with squashy cushions covered in bright floral print fabrics. Not what she'd have expected from Nik. She'd imagined grey suede, or maybe sackcloth and ashes, would be more his style.

Shelves of books, wildlife paintings clearly the work of an amateur. Nik again? Or did he have a flea-market habit when he was out here in the Boonies? No TV. Now that *did* fit with what she knew of the man.

She crept round to the side of the house. Two more windows flanking a door. On silent feet, she slithered along the wall and stretched out her free hand to grasp the handle. Out of the sun the metal was still cool to the touch.

She pushed it down and inwards. The door opened. Heart galloping, grip on the pistol butt slippery, she edged inside. With the door shut behind her, she closed her eyes and strained to catch a sound. But the house was utterly silent.

Slowly, sounds did emerge from the hiss of her own blood in her ears. A clock ticking laboriously, always seeming to be behind the beat, as if someone had a finger on the pendulum. A radio turned low, one male voice, one female. A news or discussion show of some kind. Through the open window at the front, geese honking distantly, still preoccupied with their territorial squabbles.

The front door led directly off the sitting room. Beside it sat pairs of long boots, and shorter ones for hiking. A rifle leaning against the wall. A pair of skis and poles on a rack to the left.

Three more doors. Kitchen, bedroom and bathroom, presumably.

Stella transferred her pistol to her left hand, wiped her palm then swapped hands again. She swung it open and stepped through, heart racing, gun levelled, a shout of 'armed police!' ready on her lips. Though if she found Olaf, with or without Nik, she was going to shoot unless he hit the deck immediately.

The bathroom, small, tiled in white with a waist-high dado rail of navy diamonds, was empty. She turned and advanced on the next door. Same routine. Pulse thudding against her ribs and a lump in her throat choking her, she pushed-entered-covered the bedroom. Also empty.

That just left the kitchen.

Images crowded her mind. A demonically grinning Olaf Wallin, face and hands bloody, ceremonial dagger in his hand. Nik bound and strung up to a hook in the ceiling. Oh, God! She reached out a hand for the handle. It was trembling. Changed her mind.

Stella reared back, raised her leg and booted the door in, charging in after it pistol raised, index finger curled around the trigger, ready to shoot the Devil of Axberg stone-dead and rescue her former tormentor.

The door swung all the way round, banging off the wall and bouncing back towards Stella, catching her painfully on the elbow. A dark human figure shifted in the gloomy corner: masked face, shapeless body, black legs below. She aimed and felt the screamed warning pressing against the backs of her incisors. Then she stopped, dropped her arm.

'Fucking hell!'

The intruder revealed himself as a coat stand bearing a floppy-brimmed hat of olive-green cotton, and a thornproof waxed duster with a brown corduroy collar and long skirts. Below them, a pair of turned-in green wellington boots.

She made a final rapid sweep of the house, but it was empty. That left two possibilities. Olaf had taken Nik into the forest, or they were in the boathouse.

She peered through the net curtain down to the dock and the

boat house. What would *she* do? Correction: what would *Other Stella* do?

Isn't it obvious, babe? The voice between her ears piped up. *You're a murderous nutjob with a hard-on for Satan. You've lured an SPA officer out to a remote cabin to save her colleague. You need some privacy, don't you?*

Stella nodded.

The boathouse.

56

As she drew nearer to the boathouse, Stella heard music emanating from its planked walls. A saw-edged thrashing of heavily distorted electric guitars, drums on the point of implosion from the abuse they were suffering and a thudding bassline. Bellowing vocals.

A small, four-paned window on the rear wall was the only point of access apart from making a frontal assault via the opening facing the lake. Stella stood on a sawn cylinder of birch log and peered in through the dusty glass. The sight made her breath catch in her throat.

Nik Olsson stood, or, more accurately, hung, in a narrow gap between two tall piles of wooden boxes. His arms lay across the topmost crates. Olaf had fixed him there somehow. She looked for nails, the gruesome image being the place her mind leaped to, but saw nothing. Maybe he'd used more duct tape.

Nik had his back to her. His head hung down on his neck as if unconscious. She prayed he wasn't dead.

But where was his captor? Keeping low, she squinted as she tried to see into the far corners of the boathouse. No sign of Olaf.

Had he left? Gone for beer? Or just for a walk, leaving the man he was slowly torturing to death to marinate in his own fear?

No more time for speculation. She had to save Nik, whatever the risk to her own life.

But if Olaf were inside, she wasn't going to give him an easy shot.

She made her way back to the house, keeping low and scuttling like a forest animal on the lookout for predators. There, she rounded the building and entered the lake where the small garden sloped down through sandy soil threaded with pine needles. Modern firearms were supposed to function when wet, but she was taking no chances. After making the necessary adjustments, she waded deeper.

She gasped involuntarily as the lake bottom shelved suddenly, sending her slithering down the muddy bottom until she was thigh-deep in the freezing water. She made her way over to the boathouse, keeping low and grateful for the fact that on this side of the wooden structure, there were no windows.

This close, the music was immensely loud. A roaring grinding cacophony over which the singer – if you could call him that – was alternately screeching and growling like a man possessed by demons, which presumably was the point. Was this Sepülkå, the band a much younger Olaf had been charged with babysitting as a proby?

When she was near enough to reach out and grasp the front edge of the wall, she raised her SIG up to her face again and then swung round the corner, sending ripples of water out onto the lake.

Gun arm extended, she found firmer ground beneath her feet and waded out of the water onto the floor of the boathouse.

Of Olaf, there was no sign. But the sight of her former adversary sandwiched between those two tall piles of crates sent a dagger of pity shooting into her heart. His head drooped over his bare chest. And there, bleeding into his waistband, was a crudely carved pentagram. Nik's scar from his encounter with Ulrik Ahlgren in 2003 bisected the Satanic symbol.

Stella approached him. 'Nik!' she shouted, trying to make him hear her over the metal music reverberating off the wooden walls. 'Can you hear me?'

Nik raised his head. Opened bleary eyes, which were splotched with tiny scarlet flowers where blood vessels had burst in his corneas. His lips parted.

'He's—'

The music snapped off. In the silence, Stella's ears filled with a high-pitched whine.

' – right here.'

Olaf's voice emanated from behind the pile of crates supporting Nik's right arm. Stella had no idea whether they were full or empty. A shot through the wood might incapacitate him but if she missed and he decided enough was enough he could kill Nik and probably her, too. She'd seen the kind of firepower Swedish bikers could lay their hands on.

Better to talk. For now. After all, he'd allowed her to get this close. Presumably he had something in mind. She could use his sense of grandiosity against him. Keep him talking till the cavalry arrived.

She kept her pistol aimed at the topmost crate, which sat hard up against Nik's ribcage, his arm laid over the top.

'Let him go, Olaf. Something tells me you wanted me here. I don't believe it was because you needed a witness.'

From the shadows to Nik's right, the stubby barrel of a sawn-off shotgun emerged. It met Nik's cheekbone and tipped his head up a little further.

'Smart lady. I can see why they named you the super-cop. Or did you ask them to call you that? Never mind. Turn around.'

Stella hesitated.

'I said turn around, bitch, or I'll paint his brains over the walls.'

Slowly, trying not to hunch her shoulders or show Olaf any signs of how scared she was feeling, Stella rotated on the spot until she was facing the lake. Even with her leather jacket on, she was shivering.

In the middle distance, the greylag geese were cruising in the light breeze that had sprung up. She remembered the amateur artist whose works decorated the summerhouse's walls had included a painting of this exact scene.

'If you kill us, they won't bother arresting you, Olaf. Out here, in the sticks? They'll say you were resisting arrest and shoot you dead.'

He laughed. 'Oh, I very much doubt that. This is Sweden, remember. Now, throw your gun into the lake.'

It was a positive sign. Perhaps the first. If he meant to shoot her, he could have done that at any point.

She dropped her right arm, took it behind her then swung it forwards, releasing the SIG at the end of the upswing. The pistol sailed out over the water, entering with a splash fifteen metres from the shore.

Without waiting to be told, she turned round to face Nik. The sawn-off barrels were still jabbed against his cheek, distorting the flesh there and pushing his mouth open to reveal bloody teeth.

'Why don't you show yourself, Olaf? You've got us both where you want us now.'

His boots scraped on the rough planked floor of the boathouse. Instead of emerging fully, he popped his head up over the top of the crate to Nik's right. The effect would have been comical if it weren't so grotesque. He'd smeared blood – Nik's, Stella assumed – over his face so his eyes blazed whitely from the crimson slick.

'I'm impressed, Stella. You found me. Seems you even know why I killed Joel.'

For whatever reason, he was throwing her a lifeline. And as long as they were talking, he wasn't killing either her or Nik. Maybe she could get out of this without a shot being fired.

'It was drugs, wasn't it? You had something going with Joel Varela, didn't you? You met him through Kenny. Joel offered you protection. Then, what? He got greedy? Asked for too much money? Or did he double-cross you? Either way, you decided enough was enough and you murdered him. Because you knew

Playing the Devil's Music

about Ulrik Ahlgren, you decided to throw us off by making it look like a disciple of his.'

Olaf rasped out a guttural sigh. 'Stella, slow down. You're gabbling like a goose. But you're right. You figured it all out.'

'What do you want, Olaf? Why am I here?'

'What do I want? Hmm. Well, here's the thing, Stella. Somewhere along the line, I think it was between Barbro and Fredrika, I kind of got a liking for it. And now you're the person standing between me and my new hobby. I want you.'

'What do you mean, you want me?'

'I mean, I'll do you a deal. Like with the devil. You for Nik. I'll let him go and I'll take you in his place. Or I'll complete the set of Hunter Killers and then I'll do you anyway before I disappear.'

'So I die either way.'

He giggled. 'Well, yeah. I appreciate it doesn't have much of an upside for you. But you can go down knowing you saved a brother officer. Isn't that how you guys all talk about each other?'

Stella opened her mouth to reply but Nik spoke first.

'Go, Stella. I'm done. He's carved me up too badly. I want you to save yourself.'

Olaf bared his teeth. 'Shut up,' he snarled.

He reversed the shotgun and slammed the butt into Nik's temple. He groaned and his head lolled forwards once more. Olaf grabbed the top of his head and wrenched it upright. Nik stared at Stella, his bloodshot eyes rolling.

Stella took a step forwards. 'Please, Olaf, leave him alone. OK, I'll do it. Me for him.'

She clasped her hands behind her in a gesture of submission.

Olaf was still being cautious. Apart from the top half of his face, no part of him was visible behind the crates.

'Really? You surprise me. But he's right about me carving him up. I've added a new twist to my signature. What do you think?'

He grabbed Nik's right hand and turned it palm outwards towards Stella. The action loosened the silver duct tape Olaf had used to fix it to the top of the crate.

Nik's palm bore a bloody pentagram, a replica of the larger

symbol so cruelly incised into his chest. The blood in the slashes was black and clotted. Slowly, Olaf extended his tongue and licked the back of Nik's hand, rolling his eyes between the splayed fingers.

Nik turned his head to look at his tormentor then back at Stella.

'Go,' he groaned.

Stella was rooted to the spot. Once she surrendered, Nik's life would be forfeit along with her own. Olaf would have no need to let him go. And as he said, he'd developed a taste for killing.

As if to underline her conclusion, Olaf pushed the barrels of the sawn-off shotgun harder into Nik's cheek. She saw his knuckle whitening on the trigger. In a few seconds, whatever load Olaf had selected would blast its way out of those truncated barrels and obliterate Nik's head.

Nik's bloodshot eyes were wide with terror.

'Please,' he begged her.

She nodded. 'It's all right, Nik. It's all right,' she murmured softly.

Her arm whipped up from behind her back, her spare pistol gripped in her fist. She'd transferred it from her ankle to her waistband before she'd entered the lake. And now it was swinging up and out, her index finger finding the trigger. The target just a couple of metres away.

Stella aimed instinctively. Summoned every ounce of firearms training she'd ever undertaken.

Shutting out Nik's pleas, she squeezed the trigger.

While Olaf was still rolling his eyes at her from between Nik's bloody fingers, the 9mm full metal jacket round entered Nik's right palm dead-centre on the pentagram.

The copper-jacketed lead bullet passed through the web of tendons, bones and blood vessels, tearing a ragged circle of flesh away as it exited. From there, it entered Olaf Wallin's mouth, breaking three upper incisors on the way in. It grooved a bloody trench over the upper surface of his tongue, and passed through the soft palate. Losing speed, it deviated by twenty degrees and clipped a chip of bone off the second cervical vertebra, missing his spinal cord, before lodging in the splenius capitis muscle keeping Olaf's head straight on his shoulders.

He fell sideways, hand clapped to his mouth, blood gushing through his own fingers. The shotgun clattered to the floor. Nik sagged in his bindings, but as the duct tape wrenched free with a tearing sound, he swung round and staggered, bringing the other pile of crates down on top of him.

Stella rushed forwards and dragged him clear, ripping the tape from his left wrist. She wanted to help him, but she needed to make sure Olaf was immobilised.

He was trapped in the angle between the floor and the wall, ropes of blood still pouring from his mouth and puddling on the floorboards. His eyes were rolling wildly in his head. Gargles escaped his lips.

Stella had basic first aid training, but treating a gunshot wound to the head was way beyond that. She put her pistol on the ground behind her then heaved him over onto his front; at least that way he wouldn't drown in his own blood.

As she reached for her phone to call an ambulance, she caught a movement in the corner of her eye. She turned to see Nik stretched out on the floor. His right arm snaked out in front of him towards her pistol.

In slow motion, his fingers curled around the grip and he brought the barrel up, cradling his right hand in his left palm. She just had time to curl into a ball and roll out of the way before he began firing.

The little SIG held eleven 9mm rounds including one in the chamber. Minus the round she'd fired, that left ten. All of them entered Olaf's body, which jerked with each impact. The last two found his chest, high on the left side.

Man and ammunition spent, Nik collapsed onto his face.

57

By the time the tactical support team arrived at Nik's summerhouse, all the shooting to be done had already taken place.

With nothing left for them to do, the commander had his black-clad unit members sweep the woods and the lakeshore 'looking for accomplices'. Half an hour later, having pronounced the scene safe, he ordered them back into their matt-grey Transit vans. He was already answering a request for backup on his radio as the convoy pulled out.

Stella had bandaged Nik's hands, taking extra care with the palm she'd shot through to incapacitate Olaf Wallin. As the paramedics lifted him onto a stretcher he reached out and took Stella's right hand in his left. He jerked his head sideways in a 'come closer' movement.

She crouched beside the stretcher, motioning with a hand for the paramedics to hold on, just for a second.

'They were my friends, Stella. He murdered them all in cold blood.'

She smiled down at his blood-smeared face. 'I know, Nik. It's OK.'

'But I shouldn't have done it.' He dragged in a breath. 'The rules are clear.'

She brought her lips close to his ear. 'Olaf was on the point of shooting me with the sawn-off. Despite your own severe injuries, you shot him dead protecting me. That's what I'm going to tell the investigation. You should do the same.'

One of the paramedics nudged her.

'We need to get him to the hospital.'

She nodded, and straightened, wincing as her knees popped. Suddenly the cold of the lake water soaking her jeans rushed back at her like a tidal wave, chilling her to the bones and making her shudder.

Someone appeared with a silver foil survival blanket and wrapped it around her shoulders. She looked round. It was Sven.

'You OK?' he asked, his forehead grooved with concern.

'I'm fine. Bit cold, that's all.'

'You've had a shock. Are you sure you don't want to go to the ER?'

She shook her head, looking past Sven to wave to Nik as the two paramedics rolled him into the back of the ambulance.

'Let's get the scene processed,' she said. 'But I wouldn't mind a lift to Örebro if you can find someone to ride the bike back for me.'

* * *

Owing to the complexities of the case, the wrap-up party had to wait for a couple of days. But now it was in full swing. After a couple of bottles of wine at the station, they'd decamped to a bar in the centre of Örebro. Kersten had paid for food and every officer was holding a bottle, a glass or a slice of pizza; some, all three.

The bar owner, catching the celebratory mood, had selected an ABBA playlist from Spotify. Stella, Sven and Lucy were singing along loudly, and more or less tunefully, to 'Waterloo'.

Over the heads of the cops dancing in front of the little stage they'd claimed as their own, Stella saw the door open. Her eyes widened and her face broke into a wide grin. She pushed her way through the crowd.

Jonna was smiling from the doorway as Stella emerged from the scrum of cops and hugged her, then kissed her on both cheeks.

'What the hell are you doing here?'

Jonna laughed. 'I just drove all the way from Stockholm and that's the welcome I get?'

'Sorry! It's just so unexpected.'

'And pleasant, I hope?'

'Of course. Come and get a drink. I can introduce you to the rest of the team.'

Beers procured and slices of pizza snagged from the buffet table, Stella led Jonna over to where her temporary brothers and sisters were gathered at the bar.

Roger was there, a crutch propped against a stool. He raised his beer mug.

'Nice to meet you, Jonna. I have to say Stockholm's loss is Örebro's gain.'

Jonna clinked her bottle against his brimming tankard.

'That's where you're mistaken.' She turned to Stella, eyes shining. 'Malin couldn't come in person but she wanted me to tell you as soon as possible. You're reinstated.'

Stella's mouth dropped open. 'You mean...'

'You're back in Homicide. Old rank, old pay, everything. Apparently Nik called her from the hospital. He insisted on it.'

Stella tried to process the news. Her one-time enemy had just gone in to bat for her, overturning a severe disciplinary sanction he himself had instigated.

'Wow! I'm back. We'll be working together again.'

Jonna's smile shifted. 'Actually, we won't. I got the fincrime job. I start next Monday. I'll still be based at Kungsholmsgatan though.'

Stella hugged her again. 'Jonna, that's fantastic! You did it.'

'You're not mad?'

'Don't be silly, of course I'm not! It's what you wanted.'

'Dancing Queen' blared from the PA. Roger got to his feet.

'Hey, Stella, if we're losing you back to HQ, will you at least give this mashed-up old biker a dance?'

She grinned at him. 'Come on, you old crock. Let's show the youngsters how it's done.'

Jonna flashed her a brilliant smile as she let Roger lead her onto the tiny dance floor. After a couple of minutes he winced. 'My heart's nineteen again but my body's ninety.' He held his arms wide. 'Fancy saving my dignity and turning this into a slow dance?'

Secure inside his arms, Stella turned gently on the floor as ABBA sang and the other cops joined in.

Perhaps because the victims had all been cops, the party went on long into the night. Nobody wanted to be the first to leave, and after the beer ran out, they started on aquavit.

Emboldened by the alcohol and now with a readymade excuse, Roger systematically asked every female cop there for a slow dance. As he stumbled drunkenly with Stella in his arms for a second time, Jonna caught her eye over Roger's shoulder and winked.

Somehow she'd survived. She'd caught the Devil of Axberg and saved Nik Olsson's life. He'd relented and had her reinstated in Homicide. She could move back to her flat on Mariebergsgatan and resume her daily runs with Jonna.

Could her life get any better?

Her phone rang.

She pulled it out and checked the screen. No Caller ID.

Frowning, she went outside into the cool night air.

'Hello?'

'Stella? Is that you?'

The voice was familiar, but it took her a moment to place it. Oh my God, was it *him*? Talk about a blast from the past.

'Gabriel?'

'How are you?'

'Well, a little drunk, to be honest. We just closed a big case.

How are you? It's been a while since our little jaunt to Africa. Have you and Eli tied the knot yet?'

He didn't answer. And as time stretched elastically in her befuddled state, she understood with sudden, sobering clarity why not.

'Oh no, Gabriel. Please tell me she's all right.'

'I'm afraid not. She, ah...' Another pause stretched out. Stella heard chirrups and whistles in the background. 'Eli's dead. Murdered, actually. By one of our mutual acquaintances. The woman who sent you to Sweden.'

'Gemma Dowding killed Eli?'

'Ordered it, but it amounts to the same thing. Anyway, I thought you might like to know that she's dead, too. It's safe for you to come home.'

'Did you...' Stella stopped herself just in time. 'I mean, are you sure?'

'You know me.'

'I do.'

'I have to go. See you around.'

Stella pocketed her phone. A cold breeze blew down the street, raising a swirl of dust and leaves. Behind her, the door to the bar opened, letting out a raucous blast of music and laughter.

It was Jonna. She was smiling. 'Help! I think Roger's going to propose if I have one more dance with him.'

They headed back inside, though even as she danced, Stella couldn't shake Gabriel Wolfe's words out of her head. Gemma Dowding was dead. And when she'd told him she knew him, they'd both known what that little phrase meant. He was sure in the way only a killer could be. Because he'd done it.

She really was free. Free to go back for the christening. Free to visit Elle and Jason. Free to place flowers on Lola's grave. Free to move back to England.

And then the strongest feeling came over her. Regret.

She found Jonna, tried to explain what had just happened. But her tongue wasn't obeying her brain and eventually Jonna laughed, handed her another drink and suggested getting some air.

*　*　*

Stella woke up and unstuck her eyelids to peer at the red numerals on the digital clock radio. She groaned. Well into her twenties, and even after Lola had been born, she'd been able to smother the worst effects of a hangover with extra sleep. Then she'd hit forty and it was as if someone had turned a dial in her brain marked 'waking up', setting the needle at 7:00 a.m.

She closed her eyes again and tried to recall the last moments of the party. Roger making a clumsy pass at her, grinning through a fog of alcohol. Something about 'taking a ride together'. Stella had demurred. Or had she? It was a blur of coloured lights, ABBA hits and way, *way* too much booze. There'd been drunken kissing, Stella was sure of it, but the face of her partner was elusive.

She rolled over and stretched. Her hand met the skin of someone's cheek. Interesting. No beard. Not Roger, then. She stroked downwards. No stubble at all.

She opened her eyes a second time. Recognised her bed-mate. And knew, with a fluttering heart, that even with Gemma Dowding gone, she wouldn't be moving back to England.

Stella smiled. 'Isn't sleeping with a junior officer breaking about a thousand SPA rules?'

'Not if she isn't her boss,' Jonna said, smiling back happily and holding her arm out wide.

READ ON FOR AN EXTRACT FROM SHALLOW GROUND, THE FIRST BOOK IN THE DETECTIVE FORD THRILLERS…

PROLOGUE

Summer | Pembrokeshire Coast, Wales

Ford leans out from the limestone rock face halfway up Pen-y-holt sea stack, shaking his forearms to keep the blood flowing. He and Lou have climbed the established routes before. Today, they're attempting a new line he spotted. She was reluctant at first, but she's also competitive and he really wanted to do the climb.

'I'm not sure. It looks too difficult,' she'd said when he suggested it.

'Don't tell me you've lost your bottle?' he said with a grin.

'No, but . . .'

'Well, then. Let's go. Unless you'd rather climb one of the easy ones again?'

She frowned. 'No. Let's do it.'

They scrambled down a gully, hopping across boulders from the cliff to a shallow ledge just above sea level at the bottom of the route. She stands there now, patiently holding his ropes while he climbs. But the going's much harder than he expected. He's wasted a lot of time attempting to navigate a tricky bulge. Below him, Lou plays out rope through a belay device.

Prologue

He squints against the bright sunshine as a light wind buffets him. Herring gulls wheel around the stack, calling in alarm at this brightly coloured interloper assaulting their territory.

He looks down at Lou and smiles. Her eyes are a piercing blue. He remembers the first time he saw her. He was captivated by those eyes, drawn in, powerless, like an old wooden sailing ship spiralling down into a whirlpool. He paid her a clumsy compliment, which she accepted with more grace than he'd managed.

Lou smiles back up at him now. Even after seven years of marriage, his heart thrills that she should bestow such a radiant expression on him.

Rested, he starts climbing again, trying a different approach to the overhang. He reaches up and to his right for a block. It seems solid enough, but his weight pulls it straight off.

He falls outwards, away from the flat plane of lichen-scabbed limestone, and jerks to a stop at the end of his rope. The force turns him into a human pendulum. He swings inwards, slamming face-first against the rock and gashing his chin. Then out again to dangle above Lou on the ledge.

Ford tries to stay calm as he slowly rotates. His straining fingertips brush the rock face then arc into empty air.

Then he sees two things that frighten him more than the fall.

The rock he dislodged, as large as a microwave, has smashed down on to Lou. She's sitting awkwardly, white-faced, and he can see blood on her leggings. Those sapphire-blue eyes are wide with pain.

And waves are now lapping at the ledge. The tide is on its way in, not out. Somehow, he misread the tide table, or he took too long getting up the first part of the climb. He damns himself for his slowness.

'I can lower you down,' she screams up at him. 'But my leg, I think it's broken.'

She gets him down safely and he kisses her fiercely before crouching by her right leg to assess the damage. There's a sharp lump distending the bloody Lycra, and he knows what it is. Bone.

Prologue

'It's bad, Lou. I think it's a compound fracture. But if you can stand on your good leg, we can get back the way we came.'

'I can't!' she cries, pain contorting her face. 'Call the coastguard.'

He pulls out his phone, but there's no mobile service down here.

'Shit! There's no signal.'

'You'll have to go for help.'

'I can't leave you, darling.'

A wave crashes over the ledge and douses them both.

Her eyes widen. 'You have to! The tide's coming in.'

He knows she's right. And it's all his fault. He pulled the block off the crag.

'Lou, I—'

She grabs his hand and squeezes so hard it hurts. 'You *have* to.'

Another wave hits. His mouth fills with seawater. He swallows half of it and retches. He looks back the way they came. The boulders they hopped along are awash. There's no way Lou can make it.

He's crying now. He can't do it.

Then she presses the only button she has left. 'If you stay here, we'll *both* die. Then who'll look after Sam?'

Sam is eight and a half. Born two years before they married. He's being entertained by Louisa's parents while they're at Pen-y-holt. Ford knows she's right. He can't leave Sam an orphan. They were meant to be together for all time. But now, time has run out.

'Go!' she screams. 'Before it's too late.'

So he leaves her, checking the gear first so he's sure she can't be swept away'. He falls into an eerie calm as he swims across to the cliff and solos out.

At the clifftop, rock gives way to scrubby grass. He pulls out his phone. Four bars. He calls the coastguard, giving them a concise description of the accident, the location and Lou's injury. Then he slumps. The calmness that saved his life has vanished. He is hyperventilating, heaving in great breaths that won't bring enough oxygen to his brain, and sighing them out again.

Prologue

A wave of nausea rushes through him and sweat flashes out across his skin. The wind chills it, making him shudder with the sudden cold. He lurches to his right and spews out a thin stream of bile on to the grass.

Then his stomach convulses and his breakfast rushes up and out, spattering the sleeve of his jacket. He retches out another splash of stinking yellow liquid and then dry-heaves until, cramping, his guts settle. His view is blurred through a film of tears.

He falls back and lies there for ten more minutes, looking up into the cloudless sky. Odd how realistic this dream is. He could almost believe he just left his wife to drown.

He sobs, a cracked sound that the wind tears away from his lips and disperses into the air. And the dream blackens and reality is here, and it's ugly and painful and true.

He hears a helicopter. Sees its red-and-white form hovering over Pen-y-holt.

Time ceases to have any meaning as he watches the rescue. How long has passed, he doesn't know.

Now a man in a bright orange flying suit is standing in front of him explaining that his wife, Sam's mother, has drowned.

Later, there are questions from the local police. They treat him with compassion, especially as he's Job, like them.

The coroner rules death by misadventure.

But Ford knows the truth.

He killed her. *He* pushed her into trying the climb. *He* dislodged the block that smashed her leg. And *he* left her to drown while he saved his own skin.

DAY ONE, 5.00 P.M

SIX YEARS LATER | SUMMER | SALISBURY

Angie Halpern trudged up the five gritty stone steps to the front door. The shift on the cancer ward had been a long one. Ten hours. It had ended with a patient vomiting on the back of her head. She'd washed it out at work, crying at the thought that it would make her lifeless brown hair flatter still.

Free from the hospital's clutches, she'd collected Kai from Donna, the childminder, and then gone straight to the food bank – again. Bone-tired, her mood hadn't been improved when an elderly woman on the bus told her she looked like she needed to eat more: 'A pretty girl like you shouldn't be that thin.'

And now, here she was, knackered, hungry and with a three-year-old whining and grizzling and dragging on her free hand. Again.

'Kai!' she snapped. 'Let go, or Mummy can't get her keys out.'

The little boy stopped crying just long enough to cast a shocked look up into his mother's eyes before resuming, at double the volume.

Fearing what she might do if she didn't get inside, Angie half-

Day One, 5.00 p.m

turned so he couldn't cling back on to her hand, and dug out her keys. She fumbled one of the bags of groceries, but in a dexterous act of juggling righted it before it spilled the tins, packets and jars all over the steps.

She slotted the brass Yale key home and twisted it in the lock. Elbowing the door open, she nudged Kai with her right knee, encouraging him to precede her into the hallway. Their flat occupied the top floor of the converted Victorian townhouse. Ahead, the stairs, with their patched and stained carpet, beckoned.

'Come on, Kai, in we go,' she said, striving to inject into her voice the tone her own mother called 'jollying along'.

'No!' the little boy said, stamping his booted foot and sticking his pudgy hands on his hips. 'I hate Donna. I hate the foobang. And I. Hate. YOU!'

Feeling tears pricking at the back of her eyes, Angie put the bags down and picked her son up under his arms. She squeezed him, burying her nose in the sweet-smelling angle between his neck and shoulder. How was it possible to love somebody so much and also to wish for them just to shut the hell up? Just for one little minute.

She knew she wasn't the only one with problems. Talking to the other nurses, or chatting late at night online, confirmed it. Everyone reckoned the happily married ones with enough money to last from one month to the next were the exception, not the rule.

'Mummy, you're hurting me!'

'Oh, Jesus! Sorry, darling. Look, come on. Let's just get the shopping upstairs and you can watch a *Thomas* video.'

'I hate *Thomas*.'

'*Thunderbirds*, then.'

'I hate them even more.'

Angie closed her eyes, sighing out a breath like the online mindfulness gurus suggested. 'Then you'll just have to stare out of the bloody window, like I used to. Now, come on!'

He sucked in a huge breath. Angie flinched, but the scream

never came. Instead, Kai's scrunched-up eyes opened wide and swivelled sideways. She followed his gaze and found herself facing a good-looking man wearing a smart jacket and trousers. He had a kind smile.

'I'm sorry,' the man said in a quiet voice. 'I couldn't help seeing your little boy's . . . he's tired, I suppose. You left the door open and as I was coming to this address anyway . . .' He tailed off, looking embarrassed, eyes downcast.

'You were coming *here*?' she asked.

He looked up at her again. 'Yes,' he said, smiling. 'I was looking for Angela Halpern.'

'That's me.' She paused, frowning, as she tried to place him. 'Do I know you?'

'Mummee!' Kai hissed from her waist, where he was clutching her.

'Quiet, darling, please.'

The man smiled. 'Would you like a hand with your bags? I see you have your hands full with the little fellow there.' Then he squatted down, so that his face was at the same level as Kai's. 'Hello. My name's Harvey. What's yours?'

'Kai. Are you a policeman?'

Harvey laughed, a warm, soft-edged sound. 'No. I'm not a policeman.'

'Mummy's a nurse. At the hospital. Do you work there?'

'Me? Funnily enough, I do.'

'Are you a nurse?'

'No. But I do help people. Which I think is a bit of a coincidence. Do you know that word?'

The little boy shook his head.

'It's just a word grown-ups use when two things happen that are the same. Kai,' he said, dropping his voice to a conspiratorial whisper, 'do you want to know a secret?'

Kai nodded, smiling and wiping his nose on his sleeve.

'There's a big hospital in London called Bart's. And I think it rhymes with' – he paused and looked left and right – 'farts.'

Kai squawked with laughter.

Day One, 5.00 p.m

Harvey stood, knees popping. 'I hope that was OK. The naughty word. It usually seems to make them laugh.'

Angie smiled. She felt relief that this helpful stranger hadn't seen fit to judge her. To tut, roll his eyes or give any of the dozens of subtle signals the free-and-easy brigade found to diminish her. 'It's fine, really. You said you'd come to see me?'

'Oh, yes, of course, sorry. I'm from the food bank. The Purcell Foundation?' he said. 'They've asked me to visit a few of our customers, to find out what they think about the quality of the service. I was hoping you'd have ten minutes for a chat. If it's not a good time, I can come back.'

Angie sighed. Then she shook her head. 'No, it's fine . . . Harvey, did you say your name was?'

He nodded.

'Give me a hand with the bags and I'll put the kettle on. I picked up some teabags this afternoon, so we can christen the packet.'

'Let me take those,' he said, bending down and snaking his fingers through the loops in the carrier-bag handles. 'Where to, madam?' he added in a jokey tone.

'We're on the third floor, I'm afraid.'

Harvey smiled. 'Not to worry, I'm in good shape.'

Reaching the top of the stairs, Angie elbowed the light switch and then unlocked the door, while Harvey kept up a string of tall tales for Kai.

'And then the chief doctor said' – he adopted a deep voice – '"No, no, that's never going to work. You need to use a hosepipe!"'

Kai's laughter echoed off the bare, painted walls of the stairwell.

'Here we are,' Angie said, pushing the door open. 'The kitchen's at the end of the hall.'

She stood aside, watching Harvey negotiate the cluttered hallway and deposit the shopping bags on her pine kitchen table. She followed him, noticing the scuff marks on the walls, the sticky fat spatters behind the hob, and feeling a lump in her throat.

Day One, 5.00 p.m

'Kai, why don't you go and watch telly?' she asked her son, steering him out of the kitchen and towards the sitting room.

'A film?' he asked.

She glanced up at the clock. Five to six. 'It's almost teatime.'

'Pleeease?'

She smiled. 'OK. But you come when I call you for tea. Pasta and red sauce, your favourite.'

'Yummy.'

She turned back to Harvey, who was unloading the groceries on to the table. A sob swelled in her throat. She choked it back.

He frowned. 'Is everything all right, Angela?'

The noise from the TV was loud, even from the other room. She turned away so this stranger wouldn't see her crying. It didn't matter that he was a colleague, of sorts. He could see what she'd been reduced to, and that was enough.

'Yes, yes, sorry. It's just, you know, the food bank. I never thought my life would turn out like this. Then I lost my husband and things just got on top of me.'

'Mmm,' he said. 'That was careless of you.'

'What?' She turned round, uncertain of what she'd heard.

He was lifting a tin of baked beans out of the bag. 'I said, it was careless of you. To lose your husband.'

She frowned. Trying to make sense of his remark. The cruel tone. The staring, suddenly dead eyes.

'Look, I don't know what you—'

The tin swung round in a half-circle and crashed against her left temple.

'Oh,' she moaned, grabbing the side of her head and staggering backwards.

Her palm was wet. Her blood was hot. She was half-blind with the pain. Her back met the cooker and she slumped to the ground. He was there in front of her, crouching down, just like he'd done with Kai. Only he wasn't telling jokes any more. And he wasn't smiling.

'Please keep quiet,' he murmured, 'or I'll have to kill Kai as well. Are you expecting anyone?'

Day One, 5.00 p.m

'N-nobody,' she whispered, shaking. She could feel the blood running inside the collar of her shirt. And the pain, oh, the pain. It felt as though her brain was pushing her eyes out of their sockets.

He nodded. 'Good.'

Then he encircled her neck with his hands, looked into her eyes and squeezed.

I'm so sorry, Kai. I hope Auntie Cherry looks after you properly when I'm gone. I hope . . .

* * *

Casting a quick glance towards the kitchen door and the hallway beyond, and reassured by the blaring noise from the TV, Harvey crouched by Angie's inert body and increased the pressure.

Her eyes bulged, and her tongue, darkening already from that natural rosy pink to the colour of raw liver, protruded from between her teeth.

From his jacket he withdrew an empty blood bag. He connected the outlet tube and inserted a razor-tipped trocar into the other end. He placed them to one side and dragged her jeans over her hips, tugging them down past her knees. With the joints free to move, he pushed his hands between her thighs and shoved them apart.

He inserted the needle into her thigh so that it met and travelled a few centimetres up into the right femoral artery. Then he laid the blood bag on the floor and watched as the scarlet blood shot into the clear plastic tube and surged along it.

With a precious litre of blood distending the bag, he capped it off and removed the tube and the trocar. With Angie's heart pumping her remaining blood on to the kitchen floor tiles, he stood and placed the bag inside his jacket. He could feel it through his shirt, warm against his skin. He took her purse out of her bag, found the card he wanted and removed it.

He wandered down the hall and poked his head round the door frame of the sitting room. The boy was sitting cross-legged,

Day One, 5.00 p.m

two feet from the TV, engrossed in the adventures of a blue cartoon dog.

'Tea's ready, Kai,' he said, in a sing-song tone.

Protesting, but clambering to his feet, the little boy extended a pudgy hand holding the remote and froze the action, then dropped the control to the carpet.

Harvey held out his hand and the boy took it, absently, still staring at the screen.

DAY TWO, 8.15 A.M.

Arriving at Bourne Hill Police Station, Detective Inspector Ford sighed, fingering the scar on his chin. *What better way to start the sixth anniversary of your wife's death than with a shouting match over breakfast with your fifteen-year-old son?*

The row had ended in an explosive exchange that was fast, raw and brutal:

'I hate you! I wish you'd died instead of Mum.'

'Yeah? Guess what? So do I!'

All the time they'd been arguing, he'd seen Lou's face, battered by submerged rocks in the sea off the Pembrokeshire coast.

Pushing the memory of the argument aside, he ran a hand over the top of his head, trying to flatten down the spikes of dark, grey-flecked hair.

He pushed through the double glass doors. Straight into the middle of a ruckus.

A scrawny man in faded black denim and a raggy T-shirt was swearing at a young woman in a dark suit. Eyes wide, she had backed against an orange wall. He could see a Wiltshire police ID on a lanyard round her neck, but he didn't recognise her.

Day Two, 8.15 a.m.

The two female civilian staff behind the desk were on their feet, one with a phone clamped to her ear.

The architects who'd designed the interior of the new station at Bourne Hill had persuaded senior management that the traditional thick glass screen wasn't 'welcoming'. Now any arsehole could decide to lean across the three feet of white-surfaced MDF and abuse, spit on or otherwise ruin the day of the hardworking receptionists. He saw the other woman reach under the desk for the panic button.

'Why are you ignoring me, eh? I just asked where the toilets are, you bitch!' the man yelled at the woman backed against the wall.

Ford registered the can of strong lager in the man's left hand and strode over. The woman was pale, and her mouth had tightened to a lipless line.

'I asked you a question. What's wrong with you?' the drunk shouted.

Ford shot out his right hand and grabbed him by the back of his T-shirt. He yanked him backwards, sticking out a booted foot and rolling him over his knee to send him flailing to the floor.

Ford followed him down and drove a knee in between his shoulder blades. The man gasped out a loud 'Oof!' as his lungs emptied. Ford gripped his wrist and jerked his arm up in a tight angle, then turned round and called over his shoulder, 'Could someone get some cuffs, please? This . . . gentleman . . . will be cooling off in a cell.'

A pink-cheeked uniform raced over and snapped a pair of rigid Quik-Cuffs on to the man's wrists.

'Thanks, Mark,' Ford said, getting to his feet. 'Get him over to Custody.'

'Charge, sir?'

'Drunk and disorderly? Common assault? Being a jerk in a built-up area? Just get him booked in.'

The PC hustled the drunk to his feet, reciting the formal arrest and caution script while walking him off in an armlock to see the custody sergeant.

Ford turned to the woman who'd been the focus of his newest collar's unwelcome attentions. 'I'm sorry about that. Are you OK?'

She answered as if she were analysing an incident she'd witnessed on CCTV. 'I think so. He didn't hit me, and swearing doesn't cause physical harm. Although I am feeling quite anxious as a result.'

'I'm not surprised.' Ford gestured at her ID. 'Are you here to meet someone? I haven't seen you round here before.'

She nodded. 'I'm starting work here today. And my new boss is . . . hold on . . .' She fished a sheet of paper from a brown canvas messenger bag slung over her left shoulder. 'Alec Reid.'

Now Ford understood. She was the new senior crime scene investigator. Her predecessor had transferred up to Thames Valley Police to move with her husband's new job. Alec managed the small forensics team at Salisbury and had been crowing about his new hire for weeks now.

'My new deputy has a PhD, Ford,' he'd said over a pint in the Wyndham Arms one evening. 'We're going up in the world.'

Ford stuck his hand out. 'DI Ford.'

'Pleased to meet you,' she said, taking his hand and pumping it up and down three times before releasing it. 'My name is Dr Hannah Fellowes. I was about to get my ID sorted when that man started shouting at me.'

'I doubt it was anything about you in particular. Just wrong place, wrong time.'

She nodded, frowning up at him. 'Although, technically, this *is* the right place. As I'm going to be working here.' She checked her watch, a multifunction Casio with more dials and buttons than the dash of Ford's ageing Land Rover Discovery. 'It's also 8.15, so it's the right time as well.'

Ford smiled. 'Let's get your ID sorted, then I'll take you up to Alec. He arrives early most days.'

He led her over to the long, low reception desk.

'This is—'

Day Two, 8.15 a.m.

'Dr Hannah Fellowes,' she said to the receptionist. 'I'm pleased to meet you.'

She thrust her right hand out across the counter. The receptionist took it and received the same three stiff shakes as Ford.

The receptionist smiled up at her new colleague, but Ford could see the concern in her eyes. 'I'm Paula. Nice to meet you, too, Hannah. Are you all right? I'm so sorry you had to deal with that on your first day.'

'It was a shock. But it won't last. I don't let things like that get to me.'

Paula smiled. 'Good for you!'

While Paula converted a blank rectangle of plastic into a functioning station ID, Hannah turned to Ford.

'Should I ask her to call me Dr Fellowes, or is it usual here to use first names?' she whispered.

'We mainly use Christian names, but if you'd like to be known as Dr Fellowes, now would be the time.'

Hannah nodded and turned back to Paula, who handed her the swipe card in a clear case.

'There you go, Hannah. Welcome aboard.'

'Thank you.' A beat. 'Paula.'

'Do you know where you're going?'

'I'll take her,' Ford said.

At the lift, he showed her how to swipe her card before pressing the floor button.

'If you don't do that, you just stand in the lift not going anywhere. It's mainly the PTBs who do it.'

'PTBs?' she repeated, as the lift door closed in front of them.

'Powers That Be. Management?'

'Oh. Yes. That's funny. PTBs. Powers That Be.'

She didn't laugh, though, and Ford had the odd sensation that he was talking to a foreigner, despite her southern English accent. She stared straight ahead as the lift ascended. Ford took a moment to assess her appearance. She was shorter than him by a good half-foot, no more than five-five or six. Slim, but not skinny.

Day Two, 8.15 a.m.

Blonde hair woven into plaits, a style Ford had always associated with children.

He'd noticed her eyes downstairs; it was hard not to, they'd been so wide when the drunk had had her backed against the wall. But even relaxed, they were large, and coloured the blue of old china.

The lift pinged and a computerised female voice announced, 'Third floor.'

'You're down here,' Ford said, turning right and leading Hannah along the edge of an open-plan office. He gestured left. 'General CID. I'm Major Crimes on the fourth floor.'

She took a couple of rapid, skipping steps to catch up with him. 'Is Forensics open plan as well? I was told it was a quiet office.'

'I think it's safe to say it's quiet. Come on. Let's get you a tea first. Or coffee. Which do you like best?'

'That's a hard question. I haven't really tried enough types to know.' She shook her head, like a dog trying to dislodge a flea from its ear. 'No. What I meant to say was, I'd like to have a tea, please. Thank you.'

There it was again. The foreigner-in-England vibe he'd picked up downstairs.

While he boiled a kettle and fussed around with a teabag and the jar of instant coffee, he glanced at Hannah. She was staring at him, but smiled when he caught her eye. The expression popped dimples into her cheeks.

'Something puzzling you?' he asked.

'You didn't tell me your name,' she said.

'I think I did. It's Ford.'

'No. I meant your first name. You said, "We mainly use Christian names," when the receptionist, Paula, was doing my building ID. And you called me Hannah. But you didn't tell me yours.'

Ford pressed the teabag against the side of the mug before scooping it out and dropping it into a swing-topped bin. He handed the mug to Hannah. 'Careful, it's hot.'

Day Two, 8.15 a.m.

'Thank you. But your name?'

'Ford's fine. Really. Or DI Ford, if we're being formal.'

'OK.' She smiled. Deeper dimples this time, like little curved cuts. 'You're Ford. I'm Hannah. If we're being formal, maybe you *should* call me Dr Fellowes.'

Ford couldn't tell if she was joking. He took a swig of his coffee. 'Let's go and find Alec. He's talked of little else since you accepted his job offer.'

'It's probably because I'm extremely well qualified. After earning my doctorate, which I started at Oxford and finished at Harvard, I worked in America for a while. I consulted to city, state and federal law enforcement agencies. I also lectured at Quantico for the FBI.'

Ford blinked, struggling to process this hyper-concentrated CV. It sounded like that of someone ten or twenty years older than the slender young woman sipping tea from a Spire FM promotional mug.

'That's pretty impressive. Sorry, you're how old?'

'Don't be sorry. We only met twenty minutes ago. I'm thirty-three.'

Ford reflected that at her age he had just been completing his sergeant's exams. His promotion to inspector had come through a month ago and he was still feeling, if not out of his depth, then at least under the microscope. Now, he was in conversation with some sort of crime-fighting wunderkind.

'So, how come you're working as a CSI in Salisbury? No offence, but isn't it a bit of a step down from teaching at the FBI?'

She looked away. He watched as she fidgeted with a ring on her right middle finger, twisting it round and round.

'I don't want to share that with you,' she said, finally.

In that moment he saw it. Behind her eyes. An assault? A bad one. Not sexual, but violent. Who did the FBI go after? The really bad ones. The ones who didn't confine their evildoing to a single state. It was her secret. Ford knew all about keeping secrets. He felt for her.

Day Two, 8.15 a.m.

'OK, sorry. Look, we're just glad to have you. Come on. Let's find Alec.'

He took Hannah round the rest of CID and out through a set of grey-painted double doors with a well-kicked steel plate at the foot. The corridor to Forensics was papered with health and safety posters and noticeboards advertising sports clubs, social events and training courses.

Inside, the chatter and buzz of coppers at full pelt was replaced by a sepulchral quiet. Five people were hard at work, staring at computer monitors or into microscopes. Much of the 'hard science' end of forensics had been outsourced to private labs in 2012. But Wiltshire Police had, in Ford's mind, made the sensible decision to preserve as much of an in-house scientific capacity as it could afford.

He pointed to a glassed-in office in the far corner of the room.

'That's Alec's den. He doesn't appear to be in yet.'

'*Au contraire*, Henry!'

The owner of the deep, amused-sounding voice tapped Ford on the shoulder. He turned to greet the forensic team manager, a short, round man wearing wire-framed glasses.

'Morning, Alec.'

Alec clocked the new CSI, but then leaned closer to Ford. 'You OK, Henry?' he murmured, his brows knitted together. 'What with the date, and everything.'

'I'm fine. Let's leave it.'

Alec shrugged. Then his gaze moved to Hannah. 'Dr Fellowes, you're here at last! Welcome, welcome.'

'Thank you, Alec. It's been quite an interesting start to the day.'

Ford said, 'Some idiot was making a nuisance of himself in reception as Hannah was arriving. He's cooling off in one of Ian's capsule hotel rooms in the basement.'

The joviality vanished, replaced by an expression of real concern. 'Oh, my dear young woman. I am so sorry. And on your first day with us, too,' Alec said. 'Why don't you come with me?

Day Two, 8.15 a.m.

I'll introduce you to the team and we'll get you set up with a nice quiet desk in the corner. Thanks, Henry. I'll take it from here.'

Ford nodded, eager to get back to his own office and see what the day held. He prayed someone might have been up to no good overnight. Anything to save him from the mountains of forms and reports that he had to either read, write or edit.

'DI Ford? Before you go,' Hannah said.

'Yes?'

'You said I should call you Ford. But Alec just called you Henry.'

'It's a nickname. I got it on my first day here.'

'A nickname. What does it mean?'

'You know. Henry. As in Henry Ford?'

She looked at him, eyebrows raised.

He tried again. 'The car? Model T?'

She smiled at last. A wide grin that showed her teeth, though it didn't reach her eyes. The effect was disconcerting. 'Ha! Yes. That's funny.'

'Right. I have to go. I'm sure we'll bump into each other again.'

'I'm sure, too. I hope there won't be a drunk trying to hit me.'

She smiled, and after a split second he realised it was supposed to be a joke. As he left, he could hear her telling Alec, 'Call me Hannah.'

DAY TWO, 8.59 A.M.

The 999 call had come in just ten minutes earlier: a Cat A G28 – suspected homicide. Having told the whole of Response and Patrol B shift to 'blat' over to the address, Sergeant Natalie Hewitt arrived first at 75 Wyvern Road.

She jumped from her car and spoke into her Airwave radio. 'Sierra Bravo Three-Five, Control.'

'Go ahead, Sierra Bravo Three-Five.'

'Is the ambulance towards?'

'Be about three minutes.'

She ran up the stairs and approached the young couple standing guard at the door to Flat 3.

'Mr and Mrs Gregory, you should go back to your own flat now,' she said, panting. 'I'll have more of my colleagues joining me shortly. Please don't leave the house. We'll be wanting to take your statements.'

'But I've got aerobics at nine thirty,' the woman protested.

Natalie sighed. The public were fantastic at calling in crimes, and occasionally made half-decent witnesses. But it never failed to amaze her how they could also be such *innocents* when it came to the aftermath. This one didn't even seem concerned that her

Day Two, 8.59 a.m.

upstairs neighbour and young son had been murdered. Maybe she was in shock. Maybe the husband had kept her out of the flat. Wise bloke.

'I'm afraid you may have to cancel it, just this once,' she said. *You look like you to could afford to. Maybe go and get a fry-up, too, when we're done with you. Put some flesh on your bones.*

The woman retreated to the staircase. Her husband delayed leaving, just for a few seconds.

'We're just shocked,' he said. 'The blood came through our ceiling. That's why I went upstairs to investigate.'

Natalie nodded, eager now to enter the death room and deal with the latest chapter in the Big Book of Bad Things People Do to Each Other.

She swatted at the flies that buzzed towards her. They all came from the room at the end of the dark, narrow hallway. Keeping her eyes on the threadbare red-and-cream runner, alert to anything Forensics might be able to use, she made her way to the kitchen. She supported herself against the opposite wall with her left hand so she could walk, one foot in line with the other, along the right-hand edge of the hall.

The buzzing intensified. And then she caught it: the aroma of death. Sweet-sour top notes overlaying a deeper, darker, rotting-meat stink as body tissues broke down and emitted their gases.

And blood. Or 'claret', in the parlance of the job. She reckoned she'd smelled more of it than a wine expert. This was present in quantity. The husband – what was his name? Rob, that was it. He'd said on the phone it was bad. 'A slaughterhouse' – his exact words.

'Let's find out, then, shall we?' she murmured as she reached the door and entered the kitchen.

As the scene imprinted itself on her retinas, she didn't swear, or invoke the deity, or his son. She used to, in the early days of her career. There'd been enough blasphemy and bad language to have had her churchgoing mum rolling her eyes and pleading with her to 'Watch your language, please, Nat. There's no need.'

She'd become hardened to it over the previous fifteen years.

Day Two, 8.59 a.m.

She hoped she still felt a normal human's reaction when she encountered murder scenes, or the remains of those who'd reached the end of their tether and done themselves in. But she left the amateur dramatics to the new kids. She was a sergeant, a rank she'd worked bloody hard for, and she felt a certain restraint went with the territory. So, no swearing.

She did, however, shake her head and swallow hard as she took in the scene in front of her. She'd been a keen photographer in her twenties and found it helpful to see crime scenes as if through a lens: her way of putting some distance between her and whatever horrors the job required her to confront.

In wide-shot, an obscene parody of a Madonna and child. A woman – early thirties, to judge by her face, which was waxy-pale – and a little boy cradled in her lap.

They'd been posed at the edge of a wall-to-wall blood pool, dried and darkened to a deep plum red.

She'd clearly bled out. He wasn't as pale as his mum, but the pink in his smooth little cheeks was gone, replaced by a greenish tinge.

The puddle of blood had spread right across the kitchen floor and under the table, on which half-emptied bags of shopping sagged. The dead woman was slumped with her back against the cooker, legs canted open yet held together at the ankle by her pulled-down jeans.

And the little boy.

Looking for all the world as though he had climbed on to his mother's lap for a cuddle, eyes closed, hands together at his throat as if in prayer. Fair hair. Long and wavy, down to his shoulders, in a girlish style Natalie had noticed some of her friends choose for their sons.

Even in midwinter, flies would find a corpse within the hour. In the middle of a scorching summer like the one southern England was enjoying now, they'd arrived in minutes, laid their eggs and begun feasting in quantity. Maggots crawled and wriggled all over the pair.

As she got closer, Natalie revised her opinion about the cause

Day Two, 8.59 a.m.

of death; now, she could see bruises around the throat that screamed strangulation.

There were protocols to be followed. And the first of these was the preservation of life. She was sure the little boy was dead. The skin discolouration and maggots told her that. But there was no way she was going to go down as the sergeant who left a still-living toddler to die in the centre of a murder scene.

Reaching him meant stepping into that lake of congealed blood. Never mind the sneers from CID about the 'woodentops' walking through crime scenes in their size twelves; this was about checking if a little boy had a chance of life.

She pulled out her phone and took half a dozen shots of the bodies. Then she took two long strides towards them, wincing as her boot soles crackled and slid in the coagulated blood.

She crouched and extended her right index and middle fingers, pressing under the little boy's jaw into the soft flesh where the carotid artery ran. She closed her eyes and prayed for a pulse, trying to ignore the smell, and the noise of the writhing maggots and their soft, squishy little bodies as they roiled together in the mess.

After staying there long enough for the muscles in her legs to start complaining, and for her to be certain the little lad was dead, she straightened and reversed out of the blood. She took care to place her feet back in the first set of footprints.

She turned away, looking for some kitchen roll to wipe the blood off her soles, and stared in horror at the wall facing the cooker.

'Oh, shit.'

KEEP READING

NEWSLETTER

Join my no-spam newsletter for new book news, competitions, offers and more…

Follow Andy Maslen

Bookbub has a New release Alert. You can check out the latest book deals and get news of every new book I publish by following me here.

BingeBooks has regular author chats plus lists, reviews and personalised newsletters. Follow me here.

Website www.andymaslen.com.
Email andy@andymaslen.com.
Facebook group, The Wolfe Pack.

© 2023 Sunfish Ltd

Published by Tyton Press, an imprint of Sunfish Ltd, PO Box 2107, Salisbury SP2 2BW: 0844 502 2061

The right of Andy Maslen to be identified as the author of this work has been asserted by him in accordance with the Copyright, Designs and Patents Act 1988.

All rights reserved

No part of this publication may be reproduced, stored in a retrieval system or transmitted, in any form or by any means, electronic, mechanical, photocopying, recording or otherwise, without the prior permission of the copyright owner. Requests for permission should be addressed to the publisher.

This is a work of fiction. Names, characters, businesses, places, events and incidents are either the products of the author's imagination or used in a fictitious manner. Any resemblance to actual persons, living or dead, or actual events is purely coincidental.

Cover illustration copyright © Nick Castle

Author photograph © Kin Ho

Edited by Nicola Lovick

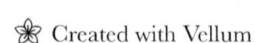

❦ Created with Vellum

ACKNOWLEDGMENTS

I want to thank you for buying this book. I hope you enjoyed it. As an author is only part of the team of people who make a book the best it can be, this is my chance to thank the people on *my* team.

For sharing their knowledge and experience of The Job, former and current police officers Andy Booth, Ross Coombs, Jen Gibbons, Neil Lancaster, Sean Memory, Trevor Morgan, Olly Royston, Chris Saunby, Ty Tapper, Sarah Warner and Sam Yeo.

For helping me stay reasonably close to medical reality as I devise gruesome ways of killing people, Martin Cook, Melissa Davies, Arvind Nagra and Katie Peace.

For her wonderfully detailed information and advice about Swedish forensic science and law enforcement, Brita Zilg.

For their brilliant copy-editing and proofreading Nicola Lovick and Liz Ward.

For his super-cool artwork, my cover designer, Nick Castle.

The members of my Facebook Group, The Wolfe Pack, who are an incredibly supportive and also helpful bunch of people. Thank you to them, also.

And for being an inspiration and source of love and laughter, and making it all worthwhile, my family: Jo, Rory and Jacob.

Andy Maslen
Salisbury, 2023

ABOUT THE AUTHOR

Photo © 2020 Kin Ho

Andy Maslen was born in Nottingham, England. After leaving university with a degree in psychology, he worked in business for thirty years as a copywriter. In his spare time, he plays the guitar. He lives in Wiltshire.

Printed in Great Britain
by Amazon